The Fine Art of Murder

By M. Ward Leon

Beacon Publishing Group
ISBN (Paperback): 9781961504158

The Fine Art of Murder

Cover Design by Jerry Parsons
Exterior Design by Lori Pace
Edited by Gerard Hernandez

Order at www.beaconpublishinggroup.com for a discount. Email to inquire about bulk purchase discounts at customerservice@beaconpublishinggroup.com

Beacon Publishing Group, New York, NY 10001
www.beaconpublishinggroup.com

Manufactured in the United States of America

The Fine Art of Murder

The Case of the Fugu Voo Doo

The Case of the Devil's Tooth

The Case of the Alphabet Killer

The Case of the Which Doctor

The Case of Our Lady of the Bone Yard

The Case of the Killer Clown Killer

The Case of the Cyclone Psycho

The Case of the God Squad

The Case of the Mamba Murder

The Case of the Fugu Voo Doo

Vincent Rainwater IV, the world-renowned art critic for the New York Times, was a man who could make or break any artist's career with just a few simple words.

Like most art critics, Vincent couldn't paint his way out of a paper bag, but he specialized in analyzing, interpreting, and evaluating art. His written critiques and reviews contributed to art criticism. Rainwater regularly appeared in the New York Times, popular art magazines, exhibition brochures, and art catalogs.

Vincent Rainwater was *the* most powerful man in the world of art.

Vincent Rainwater was born in 1927 into a world of the über rich. His father's family was one of the first families to have a seat on the Chicago Board of Trade. Since 1848, there has always been a Rainwater on the CBOT.

Vincent grew up in Lincoln Park, one of the most affluent neighborhoods in Chicago. The red brick two-story house at 2242 North Fremont Street stood apart from the other homes on the block with its large bay windows painted green to match the green ironworks of the front porch railings and the second-story iron latticework. The rest of Fremont Street homes were primarily white limestone fronts with pale brick side walls, all very traditional and unassuming. The Rainwaters were anything but. They wanted the world to know they were wealthy, *"de crème de la crème."*

Vincent was the eldest of three brothers and two sisters; they grew up wanting for nothing. They had butlers, cooks, chauffeurs, and nannies. The Rainwater children attended the prestigious Francis W. Parker School, one of Chicago's finest schools.

Following the family tradition of attending the School of Business, Vincent went on to graduate summa cum laude but decided not to continue for his MBA. Instead, after falling in love with Amy Albright, a Yale art student, Vincent chose to obtain another undergraduate degree in art history, much to the family's chagrin.

Ultimately, being that Vincent was the rebellious one of the broods, his younger brother, Theo, took the seat occupied by his father, Vincent Rainwater the Third.

Amy Albright came from a middle-class family living in Santa Monica, California. Her father, Andrew, and his brother, Peter, had a small seafood restaurant on Santa Monica Pier. Amy had an older sister, Sally, who was the complete opposite of Amy. Sally was logical, and Amy was creative. Sally was an A student; Amy was a C student. Sally was the head cheerleader, editor of the school newspaper, valedictorian of her class, and voted most likely to succeed. At the same time, Amy was a member of the Art Club and voted the most creative.

Sally got a full ride to UCLA to study medicine. Amy went to Santa Monica City College for two years, studying art. She entered the Los Angeles County Art Festival and won first place in the painting category. There was a large spread in the LA Times Arts Section, where Henry Dobbins, head of the painting department of Yale Art School, saw the article and was so impressed that he invited Amy up to Yale for an interview. Three months later, Amy was a Yalie. Just like Sally, her sister received a full scholarship. Both Albright girls seemed to be heading to fulfill their destinies.

It was in Amy's junior year, during a student art exhibit of her paintings, that she met a senior, Vincent Rainwater. Rainwater was unlike any of the boys in her circle of friends, who were free-spirited, casual, and creative; Vincent was a bit stodgy, serious, and square. She always told people what attracted her to him; they were complete opposites.

He would tell people that he, too, was attracted to her because she was so different from anyone he had ever met. He loved her free and bohemian ways. She always wore all black and would talk in an unusual beatnik vocabulary, using words like cool, hip, and daddy-o.

Once she got her undergraduate degree, she went on to earn her master's; while Vincent had earned a BA in communication, he decided to enroll in the Yale School of Art. He majored in Art History while Amy was pursuing her MFA.

After Vincent and Amy graduated from Yale in 1955, they moved to New York City. Greenwich Village and the Bowery, where the epicenter of the merging art styles of the day was beginning. Abstract Expressionism, Neo-Dada, and Pop Art were blossoming. Artists like Jasper Johns,

Willem de Kooning, Mark Rothko, Jackson Pollock, Roy Lichtenstein, and Andy Warhol were shaking up the art establishment.

Vincent and Amy moved into a fourth-floor walk-up flat in the Bowery, 79 Allen Street. The apartment had an enchanting view of the alley, where bums and hookers congregated. There was a communal toilet at the end of the hall; their bathtub was in the kitchen and doubled for the dining room table when they placed the 3X5 foot plank on top of the tub.

On the street level was a small bodega where two large tabby cats lived, Cosmo and Midnight. They were the building's mousers. On average, they would eliminate eight to ten rats a week, but occasionally, in the middle of the night, Vincent and Amy would be awakened by the snap of the steel bar crashing down on the neck of a giant Norway rat. Usually, the rat would meet a swift and fatal end, although there were times if the rat was particularly large, they would hear squealing as the poor creature would flop around in agony until it eventually died.

Vincent and Amy were young and in love. They had resigned themselves to their lifestyle, which was part of the artist's experience of suffering for one's art.

While Amy spent most of her day painting, she occasionally walked to the East Village and hung out in coffee houses, where she met other struggling artists.

Vincent found a job as an account executive at B, D, T&O, an advertising agency in midtown. He was a junior AE on the Proctor & Gamble account. Vincent was responsible for writing advertising copy and working with the art department to develop his concepts.

Vincent hated the "Ad Game." He found it shallow, self-indulgent, boorish, and made up of the same type of good old boy network that he despised at the Chicago Board of Trade.

In client meetings, they would sit around and throw out such inane patter as *"Let's run it up the flagpole and see who salutes."*

"Let's throw it on the stoop and see if the cat drags it in."

"Let's throw it against the wall and see if it sticks."

"Let's drop it down the well and see if it makes a splash."

The sad thing about it was that he was good at it as much as he hated it. The P&G client loved him and his work. He received raise after raise, promotion after promotion. Soon, he was made account supervisor on the Gillette account.

Then, out of the blue, the worst thing happened. He became his father. His life was all about money and power. He wanted to move uptown to Central Park East, but Amy was content living the bohemian life in the Bowery. Her art started gaining attention; she had several small one-woman shows, which had gotten fairly good reviews.

They were hurdling towards a crossroads that neither knew was coming.

In the summer of 1960, Amy Albright had several pieces in the New York Armory Show. During the Armory

Show, Vincent, wanting to build up some hype for his wife, sent a letter to the New York Times editorial critiquing Amy's exhibit.

"Amy Albright, at the Armory Show, presented eight oils. A Yale School of Art graduate and a denizen of Southern California, her abstractions are free of Paris's snobbery and contain an unbridled passion for American fury. Her work is personal yet universal. She has a fine sense of synthesis that preserves the individuality of each canvas."

The editorial staff was so impressed that they asked Vincent if he might be interested in providing them with additional reviews of the Armory Show. Unbeknownst to anyone outside the Times editorial staff, they were looking to replace their current critic, Derrick Sneed. Sneed had gotten himself in trouble by having a sexual relationship with a fourteen-year-old Catholic schoolgirl.

That simple paragraph Rainwater wrote about Amy set the stage for Vincent Rainwater to become the New York Times art critic and Amy Albright's rise within the art world. Her paintings were now sought after by serious collectors, the prices of her work quadrupled, and galleries were wooing her for them to represent her.

At first, Vincent's critic assignments were sporadic, minor art shows and gallery openings, but eventually, the Times made him a permanent offer to be the official art critic.

The ad agency people were caught off guard and not very happy. The client at P&G loved Vincent and wanted him to stay, even threatening to pull the account if he left.

"Vincent, we don't want to lose you. We feel you're a valuable cog in the B, D, T&O machine, and you're like family. I think you know how much we value you, and to show our appreciation, we'd like to offer you a sixty-thousand dollar a-year raise, the title of Sr. VP, a five-figure expense account, membership at the Greenwich Country Club, and a fifteen percent year-end bonus.

I don't know what the Times is offering you, but I do know that they won't be able to come anywhere near what we are.

Besides, an art critic? Really? How gauche and pedestrian. I mean associating with beatniks, bohemians, and those pretentious artists." Said Theodore "Skip" Westinghouse, head of account services worldwide.

"Skip, you do know that Amy, my wife, is an artist?"

"Well, of course I do. I wasn't referring to Amy. We all think Amy is really top-drawer, really super.

Now, you don't have to answer right now. Why don't you go home, take some time, and talk it over with the little woman? And we'll confab over lunch at the Jockey Club tomorrow 'round 1:00.''

"What do you mean no!" Skip said, stunned, mouth open, aghast.

"Well, Skip, I just don't see myself spending my whole life hyping shaving cream, toothpaste, and toilet paper. I mean, your offer was…"

"Top drawer?"

"Okay, yeah. But it's not like I need the money. My old man is worth twenty million."

"So, you would rather deal in art than in superior quality products that help millions of American housewives?"

"Nietzsche said, "We have art so that we shall not die of reality.""

"What the Hell does that mean?"

"It means thanks, but no thanks." Vincent said as he stood up and walked out of the Jockey Club, leaving Theodore "Skip" Westinghouse staring at him in disbelief as the waiter brought his fifth martini.

What Theodore "Skip" Westinghouse didn't know was that Vincent Rainwater had a master plan. It was a carefully thought-out plan to make more money than his father could ever make in ten lifetimes. Twenty million would be chump change compared to what lay in store for the New York Times art critic Vincent Rainwater.

"So, Amy, is it true that Vincent is the Times' new art critic." Asked Jasper Johns, having a coffee with Amy and Helen Frankenthaler at Caffe Cino in the West Village.

"Yes. He officially started last Monday." Amy responded, smiling.

"How do you feel about that?" Helen asked.

"What do you mean? I'm happy for him." She said.

Helen posed the question, "Well, do you think that the fact that he's your husband might influence his critique of your work?"

"God, I hope not. No! Vincent wouldn't do that. If he did, he would lose all credibility."

"Well, I've always found him as a straight shooter," Johns said.

"Sure, he just gave you a great review." Helen snipped with a grin.

"When are you having your next show, Helen?" Amy asked.

"Morris Louis and I are having a show at the Findlay Galleries mid-town in June."

"That's fantastic! I love his color field paintings." Amy stated.

Jasper sipped his coffee and dismissively said, "Yeah, he's all right."

"You artists are all the same. Conceited, arrogant with gigantic egos. I'm surprised your heads can fit through the door." Vincent said, smiling as he sat down at the table.

"Mr. Rainwater." Greeted Helen.

"Vincent, please, Miss Frankenthaler."

"Well, if we're going with first names, then it's Helen."

"It's my pleasure. I was enthralled with your painting, "Jacob's Ladder." I loved the feeling of depth and layering. The color palette gave me a soothing yet chaotic dynamic. Quite mesmerizing. Fabulous stuff." Vincent said.

"Wow. I'm so glad you like it. Morris Louis and I are having a show of new works in June." She said proudly.

"I know. It's already on my calendar. I can't wait to see it." Vincent said as he turned his attention to Jasper Johns.

"Hello, Jasper."

"Vincent."

"I must admit, I was taken aback by "Flag on Orange Field." I really like the direction that you're going. Could you tell me what you were thinking?"

"Flag on Orange was involved with having more than one element in the painting and extending the space beyond the limits of ... the predetermined image... It got rather monotonous, making flags on a canvas, and I wanted to add something - go beyond the limits of the flag and have different canvas space. I did it early with the little flags and the white below, making the flag hit three canvas edges and adding something else. And then in the Orange, I carried it all the way around."

"Well, you certainly succeeded."

"Why, thank you, Vincent."

"And Miss Albright, what new, provocative, and avant-garde ideas are you working on these days?" Vincent said as he leaned forward and kissed Amy on the cheek.

"Don't you know?" Jasper asked, his curiosity peaked.

"No. You see, my dear Amy keeps her work far from the prying eyes of this art critic. I'm sure you all will know what she is working on long before I do, as it should be. I try to be fair-minded, objective, and impartial. Right, dear?"

"Damn right," Amy said with a smile and an air of defiance.

Vincent got a call from Benny Bourgeois, owner of the Bourgeois Gallery in the Bowery. Benny had an eye for up-and-coming artists. He was one of the first to recognize Jackson Pollock as a major force in the art world. So, when Benny called Vincent with an artist he wanted him to check out, Vincent said where and when.

"Hello, Vincent. Benny Bourgeois."

"Hey, Benny. What's up?"

"Vincent, I got a kid here who's going to knock your socks off."

"Have I heard of him?"

"Nobody has. His work is like no other. He's cross-pollinating abstract expressionism with something wild. I can't explain it. You'll have to see it for yourself."

"What's his name?"

"Anthony Banta. But he only goes by Banta. You interested?"

"Are you kidding? After a build-up like that, where and when?"

"Tomorrow. 10 am."

"See you tomorrow morning."

"Au revoir."

"G'bye, Benny."

CLICK

"Hey, babe. Ever hear of a young kid named Anthony Banta?" When he got home from the Times Building on 43rd Street, Vincent asked Amy.

"Banta? Sure. He's breaking new ground. You should go see his stuff."

"I am. Tomorrow morning, at the Bourgeois Gallery."

"Aw, how is Benny?" She asked.

"He seems super excited by this Banta kid. I'm anxious to see what all the buzz is about."

"Can't wait to see what you think."

"Oh, by the way. How's your series coming? Nearly finished?" He asked, knowing not to pry too much.

Amy smiled and answered, "As Da Vinci once said, "Art is never finished, only abandoned.""

"Got it. Did you hear that Franz Kline's *Siegfried* sold at the Carnegie International for $5,000?"

"My God! $5,000, that's unreal. Wow, I can't imagine getting that much for one of my paintings."

"Well, I can. Your work is as avant-garde as Kline's, and I'm not just saying that because you're my wife."

She walked over to him and gave him a deep, passionate kiss, smiled, and said, "Well, how about because I'm your lover?"

"Oh, sure. Of course, you being my lover makes all the difference in the world."

She took him by the hand, walked him into the bedroom, took off all her clothes, laid on the bed, and said seductively, "Come on, baby and fuck me; I need a great review on my latest series."

"I'll give you a great review if you give me one." He said with a wolfish grin.

"Oh, Vinnie, come down here, and I'll show you some abstract expressionism." She purred.

Benny Bourgeois was a short, pudgy man who always wore a black suit with a matching beret. Under the beret was a crop of thinning black hair that he combed from the left side of his head to the right side. He sported a David Niven pencil mustache, which gave him an air of sophistication to his clients, mainly when he spoke French.

Vincent walked through the door at precisely 10 a.m.

"Ah, Vincent, mon cher ami!" Benny said as he walked up to Vincent with open arms and kissed him on each cheek.

The gallery felt empty and cavernous, as it did not open until noon. The thick smell of oils permeated the air, which was one of the things that Vincent liked about these older galleries. Most had the wax and polish worn off the wooden floors decades ago, and the Bourgeois Gallery was no exception. Years and years of pedestrian traffic shuffling through the gallery had developed a natural flow pattern on the floor. People would enter through the front door, automatically start on their right, and proceed in a large U pattern until they slowly returned to the front entrance.

The Bourgeois Gallery was currently showing Mark Rothko's latest works, large canvases five to ten feet in width and over twenty feet tall.

"I thought you'd be featuring Banta's work," Vincent said, slightly disappointed.

"Naw, He's not ready for a one-man show. Not yet, but soon. I have his stuff in the back. Come on back; he's anxious to meet you."

They walked towards the back room, passing through the valley of Rothko paintings, each more powerful than the next.

Benny opened the door, and there, standing next to five canvases, stood a twenty-two-year-old boy. He had a James Dean vibe to him. Unkept hair, a black leather motorcycle jacket, a grungy tee shirt, scuffed blue jeans, and motorcycle boots.

"Vincent Rainwater, this is Anthony Banta. Tony, this is Vincent Rainwater, the New York Times art critic."

"I understand you prefer Banta?" Vincent said as he reached out his hand.

"Yes, sir, Mr. Rainwater," Banta said.

"Vincent, please. Well, Banta Benny has spoken very highly of you. Do you mind if I take a look at your work?"

"No, please." The kid said, inviting the art critic as he stepped aside from the paintings.

Vincent stood silent for a few minutes, peering from one canvas to the next. Then he walked in front of each painting, not speaking but exploring every inch of the canvas. Sometimes, he approached the paintings, getting within inches, then stepped back. All the while, he took no notes, made no statements, or asked any questions.

After half an hour, he smiled, thanked the young artist for allowing him to view his work, shook hands with Benny, and left.

Banta stood by his paintings, looking gutshot, "What the Hell?"

"Don't take it personally, mon amie. That's how he works; he doesn't like to have the artist's personality influence his critique. He judges strictly on the quality of the art. Believe me, I've worked with him too many times; I know that he was impressed. You'll see, do not worry."

That Thursday, the headline in the New York Times art section read, "ABSTRACT EXPRESSIONISM MEET NEO-DADA" Introducing a radical shift in the world of modern art.

Artists such as Jasper Johns, Robert Rauschenberg, Allan Kaprow, and newcomer Banta are rebelling against the emotionally charged paintings of the Abstract Expressionists that have dominated the art world.

The artist Banta's work, in particular, provokes through surreptitious strategies more suitable to today's Cold War climate. He simultaneously scoffs and celebrates consumer culture while uniting opposing conventions of abstraction and realism. He neglects boundaries with indifference between media through experimentation with aggregation, performance, and other hybrid fusions.

Banta often encourages viewers to look beyond conventional aesthetic standards and interpret meanings through the process of critical thinking generated by inconsistencies and illogical juxtapositions rather than the internal emotions the abstract expressionist painters referenced in their abstruse works.

His work currently can be viewed at The Bourgeois Gallery, located in the East Village.

The day before the article was to be released, Vincent called Benny and bought four of Banta's canvases.

A week later, based on Rainwater's review, Artforum International magazine did a multi-page article about the up-and-coming artist. By the time Banta's opening was held at the Bourgeois Gallery, all the paintings were sold. Banta also received several private commissions for a dozen patrons and three commissions from museums:

MOMA, the Guggenheim, and the Los Angeles County Museum of Art.

Artists don't work in a vacuum; they need other artists to spark new ideas, to have friends, and, at times, not-so-friendly competition to help gain creative vision. In modern art, unlike Renaissance art, it's not the artist's technical ability so much as the conceptual abilities that separate great artists from the average.

Pablo Picasso was never stagnated as an artist. He was constantly growing, exploring new news, and trying different things. He once said, "Bad artists copy. Good artists steal."

One year after Banta's show at the Bourgeois Gallery, he died in a horrific motorcycle accident. He was riding his Harley in upstate New York, just outside of Woodstock, when a drunk driver t-boned his bike. Banta was thrown from the motorcycle and went headlong into a guardrail. The ME's report stated that it was a one-in-a-million-freak accident. The angle of his body's impact with the guardrail caused the severing of his head as he slammed into the metal railing.

The local police searched for over an hour before finding the severed head. It had rolled down the hill and landed under a large Labrador Tea plant. Police Officer Bennett said that Banta's eyes were open, staring at him as he approached. He picked the head up by the hair and carried it uphill to the scene of the accident; all the while, Bennett claims that Banta's eye kept looking at him.

The art world was stunned by a visionary so young whose life was cut too short. Who knows what great things he might have achieved? There were several memorials and tributes to the young talent. Vincent was asked to speak at one, which took place on the roof of the Marlborough Gallery in midtown. As Vincent finished his eulogy, he noticed a magnificent sunset over his left shoulder. He stopped and said, "I've always heard that whenever an artist dies, God lets them paint the sky to say goodbye. I think we're in for one beautiful sunset."

Vincent sat down next to Amy, who was crying. Everyone sat silently, watching the sunset, not saying a word until the sun finally set and the sky went black.

It didn't take long for the prices of his limited works to skyrocket into the stratosphere. The four paintings Vincent had purchased for a thousand dollars a year ago were now worth over fifty times as much. He ended up selling three of the four paintings to private collectors, keeping one for himself.

When Amy heard what he had done, she was distraught and called him a mercenary, avaricious, and money-grubbing.

"Mercenary?" Vincent said, surprised at her reaction.

"What else would you call someone who profits from someone's death?"

"All I did was sell a couple of paintings. We didn't need four of his works; I'm not running a museum. Come on, babe. Art is a commodity, you know that. Do you believe everyone who buys your work plans to keep them forever? Some do, and some buy your work to enjoy for a time, and then they'll sell them."

"You're right. I'm sorry. I'm just upset that Banta died way before his time, that's all. Forgive me?" She asked.

"Of course I do. I love you."

Vincent was having lunch at the Yale Club with his college roommate, Frank Williams Esquire, a noted criminal attorney who recently became a partner in one of New York's most prestigious law firms. They were joined by a classmate, Gary Tinterow, M.D., one of the city's best-known and renowned psychiatrists.

The Yale Club is a private club in Midtown Manhattan, New York City. Its membership is restricted almost entirely to alums and faculty of Yale University. With a clubhouse comprising 22 stories, the Yale Club has a worldwide membership of over 11,000. The club is at 50 Vanderbilt Avenue, across from Grand Central Station.

Frank Williams asked as the three sat around dishing the dirt about other alums, chowing down on the traditional Bulldog Burger.

"Vincent, I heard that you made quite the killing on the sale of three of Banta's paintings. Is that true, old man?"

"Yes, I was fortunate. I mean, I liked the paintings and bought them intending to sell them one day. Although I intended to keep the one I did, I didn't know I would turn them around so fast. It's only because of his untimely death that the opportunity presented itself." Vincent said.

"How very fortuitous for you." Dr. Tinterow said slyly.

"For me, yes. But not so much for Mr. Banta." Vincent quipped.

"Does this sort of thing happen very often in the art world?" The doctor asked.

"No, not really, especially with young artists. And it's proven that most artists live to be quite old, on average. Monet was 86 when he died, Matisse was 84, and Degas was 83."

"Well, you see, Frank and I were just musing that we might be interested in forming an art syndicate of sorts with you, of course."

"A syndicate?" Vincent asked, intrigued by the idea.

"Yes, we thought that if we each ante up ten thousand dollars into a kitty and have you made the choices of art, with the express purpose of making a good return on our investments," Tinterow said.

"We're not interested in art other than making a profit.' Williams added.

"You do know that art is like every other commodity; sometimes it's up and sometimes down. You're in one day; the next, you're out. There are no guarantees in the art world."

"Oh, but we think there is. You." Tinterow grinned.

"Me?"

"Sure. We've all seen it, Vincent. You give a glowing critique, and the artist's stock goes through the roof. All you have to do is tip us off before the review comes out. We buy a couple of art pieces, store them, wait until the right moment, and then cash in. What do you say?" Tinterow asked.

"You do realize that Banta was a flook. It usually takes years, even decades, for the price of art to increase. Often, an artist's work doesn't rise until after the artist dies."

"Yeah, yeah. Blah. Blah. Blah. You in or not?" Williams pressed.

"Okay. I'm in." Vincent relented.

"So, you're selling out," Amy said.

"No. Look, babe, like I said to Frank and Gary, art is a commodity. Not everyone buys your work because they love it and want to keep it forever. Some people and corporations buy art because they think it's a good investment and more fun to look at than a stock certificate."

"Did you buy any of mine?" She said defiantly.

"Yes, of course. It was the first one we bought." Vincent proudly said.

"Which one did you buy?" She coyly asked.

"Opus in Blue."

"Good choice. What did you pay?"

"Three thousand."

"You got a bargain," Amy said, smiling.

"Don't I know it?"

"Who else are you thinking of?"

"Do you really want to know?"

"Yes!"

"Well, there's this new kid, Roy Lichtenstein, I'm interested in. As well as this youngster showing at the Bodley Gallery, Andy..."

"Warhol?"

"That's right, Andy Warhol. He's doing some real interesting things."

"Both excellent choices," Amy said approvingly.

"I scheduled to review them for the Times next month."

"You know, Vincent, you should look into this guy, Max Albertson. He's a three-dimensional artist, very avant-garde."

"Thanks, babe. I'll look into him. Do you know where he's showing?"

"Yeah. A little gallery in SoHo called The Lost Gallery."

On the corner of MacDougal and Minetta Lane in Greenwich Village is a small club called Café Wha? It wasn't unusual to see Bob Dylan, Peter, Paul and Mary, and Lenny Bruce hanging out there.

Amy and several of her artist friends would occasionally meet there for lunch, eat, compare notes, hear each other's stories, and catch up on all the art world's goings.

Sitting around the table were Jasper Johns, Robert Rauschenberg, Robert Motherwell, Helen Frankenthaler, and Frank Stella, an up-and-coming painter working in the minimalism and post-painterly abstraction school.

Amy started the discussion by discussing the concept of art syndicates buying art and promoting artists for purely financial gain.

"What do you all think of the idea?" Amy asked the group.

Helen Frankenthaler said, "I don't see anything wrong. The idea is to get our work noticed and out to the people. Am I right?"

"Face it; artists have been relying upon patrons for centuries. Look at Botticelli, Da Vinci, and Michelangelo and their relationship with the Médicis. Back then, wealthy families were patrons; today, it's syndicates and corporations." Rauschenberg said.

"I'd be more than happy to talk to any syndicates or corporations you know looking to invest in a post-painterly abstraction artist, Amy!" Stella quipped.

Robert Motherwell laughed and asked Amy, "So, you're not bothered at the notion of syndicates or corporations investing in art, but the fact that your husband, the art critic for the New York Times, is involved in a syndicate investing in art. Even though he's purchased some of your work?"

"Well, I could see, and of course, I'm not saying that Vincent would ever do such a thing, but think about it: some art critic hypes up some undeserving or unknown artist just for the sake of manipulating the value of the critic's investment," Amy said.

"If that ever happened and it got out, I think that critic would be ruined. His reputation would forever be sullied." Jasper Johns noted.

"I agree, but it would be hard to prove unless you caught the culprit in the act of selling the works for a considerable profit. After all, the art critic was supposedly giving *his* opinion. Unless a substantial number of other critics and experts publicly disagree and discuss the reasons for their disagreement with the critic, then it boils down to it's just like his opinion, man." Frankenthaler argued.

"It is an interesting theory to ponder," Amy said.

"Enough about business. Frank, I saw your "The Marriage of Reason and Squalor, ll." Fantastic. Have any of you seen it yet?" Motherwell asked the group.

They all nodded that they had.

"Thank you, Robert. I'm glad you liked it. I did a whole series of Black Paintings. I'm replacing the romantic notion of a creative act with the actual labor used to make the painting. My Black Paintings challenge the assumption that a painting must represent an idea or communicate some profound meaning to the viewer. What you see is what you see." Stella said, smiling.

"Frank, when's the opening of your Black Painting exhibit?" Amy asked.

"Officially, in two weeks, but if your husband and his syndicate would like a preview, I can arrange it."

"I'll talk to him tonight. I'm sure you're already on his radar." She said.

"Cool," Stella said with a grin.

"Frank Stella. Yeah, I have him on my calendar for the opening. I also have Max Albertson the day after.

So, Stella said that I could come down for a preview. That's great; I'll call the Lowes Gallery tomorrow and set something up. Thanks babe. I'm going to call Frank and Gary and give them a heads up." Vincent said as he grabbed the phone and dialed Tinterow.

"Gary, it's Vincent. I've got two new prospects. But I think we'll need to ante up some more into the kitty."

"How much more?" Tinterow asked.

"I think another five grand each."

"Listen, Vincent, when are we going to start seeing some ROI?" Tinterow pressed.

"I told you guys that a quick turnaround wasn't the norm. These two artists I'm looking at will be huge in a couple of years. Trust me."

"Okay, it just seems we're investing a lot on the come."

"Well, it was your idea."

"I know. I know." Tinterow said begrudgingly.

"So, you in for another five grand."

"Yeah, sure. In for a penny, in for a pound. Say, Vincent, do you think I could come along for one of these previews?"

"Okay, how about you tag along when I meet with Max Albertson this Wednesday?"

"What time? I usually have rounds in the morning. Could we do it in the afternoon?"

"I'll set it up for Wednesday afternoon. I'll call you with the details."

"Great, maybe we can get Frank to come along too?"

"Sure, the more, the merrier. I'll ask him when I call him for his five grand."

"You sure about these guys?"

"Hey, I don't tell you how to perform psychoanalysis, do I?"

"Yeah. Yeah. I'll have the money in the account tomorrow."

"Good. I'll talk to you later."

"Goodbye."

CLICK

"Williams, here."

"Hey, Frank, Vincent. Is this a good time?" "Always for you, my friend. What's cooking?"

"I just got off the phone with Gary. Listen, I got a lead on two new rising stars, and I think we need to drop another five grand in the kitty to get in on the bottom floor. Gary's in. What do you think?"

"Get in on the bottom floor? You still have that Adman thing going, don't you? Who are these hotshots?" Williams asked.

"Frank Stella and Max Albertson."

"Sounds like a couple of Jewish delicatessen owners."

"Very funny. Are you in?"

"Yeah, I'll drop the money into the account tomorrow."

"Also…"

"There's more?"

"Gary wants to go on to the preview on Wednesday. You want to go?"

"What time Wednesday?"

"I'll know sometime tomorrow, but it will be in the afternoon."

"Good. Because I have to be in court in the morning."

"Great, I'll call you with the details as soon as I set it up."

"Sounds good. Okay, Rainwater, talk to you later. Ciao."

"Bye."
CLICK

"Gentlemen, please. Come in. Welcome to my studio." Max Albertson greeted Rainwater and his two companions.

Max's studio was located at 201 Spring Street in Soho, on the third floor of a loft building. The space had hardwood floors, exposed brick walls, and windows from floor to ceiling on the north wall. The artist also installed dozens of track lights overhead to highlight his sculptures. Although the space was cavernous, over 5,000 square feet, it felt very intimate.

"Can I get you anything to drink?" Max asked.

"No, thank you," Vincent replied.

"Ah, Mr. Albertson, pardon my ignorance; what does your art represent? All I see are large steel cubes, unpainted. Some are stacked, some side-by-side, and others are boxes in boxes. I don't get it." Tinterow confessed.

"Gary! I'm sorry, Max." Vincent said apologetically.

"No. No. It's quite all right." Max said, smiling.

Max walked over to a stack of metal boxes that looked to be arranged haphazardly; they were all jumbled, facing in different directions, and the sculpture stood over fifteen feet tall.

"Gary, tell me what you see," Max asked Doctor Tinterow.

"Honestly, I see just a bunch of boxes stacked up randomly."

"Very good. Now, look past the obvious. Concentrate on the space that you and they share; you'll become more or less conscious of your physical relation to the sculpture.

The lack of paint allows you to concentrate on the natural forms, the shapes of individual cubes and spaces, and the depth created by the voids.

The work is not meant to be just looked at by itself but to be seen in relation to the environment it inhabits.

My work is considered minimalism, which removes all nonessential forms in order to expose the purity and beauty of the art object, focusing on highlighting the very essence of the medium and material to form the art itself." Max explained.

"All I see is a stack of boxes," Tinterow said.

"My job is merely to present you with the work and leave you to interpret it however you will. As they say, art is in the eye of the beholder." Max smiled.

"Mind if I wander around?" Vincent asked.

"Not at all."

"Gary, Frank, why don't you boys have a seat while I have a look around," Vincent said.

"Let me get you, fellas, a cup of joe; follow me," Max suggested as he led them to the kitchen off in the corner overlooking Spring Street.

Max Albertson was in his mid-forties, ex-Army Ranger, butch haircut, dark complexion, slim with dark hair and brown eyes. He had a long scar down the right side of his face that he received from a German soldier's dagger, fighting in hand-to-hand combat at the Battle of the Bulge.

He and his outfit landed on Normandy Beach and slogged their way to Berlin. Max was as hard a Ranger as there ever was. He received two Purple Hearts, three Bronze Stars, and six commendations for bravery.

Max, being a Jew, was overly conscious of who he was fighting. Whenever possible, with his bayonet, he would carve the Star of David on the forehead of every dead German he killed to send his personal message to any Nazi who found their fallen comrade; don't fuck with the Jews.

"Max," Vincent said as he approached the kitchen.

"Yes? Care for some coffee?"

"Sure. I have to tell you I'm very impressed with your work. I think you're going to be a force to be reckoned with."

"Thank you so much, Mr. Rainwater. That means a lot coming from you." Max humbly said.

"In fact, I'm going to feature you in an upcoming article, probably with another artist, Frank Stella."

"I love his work," Max said.

"Max, I'm interested in purchasing one of your pieces."

"Really. Which one."

"I'm torn between "*Untitled 3*" and "*Untitled 8.*"

"I could give you a good price if you want them both," Max said.

"What are we talking?"

"How about both for six thousand?"

Vincent thought for a moment, looking at his partners, smiled, and said, "Deal."

"Fantastic," Max said enthusiastically.

"Great. I'll have somebody come by and pick them up later next week if that's all right."

"Perfect. That will give me time to crate them up for you."

"So, you'll be putting a box in a box?" Gary snarked.

"That's right. Art within art, I like the concept. Very good, Gary." Max countered, smiling.

Under Tinterow's breath, he uttered, "Smartass."

"We just paid six thousand for a couple of wooden boxes." Gary griped as the three of them walked uptown.

"Gary, let me tell you a little story. A tourist was driving in the south of France when he became lost. He pulled up to a small café overlooking the Mediterranean, where a group of men was sitting outside watching the world go by and drinking expressos.

The tourist told the men that he was lost and asked one of the men could tell him how to get to the town he was looking for.

The man took a paper napkin and, with a pen, drew a map and directions on how to get to the town. As the man was making the map, the tourist recognized the man to be Pablo Picasso.

As Picasso handed the tourist the napkin, the tourist asked, "Are you Pablo Picasso?"

Picasso smiles and says, "Yes, I am."

"Oh, Mr. Picasso, I am a huge admirer of you." The tourist says.

"Thank you very much," Picasso responded.

"May I ask if you would please sign this napkin for me?"

Without hesitation, Picasso says, "No."

"Why not?" The tourist asked dejectedly.

"Because right now, you have a map. If I sign it, you'll have a piece of art."

"Now, do you get it? It's not the object; it's what it represents." Vincent asked Tinterow.

"It's a box!" Tinterow insisted.

"Peasant." Vincent jabbed.

"Frank, help out here." Tinterow pleaded.

"Sorry, Doc. I get it. The damn thing is worth what anybody is willing to pay for it, like the napkin. If Picasso would have signed, that napkin would have been worth thousands. Right?" Williams said, gazing at Vincent.

"Exactly." Vincent happily answered that at least one of his so-called elitist friends grasped the concept of art.

"So, is this other guy, this Frank Stella? Is he a sculptor, too?" Tintrow asked.

"No. He's a painter and printmaker."

"Good. I can at least understand paintings." Tinterow said.

"I doubt it." Vincent scoffed.

"Why, what kind of pictures does he paint?"

"Well, to put it in as simple of terms as I can, he paints black stripes on unprepared canvas."

"Black stripes."

"Black stripes." Vincent reiterated.

"Hey, I could paint black stripes on unprepared canvas."

"I'm sure you could. But you didn't, he did." Vincent mocked.

"So, we're going to own wooden boxes and paintings of black stripes."

"Welcome to the world of modern art," Vincent said.

"And these guys are the future of art?"

"Lighten up, Gary. As Bob Dylan says, "Don't criticize what you don't understand.""

"Bob, who?"

"Exactly."

Two years had passed since the art syndicate formed. Over those two years, Vincent made some incredible acquisitions from artists such as Donald Judd, Willem de Kooning, Mark Rothko, Max Albertson, Roy Lichtenstein, Frank Stella, Robert Rauschenberg, Helen Frankenthaler, and Andy Warhol.

While Dr. Tinterow and Frank Williams were becoming wealthy from their respective professions, they were becoming increasingly impatient with the lack of any return on their investment, with all these works of art just hanging around their homes. At least with stocks, you get dividends.

It reached the point where Williams called Vincent, complaining, "Rainwater, every inch of wall space in my home is covered with art; I have so many sculptures that I'm living in a museum. I'm going to have to move to a bigger house soon. When can we start selling some of this stuff?"

"That *stuff* you're whining about is worth five times what your whole house is worth. And it's only going to go up." Vincent said.

"Can we at least sell one of those metal boxes?"

"The Max Albertson? We could, but I would have to say the value has risen maybe 20% from what we paid."

"That's all!"

"Frank, not all artist prices rise at the same pace."

"Fine. Forget it. But can you do me a favor and at least trade me for the de Kooning woman painting? Joanne is creeped out by it every time she sees it."

"How about a nice painting of a Campbell's Soup Can?"

"Sure. Sounds great. Anything has to be better than that woman with those large eyes and that evil grimace staring down at us."

"Fine. I'll have them switched out tomorrow."

"Thanks."

"Goodbye."

CLICK

A few weeks later, Frank and Gary happen to run into each other having lunch at the Yale Club. After finishing his lunch, Frank stopped by Gary's table and said, "Excuse me, folks, I just stopped by to say hello to Dr. Tinterow."

Doctor Tinterow was having lunch with several fellow doctors from his practice. Gary shook hands with Williams and introduced him to his colleagues. "Folks, this is my very good friend Frank Williams, attorney at law. We were roommates back at Yale."

"What kind of law do you practice, Mr. Williams?" One of the doctors asked.

"I specialize in corporate law. I'm a partner with Cromwell, Thacher, and Wharton."

"Very prestigious." The doctor replied.

"Thank you. Well, it was very nice meeting you all. I got to run. Say, Gary, give me a call when you can. I have a couple of things I'd like to talk to you about. Again, it was a pleasure meeting you. Ciao."

"I'll call you tonight," Tintrow said.

Williams and Tinterow hooked up after work that night at Pete's Tavern in Gramercy Park for some beers. Pete's Tavern has been around since 1864. It is alleged that the famous author O. Henry wrote "The Gift of the Magi" at Pete's Tavern.

"So, what's so damn important that we had to get together to talk about what we couldn't talk over on the phone?" Tinterow asked.

"Joanne and I are getting a divorce," Frank said sheepishly.

"A divorce? Why? What happened?"

"Aw, she found out that my secretary, Donna, and I are having an affair."

"How the Hell did she find out?"

"I stupidly left a receipt for some flowers I had sent her in my suit coat pocket. Joanne found it when she was going through my pockets before sending my suits to the cleaners. I am so screwed!"

"Oh, Frank, I'm so sorry. Is there no chance of a reconciliation?"

"No. She's adamant. She wants a divorce."

"Did you suggest maybe trying some counseling?"

"Gary, I tried everything. I pleaded, I cried, I begged for forgiveness. Nothing. She wants me out by the end of the month."

"So, what does she want."

"Half."

"Half?"

"The one saving grace is that I convinced her that since the artwork is owned by the three of us, it would be a nightmare trying to untangle the whole syndicate partnership thing. So, she says she'll settle for just one of the paintings, Lichtenstein's Drowning Girl."

"We'll have to get Vincent to figure out how we handle this," Tinterow said.

"I know."

"Let's see if he can join us."

"I called earlier, but he wasn't there."

Tinterow left the booth and slipped into the phone booth at the end of the bar. Williams could see that the doctor was talking to someone, and by the way, he was gesturing, he was sure it had to be Vincent. Moments later, he returned.

"Vincent will be down as soon as possible," Tinterow reported.

"Great. I'm going to have a boilermaker. You want another beer?" Williams asked.

"Make it two. Err, better make it three. I'm sure Vincent's going to need one."

"Right."

Vincent had arrived by the time Williams returned from the bar with the drinks. Tinterow broke the news to Vincent. He looked like he had been gut-shot. Frank sat on one side of the booth while Vincent and Tinterow sat opposite him.

Williams took the shot glass of whiskey and just plopped it into the mug of beer. Vincent and Tinterow followed suit.

"So, this divorce is real?"

"Oh, it's real, all right."

"So, she's getting half and wants the Lichtenstein?" Vincent asked.

"Yeah."

"Well, Frank. The auction estimate of the Lichtenstein is about a quarter of a million dollars."

"You are shitting me!" Frank exclaimed.

"No. I am not."

"But we just bought it two years ago for eighteen thousand," Tinterow said.

"How are we going to work this out?" Williams asked.

"Well, I am assuming that Gary is willing to do this. Correct?" Vincent asked the doctor.

"Yes," Tinterow replied.

"In that case, I will also agree. Now, Frank, that means you owe Gary and me eighty-three thousand dollars apiece."

"But I don't have that kind of cash. Especially now with the divorce." Franked whined.

"Or, whenever we start to sell inventory, you're in debt for one hundred sixty-six thousand, six hundred, sixty-six dollars and will see no monies until the debt is paid in full. Agreed?"

A sullen Frank Williams confirmed. "Okay, I will draw up the proper document for everyone's signature tomorrow."

"So, Frank, was it worth it?" Vincent asked.

Williams didn't say a word, but he did look up with a huge grin on his face.

Dr. Gary Tinterow and his wife Cindy were driving to their home from an opera at Lincoln Center. They were only blocks away from their apartment on the corner of 94th Street and Riverside Drive when Richard Croft, a homeless man, happened to wander into the street. Tinterow, who was in an in-depth discussion with Cindy about tonight's performance of Mozart's *La Clemenza di Tito,* didn't see Croft. He consequently rammed his Mercedes-Benz 600 into the drunk, staggering across the road, killing poor Mr. Croft.

Tinterow panicked and fled the scene of the crime. Since it was late, they didn't notice any pedestrians out walking, and the man he hit was obviously a bum, so he decided to take a gamble.

If he did get questioned, he had several that he thought were good responses.

It was dark.

He didn't see the man.

The Mercedes-Benz 600 is such a substantial automobile that he felt nothing.

Are you sure it was my car? There are a lot of Mercedes-Benz 600s in this neighborhood.

There's no damage to my car.

Tinterow took the 600 to an independent Mercedes-Benz body shop in Westport, Connecticut, the following day. He gave the man five hundred dollars for the repair and another five hundred to forget this work ever happened.

Two days after the accident, Tinterow's Mercedes-Benz 600 was showroom-perfect.

There was a small blurb in the Times about a homeless man being involved in a hit-and-run in the Upper West Side. But nothing ever came of it. The NYPD has too much actual crime to spend hours working on some bum being run over. They figured it was probably his fault anyway. The alcohol in his blood was off the charts, so the cops moved on.

Tinterow and his wife Cindy moved on, too, like it never happened. They didn't tell a soul and never spoke of it, even to each other. Sure, it was terrible, but why should a simple mistake ruin their lives? After all, Tinterow was a cardiologist; he saved hundreds of lives. The homeless man was a bum; his life was worthless compared to Doctor Tinterow's. No. It was definitely better to just move on, and so they did.

It was three months to the day that the accident occurred when Dr. Tinterow was walking Buster, his German Shepherd, on Riverside Drive. A shabbily dressed man walking in the opposite direction and said, "Beautiful dog."

Tinterow stopped, as he had often done when people commented on his dog, and replied, "Thank you."

He was about to continue when the man said, "I saw you hit that homeless man in the street with your Mercedes, and you just drove on, Dr. Tinterow."

"What! I have no idea what you're talking about. Who the Hell are you?" Tinterow demanded.

"Me? I'm just a concerned citizen. A concerned citizen who happened to witness a hit and run, doctor."

"You, sir, are mistaken."

"Oh, really. Take a look at this." The man handed Tinterow a photograph taken at night, showing a Mercedes-Benz 600 with the license plate clearly visible hitting a man in the middle of the street.

Tinterow stood silent, petrified. He could feel the blood rushing down to his feet. He looked at the man with hatred, his brow furrowed, his upper lip curled. He ripped the photograph from the man's hand and tore it up.

The man smiled and handed Tinterow another photograph, "Here. There's plenty more where that came from."

Tinterow stared at the man and asked, "How much?"

"Two hundred thousand dollars, Cash."

"No. You'll start demanding more, milking me dry."

"Look, Doc. I'm not greedy. I just want the two hundred thou, and you'll get all the photos and the negatives. I figure if I keep trying to drain you, you'll have enough and go to the cops. I'm just looking for a quick score. In and out. What do you say?"

"It will take me a week or so to get that kind of money."

"What do you take me for a fool? I know you high falutin doctors make tons of dough."

"It's all in investments. I don't keep hundreds of thousands under my mattress. I'll have to move some things around, so I'll need a week." Tinterow demanded.

"Okay, one week. Next Saturday."

"Call my office, not my home," Tinterow said as he handed the man his card.

"I'll call Friday afternoon with the details." The man turned and walked away.

Tinterow thought about following the blackmailer but was too distraught. He decided to finish his walk with Buster and think. His mind was racing with all kinds of vengeful thoughts and ideas.

Cindy was out when he finally returned home to his apartment on the fourteenth floor overlooking the Hudson River. A note was taped on the refrigerator saying she was out with her girlfriends and wouldn't be home till late. He'll have to fend for himself.

He called Frank and Vincent and said that he needed their help. Something urgent came up. They both agreed to come by immediately. Frank was the first to show up, with Vincent minutes behind.

Once they both were there, Tinterow poured them all whiskeys and had them all go into his den just in case Cindy came home early. Williams and Vincent took a seat on the Chesterfield leather couch.

Frank took a swig and asked, "Okay, Gary, what the Hell's going on."

Tinterow stood before them and began, "First of all, I need you guys to swear to God that what is said here will never leave this room?"

Frank and Vincent looked at each other and mumbled, "Sure. Yeah."

"No. I need you both to swear to God!" Tinterow commanded.

Frank and Vincent solemnly swore to God that they would never repeat what would be discussed with any living soul.

"Okay, did you guys happen to read a couple of months ago in the Times about a hit-and-run accident that killed a homeless man in this neighborhood?"

"No," Vincent said.

"Me neither," Frank added.

"Well." Tinterow took a big gulp of whiskey and said, "It was me. We were coming home after the opera, and suddenly, this bum stepped out into the street, and I hit him."

"Jesus," Williams uttered.

"Yeah, I know. Then, I panicked and left the scene. I didn't see anyone out on the street. I got the car repaired and waited for the cops to come by. They never did. That was three months ago. Then today, this guy walks up to me and hands me this photo." Tinterow handed Vincent the incriminating photograph, who looked at it and passed it to Williams.

Frank looked at the photo and asked, "How much is he asking?"

'Two hundred thousand. Cash."

"Wholly fuck!" Frank exclaimed.

"What are you going to do?" Vincent asked.

"I told him I'd pay. He promised that he'd turn over all the prints and negatives."

"No. No. No. This fucker is just going to drain you dry!" Frank insisted.

"What can I do? If I go to the police, I'll get arrested for hit and run and possibly vehicular manslaughter! Either way, I'm fucked."

"When are you supposed to meet with this guy for the payoff?" Vincent asked.

"Sometime Saturday. He's going to call me at the office on Friday."

"Okay, we need to have you meet somewhere where it's beneficial for you," Frank said.

"What do you mean?" Vincent inquired.

"Someplace where Gary's in control, in case things go wrong."

"Wrong?" Tinterow asked.

"Yeah, what if this punk pulls a gun on you? He takes all the money and keeps the photos and negs. Gary, you got to be prepared." Frank asserted.

"But I don't even own a gun."

"I do." Frank proudly announced.

"You do?" Vincent asked, surprised.

"Yeah, a Smith & Wesson .38 Special, Police Revolver."

"And *you* know how to use it?" Vincent challenged.

"Damn right," Frank said with much machismo. Then asked Tinterow, "Where could we meet?"

"We?" Vincent pressed.

"Yeah. Come on, Gary needs our help, support, and backup."

"I guess we could meet in this abandoned building where I and several other doctors are rehabbing, 315 West 125th Street, West Harlem," Tinterow suggested.

"Will there be any workers there?" Frank asked.

"No. They don't work on the weekends."

"Good. When this guy calls, you tell him where you will meet and when. Tell him you'll meet him outside the building so it doesn't look like a setup. Vincent and I will arrive an hour or two before your meeting."

"Then what?" Vincent poised.

"Then. We'll wait out of sight, and we'll be listening. If he tries to pull anything funny, we'll step in." Frank said with a big smile on his face.

"Frank, this isn't make-believe. If you bring a gun, you better be prepared to use it because if you don't, the other guy will."

"I know that."

"Gary, are you good with all of this?" Vincent queried.

Vincent could see Tinterow trying to summon some bravado before answering, "Yeah. Let's do this. You guys in?"

"Hell, yeah. I'm in," Frank said enthusiastically.

Vincent thoughtfully answered, "Yeah, if only to keep Frank from shooting someone."

Jerry Wald was a third-rate private investigator. His clients were primarily people looking to get dirt on their spouses for divorce cases, insurance companies wanting to see if claimants were filing legitimate claims or just trying to make a quick buck, along with companies looking into employees who they think might be cheating, embezzling, or stealing company secrets.

Jerry was never without his 35mm Leica IIIg camera with a 90mm lens around his neck. Three months ago, while trailing the wife of a client whose husband suspected her of having an adulterous affair with the building doorman, I was tailing her down Riverside Drive.

Wald was taking photographs of the doorman when the wife, out of the corner of his eye, spotted a man staggering into the street in front of a large Mercedes. He instinctively swung his camera and began snapping photographs.

Wald felt he had just struck pay dirt when the Mercedes driver fled. Once he got back to his studio apartment down on Henry Street and developed the film, he saw that he not only had the accident on film but also a clear image of the license plate number. Wald immediately began planning how he was going to spend all that money.

The first thing he would do was move out of that fleabag apartment, move uptown into one of those deluxe apartments, and get an office instead of working out of the dump he was living in.

He might just get himself a classy girlfriend. Betty Langston was OK. She was all right but not a real head-turner. The best thing about Betty was the convenience. She lived three floors up in the same building, was a halfway decent cook, and most nights, she was willing to let him have his way with her. Jerry liked Betty a lot, but a man can dream, can't he?

Four o'clock on Friday afternoon came, and Jerry Wald called the office of Gary Tinterow, MD, Ph.D.

"Doctor Tinterow's office." The receptionist said.

"Doctor Tinterow, please."

"Who may I say is calling?"

"Ah, Mr. Jones, the photographer. He's expecting my call."

"One moment, please."

"Hello!" Tinterow answered.

"Hello, Doc. You got the dough?"

"Yes, I have it."

"OK, here's how it's going to hap..."

Tinterow cut him off, "No. *Here's* how it's going to happen. I want this to be discreet. I'm not taking any chances. I will meet you at seven o'clock at 315 West 125th Street in West Harlem. It's a building that some partners and I are rehabbing. There's no one there, so we can complete our business in private."

"No way, Doc."

"Fine. I've already talked to my attorney, and he thinks I can walk away with a hefty penalty and community service or, at worst, a short time in a country club prison. I prefer to keep things quiet, but I will not take a chance of you pulling something. So, if you want the money, we'll do it my way." Tinterow demanded.

Wald remained silent, thinking. Finally, greed won out.

"OK. Seven o'clock tonight. You better bring the dough!"

"And *you* better bring the negatives and all the copies!"

CLICK

Frank Williams and Vincent got to the building shortly before five. They went to the second floor to wait for the meeting at seven. They arrived early in case the blackmailer wanted to scope things out or thought he might get there first to try an ambush.

They waited for seven o'clock, sitting on sizeable five-gallon paint drums, consciously staying away from windows and not making any sounds. Williams took out his pistol and showed it to Vincent. He checked to be sure the gun was loaded; he even brought extra rounds.

"What? Are you expecting the shootout at the OK Corral?" Vincent gasped.

"Trust me. It's better to be over-prepared than under." Frank snapped back.

It was seven o'clock when they heard Gary's voice outside.

"Did you bring everything?" Gary asked.

"They're all right here in the satchel. You got the cash?"

"In the briefcase. Come on, let's go inside, out of the way of prying eyes." Tinterow said as he was looking all around.

"After you," Wald said.

Tinterow fumbled with the keys, finally unlocking the two deadbolt locks. He entered first and locked the door once Wald passed him.

"Let's go in here," Tinterow said as he led the way into the kitchen, where counters had already been installed. They each slowly placed their cases on the counter facing each other. Tinterow unlocked his briefcase first, opened the top, and spun the case around. There are four neat rows of bundles of one hundred dollars; each row was stacked three high.

"Oh, hoochie, mama!" Wald squealed with joy.

"Your turn," Tinterow said.

Wald opened his satchel and reached in, but instead of revealing the photographs and negatives, he pulled out a snub-nosed pistol and pointed it at Tinterow.

"Doctor Tinterow, you're so naïve. Did you really think I would settle for a lousy 200 Gs? Oh, no, Doc, this is going to be the beginning of a long and beautiful relationship." Wald said, grinning from ear to ear.

The grin faded away quickly when he heard a voice from behind him say, "Drop the gun, shithead, or I'll blow your fucking brains all over the wall!" Williams's voice was ice cold.

"Wald did as he was told.

"Now get down on the ground, face down, spread eagle. You move. You die." Williams commanded.

Vincent walked over to the counter and looked inside Wald's bag. There was nothing.

"It's empty," Vincent said.

"Where is it?" Tinterow demanded.

"Ha. Fuck you!" Wald sneered.

"You think we're fucking around!" Williams said as he gave Wald a hard, swift kick to the ribs.

"AAGGGH!" Wald grimaced.

"Vincent, check to see if this creep has a wallet."

Vincent reached down and pulled an old, worn leather wallet from Wald's back pocket. He looked through it and found his driver's license and private investigator's ID.

Vincent read, "Jerry Wald. 127 Henry Street, apartment 1B. He's a private eye."

"That's right, Vincent. I'm going to find out who all you guys are, and then I'm going to make you all pay through the nose." Wald chuckled.

Williams reared back and gave Wald an even harder kick to the ribs.

"AAHH! AGH!"

Williams leaned down so Wald could hear what he whispered, "Listen, dick! The only thing you're going to get is a bullet in the head." Williams then cocked the pistol next to Wald's ear.

"Now. Where's *all* the goods?" Williams demanded.

Quickly trying to defuse the hostility, Vincent said, "I bet it's at his apartment. Let me go down and look around."

Williams looked at Tinterow, who nodded his approval.

"OK, get his keys and go check it out. We'll stay here with our newest best buddy, Jerry, until you get back." Williams said sarcastically.

Vincent got keys from Wald's sports coat pocket and quickly walked to the door. He walked down the block, hailed a taxi, and stood in front of 127 Henry Street by eight-forty-five.

The hallway was empty and dark. He slipped the key into the lock and silently turned it until the bolt slid back. The room was dark; he felt along the wall until he turned on the overhead light. Vincent walked over to the picture window that faced the street and pulled the drapes shut. He was mindful of using his handkerchief to open drawers and anything he touched. There was an old pea-green four-drawer filing cabinet in the corner; Vincent figured it had to be where the private dick kept all his client files.

There was no rhyme or reason to the files; they weren't filed in alphabetical order or by date. It took Vincent two hours to find the folder with the prints and negatives. Vincent had a hunch that there had to be at least another photo that this crumb would use to come back again. He was right. He found two; one was hidden, taped behind a picture on the wall, and the other was under a rag rug in the kitchen.

As Vincent was ready to leave, he turned off the overhead light, opened the curtains, and returned to the door to leave. There was a light knock on the door.

"Jerry?" A woman's voice softly said.

Vincent froze.

"Jerry? It's Betty. Open up. Come on, baby."

Vincent's heart was beating so loud that he feared that the woman on the other side of the door could hear it.

Finally, he heard footsteps walking away. Then, what sounded like someone walking up creaky stairs. He waited a few minutes before slowly opening the door to peek out. The coast was clear. Vincent eased his way out of the apartment, locked the door behind him, and made his way back out onto the street.

He walked over to East Broadway and got a cab heading uptown. Twenty minutes later, he was back in West Harlem.

Jerry Wald was still laying spread eagle on the floor when he entered the kitchen.

"What did you find?" Tinterow asked anxiously.

"I found the negatives and a dozen prints in a filing cabinet, plus I found one print behind a painting and another under a rug," Vincent said as he handed the packet to Tinterow.

"Ha! You missed a couple more that I've got hidden away." Wald said gleefully.

"Oh yeah." Williams jeered as he gave Wald a hard kick to the ribs. So hard that everyone heard two of them crack.

"AAHH! AGH! You bastard, I'll kill you!"

Wald tried to spring up and made a leap for his snub-nosed .38, still lying feet away on the floor. He grabbed it and started to roll over to shoot Williams, but his cracked ribs slowed him down. He never got off a shot. Williams reacted immediately and fired once, hitting Wald in the forehead, spattering Wald's brains all over Tinterow's eight-hundred-dollar Gucci loafers.

POW

Tinterow instinctively went into doctor mode; he knelt next to Wald's bloody body and felt for a pulse; there was none. He stood up and announced what everyone knew, "He's dead."

"He was going to shoot me! I had to." Williams franticly said.

"We know, Frank. The question is, what do we do now?" Vincent said, trying to stay calm.

"Well, we can't go to the police. I'd go to jail for murder, Gary would be arrested for hit and run and vehicular manslaughter, and you'd be an accessory after the fact." Williams stated.

"OK. Gary, what's going on here at the rehab?" Vincent asked.

"I don't know. They're rehabbing the building. Why?"

"Let's go down in the basement and see if there's somewhere down there where we can put him," Vincent suggested.

They all went down to the basement. There, they found dozens of cement bags, tools of all kinds, picks, shovels, sledgehammers, drills, and saws.

Frank walked over into a corner at the far end of the basement and said, "We'll bury him here. We'll break up the floor, bury him, and replace the floor."

"What are you fucking nuts!" Tinterow yelped.

"You got a better idea?" Williams dared.

"No," Tinterow answered.

"How about we wait until the early morning, then we weigh him down with one of these cinderblocks and dump his body in the Hudson River," Vincent suggested.

"Where?" Tinterow asked.

"Well, we'll drive over to Jersey, swing off 9, head south into Fort Lee. I know a deserted pier a little ways past the North Hudson Yacht Club. By three in the morning, there won't be a soul around. If there is, we drive on until we find a spot." Vincent said.

Frank looked at the others and said, "Let's go!"

The pier in Fort Lee was too dilapidated to get out far enough with Mr. Wald. So, they drove down River Road to Edgewater, New Jersey, where they found the deserted pier they could drive to the end. They got out of the 600 and stood admiring the skyline of Manhattan for almost a half-hour. In actuality, they were just observing the surrounding area to see if it was safe to dump Mr. Wald's corpse into the Hudson.

It was four o'clock when they opened the trunk and removed the cargo. They quickly carried the body to the end of the pier and gave Mt. Wald the old heave-ho.

"Let's get the fuck out of here," Tinterow said.

They all scrambled back into the car, and as they were driving back over the GW Bridge, Williams threw the revolver out the window into the Hudson River.

On the way back into Manhattan, Vincent told Tinterow, "Listen, Gary, there is the possibility that the police will come by to question you. Tell them that you met him at the place in West Harlem. You were going to hire him because you were suspicious that someone might be stealing supplies. You talked, and then he left. That's all you know."

"What if they see all the blood?"

"We poured two gallons of bleach on the spot. We "accidentally" spilled a pint of black paint on it and sprayed some powder concrete. There's no fucking way they're going to see blood."

Williams asked, "Why would they even come to see Tinterow?"

"Who knows what kind of records or calendar this guy kept? The place was a pigsty, but he might have written your name somewhere." Vincent said.

They sat quietly for a long time as Tinterow began to drop everyone off at their apartments. Frank was the first. When they arrived at his place, the sun started peering up over the East River. They sat silently in front of his apartment building; finally, Frank said, "Guys, we got to put this behind us. What happened was terrible, but it happened, and now it's over."

"Let's give it a couple of days before we get together," Vincent suggested.

"Good idea. See you, guys." Williams said as he got out of the car. He walked straight into the building without looking back.

Tinterow was silent all the way downtown. When they reached Vincent's place, Vincent asked, "You going to be okay?"

"I keep wondering if there was any other way we could have played it?"

"Look. You were going to play it straight; you were going to pay up. But he had to be a greedy asshole. It's his fault, not yours."

"I guess."

"Hey. This, too, shall pass. Call me if you need to talk."

"Thanks, Vincent."

Times were changing quickly within the art world. Although still a significant force, abstract expressionism was being challenged by a new league of young upstart artists who were developing an art movement known as "Pop Art."

Pop artists were challenging the traditions of "fine art" by including imagery from popular culture. They began using images from advertising campaigns, comic books, and ordinary mass-produced objects, such as a three-dimensional cardboard box labeled with the Campbell tomato juice logo and a silkscreen canvas of a Coca-Cola bottle.

The Pop-in Pop Art stands for Popular Culture. Pop Art is a style of art that is based on simple, bold images of everyday objects, usually painted in bright colors. The movement gained a massive following and was considered revolutionary. There were many cultural movements going on at that time. In the 1960s, a revolution was in the air. People wanted change; people demanded change. There was the civil rights movement, the student movement, the women's movement, the anti-Vietnam movement, the gay rights movement, and the environmental movement. Social revolution was in the air; it was a climate of turbulence, experimentation, and consumerism that a new generation of artists emerged, reflecting that change.

It was the Summer of Love, Woodstock, Hippies, and LSD; the mantra was *"Tune in, Turn on, and Drop Out."*

For Vincent Rainwater, the sixties were a time of excitement. The art world was rocking. Amy and Vincent traveled to San Francisco to review an extensive gallery showing several new artists, including those associated with the psychedelic art movement: Peter Max, Roger Niles Rick Griffin, Robert Williams, and a counterculture underground comix cartoonist, R. Crumb. Art was moving away from traditional forms. The sixties brought notoriety to artists whose medium was murals, posters, album covers, and comic books.

Of all the psychedelic artists, Roger Niles, a Coney Island resident, was considered the "Cosmic King." Niles was initially trained as a realistic painter. He developed a unique, dynamic, avant-garde, and diagrammatic style of art.

He blended archival photographs with paint, India ink, and other media to create provocative and innovative images.

His vibrant images soon appeared in TV commercials and magazine advertisements worldwide. He was a significant force in the Cultural Revolution Movement.

Coming away from reviewing the psychedelic art movement gallery show, Vincent purchased a dozen works from each artist, adding to the depleted syndicate's portfolio.

For Dr. Tinterow and Williams, life slowly returned to normal after many sleepless nights and constantly looking over their shoulders. But after a while, when the police never came to question them, the memory of the death of Jerry Wald eventually faded.

There was a tiny blip in the New York Post about Jerry Wald, a small-time private investigator who had gone missing, but that was it. Even seven months later, when his bloated, decomposed body floated to the surface of the Hudson River on the New Jersey side, nobody seemed to care. It took the police several months to finally discover who the deceased was after the fish had nibbled the flesh off of his fingers, hands, and face. They finally got a hit off of his dental records.

The New Jersey police sent detectives to his last known address. But his apartment had been rented to another tenant, his personal effects were sent to his folks in upstate New York, and his girlfriend at the time, Betty Collins, had moved back home to Gulfport, Mississippi. The NJPD filed it as another unsolved crime.

Tinterow, Williams, and Vincent didn't see much of each other for the longest time afterward, and when they finally did, none of them spoke of it. Neither Tinterow nor

Vincent ever mentioned the incident to their wives, and as time passed, it was as if it had never happened. Eventually, life as they knew it returned to normal.

But it was hardly normal. There was a new normal. Dr. Tinterow's marriage slowly started to fall apart, as it was frequently the stress and expectation that at any moment, the heavy hand of the law would come crashing down upon them. At first, they tried a trial separation, but eventually, they divorced. Murder is a heavy and lonesome burden to carry by yourself.

Tinterow's wife decided to seek a large settlement due to an undisclosed and private incident that caused her great mental anguish. The syndicate's portfolio was dwindling; it was holding on to a handful of minor unknown artists. With the divorce, they lost all of their major artists. Vincent was the only member who was doing fine financially.

One night at the Yale Club, Frank and Tinterow were bemoaning their financial woes and admitted to each other that even though they committed the mortal sin of murder that between them, they truly felt no remorse. In fact, they both found it exhilarating.

As the night went on and the wine went down, they began to hatch a get-rich scheme that would shake up the art world and even a few scores. But at the moment, it had to be kept just between the two of them…for now.

For years, Max Albertson had stuck in the craw of Tinterow. His holier-than-thou, smug attitude had always bothered him when they first met. Both Tinterow and Williams had begun following the world of art since they got involved in investing with the syndicate, as they did with all of their investments, whether it was art or stocks and bonds.

Albertson was becoming a hot property. Museums, corporations, and private collectors were hiring him for large installations. Some of his sculptures were worth tens of millions for projects in public spaces.

It was when Vincent and Amy were away in San Francisco reviewing the psychedelic artists that Frank received an invitation to a preview showing of Max Albertson's newest body of work. The fact that Tinterow didn't receive an invitation further infuriated him. He felt it was an intentional slap in the face.

Saturday night at 201 Spring Street, Soho was jumping. Williams parked his black LeBron down the block in front of a bodega. On the way to the party, Williams spotted a young vagrant sleeping on a subway grate out in front of the bodega for warmth. He wore old, grimy army fatigues. He had a scruffy beard, long, unkempt, matted hair, and a filthy face and hands.

As they passed him, they could detect the strong, fetid, foul-smelling, pungent stench of someone who hadn't bathed in months. Beside him was an old beat-up coffee can with a handful of change and a hand-scribbled sign written on a ragged piece of cardboard.

HOMELESS VIETNAM VETERAN
WILL WORK - PLEASE HELP
GOD BLESS YOU

Inside were several paparazzi snapping photographs of all the "Beautiful" people. There were Hollywood movie stars, New York stage actors, rock stars, patrons, collectors, and dozens of other pop art icons. The whole scene was one huge hippie party. Grass, uppers, downers, cocaine, and LSD were passed around like Hors d'oeuvres, Grateful Dead music was blasting, and there were at least six gorgeous women who were casually strolling around totally naked. One of which was Linda Scott, a high-fashion model, five foot eleven, with long blond hair, emerald green eyes, and legs that go from here to there and back again.

As Williams and Tinterow entered the loft, Frank presented the bouncer, a man who had no neck, dressed in all black, wearing black Ray-Bans, and weighed three-hundred and twenty-six pounds, with his invitation. The giant gorilla didn't even look at the invite; he just eyeballed the two of them, grunted, and shooed them in.

When Max spotted them walking in, he took Linda by the hand and greeted them.

"Mr. Williams, I'm so glad you could come. This is Linda." Max chirped.

"Good to see you, too," Williams said.

"I'm sorry, Dr. Tintersoll. It's nice to see you again as well." Albertson said with a slight hint of a smirk.

"That's Dr. Tinterow."

"Oh, I am sorry, Tinterow. And doctor, you are a psychologist, am I correct?"

"Psychiatrist."

"That's right. I do apologize."

Linda seemed a bit confused when she asked, "What's the difference?"

"Well, you see, psychiatrists are medical doctors, psychologists are not. A psychiatrist can prescribe medication, and a psychologist can't. Psychiatrists diagnose illness, manage treatment, and provide a range of therapies for complex and serious mental illness. Psychologists focus on providing psychotherapy to help patients." Tinterow explained.

"In other words, doll. You're a shrink, right, Doc?" Max said dismissively.

A vein popped up on Tinterow's forehead, and his face turned a bright beet red. He was getting ready to start something, but thankfully, Linda saw his anger rising, and she quickly said, "How about some champagne, Doctor Tinterow." She took him by the arm and led him to the bar at the far end of the loft.

"So, what do you do, Linda?" Tinterow asked.

"I'm a fashion model." She said.

"Fashion, huh? I'd never know it by looking at you." He said with a grin.

Throughout the night, Tinterrow and Albertson continued making jabs at each other. Tinterow's remarks were high-brow and cerebral, whereas Albertson's were gritty and funny. Which pissed off Tinterow even more, and the fact that people were laughing at him. Him, Gary C. Tinterow, M.D. Ph.D., a renowned psychiatrist, the butt of jokes, unacceptable.

They came to the party for a reason, and the fact that this man had the nerve to try and humiliate him in front of all these people was unconscionable. One does not trifle with a man like Gary C. Tinterow, M.D. Ph.D., and expect to get away with it.

Williams and Tinterow sat parked in Williams' 1968 black Chrysler Imperial LeBron 4dr Sedan across the street from Albertson's loft, waiting.

The party officially ended around three in the morning. The last of the guests to leave were Linda and the other women who paraded around the party nude. Tinterow and Williams waited until Spring Street was deserted. Williams reached over, opened the glove box, and removed a Smith & Wesson .38 Model 10 pistol. Tinterow gave Williams a quizzical look.

"It's clean. The serial numbers have all been filed off. I got it from one of my clients months ago." Williams said as he put on a pair of gloves.

They walked back to 201, continually checking to see if there was anyone out on the street. They passed the sleeping army bum, who hadn't moved an inch since 7 pm. Frank rang the buzzer.

BUZZZZZZ

There wasn't any response. He rang again.

BUZZZZZZ

"Hello?"

"Hey, Max. It's Frank Williams. Sorry to bother you, but I think I might have dropped my wallet at the party. Could I possibly come up and take a look around?"

"Sure thing. Come on up."

BUZZZZZ

When the elevator doors opened up, the last thing Max Albertson's brain registered before the fire from the muzzle from Frank Williams' Smith & Wesson .38 was Gary Tinterow smiling and saying, "So long, asshole."

POW

As Max Albertson's lifeless body lay oozing blood, the elevator doors slowly closed; Williams and Tinterow walked out of the lobby and back towards their car. As they walked past the homeless man, Williams leaned down, slipped the gun under the blanket covering the sleeping vet, and drove off.

On the ride to drop Tinterow home, Williams reiterated that the police would undoubtedly come around to interview them and everyone else at the party. They just had to casually mention the homeless guy down the block.

Tinterrow was almost giddy. Not only was the value of Max Albertson's art going soar, but he also got rid of that smart-ass pseudointellectual art snob.

The afternoon edition of the Times had a whole section about the significant loss caused by Max Albertson's death.

The Chief of Police of Manhattan, Donald Miller, stated that although they were at the preliminary stages of the investigation, he promised that this murder was an NYPD top priority. He told reporters that they already had some promising leads. Something that no criminal ever wants to hear.

"Vincent, wake up! Wake up!" Amy said as she came running into the San Francisco's Four Seasons Hotel bedroom.

"What?" Vincent responded, dazed and confused.

"Turn on the television. Max Albertson has been shot and killed."

"My God, you're kidding!" Vincent said as he scrambled out of bed and ran to turn the bedroom television on.

"Once again, our top story this morning is that Max Albertson, world-renowned New York City sculptor, was gunned down last night in his Soho apartment sometime after 3 am. His body was discovered this morning by his longtime girlfriend, Linda Saunders, a prominent model in the world of high fashion.

According to a police spokesman, Mr. Albertson had hosted a large party that night. Sources tell WJM News that the police will be looking into all the attendees for possible suspects. The guest list was rumored to be a virtual who's-who of the New York elite.

This is Biff Henderson reporting. Back to you, Skip."

"What time is our flight this afternoon?" Amy asked.

"Two o'clock. We have six hours." He said.

"What do you feel like doing?"

"Not much, now."

"Well, let's walk down to Fisherman's Wharf and have something to eat." She suggested.

"Sounds like a plan."

As they made their way to the Wharf, they spent most of that time talking about Max.

"You know, it just occurred to me that Gary and Frank planned to go to that party."

"Get out of here!"

"Yeah. I'll call them when we get back to the hotel before we head on out to the airport."

They casually walked along the Wharf, watching the fishing boats leave the harbor going out for the day's catch.

They ended up at Fog Harbor Fish House for brunch, out on Pier 39. They shared an order of crispy calamari; Vincent had the Cioppino, which consisted of crab, fresh fish, clams, scallops, and mussels stewed in a seafood tomato broth. Amy decided on the Seared Scallops & Crab Risotto. Together, they each polished off two bottles of Fog Harbor Lager. They made a quick stop at Ghirardelli Square to pick up some chocolate for friends back home on the way back to the hotel.

When they got back to the hotel, Vincent called Gary.

"Gary. Vincent, we just heard about Max Albertson."

"Yeah, it's tragic. What's really spooky is that Frank and I were there."

"Did you happen to see anything suspicious?"

"No. But it was one weird party. There were lots of celebrities and A-listers, tons of beautiful women, some of them even walking around naked, and lots and lots of drugs."

"Have you talked to the police?"

"Not yet. They said they were planning on talking to all of the guests who were there. So, I guess Frank and I will be talking to them, I'm sure."

"Well, Amy and I will be back in the City late tonight. I'd love to talk to you and Frank before writing my piece on Max for the Times tomorrow. Who knows, you might be able to give me an insight into what happened that night."

"Yeah, who knows," Tinterow said with a snicker.

The three of them sat in a booth at the back of the dining room at the Yale Club.

"Vincent, you look like shit," Frank said.

"Thanks. Our flight was delayed. We didn't get into LaGuardia until after two this morning. It was after four a.m. when we got back to our place."

"Yeah, those cross-country flights are a bitch. Especially when you're going west to east." Gary said sympathetically.

"I've been running on caffeine all day. I think I'm catching my second wind. So, tell me about the party." Vincent asked.

Sitting across from Williams, Gary gave him a look and slowly shook his head no, saying, "Like I said yesterday. It was a bizarre party, wasn't it, Frank."

"Yes, it was. It was super weird."

"What's the matter with you two?" Vincent quizzed.

Frank leaned in and whispered, "How much do you think our two Albertson's pieces are worth today?"

Vincent looked stunned and confused. He sat quietly for several minutes, looking at his two best friends, before a light bulb came on inside his head.

"Oh, sweet Jesus. No! Don't tell me that. You two didn't."

With a wolfish grin, Gary asked, "How much do you think our two Albertson's pieces are worth today?"

"Are you fucking kidding me? Vincent asked.

"How much?" Frank repeated.

"Our six-thousand-dollar investment is now worth six hundred thousand," Tinterrow stated matter-of-factly.

"You killed Max Albertson!"

"Shhhhh! Keep your voice down." Tinterow said.

"But why?"

"For the money," Williams whispered.

"And because I thought he was a pompous ass."

"You guys are joking with me, right?" Vincent half laughed, hoping they would admit they were just kidding him.

"Six hundred thousand," Tinterrow said coolly.

"Look, Vincent, it isn't like we hadn't killed before," Williams said.

"Jeez! You guys have put me in a real tight spot here."

"How so?" Williams asked innocently.

"How so! I now know that you've killed Max Albertson."

"Well, it's not like we haven't killed before," Williams said.

"That was different. Our lives were threatened. That was self-defense. He was going for his gun." Vincent explained.

"Vincent, it's hard to claim self-defense when he was shot in the back." Williams countered.

"But killing Max Albertson was just plain murder."

"So," Tinterow said with indifference.

"Gary, you're a doctor, for God's sake. What about the Hippocratic Oath?"

"Oh, grow up, Vincent. You swear an oath that's over 2000 years old to a number of *"healing gods."* If anything, it's a matter of conscience, not law." Tinterow responded using air quotes to emphasize healing gods.

"Look, Vincent, we're not asking you to kill anyone," Williams said.

"No?" Vincent asked.

"God, no. We'll do that. All you have to do is just continue discovering new artists and making purchases for the syndicate. Gary and I will do the heavy lifting, as it were when the time is right." Williams said, smiling.

"So, you're saying that I should go out and purposely find people for you to murder?"

"Well, I wouldn't put it like that. You make it sound so tawdry." Tinterow said sheepishly.

"Oh, I'm sorry. How would you put it?"

"Look at it this way, Vincent. You're finding new and talented artists. Artists who have something new and exciting to contribute to the art world. You give them something that all artists want: recognition and fame. We give them immortality." Williams elucidated.

"You kill them."

"Vincent, it's a win-win for everybody. They go out at the zenith of their career, become even more famous with all the notoriety of their death, and the collectors will receive a great return on their investments. You see, win-win." Tinterow said smugly.

"You guys are such humanitarians. Such art lovers. You're only interested in the money, that's all!"

"Vincent, we're not asking you to do anything illegal; just do your job. Art critic." Williams said.

"And it's not like we're going to be killing every artist in the world. Just once every now and then." Tinterow added.

"This is insane. Max didn't deserve to die. He didn't do anything wrong. It's not fair."

"Fairs got nothing to do with this. Life's not fair, my friend." Tinterow said.

"I gotta go," Vincent said, overwhelmed.

"Be sure to give Amy our love," Williams said with a grin.

"Max Albertson, Famous For His Natural Monumental Works Of Art, Murdered."

<u>Vincent Rainwater</u>

"Artist Max Albertson, who was known for creating monumental works of art that incorporated the natural materials and the environment of three-dimensional cubes in cities around the world, was found murdered Saturday at his home in Soho. He was 47 years old.

Albertson, born in Brooklyn in 1921, attended New York's Pratt Institute. Max joined the Army at the outbreak of WW2. He stormed the beaches at Normandy and fought all the way to Berlin. Max received two Purple Hearts, three Bronze Stars, and six commendations for bravery.

After the war, Max returned to Brooklyn and began as a painter, but Albertson is best known for his large untreated steel cube sculptures that develop a painterly green patina over time.

Today, Albertson's work is in the collections of the Metropolitan Museum of Art in New York, the Brooklyn Museum, the Museum of Fine Arts in Boston, the Hirschhorn Museum in Washington, the San Francisco Museum of Modern Art, the Whitney Museum of American Art and many other institutions."

Homicide Detective Sergeant Bobby Dufort of Manhattan South was assigned the case of Max Albertson's murder. Dufort was a hard-nosed old school detective. He'd been with the NYPD for over 28 years and with homicide for 18 of those 28 years. His partner was a new kid in homicide, a rookie named Bill Campbell.

He'd been in homicide for only two weeks. Campbell felt lucky to be working with Dufort, whose reputation preceded him. Dufort solved some of Manhattan's biggest murders: The Working Girl Murders, The Kew Gardens Massacre, and The Bobby Keaton Kidnapping and Murder.

His captain, Captain John Daniels, called Dufort and his partner Campbell into his office. Bobby, I want you and Campbell to handle the Albertson case.

"Albertson, the artist?" Dufort asked.

"Right. It's high profile, so see if you can wrap it quickly."

"Here's the file, such as it is," Daniels said as he handed Dufort the folder.

Dufort opened the file and held the one page that was stuffed inside.

"One page! You're kidding me, right?"

"Sorry, Bobby."

"Come on, Campbell."

Dufort stormed out of Captain Daniel's office with his junior following close behind on his tail. Dufort was heard mumbling obscenities all the way down the hall until he reached his office. He grabbed his Stetson Wool Felt Cranston Pork Pie hat and trench coat off the coat rack, and the two of them headed off to the coroner's office.

Dufort let his subordinate take all the notes while he fired off questions, queries, and quizzes. He conducted his interrogations at high speed.

"Hey, Doc. Whadda we got?"

"Single bullet wound to the chest." Doctor Batell, the medical examiner, answered.

"How far from the victim was our killer when he shot?"

"It's all in the report, Dufort."

"Come on, Doc. Just tell me. I find those medical reports boring as Hell. No offense."

"Oh, why would I take offense? You can read, can't you?"

Dufort turned to Campbell and sniped, "Very funny. Five thousand comedians out of work, and I'm dealing with Shecky Batell."

"All right! All right! The killer or killers were no more than ten feet away. The vic dropped where he was shot. It appears that the perpetrator shot him as he was waiting at the elevator."

"Time of death?"

"Between 3 am, and 5 am. Closer to 3 am."

"Drugs?"

"You name it. His insides looked like a Walgreens pharmacy. Marijuana, Cocaine, Black Beauties, and LSD."

"Sounds like one Hell of a party. Anything else?"

"Yeah, but nothing that would interest you."

"Okay, thanks, Doc."

"What now, Sarge?" Campbell asked.

"Now we do the grunt work. Call on everyone on the guest list. All Two hundred of them. Fuck!"

It took Dufort and Campbell over six weeks to contact and interview everyone on the guest list. They interviewed Frank Williams at his office around week four.

"Mr. Williams, thank you for taking the time to meet with us. I'm Detective Sergeant Dufort, and this is Detective Campbell. We're investigating the murder of Max Albertson. I understand that you attended a party at Mr. Albertson's loft apartment on the night he was killed. Is that correct?"

"Yes. That is correct. But we didn't stay long." Williams said.

"We?"

"Ah, Doctor Tinterow and I went to the party together."

"I see."

"Were either of you a personal friend of Mr. Albertson?"

"No. Not exactly."

"What exactly?"

"We are collectors. I received an invitation to the party and thought it would be a hoot to go and see how the other half parties."

"The other half?"

"You know. The creative types. All the parties I ever go to are stuffy, button-down, and boring. But not this one. Beautiful women were running around naked and all kinds of drugs, not that either Doctor Tinterow or I indulged,"

"Mr. Williams, I really don't give a rat's ass about the drugs. I'm here about a murder."

"Yes, of course. Sorry"

"While you were at the party, did you see Mr. Albertson and anyone having any arguments or anything suspicious?"

"No, I can't say that I did."

"What time did you and Doctor Tinterow leave the party?"

"I believe that we left around two."

"How did you get to the party? Did you take a taxi, the subway, or drive?"

"I took my car."

"And what kind of car do you have, Mr. Williams?"

"A Chrysler Imperial LeBron."

"Color?"

"Black."

"Is there anything that you can think of that might help aid our investigation?"

"Well, when we arrived, we noticed this homeless man sleeping on the street, not far from the building. He was wearing army fatigues; he was shouting obscenities. He seemed rather violent. Doctor Tinterow and I crossed the street just to be safe."

"Can you be more specific in your description?"

"He was youngish, had dark hair, was Caucasian, and had a beard. He had a sign that said that he was a Vietnam vet. And I can't be certain, but I think I may have seen the handle of a pistol in the guy's belt."

"Do you think you could identify this guy if you saw him again?"

"Probably."

"Well, thank you for your time, Mr. Williams. Here's my card. If you think of anything else, please call me, day or night." Dufort said as he handed Williams one of his business cards.

Once they were out on the street, Campbell asked his mentor, "So, what's your take on this guy?"

"Typical lawyer. I'm sure he's holding back something; they all do."

"Whad'ya mean?"

"What kind of car did that model, Linda Scott, say she saw as she and her girlfriends left at three o'clock?"

Campbell leafed through his notepad until he found it, "A large black sedan, with two men sitting inside."

"Right. Let's go have a little talk with Doctor Tinterow."

Tinterow's office was all the way across town from Williams' Eastside law office on Park and 66th Street. Dufort and Campbell snaked their way through Central Park, entering at East 65th Street and coming out on West 86th Street. His office was on the corner of 86th and Amsterdam Avenue, the second floor of the Packard Building.

They were shown right into Tinterow. Dufort figured that Williams had called him as soon as they left to get their story straight. Fucking lawyers.

"Gentlemen, please have a seat." Tinterrow insisted. It was more than Williams, the lawyer, offered.

"Thank you, Doctor. I'm Detective Sergeant Dufort, and this is Detective Campbell. We're investigating the murder of Max Albertson. I understand that you attended a party at Mr. Albertson's loft apartment on the night he was killed. Is that correct?"

"That's correct. My friend Frank Williams had gotten an invitation to the party and asked if I'd like to go with him. Which I did."

"Were either of you personal friends of Mr. Albertson?"

"Not exactly."

"What do you mean?"

"You see, Frank and I collect art. We each have purchased some of Max's pieces, so we have met, but I couldn't say we were friends."

Dufort looked around Tinterow's office and asked, "Are any of these Max Albertson's work?"

"Why, yes. Those two lithographs on that wall over there." Tinterow said proudly.

"Mmmm, very nice."

"Expensive?"

"I'm afraid art is a rich man's pleasure. Unless you happen to discover someone before they become famous."

"I bet these are even more expensive now that Albertson's dead."

"Sadly, yes."

"Bad for him. Good for you."

Tinterow sat silently, trying to look passive and calm.

"What time did you and Mr. Williams leave the party?"

"I think it was about 2 am."

"And Mr. Williams drove his car, is that correct?"

"Yes."

"What kind of car does Mr. Williams drive?"

"A black Chrysler Imperial LeBron."

"And you're sure about the time that the two of you left the party?"

"Yes. It was either a little before or a little after 2 am."

"Do you know of anyone who might have wanted to hurt Mr. Albertson, Doctor?"

"No, I do not."

"Did you happen to see altercations with Mr. Albertson and any guests?"

"No, sir."

"Anything else?"

"Oh, yeah. There was this homeless gentleman sleeping on the street, not far from the party. I think he was a Vietnam veteran. He was wearing army fatigues; he was shouting and ranting. He seemed violent and delusional. We crossed the street just to be safe."

"You're a psychiatrist. Did he strike you as someone who could have killed Max Albertson?"

"Well, Detective, anyone is capable of killing someone."

"How true, Doctor. How true."

"Did you happen to see a gun?"

"I'm not sure."

"Why aren't you sure?"

"I did see something stuck in his belt that might have been a gun. But it could have been something else."

"Well, I thank you for your time, Doctor Tinterow. Here's my card; if you happen to think of anything else, please call me, day or night." Dufort said as he handed Tinterow one of his business cards.

When Dufort and Campbell got out on the street, Detective Sergeant Dufort said to Campbell, "Right now, those two are on the top of my list for who might have done it. I got nothing definite. It's just a hunch, a gut feeling. But my hunches are usually spot on. Remember, Campbell, always trust your gut."

"Whad'ya think about this homeless guy, Sarge?"

"I think it's a red herring. I mean, what would be his motivation for killing Albertson? Maybe, if he robbed him, but just to go up and kill the guy. I don't buy it. But let's put out an APB, just in case. You never know. So, how many more on the list?"

"Twenty-two."

"I'm saying let's call it a day. We'll start back at it first thing in the morning."

Marine Corporal Luke Wilson, an ex-Vietnam veteran, did three tours of duty between 1966 and 1968. He fought in some of the bloodiest battles of the war. The Tet Offensive, The Battle of Ia Drang, the Battle of Hué, and the Battle of Hamburger Hill, among others. Luke was wounded four separate times, and he was awarded four Purple Hearts, two Silver Stars, three Bronze Stars, and the Republic of Vietnam Gallantry Cross.

When his hitch was over, he came home to a nation that held no appreciation for him and the other returning combat veterans. The political sentiment against the Vietnam War was so strong that the war-weary country took a lot of their resentment against the ex-vets.

Wilson suffered from PTSD, but at the time, there wasn't an official acknowledgment of such a disorder. After losing job after job, Luke, like so many other Vietnam veterans, Luke fell through the cracks and became just another homeless guy living out on the streets.

He took up "residence" outside the bodega for the warmth from the subway grate, and occasionally, people would drop spare change into his coffee cup. Sometimes, people even bought him a cup of soup or a sandwich.

Luke never bought liquor or drugs with the money people gave him. He went to the VA once a month for his prescribed medications, Prozac Minipress and Tenex.

The night of Max Albertson's murder, Luke had returned from the VA and was three sheets to the wind from the drugs by the time Williams and Tinterow passed by him.

It wasn't until three weeks later that Luke found the gun. It had slipped down to the bottom of his bedroll.

When he examined it, he found that the Smith & Wesson .38 held six shots. He found five live bullets in the cylinder and one spent cartridge. Luke knew that the gun only meant trouble if he kept it. So, he waited until he saw a police officer and flagged him down, knowing that it could mean hard times ahead.

"Officer. I woke this morning and found that someone placed this weapon in my bedroll."

The Officer had seen Luke many times on his beat and had never had any trouble with him. He called into the precinct for a car to take Luke to Manhattan South to be interviewed.

Detective Sergeant Dufort and Detective Campbell got a call saying that a homeless vet reported that someone planted a gun in his bedroll the night of the murder of Max Albertson. The handgun was out being tested to see if it was, in fact, the weapon that killed Mr. Albertson. It was a match.

"Mr. Wilson, my name is Detective Sergeant Dufort, and this is Detective Campbell. We're investigating the murder of Max Albertson, who was shot and killed three weeks ago."

"I don't know anything about that. I don't even know who this Max Albertson is. Like I told the police officer, I found that gun in my bedroll this morning."

"I believe you, Mr. Wilson. Do you have any idea who might have planted that gun in your bedroll?"

"I don't. I'm not a druggy or a boozer. I take prescribed medicines from the Doctor at the VA. You can check with Dr. Hoffman. He'll tell you."

Dufort gave Campbell the nod to go and see if he could get hold of Hoffman. As Campbell was leaving the office, Dufort said, "We're going to do that right now."

"Good."

"Mr. Wilson, when you take these drugs prescribed by Dr. Hoffman, how do they make you feel?"

"Sleepy and lethargic. I've been robbed a couple of times and even beat up once because I'm totally out of it."

"I understand that you were in Vietnam."

"Yeah, that's right."

"Rough?"

"Yeah, it was pretty rough. You ever been in the shit?"

"I was in the Pacific, island hopping, Guadalcanal, Tarawa, Iwo Jima, and Okinawa."

"Marines?"

"Semper Fi."

"Semper Fi," Luke said with a big grin on his face.

"Right on."

"Wow. You must have seen some shit."

"Yup. Shit up to my chin. The big difference between Nam and WW2 was that people loved us when we came home, and now they're ashamed. Just know it's not you they hate. It's all the liars in DC."

"Don't make it any easier."

"I know, son. I know."

Campbell came back into the interrogation room. He handed Dufort a note.

"Says here that Dr. Hoffman collaborated your story. Mr. Wilson, I want to thank you for coming down here and doing the right thing. I also want to thank you for your service to our country. Stay safe, my friend."

After six months, Max Albertson's case went cold. With no new leads and the heavy workload of Manhattan South homicide, along with the retirement of Detective Sergeant Dufort, the case lost steam. Occasionally, some rookie would try to crack the case, but eventually, it was put on the back burner.

The Fine Art of Murder

In the three years since Max Albertson's death, the psychedelic artist Roger Niles, better known as the "Cosmic King," had become one of the hottest artists and the darling of all the media. He was everywhere: on television, in national magazines, in radio interviews, and even doing TV commercials and endorsing products.

The public persona that Niles was presenting was that of a happy-go-lucky guy with not a care in the world. But the pressure to stay on top, keep out front of everyone else, and continually create the "next big thing" was tremendous. There were times that he even contemplated suicide. He felt that if he were to survive, he needed help. He needed a psychiatrist.

"Doctor Tinterow, Roger Niles is here to see you." Said the muffled voice of Mrs. Rotter, Tinterow's secretary was squawking through the intercom.

"Please send him in."

Tinterow was surprised at how disheveled and stressed the man people called the Cosmic King was.

"Please have a seat, Mr. Niles."

Niles took the chair opposite Tinterow.

"Now, Mr. Niles, what seems to be troubling you?"

"Stress. I am constantly under stress. When I first got into art, it was fun. A way of expressing myself. I guess, like most people, I wanted to be successful and famous, to have my art accepted and be recognized as a major force in the art world. But I didn't realize the price you have to pay these days of instant celebrities. I'm constantly under the microscope, always in the public eye, and I know that a lot of this is my fault. But that's what it takes to stay on top." Niles conceded.

"And is that the most important thing in your life is to stay on top?"

"There's a saying, Doc, in art, one day you're in, and the next day you're out."

"Well, what about someone like Picasso?"

"Picasso is still exploring, continually working, and growing as an artist. Plus, it's different for a fine artist than a commercial artist. A fine artist can take years to develop a unique style, whereas today, it's all about the now and the present.

The attitude today is, oh sure, that was great yesterday, but what have you done new and exciting today?"

"Hmmm. Sounds rough. What would you like from me, Mr. Niles?"

"I was hoping that you might give me something to take the edge off."

"Drugs?"

"Something. Take a look at me, Doctor; I'm a wreck. I haven't eaten or been able to sleep in weeks. I occasionally have had thoughts of killing myself."

Tinterow opened his desk drawer and withdrew his prescription pad. As he started writing, he said, "Now, Mr. Niles, I'm writing you a prescription to help you sleep and another, a mild sedative.

I think that a large part of your stress and anxiety is psychological, and I want you to come to see me three times a week so we can resolve some of these issues. Are you willing to do that?"

"Sure, Doc," Niles said.

It was at that moment that he stopped focusing on himself and noticed his surroundings and all the fabulous artwork that Tinterow had in his office. He stood up and walked over to the wall to his left. There were three Frank Stella geometric lithographs. On the opposite wall were three Robert Indiana silkscreen prints, and behind Tinterow's desk was a Judy Chicago painting.

"God damn, Doctor Tinterow, I just became aware of all the artwork you have. You're quite the collector. I am impressed."

"Thank you. I must admit I have a few Roger Niles' at my home in the Hamptons. I own the complete Cops and Robbers Suite."

"No, kidding. Well, you hang on to them, Doc. One day, they're going to be worth a fortune."

"Oh, I know they will," Tinterrow grinned.

Detective Sergeant Roscoe Brown was born and raised in Coney Island. He joined the NYPD right out of Queens College, City University of New York. He graduated top of his class, majored in Political Science, and at one time thought of getting into politics. Still, after talking to a representative from the NYPD on career day, Roscoe signed up then and there. He is slightly overweight for his height; he still has a great head of hair, just starting to get a hint of grey on the side. He wears a Clark Gable mustache, always dressed in a suit and tie, and is never seen without his trademark fedora. Roscoe always looked very tidy.

He's been a cop for twenty-one years. The last fifteen in homicide and rated as one of the best homicide cops in the city, partially because of his photographic memory. He's won a dozen citations, commendations for service above and beyond the call of duty, and heroism. He once saved a fellow officer's life at his peril and was wounded. He's won the respect of his peers and superiors and has been partnered with Jimmy Walsh for the last ten years. They are usually brought in for the strange and unique cases, the hard to solve ones, and the high-profile ones.

Roscoe and Walsh had just returned to the detective's squad room from having lunch at Nathan's Famous Hot Dogs down on the boardwalk when Captain O'Rourke called them into his office.

"Roscoe, Walsh, come in and shut the door."

"What's up, Captain?" Roscoe asked.

"Do either one of you know anything about art?"

Walsh shook his head as he said, "No. Not really."

"A little. I know what I like." Roscoe said.

"Good enough."

"Why? You looking to buy some art, Captain?" Walsh asked.

"Have you ever heard of Roger Niles?" O'Rourke enquired.

"The Cosmic King? Who hasn't?" Roscoe said.

Walsh and O'Rourke looked at each other in disbelief.

"The cosmic what?" O'Rourke asked.

"Oh, come, you guys. He did that great billboard in Times Square for New York City Tourism. And all those TV animated spots for 7 Up. He's been on Johnny Carson's dozens of times." Roscoe boasted.

"Oh, yeah. He did all that?" O'Rourke mused.

"Yeah. He's great. Why?" Roscoe asked.

"He's dead. The ME is heading over there now."

"Murder?" Walsh asked.

"Don't know, we just got the call. Here's the address. This is going to be a high-profile case, so treat it as such."

"Right, Captain. Come on, Jimmy."

"Where we headed?"

"1212 Ocean View Avenue," Roscoe revealed.

"That's Seagate."

"Yeah. The other side of the tracks, as it were."

"They're not going to be too thrilled having a couple of flatfoots traipsing around discommoding the island gentry."

"Especially if it is murder."

"That's for sure."

"Well, it's like someone once said, "Art should comfort the disturbed and disturb the comfortable." Except, I say, take the word art and replace it with police." Roscoe said with a smirk.

Roger Niles had been seeing Doctor Tinterow for nine months, and during their sessions, Niles had been skillfully manipulated by the good Doctor into believing that he was making progress. But all the time, Tinterow had actually been maneuvering his patient into becoming more and more unconsciously suicidal.

Tinterrow was having dinner with Frank Williams at the Yale Club when he was notified by the concierge that he had a call. The concierge brought a phone over to their table and plugged it in.

He whispered, "He says it's urgent."

"Thank you, Walter." Tinterow said as he picked up the receiver."

"Hello. Doctor Tinterow."

"Doctor Tinterow, it's Roger Niles. I apologize for disturbing you, but I really need to talk to you."

Tinterow smiled at Williams, placed his hand over the receiver, and whispered, "Niles."

"Now, Roger, you know I don't make house calls. Would you like to schedule an appointment for you in the morning?"

"Please, Doctor Tinterow. I feel as if I'm drowning. I can't breathe. Please. Please." Niles pleaded.

Tinterow said nothing for several seconds before saying, "All right, Roger. But just this once."

"Oh, thank you, Doctor Tinterow. Thank you." He said, groveling.

"I'll be there within the hour."

"Great. I'll alert the gate that you're coming. You have my address."

"Yes. I'll be there as soon as I can."

He hung up the phone and waved the concierge over, "Walter, could I have another scotch and water."

"Certainly."

The black Mercedes-Benz 600 pulled up to the Seagate guardhouse at 10:45. A man dressed in a cold gray security guard's uniform approached the car; Tinterow rolled the window down and said, "Doctor Tinterow to see Roger Niles."

The guard scanned his clipboard for the name.

"Oh, yes, I see it here. Do you need directions, Doctor?"

"No, thank you."

"Very good, sir. Have a good evening."

"Thank you. You too." Tinterow pleasantly said as he drove off, he saw the guard pick up a phone. He assumed that the guard was calling Niles to alert him that they were coming.

Williams asked, "Have you ever been out here before?"

"Once. Went to a party not too far from Niles' house."

"It's nice if you like the whole beach scene."

"Yes, but It's not the Hamptons." Tinterow proclaimed with a hint of snobbery.

"There it is. 1212 Ocean View Avenue." Williams said.

The house sat cattycorner on a lot that had to be half an acre or more. One of the largest lots in all of Seagate. A ten-foot ivy-covered brick fence surrounded the lot. The house itself was a one and a half split-level ranch. The inside was not what one might expect an artist's house to be: simple and clean with minimal furnishings. The studio where Niles worked was just the opposite. It was cluttered, messy, and chaotic looking, but the artist knew where every little thing was in that studio and could put his hand on it at any given moment.

Once inside the gate, they saw Niles standing at the door, looking anxious and fidgety.

"Thank God you're here, Doctor Tinterow."

"Roger, relax. Everything is going to be all right."

"Please come in," Niles said.

"Roger, this is my good friend Frank Williams. We were having dinner together when you called. I hope you don't mind that I brought him along. It seemed quicker, my coming straight here rather than taking him home. Is that all right?"

"Yes. Of course." Niles answered nervously.

"Now, Roger, seeing the agitated state that you're in, I must ask you, do you have any firearms in the house?" Tinterow asked.

"Yes. I have a pistol next to my bed in the nightstand. Want me to go get it?"

"No. I'll ask Frank to retrieve it while we talk, if you don't mind. Is that okay?"

"Sure."

"Frank, would you mind?"

"No. I'll be right back."

"The master bedroom is at the end of the hall on your left," Niles said.

As Williams went down the hall, he reached into his coat pocket and pulled out a pair of latex gloves, which he proceeded to put on before touching anything in the bedroom. The gun was exactly where Niles said it was: in the top drawer of his nightstand. It was a Smith & Wesson 39 .9mm semi-automatic pistol. Williams took the safety off and cocked the gun, sliding a bullet into the chamber. It was loaded.

As Tinterrow and Niles were deep in conversation, Williams slyly walked up behind Niles, placed the .9mm next to Niles' right temple, and fired one shot.

POW

Splattering the Cosmic King's brains all over the wall. Tinterow thought that, at first glance, it looked a little like a Jackson Pollock painting.

Williams placed the pistol in Niles' right hand, went into the bathroom, washed his hands thoroughly, and made sure that there weren't any blood traces on his hands. He then went to the car, popped open the trunk, and changed his shirt. Then, they went back inside just as Tinterow called 911, telling the operator they needed the police and medics.

"Yes. This is Doctor Tinterow. A patient of mine gets shot himself in the head. Please send an ambulance and police to 1212 Ocean View Avenue, Sea Gate. And for God's sake, hurry."

He hung up the phone and asked Williams, "How was that?"

"Very convincing."

By the time Roscoe got to the crime scene, the ME was already there examining the body. Outside on the street were dozens of neighbors watching the goings on and being interviewed by the uniformed officers. Roscoe's partner, Detective Walsh, was finishing up the file on another case.

Officer Ron Harris was standing outside the front door, managing the flow of traffic in and out of the scene.

"Hey, Ron. Whad'ya got?" Roscoe asked.

"Looks like a suicide. The vic is some big-time artist, Roger Niles. Apparently, he was talking to his shrink, and all of a sudden, he pulled a gun out and blew his brains out."

"Jeez, he must be one Hell of a shrink!" Roscoe quipped.

"He's the guy sitting over there, wearing the three-piece suit, Doctor Tinterow."

"Who's the other guy?"

"A lawyer, Frank Williams."

"Lawyer? Was he here, or did the good doctor call him? Roscoe asked.

"He was here with the doctor when we arrived," Harris said.

"A shrink that travels with his lawyer. That's interesting. That's fucking interesting." Roscoe mused.

"Struck me odd, too," Harris said.

"Harris, you got good instincts. You're going to make detective soon."

"Thanks, Sarge."

"Well, I'll go in and see what Doctor Tinterow has to say."

Tinterow and Williams were sitting next to each other in the dining room, observing all the machinations going on.

"Doctor Tinterow, I'm Detective Sergeant Roscoe Brown."

"Detectives. This is Frank Williams."

Roscoe nodded acknowledgment of Williams but did not speak to him.

"Doctor, what the Hell happened?" Roscoe asked.

His tone and directness threw Tinterow off his game.

"Ah, well. Ah, you see."

"Yes?" Roscoe knew immediately that he didn't like the doctor or his friend. For a professional, he seemed in over his head.

"Go on, doctor." Roscoe gently pushed.

"Well, you see. Mr. Williams and I were having dinner at the Yale Club and…"

Roscoe interrupted, "You and Mr. Williams, the attorney, were having dinner?"

"Yes." Tinterow was getting flummoxed; he wasn't used to being interrupted.

"Mr. Williams, what kind of an attorney are you?"

"Criminal," Williams said.

"Please continue, Doctor Tinterow. I'm just making sure I understand. Go on. So, you and your lawyer were having dinner."

"Oh, Frank isn't my attorney; we're just friends. But that's right; we were having dinner when I received a phone call from Mr. Niles."

"How did Mr. Niles know where you were having dinner? Do you tell all your patients where you're having dinner?"

"No, of course not. I have a phone service. They know to get ahold of me if they feel there's an emergency."

"I see."

"Anyway. It was Mr. Niles calling, saying that he was in a very vulnerable state of mind. He said that he was feeling suicidal."

"And you thought it wise to bring your attorney along?"

"No. Like I said, we were having dinner. I just thought it would be quicker to bring Frank with me than driving him home."

"Couldn't Mr. Williams just take a cab home?"

"I guess I wasn't thinking. I was focused on Mr. Niles."

"And Mr. Williams, it didn't occur to you to just take a cab home instead of tagging along with Doctor Tinterow?"

Williams was like a deer in the headlights; He had never been the one to be asked questions; that was his job. Williams sat silent for several seconds. He finally spoke, "Ah, I guess I was so wrapped up in the moment. It just didn't occur to me."

"I see. So, Doctor Tinterow, what happened when you arrived?"

"Mr. Niles was standing in the doorway. He seemed nervous. He was fidgety. And he was holding a gun."

"He was standing in the doorway holding a gun?"

"That's right."

"And you decided to go into the house with a man who was nervous, suicidal, and fidgety holding a gun."

"Yes. Well, I knew he wasn't going to shoot me."

"How did you know that?"

"Because I know him. I mean, I knew him. He was my patient, after all." Tinterow said smugly.

"Did you know that he was going to blow his brains out?" Roscoe challenged.

"Well, no."

"Then I guess you didn't know him as well as you thought, did you?"

"I guess not," Tinterow said contritely.

"So, you're in the house with Niles. Now what?"

"Well, he goes inside…"

"Excuse me for interrupting, Doctor Tinterow. Was Mr. Williams in the house, too, at the time of the killing?"

"Suicide. And yes, he was."

"Why? Why did he come inside? He's a lawyer."

"He just did!" Tinterow snapped.

"Hey, take it easy, Doc. I'm just doing my job here. Trying to get all the facts."

"I'm sorry, Detective. It's been a very traumatic experience."

"I understand. Please continue."

"Where was I?"

"You and Mr. Williams are in the house."

"Ah, yes. Mr. Niles sat on the couch, and Frank and I sat opposite him. He started rambling on about people were stalking him and spying on him. Without going into too much detail, he suffered from depression, schizophrenia, and bipolar disorder."

"Did he say anything before he shot himself?"

"No. He actually became quite calm, then all of a sudden he put the gun to his head and fired."

"Mr. Williams, what were you doing when all this happened?"

"Nothing. I was sitting next to Gary, err, Doctor Tinterow, observing."

"I see. I'm going to have the crime lab boys take some photographs of you and your clothing if you don't mind, gentlemen." Roscoe said, and before they could respond, he left them sitting there looking at each other.

Seconds later, the police photographer took photos of them and their clothes.

"Excuse me, why is this necessary?" Tinterow asked the photographer.

"It's standard procedure, right, Mr. Williams?" He said nonchalantly as he continued to snap away.

Frank glanced at Tinterow and nodded.

"Doctor Tinterow, could you and Mr. Williams please come here," Roscoe said as he stood next to the couch they had been sitting on.

As Williams and Tinterow approached, Roscoe asked, "Where were you sitting, Doctor Tinterow?"

Tinterow pointed to where he had sat, "Right there."

"And Mr. Williams, where were you sitting when Mr. Niles shot himself?"

"I was sitting there," Williams said as he pointed to a spot on the couch.

Roscoe called out to the photographer and one of the crime lab techs, "I want photos of the couch and check it out for blood splatter.

Well, thank you gentlemen. I appreciate your time. Here's my card. Please call me if you can think of anything else. If you would please provide Officer Harris with your contact information, I will probably have some additional questions for you both."

They stopped by Officer Harris and gave him their contact numbers and addresses.

As they were leaving, Roscoe shouted, "Oh, Doctor, do you know if Mr. Niles was right-handed or left-handed?"

"Right-handed," Tinterow said timidly.

"Thank you. Good night."

Once they had left, they asked the ME, "Could it be murder?"

"Doubtful, but I'll know more when we get him back in the lab."

"Make sure you swab his hands for GSR."

"Roscoe, are you telling me how to do my job?"

"Sorry, Doc. No offense intended. Well, I'm just going to check out the house."

"Why did they take pictures of our clothes?" Williams said in a panic.

"The photographer said it was standard procedure. Stop worrying." Tinterow said, trying to calm his partner in crime down.

"I can't help it. I got a bad feeling about that Detective Brown. And what kind of name is Roscoe anyway? He doesn't look like a Roscoe!"

"It's fine. They got nothing."

The rest of the ride back to Manhattan was silent. Each man had a million things going on in his head.

Did we leave any incriminating evidence behind?

Was the angle of the gun at the temple the correct angle?

Did we place the gun properly in his hand for somebody who just shot himself?

Is there something about the photos of the clothes that will undo them?

Was Niles really right-handed?

Williams slowly got out of the Mercedes, turned around, leaned into the car, and asked, "Are we okay?"

"Frank, we're golden. We just stick to our story, and there'll be nothing to worry about. Trust me. Niles shot himself. Right?"

"Right. Okay, I'll talk to you later."

"Not to worry. We're going to be okay and rich. Our collection will probably be worth nearly two million in a few months. Golden."

Williams smiled, "Golden."

Vincent Rainwater was sitting in his office at the New York Times, writing an article on the major upcoming retrospective of Impressionism at MOMA, opening next week, when the phone rang.

"Hello."

"Vincent. Roger Niles committed suicide." Amy said, upset.

"What! When?"

"I just got a call from Peter Max saying he heard that Roger shot himself last night."

"My God, that's awful. I'm going to go down and talk to the boys in the police and crime beat. I'll call you later when I know more. Love ya."

"Bye."

CLICK

Vincent made his way down to the editor's office. Lloyd Highbloom, New York Times Editor, looked to be in a casual meeting. Vincent gave a short knock on the door and stuck his head, "Lloyd, when you get a minute."

"Come on in, Vincent. Rosemary and I were just chatting. What's up?"

"I just found out from Amy that Roger Niles committed suicide. And I wondered why I wasn't told?"

"We haven't gotten all the facts yet. We were waiting until everything was fact-checked before alerting you. Sorry, you had to hear it from Amy."

"Sure, I understand. What do we know so far?"

"Well, what I know is that Niles called his psychiatrist last night, a guy named Tinterow. He told police that, when he got there, Niles and he were having a conversation when, all of a sudden, he pulled out the pistol and blew his brains out."

Vincent's face turned as white as Casper the Ghost. He felt a tightening knot deep down in his gut and slightly nauseous. It was noticeable to Highbloom, who asked, "Are you all right, Vincent? You don't look so good."

"Oh, yeah. I'm okay. It's just that I knew Roger pretty well. It's regrettable, is all. I'm just going back upstairs to my office and finish the piece on the Impressionism retrospective."

"You take it easy, Vincent. Let me know if there is anything I can do."

Vincent took the elevator back to his office, plopped down behind his desk, closed his eyes, and said to himself, "No. No. No. It can't be. They wouldn't kill Niles!"

He picked up the phone and called Tinterow.

"Doctor Tinterow's office. How may I help you?"

"Hello, Sally. This is Vincent Rainwater. Is he with anyone?"

"Hold on if you could. He's just finishing up with a client. He'll be free in a moment."

"Thank you, Sally."

"Hello. Vincent, good to hear from you. It's been a while. How are you doing?"

"Gary, tell me you didn't have anything to do with Niles' death."

"I'm shocked that you would even think that."

"So, you didn't?"

"Absolutely not."

"Good."

"Yeah."

"Look, I will be asked to do a story on him. Is there anything that you can tell me without violating doctor-patient confidentiality?"

"Sure. Why don't we have dinner tonight around eight at the Yale Club? We'll talk about Niles and catch up. Whad'ya say?"

"Yeah, okay. It's been too long."

"I'll call Frank and have him tag along, too."

"Sounds great. See you guys tonight."

The Yale Club on a Wednesday night is usually quiet, and this Wednesday was no exception. There were only a handful of patrons dispersed throughout the dining room.

Vincent, Gary, and Frank were tucked away in the corner, where they usually prefer to meet.

"So, Gary, what can you tell me about Roger Niles' suicide?"

"Well, Frank and I were eating here at the Club when we got a frantic call from Niles saying that he was feeling suicidal and asked if I could stop by.

I told him that I don't make house calls, but he pleaded, and he sounded like he was on the precipice and ready to leap.

So, we got in the car and drove to Coney Island, to the Sea Gate community. When we arrived, he was standing in the doorway holding a gun. But not in a threatening way, casually down by his side.

When we came inside, he sat on one sofa, and Frank and I sat across from him on the other sofa facing him. He was sobbing, and as we had begun to talk, he lifted the gun to his head and pulled the trigger."

"Why did Frank go?"

"That's what the police asked me. I don't see why that would be so strange. We were having dinner together; I got a call, so I brought him along instead of taking him back to his place to save time." Tinterow said with a hard edge.

Vincent turned to Williams and asked, "Why didn't you just take a cab home?"

"Didn't think of it. Everything was happening so fast." Williams replied but was constantly looking at Tinterow for affirmation.

All of a sudden, an icy cold chill ran up and down Vincent's spine because it was at that moment that he knew that they had somehow killed Niles.

Vincent decided not to let on; after all, they were responsible for three deaths. Who knew how they might react if they felt threatened by him?

"So, were there any signs before that night that he was suicidal?" Vincent asked.

Tinterow went from being a suspect to putting on his psychiatrist's hat. "Yes. I had been seeing him as a patient for over a year. He had bouts of depression, and recently, they were becoming more and more severe. Roger was on some pretty heavy-duty medication that I prescribed for him, but I believed that he recently went off his meds, which resulted in his killing himself.”

“Why do you think he wanted you to witness his death?”

“Most people don’t want to die alone.”

“Do you think it might have had anything to do with Frank being there?”

Tinterow sat circumspectly, thinking almost in a trace for a moment before answering, “Hmmm. Interesting thought. I’m not sure, but I would doubt it. He didn’t seem interested in Frank one way or another.”

“So, what did the police say?”

“Oh, they came in with a ton of lab techs looking for clues. And there were dozens of uniformed officers, the medical examiner, and a couple of Detectives. Roscoe Brown and James Walsh.” Frank said.

“Eh, they didn’t seem to be the sharpest pencils in the box. If you know what I mean.”

“So, they’ve officially ruled it a suicide?” Vincent asked.

“What else?” Tinterow remarked definitively.

“Oh, who knows about cops? They’re always looking at things suspiciously.”

“It was suicide,” Williams added.

“How terrible for you, Gary. To lose a patient that way.”

“Yes, it was. It was very tragic and traumatic.”

It was halfway through dinner when the question that Vincent had anticipated would come up did come up. He would have put money on it coming from Frank, and it did.

"So, Vincent. Just curious, how much will Niles' work go up now that he's dead?" Frank inquired.

Vincent could see the disapproving glare coming from Tinterow towards Williams out of the corner of his eye.

"Mmmm, it depends. I'm not totally aware of his total library of work. But I'm sure that, like so many other artists, they will, in time, increase significantly.

If you're thinking of selling some of our works so soon after his death, that might not be wise." Vincent advised.

"Why is that?" Williams asked.

"When it comes to the art market, one should wait and follow, not lead. There will probably be a glut of Niles flooding the marketplace initially. People looking to make a fast buck. One should wait until the frenzy has passed. That's when the serious collectors come out to play."

"What would you estimate our collection is worth, Vincent?" Tinterow queried as if he was disinterested in the answer.

"Currently, I'd say one point two million."

"And if we wait as you suggest?" Williams wondered.

"I would imagine if we waited for twelve to eighteen months, we could realize two point eight to three point five million for the Niles collection."

"Quite a tidy little sum," Tinterow said with a smile.

"Quite." Vincent agreed.

"Detective Brown, please."

"One moment." The receptionist answered.

"Brown. Homicide."

"Detective Brown. My name is Vincent Rainwater. I believe I may have some information on the murder of Roger Niles."

"Murder?"

"That's right. Murder."

"Mr. Rainwater, would you be able to come down to the station and talk?"

"You're in Coney Island, correct?

"That's right. Where are you calling from?"

"I'm in Manhattan."

"Well, I could come to you if you like."

"No. I'll come there."

"We're at 2951 West Eighth Street. Between Neptune Avenue and Surf Avenue, closer to Surf."

"Okay, got it. I'll be down as soon as I can."

"Great. Just ask for me at the Sergeant's desk. I look forward to seeing you."

"Bye."

CLICK

Roscoe hung up the phone and walked down to Walsh's cubby.

"This is interesting. I just got a call from some guy named Rainwater who said he had some information about Niles' murder. And he's coming down."

"Murder?"

"That's what I said. Let's go talk to the ME."

When Roscoe and Walsh arrived at the coroner's office, the medical examiner had completed the autopsy of Roger Niles. Niles' lifeless body lay on the slab. His chest had been stitched back up from where the ME had removed all his organs that had been examined. What little was left of his head had been thoroughly cut apart and reassembled. Poor Niles looked like a prop from a horror film; it was definitely going to be a closed-coffin funeral.

"Hey, Doc. What's your conclusion?"

"I'm going to have to say suicide."

"Well, I have a guy coming down this afternoon who says it was murder."

"Murder?"

"That's what I said." Walsh quipped.

"Is it possible that it was a murder staged to look like a suicide?" Roscoe asked.

"Hmm. Well, the trajectory angle wasn't at the usual angle we see in a suicide. The bullet entered the skull at exactly a 90% angle to the head, which is unusual. In most suicides, when the gun is placed next to the head, it's at a slightly upward angle, but Niles' was precisely perpendicular. I guess someone could have placed the gun on his temple and fired."

"Considering that, Doc. could you leave the cause of death as suspicious? At least for now, so we can still continue the investigation."

"For now."

"Thanks, Doc. I owe ya."

"A bottle of Chivas Regal would be nice."

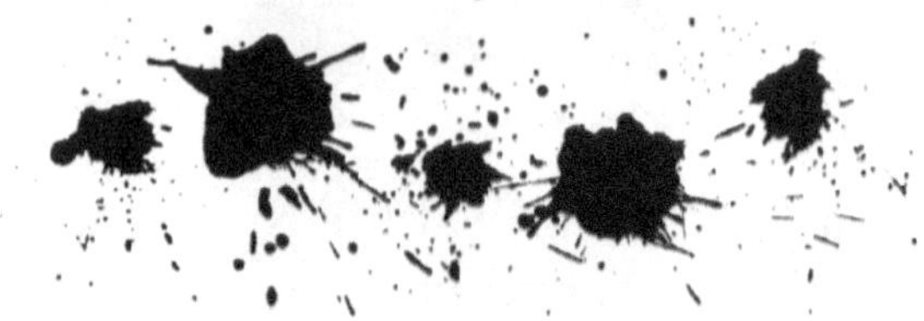

Officer Ramirez stuck his head into Roscoe's office, where he and Walsh were sitting.

"Hey, Roscoe, you got some guy named Rainwater downstairs."

"Thanks, Ramirez. Could you please show him to interview room 2? Thanks?"

"Sure."

"Come on, Jimmy. Let's see what Mr. Rainwater has to say, shall we."

They walked downstairs to the main floor, where the interview rooms were located. The door for room number two was open. Inside stood a well-dressed man in his mid-thirties, nervously pacing, which is usually a good sign of someone wanting to clear their conscience.

"Mr. Rainwater. I'm Detective Sergeant Roscoe Brown, and this is my partner, Detective James Walsh. First, we want to thank you for coming all the way down to Coney Island from Manhattan."

"How was the trip down here? Not too bad, I hope. Please have a seat."

"Not bad. I took the company car service." Vincent said as he sat opposite Roscoe and Walsh.

"Oh, where do you work?" Walsh asked.

"I work for the Times."

"A reporter?" Roscoe followed.

"No. I'm the art critic for the Times."

"Of course. Vincent Rainwater. I thought I recognized the name. I'm a big fan." Roscoe declared.

"Really? Are you a collector, Detective Brown?"

Roscoe laughed, "Hardly. Not on a Detective Sergeant's salary. No, just an art lover."

"What periods do you like?"

"All kinds, really; I like modern art. Picasso, Stella, Pollock, Lichtenstein, and, of course, Warhol."

"Outstanding, Detective Brown. And how about you, Detective Walsh? Are you an art lover as well?"

"I'm sorry to say that the only art I appreciate is the art of the fastball."

"Yankees or Mets?"

"Yankees!"

"Yeah, me too."

"Mr. Rainwater, I hate to take us off the subject of art. But I have an artist lying in the morgue with half his head blown off."

"Right," Vincent said, straightening himself up in the chair. He took a deep breath.

"Well, you see, Detective, two friends of mine and I decided several years ago to form an art syndicate."

"An art syndicate?"

"Yes, We each put an equal amount of money into a pot, and whenever I saw an artist I felt was worth investing in, we would purchase a couple of pieces for investment. Then, as the artist would gain popularity, the value of his work would go up, and at some point, when I felt the time was right, we'd place the art up for sale."

"Interesting idea."

"Well, it came out of an incident many years ago when I first became an art critic. There was this artist named Anthony Banta.

A young hotshot. He was taking the art world by storm. I liked him and his work a lot, so I purchased a couple of paintings. He was setting the art world on fire until he crashed his motorcycle into a guard rail and was killed.

It was such a waste and loss; who knows what he could have done? He could have been the next Picasso. He had that kind of potential.

Since he was so young, he didn't have a large body of work, so what work he did skyrocketed in value. When my friends heard that I made such a tremendous return on my investment, they came up with the syndicate idea."

"Your two friends wouldn't happen to be Dr. Gary Tinterow and Frank Williams Esq?"

"I'm afraid so. So, when they discovered that I made a ton of money when Banta died, they saw an opportunity to try and cash in. I explained to them that what happened with Banta was a flook. Yes, art can be a good investment, but it's not a get-rich-quick scheme.

Anyway, we formed a syndicate, and over the years, we bought really fine pieces, mostly from up-and-coming artists that would take several years for them to mature into major artists."

"What, they didn't want to wait?"

"No. What happened was that both Frank and Gary went through some rough divorces. So, we had to liquidate several pieces of our portfolio for their settlements.

Don't get me wrong, we made an excellent return on our investments, but with art, the longer you can wait, the more you can make."

"Mr. Rainwater, as fascinating as this all is, what about murder," Roscoe said.

"Sorry. I thought I'd give you a little background for context."

"That's perfectly all right; I love context."

"So, about three years ago, the artist Max Albertson was shot and killed in his loft apartment. As far as I can tell, the case was never solved."

"Yeah, I'm familiar with the case; a friend of mine was the lead detective on it."

"Well, one night after it happened, we were eating dinner at the Yale Club, and Frank and Gary confessed to me that they were the ones who murdered Max."

"They told you that they shot and killed Max Albertson."

"Right."

"And what did you do?"

"Well, at first, I didn't believe them. But the longer we talked, the more certain I was that they actually did kill Max."

"Why didn't you call the police, Mr. Rainwater?"

"Well, Detective Sergeant, I'm afraid it's at this point I'm going to request to have my attorney present."

"Frank Williams?"

"God, no. I'm going to need the best defense attorney in New York City."

Lewis Bascom, better known as "the Lawyer of the Stars," met Vincent Rainwater at the 60th Precinct. Normally, Bascom wouldn't have touched such a nonhigh-profile case as this, except that Vincent had advised Bascom on several acquisitions of significant works of art.

"Vincent. What's this all about?"

Vincent explained the whole sordid story about the art syndicate with Frank Williams and Gary Tinterow. His involvement in the blackmail attempt, the killing, and disposal of Mr. Jerry Wald's body in the Hudson River.

"Lewis, we were scared shitless. If we had called the police, then the whole story of the hit and run would have come out, and Gary's life and career would have been ruined.

Wald did go for his gun; Frank feared for his life, so he shot him. We panicked. We all decided to dispose of the body with the hope that it would go away. And it did. Until about seven months later, we read that the body had been found over in New Jersey, but nothing ever came back to us. So, we moved on with our lives.

I'm afraid if I continue exposing Frank and Gary, they will tell about my involvement in Wald's death.

Lewis, I don't want to go to jail. I wouldn't last five minutes in prison. I'll do anything. Turn state's evidence, anything. But you have to work something out so I don't go to prison.

Can you do that, please?" Vincent pleaded.

He then went on to tell Bascom about the admission of Williams and Tinterow, confessing to him about their killing of Max Albertson. And just recently, although there was no confession, his suspicion of their involvement in the killing of Roger Niles.

What Bascom initially thought to be a tedious, mundane case would turn into a major, high-profile, front-page made-for-TV movie murder case.

"Vincent, aside from your testimony, do you have any physical evidence that would corroborate your story?" Bascom asked.

"No, I don't.

"Well, right now, it's just hear-say—your word against theirs. Let me see what I can do. I think we probably work something out. But Vincent, I can't guarantee anything. Okay?"

"Okay."

"Now, from here on out, you keep your mouth shut. You say nothing unless I'm with you. Understand?"

"Yes."

"Nothing. No matter how innocent the question sounds, nothing!"

"Nothing."

"Good," Bascom said.

He got up from the table, opened the door, and called for Detective Sergeant Brown to enter the room.

Roscoe and Walsh entered interview room two, where Rainwater and his mouthpiece sat. The two detectives sat opposite them.

Roscoe smiled and said, "Mr. Bascom, I'm Detective Sergeant Roscoe Brown, and this is my partner, Detective James Walsh."

Detective Brown, my client, has information on at least three killings. He admits to no wrongdoing but would like total immunity from any prosecution that may arise against him."

"Mr. Bascom, that is something that I cannot commit to; I will need approval from the District Attorney's Office. I will need some idea what we are talking about before contacting the DA's Office."

"Hypothetically, the killing of Mr. Jerry Wald, Mr. Max Albertson, and the recent death of Roger Niles."

Roscoe looked at Walsh, who was taking notes, and said to Bascom, "Sit tight, counselor."

Roscoe and Walsh went out, closed the door, and headed to Roscoe's office.

"Whad'ya think, Roscoe?"

"It'll be the DA's call. But to clean up three murders, depending on Rainwater's involvement, I'd go for it."

Roscoe called District Attorney Charles Cooper and spelled out the possible advantages of entering into such a deal. He brought up his discussion with the ME about the apparent suicide being a homicide. In the end, Cooper agreed to at least have a conversation with Rainwater and his star-fucker attorney, Lewis Bascom.

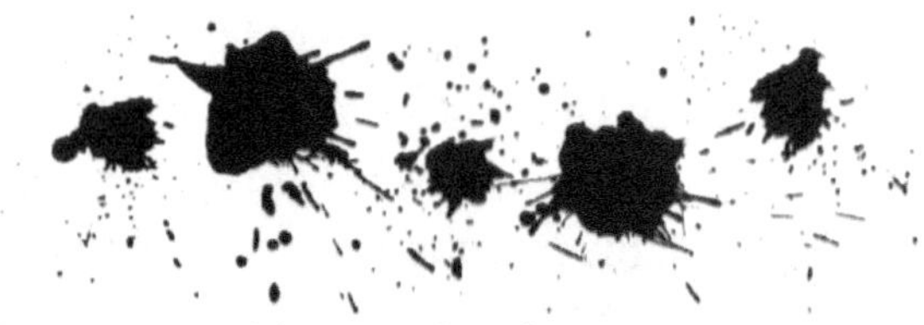

"Present at this meeting is Lewis Bascom, attorney for Vincent Rainwater. Detective Sergeant Roscoe Brown, his partner Detective James Walsh, and myself, District Attorney Charles Cooper." Cooper said to the stenographer sitting in the corner, taking notes of the meeting.

"Mr. Bascom, it's your meeting," Cooper said.

"Mr. Cooper, my client, can provide information into the deaths of Mr. Jerry Wald, Mr. Max Albertson, and the recent death of Roger Niles.

However, my client wants immunity from any charges in these deaths."

Copper sat stoically with a poker face that gave nothing away. He leaned over to Roscoe and whispered, "What do you think?"

"As long as he didn't pull the trigger, it's a win. But it has to be more than he said, he said. We need proof." Roscoe replied.

"Can Mr. Rainwater provide proof?" Copper asked.

"Not physical proof. However, my client would be willing to cooperate in any way in helping the police gather proof."

"Wearing a wire?" Roscoe asked.

"Yes."

"Allowing us to tap his phones?"

"Yes."

"Helping in any potential sting operation?"

"Anything. Provided he serves zero jail time."

"Was Mr. Rainwater in any way complicit in the deaths of any of these men?" Cooper demanded.

"No. He was not."

"Mr. Bascom, does your client know that if he doesn't tell the complete truth and live up to his side of the deal, the immunity offer is null and void, and he will be prosecuted to the full extent of the law?"

"Yes, Mr. Cooper. He does."

"All right, Mr. Rainwater, you may begin."

"Well, it all started about five years ago. When Frank Williams, Doctor Gary Tinterow, and I started an art syndicate."

"Art syndicate?" Cooper asked.

"That's where the three of us would each put an equal amount of money into a pot, and whenever I saw an artist I felt was worth investing in, we would purchase a couple of pieces of art for investment. Then, when the artist would gain popularity, the value of his work would go up, and at some point, when I felt the time was right, we'd place the art up for sale."

"Go on," Cooper said.

"Things were going well until one night, Doctor Tinterow was driving home late at night when he hit a homeless man with his car. Gary didn't stop; he continued on home.

The man he hit died. Since it was late and the streets were deserted, Gary thought nobody had witnessed the accident. The next day, he drove upstate and had his car repaired. He paid a lot of cash to keep things on the hush-hush.

A couple of weeks later, he gets an envelope in the mail with a photo of his car hitting the man. The person wanted 200,000 dollars, or he'd go to the police.

So, Gary had the blackmailer; this guy, Jerry Wald, met him in West Harlem at a house that Gary and some other doctors were rehabbing for the payoff. The apartment building was vacant and under construction. Gary asked Frank Williams and me to come along for support.

We hid in another room but could hear what was happening. As it turned out, Wald wasn't willing to give Gary all the prints and negatives; he wanted more. He said it was just the first installment. He then pulled out a revolver and pointed it at Gary.

That's when Frank came bursting in with his gun and told Wald to drop his weapon, which he did. Frank then made Wald lie down on the floor. The plan was that Frank and Gary would keep him there while I went to his apartment and try to locate the negatives. We'd let him go once we had all the prints and negatives.

I went down to his apartment and found the negatives and a bunch of prints. When I returned to West Harlem, Wald was still on the floor. As I was showing Gary the negatives and prints, Wald saw an opportunity to make a move for his weapon. When he did, Frank fired one shot, striking him in the head."

"Was he dead?" Roscoe asked.

"Oh yeah, the entire back of his head was gone."

"What did you do?" Cooper asked.

"We knew we couldn't call the police. Not only would we be in deep shit for the shooting, but the whole hit-and-run thing would have ended up ruining Gary's career and life. So, we decided to dispose of the body. We drove him over to New Jersey and dropped him into the Hudson River."

"The guns?" Roscoe asked.

"Frank threw them into the Hudson as we drove back from Jersey."

Lewis Bascom looked at his watch and said, "Gentlemen, it's getting late. What do you say we pick this up in the morning?"

Cooper looked at Roscoe and Walsh and nodded. "Very well. We'll reconvene back here at nine o'clock tomorrow morning."

When Vincent slinked in, Amy was standing at the base of an eight-foot by twenty-foot canvas, putting the finishing touches on a commission piece for IBM Corporate.

The painting *Athena by Moonlight #2* was in the style of a new school of art, Pop Expressionism. It was a gallimaufry of Pop Art and Abstract Expressionism styles. It was a bit unsettling when first viewed as a total bastardization of both styles that, in theory, should be a disaster, but in reality, it somehow worked when meshed together.

Amy was one of the pioneers of the Pop Expressionism movement. Her ethos was "If it disturbs you, it's art." The movement was still in its infancy but gaining popularity. Amy was beginning to grow as an artist and gaining recognition and a large following. Life was good, but all that was about to change.

"So, what do you think?" Amy asked Vincent for his opinion of *Athena by Moonlight #2*.

"It's fabulous. I think it's one of the best things you've ever done."

"Really! Do you really think so?"

"Honest."

Amy ran over to him, threw her arms around him, and gave him a deep, passionate kiss.

"Mmmm, I love you," she said, smiling.

"We got to talk," Vincent said in a severe tone.

"Why? What is it?"

"I've really fucked up royally this time."

"What, babe? Tell me."

Vincent told her about the art syndicate, and he recounted the story about the killing and dumping of Jerry Wald's body. About his involvement and how now that he's trying to do the right thing, it has the potential to blow up in his face, ruining his career, and he's praying not his marriage.

He told her about Frank and Gary's confessing to the murder of Max Albertson and their skirting around and hinting that they had a hand in the killing of Roger Niles.

"I went to the police today. I couldn't continue to let Frank and Gary get away with murdering artists just so they can enrich themselves and, by proxy, me."

Amy sat in stone-cold silence, crying, not bearing to look at her husband.

"Lewis Bascom is trying to work out a plea agreement with the DA, so I won't have to do any prison time. I've told the police I will do anything they need to help get Frank and Gary. Wiretaps, wear a recording device, anything."

He knelt down beside her, took her hands, and said, "Please, can you ever forgive me?" He pleaded.

"I don't know. I need time to think." She said as she got up from the couch and went into the bedroom, shutting the door behind her.

"Lewis Bascom, attorney for Vincent Rainwater. Detective Sergeant Roscoe Brown, his partner Detective James Walsh, and I, District Attorney Charles Cooper, are continuing the plea agreement meeting from yesterday afternoon regarding Vincent Rainwater. Mr. Rainwater, please continue."

"It was over three years ago; my wife and I were in San Francisco. I was doing a piece on an exhibit of psychedelic art when Amy heard from a friend here in New York that Max Albertson had been murdered. Apparently, he had just thrown a large party in his studio down in Soho. Hundreds of guests attended, including movie stars, politicians, other artists, and private collectors.

We got an invitation since Frank, Gary, and I were collectors through our syndicate. I couldn't go since I was going out of town, Gary and Frank went.

Days after I got back into town, we all got together, like we always do at the Yale Club for dinner. We usually get together at least once or twice a month just to shoot the shit.

But on this occasion, they alluded that they were responsible for the murder of Max Albertson. Frank said they waited in Frank's car on the street until everyone had left. They then went back to the building and rang Max's buzzer. Frank told me that he said that he thought he might have lost his wallet at the party.

Max buzzed them up, and when the elevator doors opened up, Frank fired one shot, killing Max. They immediately went back down, got into their car, and drove back uptown."

"Did either one of them say why? Why did they shoot and kill Mr. Albertson?" DA Cooper asked.

"Frank said for the value of the art to go up, and Gary because he just didn't like Max. He thought Max was always making fun of him and his ignorance of art."

"Why didn't you go to the police, Mr. Rainwater?" Cooper asked.

"Well, for one thing, I didn't have any proof. And because I was scared that they would bring up my involvement in the killing of Jerry Wald."

Detective Brown asked, "Did you believe them?"

"I did."

"How much did the value of Max Albertson's work increase?" Cooper inquired.

"At least ten-fold. But since Max was best known for his large outdoor sculptures, his individual smaller pieces didn't increase as much as his larger works."

"Did you end up selling the Albertson pieces?"

"We did. You see, it only takes two out of three to decide to sell part of the syndicate's holdings. Now, if there were a piece that one of us wanted to keep, he could buy out the other two and keep the work as a private personal piece."

"So, how much profit did you realize on the Albertson's pieces?"

"Hmm, let's see. We bought two pieces for six thousand and ended up selling the pair for one hundred and twenty thousand."

"A very handsome return," Cooper remarked.

"How much would those pieces be worth if Albertson were still alive today?" Roscoe asked.

"Oh, I'd say probably half. About sixty thousand for the pair." Vincent replied.

"And Williams and Tinterow killed Mr. Albertson primarily for money?" Cooper asked.

"Well, they both had just gone through pretty messy divorces. They both were used to rather lavish lifestyles."

"What can you tell us about Roger Niles's death?" DA Cooper inquired.

"Recently, we had another dinner at the Yale Club. It was a couple of days after I had heard about Niles' apparent suicide.

They didn't come right out and say they killed Roger, but Frank especially was interested in what his death would do to the price of his work.

You see, we, as the syndicate, bought several pieces, but we also individually each bought several works of art. I had discovered him relatively early in his career, so we were each able to purchase several dozen of his works.

I told them again that it pays not to rush into the art world. If they sold now, they would each realize about seven to eight hundred thousand each, but if they sit patiently for a couple of years, the work could be worth as much as one point eight to two point seven million each."

"Per piece?" Walsh gulped.

"No. No, for their whole collection." Vincent smiled.

District Attorney Cooper looked at Bascom and said, "Right now, all we have would be his word against theirs. Mr. Rainwater must do more for me to grant him total immunity. Detective Sergeant Brown will need to develop a sting operation with the cooperation of Mr. Rainwater to catch these two murders. Until such time, Mr. Rainwater, I suggest you stay available. If, for some reason, you need to leave town for work, be sure to contact Detective Brown."

"My client intends to cooperate fully with Detective Sergeant Brown and the police. Mr. Cooper."

"Very good. Detective Brown, please keep my office apprised as to the progress in this endeavor. Don't hesitate to ask if you need any support from this office. The sooner we get these two killers off the street, the better. I will be sure to get in touch with Captain O'Rourke and let him know that this has top priority."

"Thank you, sir. Detective Walsh and I will be contacting Mr. Rainwater in the next couple of days to start formulating the plan of operation *Trompe-l'oeil*." Roscoe said.

"Operation *Trompe-l'œil* ! Bravo! Excellent choice, Detective Sergeant." Vincent said, impressed.

"What does that mean?" Cooper asked.

"It's French for "deceive the eye." It's an art technique that uses realistic imagery to create an optical illusion." Roscoe admitted.

"Hello?" Said a soft-spoken woman who seemed surprised that anybody would be calling this number.

"Hello. This is Detective Sergeant Roscoe Brown with the NYPD calling. Would Bob Dufort be at home?"

"Why, yes, he is. Hold on, please."

Roscoe could hear her placing the receiver down and calling for her husband.

"Bobby. Telephone!"

"Who is it?"

"A Detective Brown."

There was a rustle of the receiver being picked up and then, "Hello."

"Detective Sergeant Bobby Dufort? I'm Detective Sergeant Roscoe Brown with the six O, Coney Island." Roscoe asked.

"Yes, Detective, what can I do for you?"

"I'm working a homicide here in Sea Gate that may involve one of your cases. The murder of Max Albertson."

"Max Albertson, the artist. That case turned cold after I retired."

"I was hoping that we could get together."

"Well, I've been retired for over three years now. Have you requested the file from Manhattan South?"

"Yeah. I got it right here. But I'd like to talk to you. I find there's so much more you can get from someone who was waist-deep in the case than just reading notes in a file."

"Okay, well, let's see here," Dufort said, thinking of his calendar and everything on his honey-do list.

"Hmm, how about tomorrow morning? Should I come to you?"

"That would be great if you could."

"How about ten tomorrow morning?"

"Terrific. I look forward to seeing you tomorrow."

"Goodbye."

"Bye."

CLICK

The following day, at ten o'clock on the nose, ex-Detective Sergeant Bobby Dufort walked into the sixtieth precinct and asked the Desk Sergeant to see Detective Sergeant Roscoe Brown.

"Detective Sergeant Dufort, Roscoe Brown. It's a pleasure to meet you, sir." Roscoe said, extending his hand.

"Bobby, please, and the pleasure is mine," Dufort said as he shook Roscoe's hand.

"Shall we head up to my office, where we can talk?"

They walked up the two flights of stairs to the Homicide Division. When they reached Roscoe's office, Detective Walsh was waiting for them.

"Bobby, this is my partner Detective James Walsh."

"Detective, nice to meet you."

"And you, sir. We want to thank you for coming all this way to help us out." Walsh said.

"Well, we'll see how much help I can be," Dufort replied with a grin.

"We've gone over the Albertson file and would like to hear your thoughts," Roscoe said.

Dufort reached into his coat pocket and pulled out an old, worn-out, chewed-up black leather-bound pocket notepad. He began flipping through his journal until he came to a page that had been marked and dog-eared.

"Ah, here we are. Yeah, I remember now. Of all the people who had attended the party, there were two guys, Doctor Tinterow and his sidekick, a real slick shyster named Williams, Frank Williams, that stood out as potential suspects.

I told my partner, Bill Campbell, a rookie in homicide at the time, that I'd put dollars to doughnuts that these two were our killers. Unfortunately, we had nothing to tie them to the murder: no evidence, no motive, and no witnesses.

You know, back in the old days, we would have brought those two mugs into the interrogation room and slapped them, sapped them, and zapped them until we got to the truth.

No, those days are over. Now, we have to read them their rights and treat them with respect. You know Roscoe, I admit it, I'm an old-school copper. Back then, we got results. Oh, I'm sure there were a few times when we got it wrong; somebody would go over who didn't do it. But I'd say 99% of the time, we got the right guy.

Do the ends justify the means? I don't know, but I'll tell you this: if I could have spent a couple of hours alone with Williams and Tinterow, They'd be in Attica right now."

"Well, Williams and Tinterow have confessed to someone, but we got no proof. Right now, it's just a "he said, he said."

Was there anything about the gun that was found with that homeless vet that might be able to help us with?" Roscoe said.

"I remember the vet, Luke Wilson, was a war hero, but his head was all fucked up. I knew he didn't have anything to do with it. He turned in the murder weapon, a .38 Smith & Wesson. I believed his story that someone planted the piece on him, hoping we'd tag him for the murder.

But two things bothered me. One was that a .38 wouldn't be a gun an ex-vet would have. He'd be packing something like a .45 semi-auto. And two, why would he kill Albertson? He didn't know him, and there was no robbery. No, I'm thinking Williams or Tinterow planted that gun on him after they shot Albertson. I still don't have a motive why those two would have killed him."

"Money," Walsh said.

"But nothing was stolen?" Dufort challenged.

"They killed the Albertson, so their works of art by Albertson that they owned would increase in value," Roscoe said.

"Did it work?"

"Like a charm," Walsh noted.

"But not as much as they would have liked. So, we believe they recently killed again. This time, the artist Roger Niles. We think they tried to make it look like a suicide." Roscoe noted.

"You know, about that .38. Isn't Williams a criminal attorney?" Dufort asked.

"Yeah," Walsh answered.

"Maybe he obtained it from a client of his," Dufort said.

"See Walsh. Sometimes, it's good to get another set of eyes on a case. Even a pair of old-school eyes. Thanks, Detective Sergeant Dufort." Roscoe said.

"Glad I could help. It felt good to get back in the saddle again." Dufort said with a grin.

Amy was having lunch at Café Wha with a group of fellow artists. They were discussing all that was happening in the art world and chatting about who was hot and who was not. Jasper Johns said he invited a young artist, Tony Romeo, to attend the lunch.

Johns had seen some of Tony's work at a gallery in Chicago. Romeo was a New York Artist who had just moved back from studying with the San Francisco artist Richard Diebenkorn, a leader of the Bay Area Figurative Movement.

Amy said, "I've always loved his Ocean Park series."

"Yes, quite the visionary." Helen Frankenthaler added.

From behind Amy came an unfamiliar voice, "Hello, everyone. Hello, Jasper."

Johns stood up, shook the young man's hand, and began the introductions.

"Everyone, this is Tony Romeo, the young man I told you about. Tony, this is Helen Frankenthaler, Frank Stella, Robert Motherwell, and Amy Albright."

Having just arrived from California, Tony looked more like a surfer or a beach bum than an aspiring artist. He was tall and thin, with shaggy blonde hair and sapphire blue eyes.

He sat at the table next to Jasper Johns and directly across from Amy. For over an hour, he talked about his time in California working with Richard Diebenkorn and Wayne Thiebaud. Thiebaud is known for his colorful works depicting commonplace objects–pies, paint cans, ice cream cones, and hot dogs.

It was close to four in the afternoon when the artist's round table broke up. Amy and Tony Romeo were making passionate love in his loft apartment by five o'clock.

Amy, who was ten years his senior, felt a feeling she hadn't felt in years with Vincent.

"Detective Sergeant Brown is here to see you, sir." Tinterow's secretary said. She smiled and said, "You may go in," as she hung up the phone.

Tinterow was sitting at his George Nelson L-shaped Executive desk, with an attached sideboard, trying to look busy.

"Doctor Tinterow, I want to thank you for taking time out to meet with me."

"Please have a seat, Detective Brown."

"Thank you," Roscoe said as he sat in the Marcel Breuer Armchair across from Tinterow.

"What can I do for you, Detective?"

Roscoe was looking around the doctor's office, admiring all the artwork. "You have quite the collection, Doctor. Very impressive."

"Thank you. Yes, I'm very proud of the pieces."

"Are any of these Roger Niles'?"

"As a matter of fact, those two over by the aquarium are Niles."

Roscoe stood up, "Mind if I take a look?"

"Not at all."

Roscoe walked over and looked closely at the two lithographs.

"Very nice. I really like the colors, the layering of textures, and the overall sense of dimension."

"Mmmm, sounds like you know something about art, Detective Brown."

"Ah, I know what I like. Oh wow, is this a saltwater aquarium?"

"Yes, it is."

"Oh, I've always wanted one, but I hear that they are very temperamental. Everything can die if you don't get the chemical balance just right."

"I have a man come in once a week to maintain the *pH balance, temperature, and salinity* and control the proper lighting."

"Can I ask where you got this?" Roscoe inquired.

"I got the tank and all the gear from the Fish Factory. In Brighton Beach."

"The fish, too?"

"Everything."

"How big a tank is this?"

"I think it's something like two hundred and forty gallons."

"Fantastic. And you have some amazing specimens. You got some clownfish, pipefish, tiger pufferfish, triggerfish, eels, groupers, and oh cool, you got a baby hammerhead shark!"

"You know your fish, Detective."

"They're kinda a hobby of mine," Roscoe said, then remembering why he was there, he changed gears back to being a detective.

"I'm sorry, Doc. I digress. Now, what can you legally tell me about Roger Niles?"

"Not a lot, Detective Brown. Mr. Niles suffered from depression; he had schizophrenia, he had difficulty concentrating, he was suspicious of everyone, and he had hallucinations."

"And with all that, he was a functioning adult. It sounds to me that he should have been hospitalized."

"I know it sounds daunting, but he was improving with the drugs and therapy. Unfortunately, he must have stopped taking his medication."

"What was he prescribed?"

"Aripiprazole for schizophrenia, Fluoxetine for depression, and Buprenorphine for suicidal thoughts."

"And those were working?"

"Yes, they were. I believe that Mr. Niles would still be alive today if he had continued taking them."

Roscoe was flipping through his little black notepad when he stopped, smiled, and asked, "Now, I'm just going over my notes from the night Niles was killed."

"Not killed, Detective. Committed suicide." Tinterow snaped.

"Ah, right. Suicide. You said that when you arrived, you saw Mr. Niles holding a gun."

"Yes, that's right."

"And was he agitated or calm before he shot himself?"

"He was quite agitated, fidgety, and nervous."

"Do you now, thinking back on it, think that Mr. Williams's presence might have affected Mr. Niles?"

"No."

"You said that Frank Williams was sitting next to you when Mr. Niles shot himself. Is that right?"

"Yes, we were sitting next to each other on the couch opposite Roger when he put the gun to his head and pulled the trigger."

Roscoe continued to finish writing his notes in the notepad. He closed it by flipping the lid over onto the pad and said, "Is there anything else that you can tell me, Doctor Tinterow, or think that I should know?"

"I'm afraid not, Detective Brown."

"Well, thank you again for taking the time to meet with me."

"I hope I was of some help."

"Oh, you were Doctor. You were. More than you could know. Bye." Roscoe said with a big grin on his face.

"Goodbye."

Tinterow felt a small knot in his stomach. Did he say too much or not enough? Was the detective being coy, deliberately being reserved, and playing his cards close to his vest?

Tinterow felt uneasy and not in control; it was a feeling that he did not like.

Vincent Rainwater sat in Roscoe's office with Detective Walsh, developing a sting operation to snare Williams and Tinterow.

"I'm just spit-balling here, but as far as I see, there's a couple of ways we can play this," Roscoe said out loud to no one in particular.

"Yeah?" Walsh asked.

"We can try and set up an artist as bait. That is, if we can find one who'd be willing to help. Or we can make Rainwater here the bait by him telling them that he's had enough and is going to squeal to the cops." Roscoe concluded.

"What about Niles' murder?" Vincent asked, looking to avoid becoming the target.

"Yeah. We're working on it. Getting all the test results back from the various labs takes time. In the meantime, I want to put the pressure on them.

Now, getting an artist to become the target would mean having them target an artist from whom they have already purchased art. Is there anyone that they could feel was ready for the slaughter?" Roscoe asked.

"There is one artist who is on fire. Andy Warhol." Vincent admitted.

"The soup can, guy." Walsh quipped.

"Think he'd do it?" Roscoe asked.

"Maybe. I could ask him. I could call him." Vincent said.

"No. It is something better done in person. See if you can arrange a meeting at his studio in the next day or two."

"Okay. I'll call him tonight. He's a bit of a night owl."

"If Warhol doesn't pan out, Mr. Rainwater, I'm afraid you're in the snare."

"Vincent, welcome back to the Factory," Andy said with open arms.

"Andy. Good to see you. It's been a while." Vincent said as he hugged Warhol.

"Andy, this is Detective Sergeant Roscoe Brown and his partner, Detective Sergeant Walsh. Is there somewhere we can go to talk?"

Andy looked perplexed as he led them through the unfinished loft to an office in the corner. "The Factory" was Andy Warhol's New York City studio. It was on the fifth floor at 231 East 47th Street in Midtown Manhattan. To

Roscoe, it looked more like a crash pad than a studio, with exposed brick walls, water pipes running overhead, and unfinished wooden floors. An old, beat-up red sofa sat in the middle of the enormous loft. On the walls were pinned-up silkscreens of some of his latest works.

The place was packed with people. It wasn't called the Factory for nothing. There was an assembly line of people working on silkscreens while others were filming screen tests or just hanging out. It all looked chaotic to Roscoe, but no one seemed stressed out or confused.

Once inside the office, Roscoe explained why they were there.

"Mr. Warhol…" Roscoe started.

"Andy, please."

"Andy. I'm sure you are aware of the tragic deaths of Max Albertson and Roger Niles. Well, it's our belief that they were both killed by the same killers."

"Why would anyone want to kill Max and Roger?"

"We believe that they murdered them to increase the value of their collections," Roscoe explained.

"Whoa, fuck me! So, do you think these guys are after me? Is that why you're here?"

"Not yet," Roscoe said.

Warhol looked at him quizzically. "Huh?"

"You see, Andy, we were hoping you might allow us to use you as bait so we can catch these guys in the act."

"You want me to be used as…"

"Bait. Of course, you'll be under twenty-four-hour police surveillance and protection." Roscoe said reassuringly.

"Mmmm, I don't know. What do I have to do?"

"Nothing. You just go about your business. Vincent told us that you usually travel with a small entourage. Is that correct?"

"Yes, most of the time."

"Well, we would have an undercover plain clothes police officer with you at all times. Also, we will have undercover officers constantly watching you and your residence."

"Any idea how long this would go on?"

Roscoe looked at Vincent. "Vincent, do you care to field this one?"

"I imagine it wouldn't be more than six weeks," Vincent said.

"What does Vincent have to do with any of this?" Andy asked.

"Well, Andy, funny thing. You see, these two murders happen to be friends of Vincent's." Roscoe elucidated.

In disbelief, Andy approached Vincent and asked, "Do I know these guys?"

"Roscoe interrupted before Vincent could answer.

"Andy, this has to be strictly on the QT. I don't know if, in fact, you do know them, but we can't tell you because if you decide to help us, your knowing might interfere with our ability to capture these guys."

Do you need an answer right now?"

"No. How about by the end of the week?" Would that be okay?" Roscoe posed.

"Sure."

"Now, Andy, no one must know anything about this, understand? Whether you agree to do it or not, I must ask you to keep it a secret until we catch these guys."

"I understand."

"Great. Here's my card. Call me with any questions that you might think of. I look forward to hearing from you on Friday."

Andy took Roscoe's card, looked at it, took a deep breath, smiled, and said, "I'm not afraid to die; I just don't want to be there when it happens."

Back at the six O, Roscoe, Walsh, and Vincent were discussing how to play the con.

"You know, Mr. Rainwater, whether Warhol's in or out, you're still in it up to your eyeballs."

"I know," Vincent admitted solemnly.

"When's your next dinner at the Yale Club?"

"This Friday."

"Great. Hopefully, Andy will agree to participate. You okay with wearing a wire at dinner?"

"Yeah. How clunky is it? Will they spot it?" Vincent asked.

"Hey Jimmy, would you mind getting Crenshaw? Have him come up and fit Mr. Rainwater with a wire so he can try it on for size."

Detective Terry Crenshaw came plodding into Roscoe's office from the basement level of the precinct. Terry was the head of the audio/visual department, which was in charge of all surveillance equipment.

Terry was one year away from retirement; he was sixty-four and looked every year of it. He had been in the force for over thirty years. He'd seen it all: mafia wars, street gangs, narcotics, prostitution, homicide, sex trafficking, and child abuse. Above all, child abuse was the worst; it really takes its toll.

Terry was six feet tall when he joined the force, and today, he's slump-shouldered and maybe five-ten, maybe. He wears orthopedic shoes that squeak when he walks through the halls. Yet, nobody ever makes fun of Terry because there, for the grace of God, go I.

When the elevator doors opened, the squeaking began. "Here comes Crenshaw," Walsh announced.

Moments later, Detective Crenshaw walked into Roscoe's office holding the wire.

"Hey, Terry," Roscoe said.

"Howdy, Roscoe. Jimmy. This our boy?"

"Mr. Rainwater, this is Detective Crenshaw."

Vincent stood up and shook Crenshaw's hand.

"Nice to meet you, Mr. Rainwater."

"Likewise, Detective."

"Now, this won't hurt a bit. Just unbutton your shirt and loosen your belt. We're going to hook this clip to your belt in the back and run the wire with the microphone around to the front of your shirt, like so. There you go. Easy peasy."

Do you usually wear a coat and tie at these meetings?" Roscoe asked.

"It's required, dress code."

"Perfect. You can either come here to get fitted, or, better yet, we'll come to you. That might be the best since we'll be around listening in."

"Okay. Come to my home. Not work."

"Sure. Whatever. Now, depending on what Warhol decides, you'll either talk him up or talk about how you're feeling stressed and thinking about going to the police. Got it?"

"Got it."

"Homicide. Detective Brown." Roscoe said as he answered the phone.

"Detective Brown, this is Andy Warhol. I'm in, I'll do it."

Roscoe was taken aback since he never thought the famous artist would agree to become involved.

"That's wonderful."

"I'm doing it for Max and Roger," Andy confessed.

"Well, Mr. Warhol, rest assured you'll not be in imminent danger. I will assign my partner, Detective James Walsh, as your undercover bodyguard.

Would it be possible for us to stop by sometime today and discuss the details of the operation?"

"Would four o'clock work?"

"Four o'clock would be great. We'll see you then." Roscoe confirmed.

CLICK

"New York Times. How may I direct your call, please?"

"Vincent Rainwater."

"One moment, please."

"Vincent Rainwater."

"Mr. Rainwater. Detective Sergeant Brown here."

"Yes, Detective Sergeant Brown?"

"Warhol has agreed to help."

"That's terrific!"

"We're meeting with him at his studio at four o'clock this afternoon to review the details. I think it would be in your best interest to be there." Roscoe said.

"I'll be there, Detective Sergeant Brown."

"See you there, bye."

Goodbye, Detective."

CLICK

Roscoe's partner, Detective Walsh, came into Roscoe's office.

"What's the good word?"

"Warhol's going to do it."

"You're kidding! Why?"

"He says he's doing it for Albertson and Niles."

"The guys got guts."

"How would you like to be one of Andy Warhol's Superstars?"

"What do I have to do?"

"The most important thing is to blend in and not look or act like a cop."

"I can do that."

"Okay, superstar, after lunch, go home, find your most nonconformist outfit, and meet me at Warhol's studio at four o'clock. But first, let's head over to Nathan's Famous for a couple of dogs."

Detective Sergeant Roscoe Brown and his partner walked down to 1025 Boardwalk to Nathan's Famous Hot Dogs, across from the world-renowned Cyclone Rollercoaster. As they walked in, Vinnie, the counterman, shouted to the cooks, "Roscoe's here. Gimme the usual."

The usual for Roscoe was two chilidogs, an order of crinkle-cut French fries, and a Coke. And by usual, it was what Roscoe ate every day.

"Hey, Vinnie, give my superstar here the same as me," Roscoe ordered.

"Aw, Roscoe, you're too kind."

"Now. Now. Nothing's too good for a superstar."

"Roscoe, don't you ever get tired of eating hot dogs for lunch every day?

"Walsh, I'll have you know that Nathan's chili dogs and fries fill all my nutritional needs in one healthy meal."

"Oh, this is going to be good. How so?"

"Well, you got your meat, which is your protein; you got your beans for carbohydrates; you got your cheese for your vitamin D, C, and B12; you got the bun, which is your fiber; and finally, you got your French fries for your potassium. So, you want to grab a dog?"

Walsh stood there, stunned, with his mouth open in amazement, "Okay, sure."

"You know, Walsh. Sometimes, you surprise me."

The four of them met in the same office in the Factory where they had initially met three days ago. Andy and Vincent sat quietly, taking in the details of the operation.

Roscoe began to lay out the plan.

"Andy, Vincent will have contact with the two suspects, Frank Williams and Doctor Gary Tinterow. He is not going to suggest that they target you overtly. That would be entrapment. He's just going to discuss with them how valuable your work is and how much more valuable it will be in the future, along with a couple of other artists, so as not to sway them towards you." Roscoe explained.

Andy turned to Vincent and asked, "Do I know these guys?"

"You've met them a couple of times at gallery events. But compared to most of the people you hang out with, they are pretty forgettable." Vincent said.

"Now, Andy, Detective James Walsh will be assigned to be your undercover bodyguard. No one must know that he's a police officer. Is there some pretext that you can think of why he would join you here at the Factory?" Roscoe asked.

Warhol studied Detective Walsh for several minutes, looking him up and down. Detective Walsh was in his early thirties, with rugged good looks, a good physique, pitch-black hair, and a smile that melted many a girl's heart.

Warhol smiled and said. "Mmmm-hmm, James, you'll star in my next film."

"But I'm not an actor."

"Most of my actors aren't actors. I like real people. Don't worry, you'll fit right in."

"Well, congratulations, Jimmy. Who knows, this could be your big break." Roscoe teased.

Warhol chuckled, as did Vincent and Roscoe. Walsh couldn't find the humor in it.

Warhol said, "We'll need a back story. Like, where are you from? How'd you two meet? You know, stuff like that."

"The best thing is to stick to the truth as much as possible. That way, neither of you has to remember a bunch of lies." Roscoe suggested.

"So, for instance, we can say we met through Vincent," Warhol said.

"Exactly. Say, Walsh, didn't you have some odd jobs in college?" Roscoe asked.

"Yeah, I was a waiter, I worked for a moving company, and I worked as a bartender at Teddy's Bar & Grill."

"Where did you work as a waiter?" Andy asked.

"Peter Luger's Steak House."

"No. I like Teddy's Bar." Warhol said.

"So, you met Jimmy through Vincent at Teddy's Bar & Grill." Roscoe intonated.

"I liked his looks and asked if he'd like to come down and work as one of my art-workers."

"Great. What do you think, Jimmy?" Roscoe asked.

"I like it. The simpler, the better." Walsh answered.

"So, when do I start?"

"Tonight. I'm having a party. So, come around eleven."

"How should I dress?"

"I think you should wear black jeans and a black tee shirt. Oh, do you have a leather jacket?"

"Yeah. An old motorcycle jacket. It's pretty beat up."

"Perfect. Wear it."

"Vincent, does the subject of art usually come up?" Roscoe asked.

"It's one of our main topics."

"When the subject of art comes up, casually mention the name Andy Warhol. You might want to suggest that the syndicate purchase some of his latest works. But don't oversell; remember, it has to be their idea. And I wouldn't bring up the subject of Niles; it might make them nervous. Just play it cool. Think you can do that?"

"I think so."

"No pressure, but if you screw any of this up, the deals off."

"I understand," Vincent said, looking for some tell of humor. There was none.

"Call me before you leave to go to the Yale Club."

"I will," Vincent replied as he rose to leave.

"Bon Appetit," Roscoe smirked.

Detective James Walsh arrived at the Factory a little after eleven, dressed in all black: a beat-up motorcycle jacket, worn-out and torn black Levi's 501s, a black T-shirt, and black motorcycle boots. The only thing that was missing was a motorcycle.

Sandwiched in the doorway was a large black man. He, too, was wearing all black, including black-rimmed Ray-Ban sunglasses. He was holding a clipboard. There was a line of over forty people wanting to get in. Some were allowed in, but most were not. As Walsh approached the doorman, he held up his enormous hand and asked in a deep, guttural voice, "Name?"

"Walsh. Jimmy Walsh."

"Okay, come on."

When Walsh got to the elevator, there were several people waiting. Most were people he had never seen before. Still, there were a couple of big-name celebrities, Mick and Bianca Jagger, Grace Jones, and Liza Minnelli, all standing around waiting for the lift to arrive, making small talk with one another.

As Walsh stood star-stuck, a beautiful blonde woman wandered up next to him.

"Hello. I haven't seen you here before." She said in a low, sexy voice.

"It's my first time here," Walsh said.

"Mmmm, you're cute. What's your name, darling? I'm Candy. Candy Darling."

"Hi. I'm Jimmy Walsh."

"What do you do, Jimmy Walsh?" She asked.

"I'm an actor." He muttered.

"Me too!" She squealed.

"Have you done any films?" Walsh asked.

"You might have seen me in Andy's film, *Flesh*. Did you see it?"

"I'm sorry. I'm afraid I haven't." Walsh admitted.

"Well, that's okay, darling. I'll just have to screen it for you privately." She whispered with a big smile.

The elevator doors opened, and the fifteen people waiting rushed in. The boy operating the lift shouted, "Next stop, the Silver Factory!" Up they went, ever so slowly as freight elevators tend to do.

When the doors opened, there were hundreds of people in various stages of drunkenness and drug-induced delirium. The live music was overpowering by a band Walsh had never heard of The Velvet Underground.

It was like nothing Walsh had ever seen or experienced. In one corner, people were painting; in another, someone was filming a movie. Over near the elevator, people were sitting on a red couch snorting cocaine and smoking grass. Down by the office, where they all had met earlier, there were couples having sex, men and women, women and women, men with men.

Candy Darling took Walsh's hand and yelled over the cacophony of sounds, "Let's go get a drink."

Walsh let her guide him through the crazy maze of people to get to the bar where Andy Warhol was standing. The bartender rushed over to see what they'd like to drink.

Candy said, "I'll have a Manhattan, and you?" Candy asked Walsh.

"Could I just get a beer?" Walsh said.

"Be right back, darling." She said.

"Hey, Jimmy, glad you could make it. I see you've met Candy." Andy shouted.

"Yes, she's been very nice."

Andy leaned close to Walsh's ear and said, "She's a he."

Walsh jerked back in disbelief; no way, this was one of the most beautiful women he had ever seen.

"No way!" Walsh said.

Andy smiled and said, "Okay. I guess you'll just have to find out for yourself. She's a wonderful human being. Be careful, don't hurt her."

Candy returned with her drink and a beer for Walsh.

"What'd I miss?" She asked.

Andy winked and said, "Nothing. Just guy talk."

"Mmmm, sorry, I missed it." She quipped.

"Now, Candy, don't be selfish with Jimmy. This is his first time here, so take him around and introduce him to everyone."

She looked at Andy with big puppy dog eyes and pouty lips."

"Promise!" Andy said.

"I promise," Candy said with a tone of disappointment in her voice.

She took Walsh by the arm, smiled, and said, "Come on, darling. Let's mingle."

That night, he had met many of the Factory regulars: Paul America, Johnny Dodd, Penny Arcade, Jean-Michel Basquiat, William S. Burroughs, Mick and Bianca Jagger, Grace Jones, Liza Minnelli, Billy Name, Lou Reed, Viva, Ultra Violet to name but a few.

By the end of the night, he couldn't remember half their names, between all the beers he had and the cumulus clouds of marijuana smoke that filled the room like a foggy day in old London town.

"So, Vincent, what's happening in the art world?" Williams asked.

"Oh, I've been working on a big article on the upcoming Impressionist retrospective opening at MOMA this weekend."

"I always liked them," Tinterow remarked.

"They're okay. But me, I really like the post-impressionists. Van Gogh, Cézanne, Gaugin, and Matisse.

Monet, Manet, and Degas are a little too foo-foo for my taste." Williams smirked.

"Well, that's the great thing about art. There's something for everybody." Vincent said.

"I didn't tell Frank, but I had a visit from the Detective who's working on Niles' suicide, Detective Sergeant Brown."

"What did he want?" Williams asked with a hint of anxiety in his voice.

"Oh, he was primarily asking about Niles' illness. And the drugs he was on."

"So, what did you tell him?" Williams asked.

"The truth. That Niles must have stopped taking the medications that I prescribed for him, as so many sick people sometimes tend to do."

"Why is that?" Vincent inquired.

"Most of them feel that they don't need it since they're feeling better, and some because they don't like some of the side-effects."

"Sad," Vincent said.

"Let's change the subject; it's too depressing. Say, Vincent, I thought maybe we should consider selling off some of our existing pieces and adding something new to our portfolio." Tinterow suggested.

"Who did you have in mind?" Vincent asked.

"You tell us. Who's hot?" Williams queried.

"Who do you guys think we should sell?"

"We're thinking either our Jasper Johns, Arthur Strong, Mark Rothko, or Andy Warhol." Williams volunteered.

"Really!"

"Yeah, we're tired of them," Tinterow said.

"Tired of them?"

"Yeah, time for a change. Gary and I have had them in our offices and homes, and we're ready to move on." Williams stated.

"Who would bring top dollar?" Tinterow asked.

"I would say that it would be between Johns, Strong, and Warhol. Both Strong and Warhol are doing some very exciting things these days." Vincent answered.

"Are all these guys here in New York?" Williams asked.

"I heard that Johns, although he has a studio here, has started working in his studio in Saint Martin. Rothko has begun working on a chapel in Houston, but both Strong and Warhol have their studios in midtown. Why?"

"Just curious." Tinterow mused.

"Are you wanting me to put some feelers out for potential buyers?"

Williams and Tinterow glanced at each other before Williams replied, "No. We're just toying around with the idea. What's your feelings about selling?"

"I guess I'm more of a long-term collector. Not keen on quick turnarounds. But, as we agreed, the majority rules, so just let me know when and if you want to sell." Vincent said.

"Say, speaking of selling. Do you have a pulse on the Niles market? Or is it still too early?" Tinterow queried.

Roscoe was sitting in an unmarked car parked on Vanderbilt Ave in front of the Yale Club, listening in on Rainwater's wire device.

"Oh, shit. Play it cool, Vincent." Roscoe uttered to himself.

Vincent spoke without hesitation, "It's only been a week since his suicide. Usually, when an artist dies the art market, the establishment won't react for several weeks out of respect."

Roscoe breathed a sigh of relief, "Nicely handled."

"That seems like a very decent thing to do," Williams said.

"Say, Vincent, do you know a Times reporter named Sharon Fiyalka?"

"Sharon. Yeah, why."

"She keeps calling my office wanting to set up an interview about Roger."

"Really?"

"What do you think? I mean, with my doctor-patient confidentiality and all."

"Well, I know there would only be so much that you could say with your professional boundaries. But whatever you could say might enhance the value of his work." Vincent suggested.

"Nice play," Roscoe said to no one.

"Hmmm, maybe I'll agree to it then. You know, say some comforting things about him to help Roger's family cope."

"That would be nice," Vincent said.

TAP TAP TAP

Roscoe was startled by the sound of the nightstick of Officer Chris Giles tapping on his window. Roscoe rolled down his window.

"Sir, you can't park here." Officer Giles said.

Roscoe showed his badge and ID to the officer, "Detective Sergeant Roscoe Brown, homicide. I'm here on an undercover stakeout, officer."

"Sorry. Are you in need of any assistance, Detective Brown?"

"No, thank you, officer. I think I'm done for the night. I thought my department contacted Midtown South to let them know I would be here."

"I'm sure they did; I'm actually with the one seven. The division line is just a couple of blocks over. Hope I didn't muff it up for you, Detective?"

"No. It's good. No harm, no foul."

"Well, have a good evening, Detective Brown."

"You too, Officer?"

"Giles, sir. Officer Giles."

"Stay safe, Officer Giles."

Walsh opened his eyes with great difficulty. That's what a night of excessive drinking and a headful of marijuana nimbostratus clouds will do. His head felt like an elephant had been sitting on it, squeezing it like a vise. He was gazing up at a ceiling that was totally alien to him. He slowly rotated his head to the left and realized that he was definitely NOT in his nor anybody's bedroom that he had been in before. It was most certainly a woman's bedroom, but whose?

He turned his head to the right, and there lying beside him was Candy Darling, fast asleep on her stomach. Walsh, ever so slowly, lifted the covers and discovered that he and Candy were both naked.

A tsunami of panic swept over him; he broke out in a cold sweat. As hard as he tried, he couldn't for the life of him remember what, if anything, happened last night. The last thing he remembered was talking to William S. Burroughs about the tenets of National Socialism compared to nihilism. Then a blackness fell over him, then nothing. Now, he lay naked next to a transsexual.

Walsh eased out of bed; sitting on the bed's edge, he looked at his watch: seven forty-eight. He stood up and walked to the chair next to his side of the bed, where his clothes were neatly folded—something he would never do.

He slipped on his boxers, tee shirt, and jeans. He had just zipped up his Levi's when he heard a sultry voice say, "Good morning, darling."

He turned to see Candy propped up against the pillows with the covers tucked under her arms.

"Good morning." He uttered.

"Sleep well?" She asked.

"Like a rock. I honestly can't remember a thing after talking to William S. Burroughs. How did I end up here?"

"You really don't remember?"

"Sorry. But it's a total blank. What happened?" He asked, fearing the answer, but he had to know.

Candy saw the terror in his eyes; she smiled and said, "Nothing. Nothing happened."

"But…"

"You were in no shape to leave on your own, so I brought you here. I tucked you into bed, and we went to sleep."

"So…"

"Listen, darling, I would never take advantage of a nice boy like you."

"I appreciate that, Candy."

"Listen, but if at some point you'd like to. You know where I live."

"I'll keep that in mind. I better go." He said as he picked up his boots.

As he left the bedroom, she asked, "Aren't you even curious?"

He stopped, leaned over, kissed her on the cheek, and said, "Candy, if and when I do find out, I want it to be my idea. Thanks."

"See ya around, darling."

"See ya."

After a six-week affair with Tony Romeo, Amy Albright Rainwater decided to try to work things out with Vincent on the condition that they go to a marriage counselor. It wasn't so much that he made a foolish mistake but that he didn't confide in her. She was proud of him for deciding to do the right thing and help the police. He was, after all, a good man who just happened to fuck up royally. He told her that he was prepared to face the consequences, whatever they may be.

Seeing if they could make the marriage work was more about how she felt about Tony, not Vincent.

Before Vincent went undercover, Detective Sergeant Roscoe Brown and partner Detective James Walsh had spoken with her once when they came to talk to Vincent.

"Mrs. Rainwater…" Roscoe said.

"I go by Albright, my artist's name, Detective." She interjected.

"Excuse me. Ms. Albright, the NYPD appreciates your husband's assistance. We are asking that you keep all of this confidence. You mustn't speak of this to anyone. It's imperative that no one knows anything about what your husband is doing."

"But these creeps are killing artists. Shouldn't they know that some of their lives might be in danger?"

"If word gets out, these men will just cease, at least for a while, and we might never be able to catch them. We need the element of surprise. We are keeping both of these men under surveillance, plus we have a pretty good idea who they might plan to attack next, and we are placing an undercover police officer close by. Do you understand?" Roscoe asked.

"Yes, I do. Is Vincent in any danger?"

"No. Not unless they find out what he's doing. Again, that's another reason we must keep this whole thing a secret."

"I understand." She said.

Once Brown and Walsh left, she realized that this wasn't a game and just how truly dangerous it was.

"How could Frank and Gary be so ruthless as to kill in cold blood for money?" She wondered.

"I don't know. They aren't the same guys I knew in college. They were fun-loving, easy-going, and not violent in any way. I guess life's circumstances can be a huge influence on one's destiny. Gary's hit and run, Frank killing that private detective, a couple of bitter divorces, and a couple of professional setbacks. All those things can drive you to do desperate things, I guess. And once you get away with something, well, I suppose you think you can keep on getting away with it. "

"Do you think you'll have to go to jail?"

"Maybe, I hope not. Bascom thinks as long as I keep up my end of the bargain, I should be okay."

"What about your job with the Times?"

"Ah! That could be a problem. It's not as bad as sleeping with a fourteen-year-old, but…"

"Yeah, but you could have kept quiet!" Amy said, pointing out the positive.

"True. I guess it could go either way. Of course, I can't say anything just yet. Can't jeopardize the case."

Vincent patted the couch, wanting Amy to sit next to him. She walked over sheepishly to him and sat down. He took her hand and whispered, "I love you so much." He said and kissed her hard. They made love on the couch. Something they hadn't done since they were first married.

The following day, Amy woke up early before Vincent, dressed, and left the loft. She went to her lawyer's office in midtown. She needed answers to several questions that she had.

Walsh went over to Nathan's Famous on the Boardwalk to meet Roscoe. He saw him sitting on a bench facing the ocean, eating his two chilidogs and fries.

Walsh sat on the opposite side of the bench. He wore a black baseball cap, aviator sunglasses, and the outfit he wore the day before.

Looking straight ahead, Walsh asked, "How'd it go last night with Vincent?"

"They were fishing for a name. He cast his line out, and they nibbled."

"Did they bite?"

"No. Not outright. I think it's going to be a bit of a cat-and-mouse chase. I don't get the sense that they fully trust him completely."

"Rainwater do, okay?"

"Yeah, he played it pretty cool."

"Great. So, what about Warhol?" Walsh asked.

"Stay with him. I'm sure he's on the top of their hit list."

"Will do."

"Say, how was the party last night?"

"Wild and crazy. Lots of drugs, drinking, and a ton of famous people."

"Yeah, like who?"

"Oh, there was Mick Jagger, Liza Minnelli, William S. Burroughs, Jean-Michel Basquiat, Paul America, Johnny Dodd, Penny Arcade, Grace Jones, Billy Name, Lou Reed, Candy Darling, Viva, and Ultra Violet."

"You lost me after Jean-Michel Basquiat."

"Most of the others are what is known as Andy's Superstars. People he puts in his movies or people who help him in his art studio."

"I hear that you left with a hot looking blonde."

"Where did you hear that!" Walsh said, alarmed.

"Did you forget we have Andy's place under surveillance?"

"Oh yeah." He said as he remembered. Walsh was still in a bit of a fog from last night.

"So, who was she?"

"Her name is Candy Darling. She's one of his actresses."

"And?"

"And nothing. She was kind enough to let me crash at her place. I was a bit too far gone to have made it home. But nothing happened." He said emphatically.

"Okay. Lighten up. I'm just asking."

"Sorry. I'm still a little off my game."

"Well, don't let this become a habit. Remember, you're working the party, not partying the party."

"Got it, Roscoe."

"Want a chilidog? That'll straighten you right up."

"Mmmm, no thanks. I better get going. I'll check in with you tomorrow."

"Okay. Be careful."

Williams and Tinterow met with Vincent for lunch after dinner the night before. They decided to have lunch somewhere different: Fuji Sushi, one of the oldest Japanese restaurants in Manhattan. They met outside the restaurant on West 56th Street. The restaurant was long and narrow, and the hostess wore a traditional Japanese Kimono, scarlet red, with a terra-cotta orange obi sash tied around the waist. She asked if they would like a table or sit at a booth.

"Would it be possible to have a tatami room?" Williams asked.

She gave a slight bow and said, "Oh, sorry. Tatami rooms only for special occasions."

Tinterrow reached into his wallet, handed her a fifty-dollar bill, and said, "Is this special enough?"

She bowed, smiled, and said, "Right this way, gentlemen."

They followed her to the back of the restaurant through an arched doorway. Inside the room, a traditional navy blue noren decorated with a diamond-shaped shibori pattern curtain hangs in the doorway. The walls are covered with beige rice paper, and the floors are bamboo. Eight red silk pillows surround the twelve-inch-high oak table.

"Please remove your shoes." The hostess said as she gave a short bow.

As Williams and Tinterow took off their shoes, the host asked, "Would you gentlemen care for some tea?"

"Yes, please," Williams answered.

"Ichika, your waitress will be right in." She said as she gave a short bow, turned, and left the room.

While waiting for Ichika to bring their cocktails, Williams said, "I'm thinking Warhol may be too big a risk at the moment. What's your thought?"

Before he could respond, a tall, beautiful woman dressed in a sea-green kimono entered the room carrying a tray with a teapot, two teacups, and steamed towels. She placed the tea in front of them and handed each a steamy hot towel. The waitress had them place the towels on the tray as she handed them a menu.

"Now, if you'll excuse me, I shall be back after you've had time to review the menu. If you have any questions, I will be more than happy to answer them."

"Thank you," Williams replied.

Ichika bowed, smiled, and left the room.

"Now, getting back to the business at hand. I tend to agree with you about Warhol. I'm thinking that he will probably or should be our last." Tinterow stated.

"Good. We agree. Arthur Strong is to die."

"Yes. But no more guns. Too dangerous. These next two, Strong and eventually Warhol, will have to look like they died naturally."

"How do we do that? Niles was a lucky coincidence, with you being his shrink and all. And him being suicidal."

Ichika came into the room. "Do you have any questions?" she asked. Neither man acknowledged that they had questions.

Tinterow ordered first, "I'll start with the Uni Chawanmushi, and I'll have the Hamachi & Quail Egg Sushi for my main course.

"Excellent, and for you, sir?"

"I'll have the Tetsu-Nabe Gyoza, and then I'll have the Seared Toro & Wasabi Vinaigrette."

"Very good. Would either of you care for some sake?"

"Sure. We'll both have a tokkuri. Thank you." Williams said.

"Would you like hot sake or cold?"

"Hot."

Once Ichika left the room, the conversation turned deadly.

"We have to become friendly with Mr. Strong," Tinterow said.

"How do we do that?"

"We buy more work from him directly. Maybe have a commissioned piece done."

"And that helps us how?" Williams asked.

"We need to become engrained into his social circle. Invite him to some of our gatherings, and hopefully, he'll invite us to some of his."

"Yeah, then what?"

"Oh, I have something special planned for Mr. Strong. A little something from the land of the rising sun."

"Hey, Jimmy. Did you have a good time last night?" Andy asked with a big smile on his face.

"Yeah. What I can remember of it."

"What did you think of Candy? She's quite a special girl."

"Yes, she that," Walsh said with a grin.

"So, what are your plans today?"

"Just hang around and make a nuisance of myself."

"Would you like to be useful?"

"Sure, as long as I still have you in sight."

"Do you think these guys would try something so bold with a lot of witnesses about?"

"Probably not. But they will probably be looking for an opportunity or spot some weakness. It's best just to be safe."

"I guess you're right."

"So, what can I do to make myself useful?"

"I'm expecting a new batch of silkscreens today, and I could use your help augmenting them if you don't mind."

"Augmenting?"

"Each print is the same until one of my team, or I add some individual touches to each piece. Then, when I approve the piece, I will sign and number them."

"But..."

"Look, Jimmy, Leonardo Da Vinci, Rafael, even Michelangelo, they all had assistants, and nobody questions their work, now do they?"

"No, I guess not."

"Oh, I almost forgot. This afternoon, I'm going to be shooting a movie. I'd like you to be in it. Just a small part. Whad'ya say?"

"Me? Naw, I can't act."

"You don't have to really act. There isn't any script; it's all ad-lib. It'll be fun, you'll see."

"Okay. Sounds like fun."

"That's it! It'll be fun."

"What's about?"

"It's called "A Symphony Of Sound." It depicts a rehearsal of the band The Velvet Underground and Nico. It will be essentially one long take of them rehearsing, and at the end, it'll be a bunch of people and the band in private conversation. That's where you'll come in and walk around and talk to the band. It'll be fun."

"Sounds easy enough. No acting?"

"Just be yourself."

"Hey, I can do that."

"Perfect."

"Hello, I'm Sharon Fiyalka. I'm a reporter for the New York Times. Doctor Tinterrow is expecting me." She said to Tinterow's secretary.

"You're a little early, Ms. Fiyalka. The Doctor is in with a patient. Would you care to have a seat?"

"Thank you," Sharon said as she sat on one of the two couches in the waiting room. She and the secretary were the only ones there. Sharon picked up a Life Magazine and began thumbing through it as the secretary was busy typing some correspondence.

A few moments later, the secretary's phone buzzed.

"Hello?" All right, I'll let her know." She said as she hung up the receiver.

"Ms. Fiyalka, Doctor Tinterow will see you now."

"I thought that he was with a patient?"

"Patients go out a separate exit."

"I see. Thank you."

Sharon Fiyalka, the investigative staff writer for the New York Times, was a short, demure, attractive-looking woman in her late thirties. She had straight brown shoulder-length hair, an olive complexion, and crystal blue eyes hidden behind a pair of green-tinted Ray-Ban sunglasses that she only ever took off when she went to sleep.

Sharon worked on some of the year's biggest stories. She was among the first female reporters to be embedded in an Army unit during the Tet Offensive.

She was only a few feet from Robert Kennedy when a lone gunman, Sirhan B. Sirhan, assassinated the Senator. She was one of the people who tackled the assassin to the ground. And that same year, she won a Pulitzer Prize for her coverage of the police brutality used against the students at the Chicago Democratic Convention.

People were often misled and taken in by her soft and feminine appearance, but underneath lay the heart of a tiger, a real maneater.

"Doctor Tinterrow, Sharon Fiyalka, New York Times." She said as she shook his hand.

"It's my pleasure, Ms. Fiyalka. I'm a big fan of your work."

"Why, thank you." She said with a smile as she sat in the chair across from his desk.

"Now, Ms. Fiyalka, I'm busy, as I am sure you are. What can I do for you?"

As she took out her notepad and pen, she said, "Well, Doctor, I'm doing a piece on the life and death of Roger Niles. I understand that he was under your care. Is that correct?"

"Yes. He had been a patient of mine for a little over two years."

"I have spoken to his family, and they informed me that he suffered from depression and schizophrenia and had bouts of hallucinations. Is that correct?"

"That's correct."

"You were there when he killed himself?"

"That's right."

"So, it was just you and him."

"Well, no. You see, I was having dinner with a friend when Mr. Niles called me. He said he was in distress and asked if I could come see him. So, my friend and I drove down to Sea Gate."

"And your friend would be Frank Williams, the criminal attorney?"

"That's right. Like I said, we were having dinner when I got the call."

"Do you think the fact that Frank Williams was with you might have played in any way in the suicide of Niles?"

"No, I do not."

"Had Niles and Williams ever met before?"

"Not to my knowledge."

"So, you don't think that the introduction of a complete stranger into an already volatile situation didn't contribute in any way to Niles' death."

"No."

"Was Williams in the room when Niles blew his brains out?"

"Yes. He was sitting on the sofa next to me."

"Might Niles have felt that he was being ganged up on?"

"Certainly not. When we walked into the room, he was calm, non-agitated, and serene."

"But you knew that he was in an unstable state, or why else would you have interrupted your dinner and gone all the way from Manhattan to Coney Island if there wasn't something to be concerned about."

"Believe me, if he had shown any signs of unstableness, I would not have allowed Mr. Williams to enter the house."

"Did you know that he had a gun?"

"I Knew he owned a gun."

"But did you see that he had a gun when you arrived?

"No."

"Did he say anything before he shot himself?"

"Nothing."

"Don't you find it odd that he asked you to come out to see him all that way and not say anything at all?"

"Of course I do. I wish to God he hadn't shot himself before I could have talked to him."

"Do you think he just wanted an audience?"

"Possibly."

"Why you?"

Tinterow said nothing; he just gazed at the Times reporter. Regretting that he allowed this inquisition and wondering how long it was to last.

"Did he leave a note?"

"No note."

"Can you tell me what medications he was taking?"

"I'm sorry, that's confidential information."

"His sister said that he was taking Aripiprazole, Fluoxetine, and Buprenorphine. Is that true?"

"I cannot say."

"Isn't one of the side effects of Aripiprazole anxiety and the feeling of agitation and distress?"

"In some patients."

"With Fluoxetine, aren't some of the side effects anxiety, nervousness, trouble sleeping, decreased sex drive, and having trouble having an orgasm?"

"In some patients."

"And if he weren't taking his medication, with Buprenorphine, aren't the mood swings experienced would be like those found in heroin addicts?"

"In some patients."

"Those are some powerful drugs."

"Yes, they can be if not monitored. I monitor my patients very carefully, Ms. Fiyalka."

Sharon smiled as she busily scribbled into her notebook. She stopped, looked around his office, and spotted the two Niles prints hanging over the saltwater aquarium.

"Oh, are those Roger Niles lithographs?" She asked.

"Why, yes, they are," Tinterow said proudly.

"And those. Max Albertson?"

"Yes. Those are a couple of pieces from his last series."

"Doctor Tinterow, I must say you have a very nice art collection."

"Thank you."

"Does your collection extend to your home as well?"

"It does."

"So, you're a patron of the arts."

"I like to think so."

"Doctor Tinterow, do you take any responsibility for the death of Roger Niles committed right in front of you?"

Tinterrow sat seething, staring at this upstart reporter. She had the advantage over him, she could look into his eyes, yet he was blind to hers, hidden behind those damn sunglasses.

"No, I do not." He sneered.

"None?"

"Listen, young lady, psychiatry is not like mending a broken arm. The mind is a complex organism. Do I feel bad that Mr. Niles committed suicide? Yes, of course. I keep asking myself, what should I have said that I didn't or shouldn't have said that I did? Could I have done more, or did I do too much?

I just wish I could have seen any signs that he was failing, but I do not accept blame for his death. Now, I think it best that you leave."

"Just one more question, Doctor Tinterow. If Roger Niles did feel threatened by Frank Williams's presence, then you are, in fact, responsible for his death. Are you not?"

"Good day, Ms. Fiyalka!"

"Arthur Strong, Father of Color Field Painting, turns seventy-five today."

<u>Vincent Rainwater</u>

Arthur Strong, one of the founding fathers of Color Field Painting, along with Mark Rothko, Barnett Newman, and Clyford Still. Color Field Painting marked a significant development in abstract painting, turns seventy-five today.

Color Field Painting was the first style to decisively avoid the suggestion of a form or mass standing out against a background. Now, with Color Field Painting, figure and ground are one, and the amplitude of the picture, perceived as a field, seems to spread out beyond the boundaries of the canvas.

Like Mark Rothko, Strong considered color to be an instrument that served a greater purpose. He believed his fields of color were spiritual planes that could tap into our most basic human emotions. For Rothko and Strong, color evoked emotion. Therefore, each of their works was intended to evoke different meanings depending on the viewer.

Strong was concerned with brushstroke and paint texture, but he soon came to view color as the most powerful communication tool. His bands of color were meant to strike a chord of homogeneity with the spectator's deep awareness, to provide an introspective, reflective space in which to visually explore one's own moods and connection with the chosen color palette. Strong sought to extract the quintessence or natural origins out of the collection of hues.

Along with his friend, the painter Adolph Advair, Strong wrote a series of statements in 1963 to explain his work. In one, they wrote: "We try to facilitate the elementary expression of the multifarious thought."

It was a week before the Collingsworth Gallery in midtown was having a show of the new works of Arthur Strong at a gallery gala when Vincent got a call from Tinterow.

"Vincent, how are you doing? Gary here."

"Hey Gary, how's by you?" He said as he switched on the recorder that Detective Brown and the NYPD had installed on his phone.

"Good. Good. Listen, I got wind of an art exhibit that Frank and I would really like to attend. Wondering if you might be able to help us get a couple of invites."

"I'll see what I can do. Who is it?"

"Arthur Strong."

"I'm scheduled to attend that as well. I'll call over to Linda at Collingsworth and see if I can add you guys on to my invite I'm taking Amy, do you guys want to bring dates?"

"Ah, no. We'll be going stag."

"Okay, I'll call over once we hang up. Are we still on for dinner on Friday at the Yale Club?"

"You bet."

"Great. See you guys then."

"Look forward to it. Thanks again for the invites."

"No sweat. Goodbye."

"Bye."

CLICK

"Detective Brown, please."

"One moment." The receptionist answered.

"Brown. Homicide."

"Detective Brown, this is Vincent Rainwater."

"Yes, Vincent, what's happening?"

"I just got a call from Doctor Tinterow requesting a couple of invitations for him and Frank Williams to attend the new Arthur Strong opening next week at the Collingsworth Gallery. What should I do?"

"Are you going to be there?"

"Yes, Amy and I are going."

"Okay, get them the tickets. I'll talk to the gallery and get tickets for a couple of undercover cops to attend."

"Ah, it might be better if you let me get the tickets," Vincent suggested.

"Good idea."

"Do you think they might pull something with at the opening?"

"Have they ever asked for invites in the past?"

"Sure, all the time. They like to be seen as art connoisseurs."

"So, it could be nothing. But just to be on the safe side, I'll have some of my men there to keep an eye on things."

"Should I wear a wire?"

"Any time you talk to them or get together with them, wear the wire. Are you planning on seeing them before the gallery opens?"

"This Friday night."

"Yale Club?"

"But of course. Where else would we go."

"Okay. Keep me posted."

"Will do, Detective."

CLICK

"Camera!" Andy shouted.

"Speed!" The camera operator yelled.

"Sound!"

"Rolling." Soundman wailed.

Somebody grabbed the clapboard with Scene One / Take One scribbled on it and slapped the clapper down in front of the lens.

CLAP

"And…Action!" Andy shouted.

The camera is in a tight close-up of Nico, the German singer, musician, model, and actress. The sound is of the band Velvet Underground tuning their guitars for over three minutes. The camera pulls back to reveal Nico sitting on a bar stool, surrounded by the band members playing the maracas. At her feet is a young blonde boy about age three who occasionally stands up, dances, and sits back down.

This went on for over an hour. Walsh stood behind the cameraman, watching him smash zooms into the band members' faces and instruments and swish pans back and forth from one player to another.

After an hour of nonstop improv, the band suddenly stopped playing because a police officer came up from the street and told Andy they had to stop. People complained about the noise left in the film. After all, this was experimental filmmaking—very avant-garde.

The band stopped playing one by one, got up, left their instruments behind, and exited the stage. Andy then had some of the "actors" walk in front of the camera, not speaking but meandering around.

Walsh must have walked across in front of the camera a dozen times. At one point, he was brought into a conversation with Lou Reed from the band, who was reading a copy of the Village Voice Newspaper. They talked about the band's upcoming gig in the East Village. Andy soon joined them, and the entire band, crew, and several actors stood before the camera for a minute or so until someone shouted, "Cut!"

"That was great, everybody. That's a wrap!" Andy proclaimed. As Andy walked by dispersing the group, he gave Walsh a tap on the butt and said, "Nice job."

"Er, thanks," Walsh said, thinking all I did was walk by the camera a few times.

"Hey. Good job." Billy Name said with a slap on the back.

"All I did was walk back and forth in front of the camera a few times," Walsh answered.

"Look, kid. As George Burns once said, "Acting is all about honesty. If you can fake that, you've got it made."

Sharon Fiyalka placed a call to Roscoe when she got back to the office.

"Detective Brown, please."

"One moment." The receptionist answered.

"Brown. Homicide."

"Detective Brown, this is Sharon Fiyalka, New York Times."

"Hello, Ms. Fiyalka. How can I help you?"

"Well, actually, I might be able to help you."

"Oh?"

"I just came back from interviewing Doctor Tinterow."

Roscoe decided to play innocent. "Really. And why do you think I would be interested?"

"Because I have an unnamed source who tells me that Doctor Tinterow is a person of interest in Roger Niles's apparent suicide."

"An unnamed source, huh?"

"Yup." She said proudly.

"Whad'ya want?"

"An exclusive."

"Okay, but only when I'm ready. I don't want any leaks. Got it?"

"Got it. Deal?"

"Deal."

"Great. I'll drop off the text of the interview this afternoon."

"When is the article supposed to break?"

"I don't want to mention that you, especially the NYPD, are looking at him as a suspect in any way."

There was a long silence before Roscoe said, "It's a deal breaker."

"Oh, all right. I sent it over ASAP."

"Super. Now, I'm off to go get lunch."

"Nathan's Famous?"

"Damn. You are good."

"Bon Appétit."

Roscoe was sitting on a park bench facing the Atlantic Ocean, finishing off the second of his two chilidogs, when Detective Walsh came and sat at the opposite end of the bench.

"Hey, Roscoe."

"Jimmy. How are things in the life of a superstar?"

"Glamorous."

"Yeah?"

"Yeah. I was in an Andy Warhol movie last night."

"Were you naked?"

"No! It's a film about this band. The Velvet Underground."

"Never heard of them."

"Me either. They set the camera up in one spot and filmed them practicing and playing for an hour. They're going to screen it tonight."

"So, what did you do? You didn't play in the band, did you?"

"No. I just walked in front of the camera a couple of times. Then, at the end of the film, they had me and a bunch of others just milling around."

"It sounds like an Academy Award-winning performance to me. Look out, Brando."

"Ha. Ha. So, what's cooking?"

"I got a call from Rainwater last night. It seems that Tinterow and Williams want to attend Arthur Strong's opening at the Collingsworth Gallery."

"What are you thinking?"

"Could be nothing, or it could mean they're interested in Strong instead of Warhol."

"Change of plan?"

"No. Not until we see what their intentions are. I want you to stay with Warhol. I'm going to have Harris and Tupperman go undercover to the opening. Once we understand what they're planning, I might pull you off the Warhol detail."

"Until then?"

"Carry on being a superstar."

"Cute."

"Say, I got a call from that New York Times reporter, Sharon Fiyalka."

"What did she want?"

"She just got through with an interview with Tinterow."

"Really.

"Yeah, and she's going to send me a transcript of the interview."

"Why would she do that?"

"She said that someone told her that Tinterow is a person of interest."

"Who?"

"She wouldn't say. But there aren't that many people who know."

"Rainwater, he works at the Times."

"That's what I first thought. But why would he leak something like that when trying to keep things close to the vest? And it wouldn't be Warhol. No, I'm thinking maybe someone here on the force."

"Ooh, that's not good."

"If whoever it is, fucks this up, his ass is grass!"

"Is there anything that you need from me, Roscoe?"

"How's Warhol doing?"

"So far, things look to be normal. Whatever that is."

Okay. Keep me posted if you need anything."

"Same with you."

"Oh, let me know if Warhol is going to the Strong opening."

"Okay, boss. I'll see ya."

"Yeah. See ya, superstar."

After all the ritual greetings and small talk, Vincent presented Tinterow and Williams with invitations to the Arthur Strong gallery opening.

"Hey, thanks, man. We're looking forward to going." Tinterow said.

"So, do you guys want the syndicate to see about purchasing a painting? I think they're starting at forty thousand a piece." Vincent said.

"Well, we were thinking it might be a solid investment. What do you think?" Williams asked.

"There's no doubt about it, Arthur Strong 's work is legendary."

"Do you know him?" Tinterow inquired.

"I wouldn't say we're friends, but I have met him several times."

"Think we could get a sneak preview?" Williams asked.

"We? What we? I can't go and ask to get a sneak preview and schlep you two along."

"Okay. Okay, you don't have to get your panties in a wad. Just asking."

"How much are you thinking of spending?" Vincent asked.

Tinterow replied, "We have about eighty thousand in the kitty. I'd say we'd feel comfortable with sixty."

"Okay, are you comfortable to go higher if we have to?" Vincent said.

"No higher than the eighty in the pot." Williams adamantly replied.

"Well, hopefully, it won't come to that," Vincent said.

"Is Strong a nice guy or a dick?" Tinterow queried.

"The couple of times I met him, he was a sweetheart. He's down to earth, cordial, and very outgoing."

"Great. I hate supporting someone who is arrogant and full of himself." Tinterow proclaimed.

"I'm looking forward to meeting him," Williams said.

"When do you think you'll go see him?" Tinterow wanted to know.

"I'll call him tomorrow and see when it's convenient for us to get together."

"Call us when you set it up," Tinterrow said, seemingly over-enthusiastic about the prospect.

"Oh, you'll be the first to know." Vincent quipped.

Roscoe was again parked outside the Yale Club on Vanderbilt Avenue, listening in on the art syndicate's conversation.

TAP TAP TAP TAP

Roscoe rolled down the window to see Officer Giles smiling down at him.

"Good evening, Detective Brown," Giles said.

"Ah, Officer Giles. Good to see you again."

"I saw it was you and wondered if everything was Jake."

"Couldn't be better."

"This is my beat. So, if you ever happen to need backup. Know that I'm around."

"I appreciate that. Really, I do."

"Well, it looks like you're in no need of assistance. So, have a good night."

"Thanks for looking out for me. See ya, Officer Giles."

Walsh arrived back at the Factory around two o'clock after meeting with Roscoe down on the Coney Island Boardwalk.

"Hey, Walsh, Just in time for the screening of the Underground flick. Come have a seat." Billy Name shouted out. He was sitting next to Candy Darling on the red couch.

Candy wiggled over, making room for Walsh to sit down next to her.

"How you doing?" She asked.

"Doing good. You?"

"I'm okay. I hear you're in the film."

"Yeah. A couple of walk-ons. That's all." Walsh said nonchalantly.

"No. That's great. Andy likes to test people with walk-ons to see if they have "it." Candy said enthusiastically.

"It?"

"You know "it," star quality."

"Well, I know for a fact that I don't have "it." Walsh declared.

"Mmmm, the people who say they don't have it are usually those who do."

It wasn't too long before the area was packed with all of Andy's "superstars" assembled to view the new film; even the Velvet Underground made an appearance.

Andy threaded the 16mm projector himself; he hit the light switch, and the film started seconds later. At first, everyone was quiet, but soon, people started making comments about Nico, the band, the little kid, and the music.

Walsh made what he thought was a humorous, off-handed comment about how the cameraman's excessive swish pans and smash zooms were making him nauseous. Several others in the group quickly admonished him, letting him know in no uncertain terms that those camera techniques were very edgy, avant-garde, and cutting-edge.

Walsh leaned over to Candy and whispered, "They can call them what they want. I still feel nauseous."

She giggled and said, "Maybe that's the point."

Finally, the band stopped playing, and it was time for Walsh's big film debut—his moment of fame. In the darkness, there came some catcalls and positive shout-outs.

"Hey! There's Jimmy!"

"Looking good!"

"He's a natural."

"He's cute."

Candy shouted out, "He's sexy!"

After the film ended and the lights came on, everyone cheered and clapped for Andy and Paul Morrissey, who stood and took their bows. Then everyone got up and went and did their own thing. Andy went to the print-making area and started working on his new series, "Cows." An entire series of silkscreens of a cow head.

Walsh walked to where Andy was working and asked, "Need any help?"

"No, thanks. Not at the moment."

Walsh turned and started to leave when Andy asked, "I'm doing a new film in a couple of weeks. The Chelsea Girls. I'd like you to be in it. Would you like to?"

"You mean like what I did with the Velvet Underground. Be in the background?"

"No. As one of the main characters. Listen, don't answer now. A bunch of us are going to Max's Kansas City later. We'll talk about it then."

"Okay," Walsh said hesitantly.

"It'll be fun. You know Jimmy, in the future, everybody will be famous for fifteen minutes." Andy said with a grin.

Officer Walden stuck his head into Roscoe's office. "Hey, Roscoe, You got something dropped off by a New York Times courier. You subscribe to the Times, now?" Walden said as he flipped the envelope on Roscoe's desk.

"Maybe. What's it to ya?"

"Jeez, I thought you were a Daily News guy."

"Well, you thought wrong."

"Pardon me for living," Walden said with a smirk.

Roscoe opened the envelope and read the transcription of Sharon Fiyalka's notes of Doctor Tinterow's interview.

As he read the transcription of her notes and compared her interview with his official police interview, there were several discrepancies.

He had told Roscoe that Niles was holding a gun when he first saw him standing in the doorway, but he said Fiyalka that he did see a gun until he shot himself. Tinterow told Fiyalka that Niles was calm and serene when they arrived, but he told Roscoe that he was wired and nervous.

Roscoe decided it was time to pay a little visit to Doctor Tinterow, but not until Sharon Fiyalka's piece came out in tomorrow's Times. He didn't want Tinterow to know that he and Sharon Fiyalka were comparing notes.

Vincent called Tinterow after purchasing "The Odyssey," an Arthur Strong color field painting. It was two canvases placed side by side. The left canvas is geometric, a green field with three horizontal bands. The top band is orange, the middle band is yellow, and the bottom band is red. Each band is a different width, thick, thin, thick. The right canvas is organic. A yellow background with numerous red, white, and black swirls and splatters that seem to be floating above the golden environment below. The painting was the largest they had bought, measuring twenty feet long by ten feet tall.

"Gary, we are now the proud owners of an Arthur Strong painting."

"How much?"

"I got a deal."

"How much?"

"A hundred and twenty."

"A hundred and twenty thousand dollars!"

"We can sell it tomorrow for double that. And in a couple of years, it will be worth millions, possibly tens of millions. So, stop whining. You wanted an Arthur Strong, and now we own one. You're welcome."

"Oh, sorry. I didn't mean to be a stickler. It just caught me off guard. What are we going to do with such a large painting?"

"I suggest we put on loan to MOMA for the time being. We can always reclaim it if and when we want to sell it. Plus, in the meantime, we can claim it as a charitable deduction. Every year, it gains in provenance; it adds extra cache and value."

"I like that idea. I'll give Frank a call and break the good news."

"Great. And tell him that when you guys get a chance, drop another $14,000 in the kitty."

"Will do. So, I guess we'll see you and Amy at the gallery opening tomorrow night."

"Yeah, we'll see you guys there."

"Bye."

"Bye."

CLICK

"Frank. Hey, it's me. I just got off the phone with Vincent. We are now the owners of an Arthur Strong painting."

"Okay. How much?"

"A hundred and twenty."

"A hundred and twenty! Thousand?"

"Ha, that's what I said. But Vince thinks it will be worth millions in a couple of years, possibly tens of millions."

"How much more do we have to deposit for this beast?"

"Only fourteen thousand a piece."

"Shit. At this rate, I'm going to have to start raising my fees."

"But Vincent said that until we're ready to sell, we can loan it to MOMA for the time being. Then, we can always reclaim it if and when we want to sell it. In the meantime, we can get a tax break every year, and it gains in the provenance, which Vincent says will add extra cache and value."

"Whatever. What time are you coming tomorrow to pick me up?"

"The invitation says it starts at seven, so I'll pick you up at seven."

"It's not a black-tie affair, is it? I hate black time affairs."

"Hell no. Just wear a sports coat. I'm not wearing a tie; I'm just going to dress casually."

"That sounds better."

"Okay, then I'll see you at seven."

"Goodbye."

"Bye."

CLICK

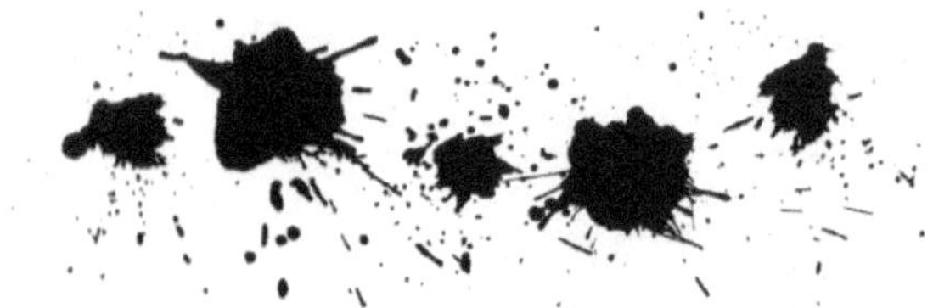

The Collingsworth Art Gallery is located on Madison Avenue and 72nd Street, on the east side of the street. By the time Vincent and Amy arrived, which was a little after eight, Frank and Gary were already there, schmoozing and mingling, trying to cultivate a friendship with Arthur Strong. They had him backed into a corner of the gallery. It was like watching a wrestling tag-team match.

It just so happened that Strong's eldest son, Jeremy, had recently been picked up on a drug charge, and they had been looking for a criminal lawyer.

"Mr. Strong, I'm a criminal attorney. I'd be more than happy to take a look at your son's case. If it's his first offense, I'm sure we can get his case either dismissed or, at the worst, probation." Frank offered.

"That's very kind of you, Mr. Williams."

"Frank, please. It's nothing. I'd love to be able to help."

"Mr. Strong, Frank here is one of the best Criminal attorneys in New York. He got David Greenlight acquitted, Samuel Rosen, the Hamptons Doctor, probation. He's one Hell of a lawyer. One of the best." Tinterow bragged.

"Well, Frank, how about if Jeremy and I stop by your office Monday if that would be all right."

Williams handed Strong a business card and said, "Just call my secretary Monday morning, and we'll set something up for Monday afternoon."

"I can't tell you how much I appreciate your kindness."

"It's my pleasure."

Vincent and Amy approached Strong and his two new best friends.

"Andrew. It's so good to see you. Your exhibit looks marvelous." Amy greeted him, kissing him on the cheek.

"Andrew, I see you've met my two partners in our art syndicate," Vincent said.

"Ah! Frank and Gary are also the owners of The Odyssey. I hope you like it."

Tinterow got a serious look on his face and replied, "Actually, I don't like it."

There was deathly silence, and the atmosphere turned cold until he smiled and said, "I don't like it…I love it."

A mixture of nervous laughter and timorous chortling. Vincent, wanting the awkward moment to pass, said, "Arthur, we have decided that we're going to have MOMA hang The Odyssey in their modern art wing of the museum."

"Oh, that's great!"

Amy took Strong by the arm, leading him away from the group, and said, "Come, I want you to tell me all about your collection. I am particularly intrigued with your technique on the "Romulus and Remus" piece. However, did you get that texture?"

Vincent looked at Tinterow disapprovingly. "What was that?"

Tinterow looked innocently at Vincent and said, "What? It was a joke. Hey, come on, lighten up, Vincent."

"Yeah, Vincent. Can't artists take a joke?" Williams chimed in.

"Some can and some can't. I don't know Arthur all that well. You're lucky; I've known artists to cancel acquisitions for much less."

"Well, I think we're good. I mean, Frank has offered to help him out with a little legal assistance pertaining to the guy's son." Tinterow said.

"His son?"

"Yeah, apparently, young Jeremy Strong has found himself on the wrong side of the law. It seems he has acquired a taste for wacky-tobaccy. Frank here is going to see what he can do."

"Marijuana?"

"Yup. I offered to try and get the case dismissed." Frank said.

"Think you can?" Vincent asked.

"Probably. If it's the kid's first offense and he wasn't dealing."

Tinterow said with a wolfish grin, "Vincent, I think we might be Strong's newest best buddies."

Roscoe stood in front of Tinterow's secretary with a copy of the New York Times under his arm.

"Doctor Tinterow is with a patient at the moment. If you would you care to have a seat, Detective." She said, showing no emotion.

"Thank you."

He and the secretary were the only ones in the waiting in the reception area. Roscoe opened the Times to the crossword page and began the arduous task of trying to solve the puzzle.

First clue, one across: *They come in last* (3 letters).

Roscoe knew that with the Times crossword puzzle, nothing is as it seems. Most people would probably jump to a form of competition.

Answer: XYZ, they're the last letters of the English alphabet.

The next clue is four across *Strips in geography class* (6 letters).

Geography wasn't one of Roscoe's strong suits in school, but he did remember that an isthmus was a narrow strip of land that connected two larger areas across a body of water. Now, what would the plural of isthmus be?

He was pretty good at biology and zoology; Roscoe determined that hippopotamus and isthmus both ended in *mus* and that the plural of hippopotamus is hippopotamus; ergo, the plural of isthmus would be isthmi.

Answer: isthmi.

Roscoe was feeling pretty good about the puzzle so far. But, like with most things in life, you should never get too cocky. The next clue was a real stumper.

Clue: *whirlybird* (9 letters)

Roscoe was deep in thought, concentrating so hard on the puzzle that he didn't hear the secretary when she called out to him, "Detective. Detective Brown."

The thought bubble burst when he snapped back to the present."

"Yes?"

"Detective Brown, Doctor Tinterow will see you now."

"Thank you," He said as he rose from the couch and entered Tinterow's office.

Tinterow was sitting behind his desk, finishing up with the last patient's notes from the session. Without looking up, he said, "Detective Sergeant Brown, please have a seat. What can I do for you, sir?"

Roscoe took the chair opposite Tinterow, sat down still holding the section with the crossword, and asked, "Doctor, do you do the Times crosswords?"

Tinterow stopped writing; he peered over his reading glasses at Brown quizzically and said, "What?"

"Do you do the Times crossword puzzle?"

"Yes, why?"

"Did you do todays?"

"No. Not yet."

"Well, I was hoping you might be able to help me with this one clue. The clue is *Whirlybird*, nine letters. I'm sorry, I don't have any letters."

Tinterow sat staring at Brown, wondering what in the world this fellow was up to. He thought that maybe the detective was trying to trip him up in some way. But he'd play along; it would take someone more intelligent than some flatfoot from Coney Island to best him.

"Whirlybird, so say."

"Yeah, nine letters."

Tinterow thought for a few minutes, then said, "Eggbeater."

Roscoe said, "Eggbeater?" as he wrote the answer into the puzzle.

Tinterow explained, "Whirlybird and eggbeater are both antiquated synonyms for a helicopter."

"Ah, very good," Roscoe said, complimenting the doctor for being so astute.

"Now, Detective Sergeant Brown, I'm sure you didn't come all the way from Coney Island to help you with the Times' crossword. Did you?"

"Actually, no. Am I to assume that you haven't read this morning's Times, doctor."

"You assume correctly."

"Well, there's an interesting article here about Roger Niles."

"Oh, I see. Yes, I talked with Ms. Fiyalka last week about Mr. Niles."

"It's a fascinating article. I just have a couple of questions about your interview with Ms. Fiyalka."

"Okay."

"You see, doctor, some of the things you said to Ms. Fiyalka don't quite jive with the statements that you gave me."

"Really."

"Yes, really."

"Like what?"

"Oh, the fact that you told me that Mr. Niles was holding a gun in plain sight when you arrived. That you clearly saw him holding the gun in his hand when you saw him standing in the doorway.

You told Ms. Fiyalka that you didn't see the gun until he pulled it to shoot himself. Which is it, Doctor Tinterow?"

The problem with lying is that no matter how good a liar you think you are, the truth is that you're not.

"I must have gotten it wrong when I spoke to her. His taking his life understandably threw me for a loop. You can understand that."

"Sure, but you told me that you saw Mr. Niles holding a gun when you arrived at his house standing in the doorway. Twice. Once at the scene and another time when I came to speak to you here in your office. Why would you tell her one thing and me another?"

"Trauma can play havoc with one's memory for specific facts, Detective Brown."

"Umhuh. What about when you told Ms. Fiyalka that Niles was calm and serene when you arrived, yet you told me that he was nervous, despondent, and sobbing? Which story are you sticking with, Doctor Tinterow?" Roscoe asked.

"Look, Detective Brown, she must have misquoted me. What I told you is the truth." Tinterow insisted.

"Thanks, Doctor Tinterow; I'm glad we got that all settled. Well, I'll be off." Roscoe said as he stood up.

As he was walking out, still looking at the crossword section, he uttered another clue loud enough so Tinterow would hear.

"Eighteen across. *Crows sailing from Ethiopia to Egypt.* Fifteen letters. Bye, Doc; I'll be speaking with you soon."

"Arthur, Jeremy, please have a seat," Williams said as he gestured to the two leather wingback chairs opposite his large oak desk. Williams was part of the prestigious Claymont, Levine, Kravitz, Roth & Partners law firm located at 460 Park Avenue, 37th Floor. Williams had a corner office overlooking Park Avenue and 57th Street.

When Arthur Strong and his son entered Williams' office, he was taken aback by the artwork in his office.

"Frank, are these all your own personal pieces of art?"

"Yes. Well, actually, since Gary, Vincent, and I made up our small art syndicate, we rotated our artwork from time to time so we all could enjoy each piece."

"My, I must say that I am truly impressed. An art syndicate, what an ingenious idea."

"Thank you. So, you must be Jeremy."

"Yes, sir. I want to thank you for taking my case."

"Well, you're quite welcome."

Jeremy Strong was currently a student at NYU, studying filmmaking. Jeremy and four of his fellow film students were clubbing down in the East Village on the night in question. They had just walked out of the Café Wha when, according to Jeremy, two undercover cops that had followed them out of the café pulled out their badges and patted the four of them down. They found two of the students, including Jeremy, had a small amount of grass in their possession.

"How much?" Williams asked.

"Maybe an ounce," Jeremy replied.

"And they busted you?"

"Yeah."

"Were any of you smoking in the café?"

"My friend Graham smoked one joint in the club."

"So, why did they hassle you all?"

"I don't know."

"And they arrested you all?"

"Yes, sir."

"Is this your first time being arrested for anything?"

"He's never been in trouble for anything, Frank," Arthur said defiantly.

"Okay, do you have a copy of the arrest report, Jeremy?"

"Yeah, here." He said as he handed the sheet of paper to Williams.

Williams scanned the record and smiled, "Hell, this has so many holes in it I could drive a Mac truck through it.

Don't worry, Jeremy; I think I can make this whole thing disappear. Let me see what I can do."

"Thank you, Mr. Williams. I really appreciate your help."

"No problem. But remember, when you're going out, be smart from now on. I don't want to make you paranoid, but you never know who's a Narc these days."

"Frank, thank you so much."

"I'm glad to help. Maybe you, me, and Gary could grab a bite sometime."

"That would be great. Thank you again."

"Arthur, Jeremy, I'll keep you posted," Williams said as he shook their hands goodbye.

"Mr. Rainwater, counselor. What do I owe the pleasure?" Roscoe asked.

Lewis Bascom, attorney for Vincent Rainwater, answered. "We or I should say, Vincent, think that Williams and Tinterow have set their sights on a new target, Arthur Strong."

"Really, why is that? Did they say anything?"

"No. But at last week's gallery opening, they seemed to be cozying up to Arthur in a big way, and the last time they became friendly with an artist, it was Max Albertson."

"I see."

"I happen to know that Frank is representing Jeremy Strong, Arthur Strong's son, in a minor drug possession case."

"Hmmm, interesting."

"The kid got caught with a small baggie of marijuana. Frank offered to handle the case for nothing."

"What do you think they're after?"

"As you know, we purchased a painting and will have it on loan to the Museum of Modern Art in Manhattan. Presently, its value is in the neighborhood of a quarter of a million dollars. As you know, when a major artist dies, the value can skyrocket. Our painting's worth could…"

"Triple?" Roscoe asked.

"More like octuple or dozenth, maybe higher," Vincent said.

"So, I'm guessing we should pull our undercover officer from watching Andy Warhol and move him over to keep an eye on Arthur Strong."

'That would be my recommendation." Vincent said.

"Would you be able to set up a meeting with Strong and me?" Roscoe inquired.

"I'll call him when I get back to the Times. Any particular day best for you, Detective?"

"No. But, probably the sooner, the better."

"Very good."

"Mr. Rainwater. Mr. Bascom. Thank you both for coming down."

"Sorry, I'm late, Roscoe. I was helping Andy set up for a film shoot at the Chelsea Hotel." Detective Walsh said as he sat on the boardwalk beach where Roscoe was having his lunch.

"Well, I've got some bad news for you, superstar."

"What?"

"It's been determined that Warhol isn't, in fact, the target. At least not at the moment. So, you're being reassigned to another artist."

"You're kidding!"

"I kid you not."

So, whose life is in danger?"

"Arthur Strong."

"Never heard of him."

"Arthur Strong. He's more of a traditional artist. Unlike Warhol, who experiments with all mediums, Strong is just a painter. No glitz. No glamour. Just oils and canvas. Sorry, I know you would be starring in Warhol's newest feature film."

"No. No, I wasn't going to star. I was going just to have a small part. That's all."

"Now, Jimmy, you know as well as I do that there are no small parts, only small actors."

"Shut up, Roscoe."

"Ew, touchy, touchy. You actors are all the same, a bunch of prima donnas."

"When do I switch?"

"We're going to have a meeting with Strong this afternoon at three. Can you make it, or must you check with your agent?"

"You're really enjoying this, aren't you?" Walsh snapped.

"No, definitely not! Well, maybe a little." Roscoe said, smiling.

"Roscoe, you're such a dick."

"Okay. Okay, seriously, it seems that Williams and Tinterow are starting to cultivate a friendship with Arthur Strong. Rainwater came by this morning and shed light on the apparent switch from Warhol to Strong. I'm thinking that they feel Warhol might be too big a target at this time. Strong, although he is a major player in the art world, he's not a media darling."

"Okay, well, I'll return to the Chelsea Hotel and let Andy know what's happening."

"Good idea. Here's the address of Strong's studio. So, I'll meet you there at three. Can I buy you a dog?"

"No time, gotta run. See you at three."

The five-story walkup brownstone at 40 Morton Street in the West Village sits among a row of ten cookie-cutter brownstones. Arthur Strong purchased the building in the early fifties. His working studio is on the fifth floor, where he had the roof refitted with wall-to-wall skylights. The fourth floor is his paint, canvas, and miscellaneous art supplies storeroom. Strong also keeps his finished paintings stored there until he is ready to display them in galleries.

Roscoe and Walsh arrived within minutes of each other in front of 40 Morton Street.

"Hey, Roscoe." Walsh greeted.

"Why, Detective Walsh, I hardly recognized you, all shaved, showered, and spit-shined. Good to have you back."

"Detective Walsh reporting for duty." Walsh snapped, giving a British Army salute.

"Very good. Shall we." Roscoe said, gesturing to Arthur Strong's doorway.

Walsh rang the doorbell.

BRINNNNG BRINNNNG

Through the glass door panels, they saw a young man walking towards the door.

"Hello, may I help you?" The young man asked.

"Hello, I'm Detective Sergeant Brown, and this is Detective Walsh. We're here to see Arthur Strong."

"Is there something wrong?" The boy asked anxiously.

"No. Nothing's wrong. Is he here?"

"Come in."

The boy closed the door, turned, and ran up the stairs, shouting, "Dad, some police are here to see you!"

A voice beckoned from somewhere out of sight, "Come up to the fifth floor if you'd be so kind."

Walsh smiled and said to Roscoe, "Well, you'll get a chance to work off some of those two chilidogs you had for lunch."

"It's called power fuel. You'll see. Come on." Roscoe retorted as he led the way up the stairs.

By the time they reached the fifth floor, they were both winded. Standing in the middle of the room was Arthur Strong, holding a large paintbrush; his clothes were all covered with splatters of paint. The canvas that he was working on was lying on the wooden floor. It looked over ten feet long and five wide with broad bands of different shades of blue and green.

Sitting in the corner on a ratty beat-up couch was Vincent Rainwater reading a copy of Artforum Magazine.

"Ah, Detective Brown, I'd like to introduce you to Arthur Strong."

"Mr. Strong, I'm Detective Sergeant Brown, and this is my partner Detective Walsh."

"Gentlemen, you'll excuse me if I don't shake your hands." He said as he held up his paint-covered hands.

"Of course, sir. Might we talk?"

"Certainly," Strong said as he placed his brush in an old Chock full o'Nuts coffee can filled with turpentine.

"Now, what can I do for you, Detective Brown?" Strong asked.

"Mr. Strong, I'm sure you are aware of the deaths of Max Albertson and Roger Niles."

"Oh, sure."

"Well, we believe that Frank Williams and Doctor Tinterow are responsible for their deaths. And we think that they are currently plotting against you."

"You think they're planning on killing me?"

"Yes, sir."

"But why?"

"For the money."

"What money?"

"They recently purchased a rather expensive painting of yours. The idea is that the painting's value will increase greatly when you die."

"Is that why Max and Roger died?"

"I'm afraid so."

"Vincent, are you a part of this?"

Roscoe interjected before Vincent could answer.

"Mr. Strong, we asked Mr. Rainwater to arrange for them to meet you. We are currently setting up a sting operation. We hoped you would agree to help us so we can catch them."

"But my family. Would they be endangered?"

"No, sir. We want Detective Walsh here to go undercover and appear to be your assistant."

"Oh, I just remembered that Frank Williams is acting as my son's attorney."

"We know of that. And we believe that is his way of ingratiating himself to you. I've alerted the district attorney's office. They're watching to make sure nothing irregular is going on. But I'm sure he will do his best to get your appreciation."

"What is it you'd like me to do? Both Max and Roger were very close friends of mine."

"Well, for one thing, do not let on that you suspect anything. Secondly, be sure that Detective Walsh is always present whenever you get together with them. We will be watching, so you have nothing to fear."

"Vincent, what do you think?"

"Arthur, these are evil men. They need to be taken off the streets."

"All right, I'll do it. Besides, I could use an assistant. My son Jeremy is a college student and has no time for the old man."

"Oh, now, Mr. Strong. No one must know about this. Not your wife, children, or friends. It must remain a secret." Roscoe insisted.

"I understand."

"Excellent. We really appreciate your cooperation."

Amy Albright had been in talks with several galleries to see which one she would exhibit her collection in. There were a couple in Soho and a couple in Midtown. She had just finished discussing the possibilities of an exhibit with the owners of the Wilson Gallery on East 56th Street and Madison Avenue when she ran into Frank Williams.

"Amy!" Frank yelled.

"Frank? What are you doing out and about this time of day?" Amy asked.

"Oh, I just needed to get out and clear my head. Where are you going? Want to grab a bite?"

"Yeah, sure. Where?"

"What are you in the mood for? I know a nice Mediterranean place around the corner."

"I haven't had Mediterranean in ages. Sounds good."

"Great."

Orion's Mediterranean Cuisine was a small family-owned restaurant that's been around for over forty years. Orion, now 82 years old, sits inside by the door in a captain's chair and greets you as you enter the restaurant. The old man has shaggy snow-white hair and a matching bushy mustache and wears the traditional Greek fisherman's cap and a roll-neck sweater.

"*Kalos irthate*. Welcome." The old man said.

"Thank you," Williams said.

Holding two menus, the hostess approached them, "Please, right this way."

"I've never eaten here before," Amy said.

"Oh, if you like Mediterranean, this is the best in town."

They sat in a booth in the window, looking out at the people walking by on 56th Street. After perusing the menu, a waitress came over to take their order.

"You go first," Amy said.

"All right. I'll have the Kaufta Kabob with a side of Baba Ganoush."

"I'll start with a small Greek Salad, and I'll have the Chicken Shawarma for my main dish."

As the waitress left the table, Williams leaned across the table and asked, "So, what's new with you?"

"Well, I've been going around scoping out galleries to see who I want to host my exhibition of new works."

"Yeah, so how's that going?"

"I'm thinking I might go with the Collingsworth Gallery."

"Oh, the one where Arthur Strong had his."

"Frank, can I ask you a question?"

"Sure."

"Roger Miles was a good friend of mine. Did he really commit suicide?"

"Of course. Gary and I were there when he did it. It was horrible." Williams said, feigning sadness.

"The police came by our place a week or so ago asking a lot of questions."

"About what?"

"Oh, about Roger and you and Gary."

"Hmmm, Vincent didn't say anything to us at dinner last Friday."

"Well, it wasn't like the policeman was accusing you of anything; he came by just to see if Vincent would come down to the station and talk to them."

"Did he?"

"Did he what?"

"Go and talk to the police?"

"Yes."

"Do you know what the police wanted?"

"I don't know for sure. He said that they asked him a bunch of questions, mostly about Roger."

"Oh."

"And some about you and Gary. Of course, he had nothing but positive things to say about you guys."

"Of course."

It was then that the waitress brought the food. She placed the dishes in front of them, smiled, and said, "Enjoy."

"Mmmm, looks delicious," Amy said with a wolfish grin.

"Of course," Williams uttered.

Arthur Strong answered the doorbell. Standing in the doorway was Frank Williams. He was smiling, holding up an official-looking document.

"Hello, Arthur. I come bearing good news about Jeremy."

"Ah, please, come in. Let's go into the living room."

Strong showed Williams into the living room, which was relatively sparse. There were dozens of finished canvases leaning against the walls, and in the center of the room were two sofas facing each other, separated by an old telephone wire spool doubling as a coffee table, and that was it.

"Please have a seat. Shall I get Jeremy?" Strong asked.

"That might be a good idea," Williams said.

"Jeremy! Could you please come down?" Strong shouted.

Moments later, Jeremy and Detective James Walsh came down to the living room.

Arthur said, "Jeremy, Mr. Williams says that he has good news."

"Great," Jeremy said excitedly.

Williams was distracted by this new face that he hadn't seen before. Walsh could see that Williams was intrigued by this unknown presence.

Walsh walked up to Williams and introduced himself.

"Hello, I'm James; I'm Arthur's assistant."

Arthur seemed genuinely embarrassed, and he quickly apologized.

"I'm sorry, Frank, I guess my mind was on the news. This here is my new assistant, James Walsh. I was lucky to get him. I stole him from Andy Warhol."

"No kidding. Andy Warhol. Wow. What's he like?"

"Have you heard the rumors?"

"Oh, yeah."

"Well, they're all true. Parties till four in the morning, drinking, drugs, sex. I couldn't keep up; I got burned out."

"No kidding."

Strong stepped in and asked. "So, Frank, the news?"

"Huh. Oh, sorry, I got Jeremy off with a small fine. There are no charges and, more importantly, no record, but you can't mess up again. This was a one-time deal. Next time, I can't guarantee anything. This was done for me as a favor." Williams bragged.

"Gee, that's fantastic, Mr. Williams. I really do appreciate it!" Jeremy said humbly.

"Jeremy, so from now on, keep your nose clean." Williams pointed out.

"Yes, sir." Jeremy shook Williams' hand, hugged his dad, and ran upstairs singing.

Arthur stood up and said, "This calls for a drink. Name your poison."

"Bourbon, if you have it," Williams said.

'Bourbon it is, and for you James?"

"I'll have the same," Walsh answered.

"Easy enough. Three bourbons." Strong said as he went into the kitchen to get the drinks.

Williams wasn't quite at ease with this unknown player being around. He didn't look like an artist, not edgy enough. He was a bit too square.

"So, James, are you an artist, too?" Williams probed.

"Well, I'm still learning and developing my own style. That's why I've worked with different artists. I'm trying to learn from as many different artists as I can. Their philosophies, sense of awareness, techniques, and conceptual consciousness."

"What sort of things do you do for Mr. Strong?"

"Oh, I stretch canvases, mix paints, clean up, and on occasion, I actually put paint on canvas under the eye of the master."

"I see. If you don't mind my asking, how old are you, James?"

"I'm thirty-five."

"Kind of old to get started as an artist, aren't you?"

"Art isn't only for the young, Mr. Williams. Grandma Moses didn't start painting until she was seventy-eight."

"Still, you don't look like an artist."

"What does an artist supposed to look like? Maybe if I wore a beret or dressed all in black and had a goatee." Walsh said with a twinge of sarcasm.

"Oh no, I'm sorry. No offense intended." Williams said, still unsure about Walsh. He had a sense of apprehension that he couldn't shake.

"None taken."

Strong came into the room holding three glasses, "Here we are, gentlemen. Frank and James, here you are." He said as he handed each of them a glass.

He held up his glass and toasted, "Cheers."

"Cheers."

"Cheers."

Williams downed his bourbon in one gulp, smiled, and asked, "Arthur, my friend Doctor Tinterow is having a small dinner party this Saturday night. He asked me to invite you and the misses as his guests. What do you say?"

Strong finished his drink, looked at Walsh, smiled, and said, "Frank, that's very kind. Let me check with Melinda when she gets home."

"Great. It'll be just an intimate dinner with eight guests. Vincent Rainwater and his wife Amy will also be attending."

"Oh, Vincent and Amy. Sounds delightful."

"It's a themed dinner. Japanese cuisine, Yakitori, Udon noodles, Tempura, and Sushi. He's having several different types of Sake, like a wine tasting."

"Oh, we love Japanese food," Strong said.

"Great. Here's Gary's card with his number on it. Just give him a call after you talk to your wife. Well, I'd best be going. Thank you for the bourbon." Williams said as he handed Strong Tinterow's business card.

"Frank, I can't thank you enough for helping Jeremy," Strong said.

"Hey, what are friends for? See you Saturday night. Good night."

"Good night."

Strong and Walsh watched Williams hail a cab and drive away before speaking.

"Strong looked at Walsh and asked, "What do you think?"

"I think your wife shouldn't attend. Tell them you accept. Then we'll show up and say that she wasn't feeling well."

"Do you think they'll try something?"

"Not sure. I wouldn't think so with Vincent and his wife there, but you never know. I'll talk to Detective Brown, and we'll formulate a plan."

Williams sat on Tinterow's office sofa, which he occasionally uses with his patients, and listened to him call Vincent.

"Vincent, Gary here. Frank and I are having a small soiree this Saturday night at my place with Arthur Strong and his wife, and we were hoping that you and Amy could come.

You can! That's wonderful. We're having Japanese and Sake.

We'll be having Sake tasting and appetizers around seven, then dinner at eight.

Great. We'll see you then. Oh, and we're still on Friday for our Yale Club dinner, right?

Okay, pal, see you at the Yale Club.

Ciao."

CLICK

"I take it they're in?" Williams asked.

"They're in. Now, tell me what exactly Amy said about Vincent talking to the cops."

"We were having lunch, just chit-chatting, and all of a sudden, she said, when the police came by their place a week or so ago and asked a lot of questions, And I said, about what?

She said about Roger, you, and me. Funny, Vincent didn't mention anything about that when we had dinner at the Yale Club."

"What did she say to that?"

"She said it wasn't like the cops were accusing us of anything; they just wanted to see if Vincent would come down to the station and talk to them."

"I asked if he went down and talked to the police. And she said he did."

"I asked if she knew what the police wanted. She said that Vincent told her that they asked him a bunch of questions about Roger and us."

"So, I asked, like what? She didn't say anything specific, but he told her he only said positive things about us."

"Why didn't he say anything to us during dinner last week? Something's not right. I told you Detective Brown came to my office the other day."

"Yeah, you said he was asking a bunch of questions about Roger and your fish tank."

"Right, but he also was playing with me. He asked me a couple of crossword puzzle questions, trying to see if I was good at deciphering clues."

"Like what?"

"So, he walks into my office working the New York Times crossword, sits down, and says to me, the clue is, whirlybird, nine letters. He says I'm sorry, I don't have any letters.

I think for a minute, then say, eggbeater."

"Eggbeater?"

"Yeah, whirlybird and eggbeater are both antiquated synonyms for helicopter," Tinterow explained.

"Okay?" Williams said, not totally understanding the jest of where this is all leading.

"Then, after all the questions about Roger, as he is leaving, he mutters to himself loud enough for me to hear him, he said, "Eighteen across. Crows sailing from Ethiopia to Egypt. Fifteen letters."

"What does that mean?"

"It means they think that they are on to us."

"Huh?"

"The clue is Crows sailing from Ethiopia to Egypt. Do you know what a group of crows is called?"

"No idea."

"A murder," Tinterow said.

"Murder. Okay."

"And to travel from Ethiopia to Egypt, you have to travel down the Nile."

"So, the answer is Murder on the Nile," Williams said, still not grasping the significance of the clue.

"Don't you get it! Murder on the Nile. And the *murder* of Roger *Niles*."

"Oh shit." Williams gasped.

"Oh, shit is right." Tinterow agreed.

"You don't think Vincent has turned rat, do you?" Williams asked.

"I don't know, but let's not bring it up. Let's see if he does. If he doesn't, then we'll have to terminate our syndicate partnership."

"Terminate?"

"With extreme prejudice. Him and maybe even Detective Sergeant Roscoe Brown." Tinterow sneered.

Roscoe and Walsh sat in his office discussing how Walsh would look after Arthur Strong at the dinner party without scaring off Williams and Tinterow. Roscoe felt good having a man on the inside with the suspects, Vincent Rainwater and Walsh on the inside next to the potential victim, Arthur Strong. Plus, they would have undercover policemen in and around both victims and suspects, keeping a close eye on them all.

"So, they've invited Vincent and his wife, Strong and his wife, and the two of them, supposedly with dates. That's a lot of eyewitnesses. I'm guessing that Williams and Tinterow are just cozying up to them for a hit at a later date." Walsh surmised.

"Yeah, that makes sense. I'm going to call Rainwater and see what he knows." Roscoe said as he picked up the phone.

RING RING RING RING

"Hello, Vincent Rainwater."

"Vincent, Detective Brown here."

"Yes, Detective Brown, what can I do for you?"

"What can you tell me about Tinterow's party this Saturday night?"

"I just got off the phone with him. He invited me and Amy to a dinner party with Arthur Strong and his wife this Saturday night."

"And?"

"And that's all I know. The three of us are planning on having dinner at the Yale Club this Friday, but beyond that, I don't know anything else."

"Did you record the phone conversation?"

"Yes, Detective, I've been recording all my phone conversations and wearing the wire when I meet them in person."

"Good. I'm going to send a tech over there tomorrow and collect everything you have so far."

"Could you have them call before they come? I might have a preview to attend, and the time hasn't been determined."

"Will do. If you hear of anything, keep me in the loop."

"Yes, sir."

"Goodbye."

"Goodbye."

CLICK

Tinterow pointed at his saltwater fish tank, "Frank, see that brown and white fish there."

"Yeah, that's one ugly fish. What is it?"

"That my friend is a Tiger pufferfish."

"A what?"

"A pufferfish or, better known in Japan as the fugu."

"People eat that thing?"

"Oh, it takes a brave soul to brave the mighty fugu. In Japan, people pay up to $300 to taste the fugu."

"Is it that delicious?"

"It's that deadly."

"Deadly?"

"Oh yes. In Japan, it's considered a delicacy. Its inner organs, especially the liver, the ovaries, eyes, and skin, contain a poison more toxic than cyanide. One drop can kill a man within 24 hours by paralyzing the muscles while the victim stays fully conscious; the victim is unable to breathe and eventually dies from asphyxiation. Only licensed sushi chefs can serve fugu. I understand it's quite delicious."

"No thanks, I'm not interested in pressing my luck."

"Guess what we're having for dinner Saturday night. Well, I should say what some of us are having for dinner Saturday night."

"Fugu?"

"Fugu. I have a client who's a licensed fugu chef. He happens to owe me several thousand dollars in fees. Master Akira Fujimoto will serve as our chef for Saturday night's dinner party."

"But won't the police find out how he died?"

"Sure, but that's the beauty of it. Even the most skilled fugu chefs have been known to have customers die from accidental poisoning. That's why fugu is so exciting; people like living on the edge of death."

"Don't people have to be warned of the danger?"

"Oh, they will be."

"But what if Strong doesn't want to live on the edge of death?"

"Did I mention that master chef Fujimoto is going to tell everyone? But unfortunately, he doesn't speak English too well."

"So, are you thinking of just Strong getting the killer fugu?"

"Depends."

"Depends on what?"

"Depends on what Vincent has to say at dinner Friday night."

Walsh met Roscoe on the boardwalk as the sun set and a cool breeze blew in off the Atlantic.

"So, Roscoe, Williams invited Mr. and Mrs. Strong to a dinner party for this Saturday night. Apparently, it's going to be a small affair. Vincent and Amy, the Strongs, Williams, and Tinterow, plus their dates."

"No way is Mrs. Strong going; we're not putting her life in danger."

"I discussed that with Strong already. I suggested that at the last minute if she gets ill, I will go in her place to keep an eye on things."

"I agree. I'm guessing that they might be thinking of trying something. So, you be extremely careful. We'll have Vincent wired and cops outside Tinterow's residence.

I'm sure Tinterow figured out the crossword clue and is panicking." Roscoe said.

"You mean that Murder on the Nile thing?"

"Yeah."

"Weren't you being rather conspicuous?" Walsh asked.

"Oh, on the contrary, Walsh. It's so overt, it's covert." Roscoe smirked.

"So, why a dinner party with Arthur Strong?" Vincent asked.

"I really enjoyed meeting him at the opening, and Frank helped his kid avoid going to jail. Just thought it would be nice." Tinterow said. He sat opposite Vincent and Williams.

"His kid avoid jail. What did the kid do?"

"Oh, it was nothing. He got stopped in the village carrying a small amount of grass. The cops overreacted; I got the kid probation." Williams said nonchalantly.

"Cops!" Tinterow snapped.

"What about them?" Vincent asked.

"That damn Detective from Coney Island, Brown, came snooping around asking me a bunch of questions about Roger, and that night he killed himself as if he didn't believe me. He thinks that me and Franked shot him." Tinterow ranted.

"Yeah, he came to see me too. Treating me like a criminal and all. If he keeps it up, I might just sue him for harassment," Frank said.

Vincent was torn. Should he mention that Brown had spoken to him, too? He thought better of it and said nothing.

"That's terrible. Maybe you should complain to his supervisor." He said.

Tinterow thought he'd push, "Did you happen to talk to the cops?"

"Me? No. Why would they talk to me? I mean, you know that I knew him, but I wasn't a close friend."

"Ah, just wondered." Tinterow mused.

"So, we're having sushi tomorrow?" Vincent said.

"Yeah, it's going to be something special. I have a master sushi chef coming over to prepare fresh sushi. Nothing like you've ever had before." Tinterow bragged.

"Amy's not crazy about sushi."

"Not to worry. I said I would have Yakitori, Udon noodles, and Tempura. And for those sushi lovers, there will be among some secret dishes, Mirugai, Chuka Idako, Shirako, Ebi, Hamachi Toro, Sake, Kanpachi, and of course, Ahi."

"Stop it. You're killing me, I can't wait." Vincent said, laughing.

Tinterow and Williams glanced at each other and began to laugh, too.

Roscoe was downstairs of the Yale Club, parked on Vanderbilt Street, listening in on Vincent's conversation with Tinterow and Williams when he heard a call come in on the police scanner about a shooting in Grand Central Station. Officer down, needs assistance.

Roscoe jumped out of the car and ran into the train station, gun drawn. He entered from the east entrance and heard screaming coming from the rotunda. He bounded down two flights of stairs and saw two men wearing bandanas covering their faces fleeing, carrying shotguns.

Roscoe positioned himself behind a large metal garbage can, knelt, and took aim.

"Police! Freeze!" Roscoe shouted.

Both men turned and fired wildly in Roscoe's direction. Neither shot came close to their intended target. Roscoe fired two consecutive shots, both hitting their mark.

POW POW

One man was struck in the left leg in the upper thigh, and the second thug was hit in the stomach. Roscoe slowly approached the two fallen criminals. When he was meters away, the man with the leg injury grabbed his Remington Double Barrel shotgun and attempted to shoot his assailant. Unfortunately for him, Roscoe had anticipated such a move and fired another round, hitting the man in the chest and killing him instantly.

Seconds later, uniformed police arrived at the scene, as did the paramedics. Roscoe ran over to the downed officer, who was lying face down. As he turned him over to administer CPR, he recognized the officer as Officer Chris Giles of the 17th precinct. Chris Giles was the policeman who stopped by Roscoe's car while parked downstairs at the Yale Club.

"Come on, Giles. Stay with me! Stay awake. Come on!" Roscoe urged. Giles had a massive wound in the lower abdomen; Roscoe used his sports coat to apply pressure, trying to stop the bleeding.

One of the paramedics rushed to where they were and took over from Roscoe, saying, "It's okay. I'll take over now, sir."

Dozens of bystanders, gawkers, and rubberneckers stood around watching. Roscoe stood up, his clothes soaked in blood, and shouted, "If there are any eye-witnesses, stick around. If not, get the Hell out of here!"

One of the responding officers walked up to Roscoe and said, "Excuse me. Just who the Hell are you?"

"Detective Sergeant Roscoe Brown, out of the six 0. I was over on Vanderbilt Avenue on a case when I responded to the 10-999. I spotted the two suspects fleeing the scene carrying shotguns. I ordered them to stop. They took a shot at me, and I returned fire, striking them both. That's who I am. Now. Just who the Hell are you."

Roscoe drove over to the seventeenth precinct on E. 51st Street and Third Avenue to give his statement to Internal Affairs. He didn't get back to Coney Island until 3 AM. On the way back home, he called in to check on Giles. Dispatch said that he was in critical but stable condition. The next twenty-four hours would be critical.

Roscoe got back to the apartment, threw his blood-soaked clothes in the garbage, took a shower, and crawled into bed. He cuddled up to the misses and crashed until ten.

Roscoe wandered into the kitchen in his boxers and t-shirt, hair mussed up and looking bleary-eyed.

"Whad'ya let me sleep so long?" He asked.

"I called in and told them you'd be a little late. Not to worry. They'll muddle through until you get there." Betty answered, placing a plate of scrambled eggs, bacon, and toast next to a steamy hot cup of joe.

"Thanks, babe."

"Why so late?"

"I was on stake out when I heard on the radio that an officer was in trouble in Grand Central. When I got there, I spotted an officer down and two men with shotguns fleeing. I called out to them to halt. But they turned and fired. I returned fire, putting both men down. Wounding one and killing the other." Roscoe said softly.

"What about the officer?"

"He's in the hospital in critical but stable condition."

"Thank God you're all right."

"Yeah, I'm fine. I pray that Giles will make it."

"You knew him?"

"Yeah, he stopped by a few times when I was in Manhattan listening on a wire and chatted. A real nice kid."

"I'll say a prayer for him at Mass Sunday," Betty said.

As he sat down for breakfast, he put his arm around her waist and whispered, "I love you."

She kissed him on the top of the head, "Better eat up. I'm sure they're starting to panic down at the six 0."

"Where's Mrs. Strong?" Tinterow asked, openly disappointed.

"She sends her apologies. Our youngest has a fever, isn't feeling well, and needs her mother." Strong explained.

"Oh, I am sorry. I was so much looking forward to meeting her."

"She, too, was disappointed. She does so love sushi. I hope you don't mind my bringing James as my number two?" Strong asked.

"No. Not at all. So good to see you again, James."

"Thank you, Doctor Tinterow," Walsh said.

"Gary, please."

"Gary."

"Pardon me for saying so, but James, you look a little under the weather."

"Yeah, I think I might be catching a cold."

"Well, I know a great cure for the common cold."

"Oh, yeah. What's that?" Walsh asked.

"Sake, and lots of it. So, you're in luck. Come on in and meet everyone."

Tinterow showed Strong and Walsh into the living room, where Frank Williams, Amy, and Vincent sat around a large round coffee table.

"Arthur, I believe that you know everyone. Everyone, this is James Walsh; he is Arthur's right-hand man. James, this is my good friend Frank Williams, attorney at law, Amy Albright, fine artist, and her husband Vincent Rainwater, art critic at the New York Times."

"A pleasure to meet you all. I must admit that I am a big fan of Amy's work, as well as yours, Mr. Rainwater."

"Thank you," Amy said.

"Thank you, as well. And please, Vincent."

"Now that the introductions are done, Can I offer you all some sake? We have both cold and hot," Tinterow announced as he handed out cards describing the different varieties of sake.

Entering the room was a man dressed like a butler, in a white shirt and a black tie, wearing a grey pin-striped waistcoat carrying a silver tray.

"May I take your orders?"

"Everyone, this is Gerald. He will be serving us this evening. Now, for you novices, sake can be served chilled or warm. Just an FYI, premium sake should only be served chilled. Not that the warm sake is inferior by any means. Amy?"

"I'll have chilled."

"Vincent?" Tinterow asked.

"I'll try hot, then we can compare."

"Arthur?"

"I love chilled sake."

"James?"

"Hot, please."

"Frank?"

"Chilled."

"And Gerald, make mine chilled as well."

"Excellent, sir," Gerald said as he headed to the kitchen.

As Gerald got the drinks, an attractive young Japanese woman dressed exactly like Gerald brought out appetizers—a bowl of edamame, chicken teriyaki skewers, fried vegetable spring rolls, and tuna tatar.

"Folks, this is Himari; she will be assisting Gerald."

The young woman gave a short bow to everyone and said, "*Kon'nichiwa.*"

"Dig in; the sake should be out any minute," Tinterow said as he took a chicken teriyaki skewer.

Gerald appeared carrying the tray with the sake cups. White cups decorated with golden dragons contained the chilled sake, and Red cups with a golden tiger held the hot sake.

Amy took one sip and said, "Mmmm. Oh, my lord. Gary, this is fabulous."

Tinterow, never one to be modest, replied, "It should be its six thousand dollars a bottle. So, savor it, don't guzzle."

"You're kidding!" She cried.

"It's Longquan Daiginjo. The distillery was founded in 1615 in the town of Akaoko."

"This hot sake is delicious," Vincent commented.

"That is Tsugu Asahi Shuzo. Even though it's not as expensive, it has a soft and rich aroma, a delicate but deep flavor, and a beautiful aftertaste."

They sat in the living room for over an hour while Master Akira Fujimoto, fugu chef, prepared several dozen rolls, pieces of sushi, and sashimi.

When Fujimoto was ready to serve, he picked up a bamboo mallet and stuck a small gong, calling the guest to dinner.

GONG

"Ah, that means Master fugu chef Akira Fujimoto has finished preparing our dinner. Won't you please follow me?" Tinterow announced.

He led everyone into the dining room, which had been converted into a sushi bar. Chef Fujimoto took a stoic pose, wearing a blood red happi like Minani Katsuragi chef jacket.

The lapels were black with gold Japanese characters that read "Ryōri-chō," Master Chef. He sported a traditional *Seigaiha* (Blue Ocean Waves) patterned apron from his waist to below his knees and black Jinbei pants.

He wore a white headband called a Hachimaki on his head, with a solid red circle, a symbol of Japan's rising sun.

Tinterow had name cards where people would sit. Arthur and James' first two seats, Vincent and Amy's seats three and four, and Frank with Tinterow seated at the end. The sushi bar was curved so people could see everyone. They sat on padded bar stools.

Chef Master Akira Fujimoto stood behind and took command of dinner. He gave the traditional Japanese bow and curtly grunted in a deep voice, *"Kon'nichiwa."*

Tinterow said, "Lady and gentlemen, I'd like to introduce our chef. This is Chef Master Akira Fujimoto. He has prepared a wide variety of delicacies for us tonight. I suggest that we allow him to serve us some of his masterpieces initially, and then afterward, you can order more of the ones you like.

Amy, we have a multitude of non-sushi dishes. You have your choice of different types of Yakitori, Udon noodles, and Tempura. Himari will take your order of anything you'd like. There's a menu before you, so please order whatever you'd like."

As Fujimoto placed the plates with several different types of sushi and sashimi delicacies in front of everyone, Tinterow made an announcement.

"Master Akira Fujimoto is one of only fifty master fugu chefs worldwide. And that means that one of the dishes he is serving is fugu. Now, fugu is a puffer fish that, if served by any inexperienced sushi chef, can be fatal because of the toxins in the puffer fish's liver. But fear not, Master Akira Fujimoto fugu chef has had over three years of training and has passed many rigorous state tests to obtain the title of master fugu chef. I will taste the fugu sashimi to prove it's safe."

Tinterow picked up the white sliver of fugu on his plate with his ivory chopsticks and slowly placed it on his tongue. As he did, all eyes were on him, even Fujimoto. Tinterow chewed it, making a pleasurable sound as he ate it.

"Mmmm, fantastic. The flavor is indescribable."

He picked up another piece and said, "Come on, you're in for a real treat."

Frank took a piece and ate it, "Amazing."

Arthur looked at Tinterow and said, "Maybe later, after I've tried some more of the traditional ones I know."

"I understand, saving the best for last. How about you, James?"

"I think I need to work up to it," Walsh replied.

"Fair enough," Tinterow said as he took another piece of fugu.

As the evening wore on, the group talked about various topics, although most were centered around the subject of art. Tinterow kept a keen eye on Arthur's plate, and the target had yet to try the fugu. Tinterow did have a backup plan that he and Fujimoto had cooked up. If, after half an hour, Strong hadn't tried the fugu, Fujimoto would mix some fugu into whatever sushi that Strong favored.

By the end of the evening, Strong, Vincent, and Walsh had been given various amounts of fugu. Even Tinterow and Williams had gotten a measured amount, so they too would suffer a small bout, but nothing fatal.

After finishing off a dozen sushi and sashimi pieces, Walsh felt slightly nauseous. He excused himself and made his way to the bathroom, where he vomited his dinner. He felt terrible, but that act saved his life.

When he returned to the dining room, Himari brought a bowl of vanilla *Mochi* (Japanese ice cream) to cleanse their palate. Walsh ate it to help soothe his upset stomach.

The effects of the fugu would not take effect for a couple of hours; after that, they would all be far away from Tinterow's. By the time they started to feel the effects of the fugu, Chef Fujimoto would be on a flight back to Tokyo.

As his diner guests left, Tinterow walked them to the door, bowed, and said, "I hope you had a wonderful evening. Thank you for coming. Oh, and James, I hope you feel better soon. *Sayōnara.*"

After receiving a call at four in the morning, Roscoe stood outside Walsh's apartment door, banging for over a minute. He was getting ready to break the door in when Walsh opened it.

"What the Hell happened to you? You look like death warmed over?" Roscoe said.

"I feel like crap. I can hardly breathe. Take me to the ER." Walsh said, gasping for air.

Roscoe helped Walsh down to the car and drove like a man possessed, sirens blaring and lights flashing all the way to the ER at Coney Island Hospital.

"What seems to be the problem?" The ER doctor asked Roscoe.

"He's having trouble breathing!"

They rushed Walsh into an ER examination room. They began to give respiratory and circulatory support, as well as activated charcoal and gastric rinsing out of the stomach and colon with a medicated solution.

Over the hospital's intercom, the call came: "Code Blue! Bring the crash cart to the ER, stat!"

At one point, Walsh went into cardiac arrest and respiratory failure. No less than sixteen doctors and nurses were trying to revive Detective Walsh.

Roscoe felt powerless, pacing around in the ER admittance area, waiting for some news, fearing the worst.

"Detective Brown. I'm Doctor Robinson." A doctor dressed in green scrubs approached.

"How is he, doc?"

"He's a fortunate man. Had he gotten here ten minutes later, he'd be dead."

"Is he going to be all right?"

"He's young and strong. He should recover, no problem."

"Can I see him?"

"Maybe tomorrow, Detective."

"So, what was it?" Roscoe asked.

"We think he ingested some kind of tetrodotoxin."

"You mean poison from some fish?"

"That's right. Your friend must have eaten some kind of fish, amphibian, octopus, or shellfish containing the poison.

We've had two other patients brought in tonight with a similar condition. Unfortunately, they weren't so lucky."

"They died?"

"I'm afraid so."

"Do you happen to know their names, doctor?"

The doctor walked over to the ER nurse's station and looked at a login book.

"Vincent Rainwater and an Arthur Strong."

"Those sons of bitches!"

The doorbell at Doctor Tinterow's townhouse came to life at four-thirty AM. Simultaneously, Roscoe began pounding on the front door, shouting, "New York City Police, open up!"

A bleary-eyed Tinterow cracked open the door. The flimsy door chain keeping the door from opening entirely.

"What the Hell is this!" He demanded.

"Get dressed. You're coming down to the precinct now. Open the door!"

"I'm not going anywhere," Tinterow said defiantly.

"You're either coming voluntarily, or you're going in cuffs. Your choice. Now, open the door!"

Tinterow unlocked the chain and let Roscoe into the foyer.

"I want to call my lawyer."

"You can do that at the station. Get dressed unless you want to go in your pajamas."

Roscoe followed him to his bedroom, watched him get dressed, then led him out to the police car and placed him in the backseat. There were people out on the streets and watching from windows, attracted by the red and blue flashing lights.

From Tinterow's townhouse, Roscoe drove to Frank Williams' apartment, where he brought Williams down in handcuffs and placed him in the backseat with Tinterow.

"Detective Brown, expect my attorney to bring charges against you for harassment and false arrest." Tinterow threatened.

"First of all, Doctor, you're not under arrest. At least not at the moment. And secondly, if you don't shut the fuck up, I'm going to pull this car into some dark alley and pistol whip the shit out of you. You got it!"

They arrived at the six 0 around five forty-five. Roscoe first brought Tinterow to the station house, placing him in interrogation room one. He then returned to the squad car and brought in Williams, putting him in interrogation room two.

When Roscoe came out of the room where Williams sat, he went to the desk sergeant and alerted him that under no circumstances was anyone to go into either room unless he gave the okay.

"Right, Detective Sergeant Brown.

Roscoe then headed back into Manhattan, where he went to Vincent Rainwater's apartment in Soho. He knocked on the door, and Amy Albright answered it moments later.

Roscoe could see she looked tired as if she had been run through the wringer. But he didn't detect any signs that she had been crying. Her eyes weren't red or puffy.

The years in homicide had taught Roscoe that not all people grieve the same; some howl and cry, and others suffer silently. Who was he to judge?

Roscoe held up his badge and said, "Hello, Mrs. Rainwater, Detective Sergeant Brown. May I come in?"

She left the door open and walked into the living room. Roscoe followed her and closed the door once he was inside. Amy wore the same dress she wore earlier at the dinner party—a simple black dress with long sleeves.

"Mrs. Rainwater, I first want to tell you how sorry I am for your loss."

"Thank you, Detective Brown. I just got home from the hospital."

"I know it's an inconvenience, but could you make a statement?" Roscoe asked.

"Now?"

"If you could, while everything is still fresh in your mind."

"All right. Give me a few minutes to get dressed."

"May I use your telephone?"

"Yes, of course." She said as she went into the bedroom.

Roscoe phoned the hospital to check on his partner Walsh's condition.

"Doctor Robinson, please. Detective Sergeant Brown calling."

"Hello. Doctor Robinson."

"Hey, Doc. It's Detective Sergeant Brown. I'm just calling to check on James Walsh."

"Mr. Walsh is off the critical list and is recovering nicely."

"That's great, Doc. Will I be able to see him sometime today? Just for a few minutes?"

"I would say if you came by around four this afternoon, you could visit him for no more than fifteen minutes."

"Thank you, Doc. I really appreciate all you've done."

Amy entered the room wearing a pair of old NYU sweats just as Roscoe finished his call.

"What's happened to Mr. Walsh?" She asked.

"He was extremely lucky that he threw up when he did, or else he would have passed like Vincent and Arthur Strong. The doctor said it looks like Walsh's going to make it."

"Arthur Strong is dead? Oh, his poor wife." She said, shocked.

"You didn't know?"

"He died of the same tetrodotoxin poisoning that Vincent did from eating toxic fish?"

"They were serving some of that fugu last night. Tinterow had a special master chef, one of only fifty in the world who was supposed to have been licensed to prepare that kind of fish."

"Did Vincent eat some?"

"No, not knowingly." She said.

"Did anyone eat some?"

"Gary and Frank did. They made a point of eating some to show everyone it was safe. Gary then specifically asked if anyone was willing to try some, but nobody did."

"All it takes is for the fugu to contaminate and poison the other fish just by the poison fugu touching the nonlethal fish."

"Did you eat any fish?"

"No. I don't like sushi. I ate all tempura and cooked dishes."

"Do you remember the chef's name?"

"I think it was Fujimoto. He is supposed to be some kind of a master fugu chef. Oh, and there was an assistant, her name was Himari. I'm sorry, they never said her last name. Just Himari."

"What did this Fujimoto look like?" Roscoe asked.

"Well, he was Japanese, not Japanese American. He was in his early forties, had a shaved head, weighed about 200 pounds, and wore glasses. He spoke broken English and not much of it.

Now, Himari looked to be in her early twenties; she is Japanese American, and she was just there to serve dishes and clean up, fill drinks, that sort of thing. She seemed well-educated and had a good vocabulary. Probably an NYU student."

"How was Tinterow and Williams' demeanor? Did they seem hostel or angry?"

"No, just the opposite. They did seem disappointed that Arthur did bring his wife, but aside from that, they seemed very upbeat and friendly."

"So, how many guests were there?"

"Six."

"Six? Tinterow and Williams didn't have dates?"

"No. Vincent said that they told him they were going to have dates. But when we got there, they never brought the subject up."

"Did you find that odd?"

"I did, and I asked Frank about it."

"And?"

"He told me that their dates were sisters. At the last minute, one of them got a cold, so the other decided to stay home and be with her sister."

"Why do you think they murdered Vincent?" Roscoe asked flat out.

"You think it was murder and not an accident?"

"Oh, it was murder. I know why they wanted Strong dead. To boost up the value of his work, but why Vincent?"

"I don't know, Detective, Unless they wanted him out of the way to get his share of the syndicate."

"But you'll inherit Vincent's share in the case of his death."

"Maybe they figured to get rid of him now and eliminate me at some later date, too."

"Maybe. You didn't get a sense that they knew about Vincent working with us, did you?"

"No. If they did, they sure didn't let on."

"Thank you, Mrs. Rainwater. And again, I'm so sorry for your loss."

"Detective Brown, you're sure it was murder."

"Without a doubt."

The desk sergeant stopped Roscoe as soon as he entered the precinct.

"Captain wants to see you now!"

"Right. How's our guests doing?"

"None too happy."

"Good," Roscoe said as he headed towards the staircase that led to Captain O'Rourke's office. He gave a quick knock and entered.

O'Rourke sat behind his desk, leaned back in his chair, and asked, "How's Walsh?"

"Looks like he's going to be okay."

"What the Hell happened?"

"I've got two suspects sitting in interrogation rooms one and two, who I believe knowingly and with malice fed poison fish to three people at a sushi dinner party. Two men have died of tetrodotoxin poisoning, and Walsh survived by a fluke, was able to survive. You see, there is no known antidote for this kind of poisoning."

"I want this done strictly by the book, Roscoe. I don't want anything to come back and let these guys off. If you don't think you can be objective, let me know, and I'll have one of the other detectives handle the case. Understand."

"Yes, sir. Strictly by the book."

Roscoe took Officer Ron Harris into interrogation room one, where Doctor Tinterow waited impatiently.

"I want to know what the Hell is going on! I want to speak to my attorney. I'm not saying a word without my attorney present. I know my rights."

"You want to know what's happening. You're being charged with three counts of capital murder. That's what's going on, Doctor Tinterow. Roscoe said, deciding not to let him know that Walsh was still alive.

Just to be above board, You have the right to remain silent. Anything you say can and will be used against you in a court of law. You have the right to an attorney. If you cannot afford an attorney, one will be provided for you.

Do you understand these rights that I've explained to you?"

"I want to call my lawyer," Tinterow demanded.

"Very well. Doctor Tinterow, I am arresting you for the murders of Vincent Rainwater, Arthur Strong, and James Walsh. You are going to be booked, photographed, and fingerprinted. Then you'll be transferred over to Rikers Island, where you'll be able to call your lawyer."

"But I want to call my lawyer right now so I don't have to go to jail."

"Sorry, Doctor, that's not how it works. Officer Harris, would you have someone process Doctor Tinterow? I'm going to go talk to Mr. Williams and see what he has to say." Roscoe said as he left Tinterow, ready to pee in his pants at the thought of mingling with hardened criminals in Rikers Island.

"Detective, why am I being detained?" Williams asked.

"Frank Williams, You have the right to remain silent. Anything you say can and will be used against you in a court of law. You have the right to an attorney. If you cannot afford an attorney, one will be provided for you.

Do you understand these rights that I've explained to you?"

"Yes, but why am I being arrested?"

"I am charging you with the murders of Vincent Rainwater, Arthur Strong, and James Walsh. You are going to be booked, photographed, and fingerprinted. Then you'll be transferred over to Rikers Island, where you'll be able to call your lawyer."

"Do you wish to speak to me?"

"Sure. I've got nothing to hide." Williams proclaimed.

Roscoe sat across from Frank Williams, placed a cassette tape into the tape machine, hit record, and said, "The time is twenty minutes till ten, Sunday morning; present in the room are me, Detective Sergeant Roscoe Brown, and Officer Ron Harris. I am speaking with Frank Williams. Mr. Williams, would you please state your full name and address?"

"Frank Emerson Williams. I live at 429 East 66th Street, apartment 55B, Manhattan, New York."

"Mr. Williams, what is your occupation?"

"I am an attorney at law."

"Would you please tell me your whereabouts last night from the hours of 5 PM until 2 PM last night?"

"I was attending a dinner party at the townhouse of Doctor Gary Tinterow at 94th Street and Riverside Drive."

"Please tell me who all was in attendance."

"Well, there was me, Gary, Doctor Tinterow, Vincent Rainwater and his wife, Amy, Arthur Strong, the artist, and his assistant, James Walsh."

"Was there anyone else?"

"Oh, yeah. It was a sushi dinner, so there was the sushi chef and his assistant."

"And their names, Mr. Williams?"

"The sushi chef was Master Akira Fujimoto, and his assistant was a young woman named Himari something. I'm sorry, I don't know her last name, Detective Brown. Doctor Tinterow would know. He hired them both."

"Any idea where I might find Mr. Fujimoto or Himari?"

"I'm afraid not."

"Do you know if Master Akira Fujimoto is a fugu chef?"

"Yes. Doctor Tinterow told me."

"And are you aware that preparing and serving fugu in New York City is illegal, Mr. Williams?"

"I'm afraid I did not know that."

"Are you aware of the dangers of eating fugu?"

"Yes, I am."

"And what are they?"

"Fugu is a pufferfish that, if prepared by anyone other than a trained and licensed fugu chef, can lead to death."

"Did Master Akira Fujimoto prepare and serve fugu last night?"

"Yes."

"Were the guests aware of the deadly consequences of eating fugu?"

"They were. Doctor Tinterow told the guests that there was fugu and that no one was obliged to try it. But everyone, with the exception of Amy Rainwater, agreed to try some."

"So, it's your assertion that Vincent Rainwater, Arthur Strong, and James Walsh all agreed to eat fugu after being told they could die." Roscoe pressed.

"That's right, Detective."

"Did you have some?"

"I did. It was quite delicious and exciting."

"Did Doctor Tinterow also have some fugu?"

"Yes, he had several pieces, as did I."

"You do know that the medical examiner will be conducting an autopsy of Mr. Rainwater and Strong. Do you believe he'll find evidence that they had eaten pufferfish?"

"I really don't know what he'll find."

"Well, for your sake, you better pray he does because if he doesn't, then you and Doctor Tinterow will be looking at first-degree murder charges."

"I'm sure the ME will find fugu in their stomachs," Williams said with confidence.

"How was your relationship with Vincent Rainwater?"

"We were old-school chums—Yale class of '55. We had formed an art syndicate, Vincent, Gary, and me. We'd pool our money to be able to buy art, hold on to the works for several years, and then turn around and sell them for large sums of money. No, Detective Brown, Gary, and I had no reason to want Vincent or even Arthur Strong dead. Although we were a bit surprised when we learned he was working with the police."

"Working with the police?" Roscoe feigned surprise.

"Yeah, that's what Amy told me."

"Do you have anything else you'd like to tell me?"

"No."

"All right, Mr. Williams, you are going to be booked, photographed, and fingerprinted. Then you'll be transferred over to Rikers Island, where you'll be able to call your lawyer and go about getting bail."

Williams didn't say anything; he went through the booking process and eventually caught up with Tinterow, where they were both taken to Rikers Island.

Four hours later, they both were out on one-million-dollar bail.

Roscoe headed over to Coney Island Hospital to visit his partner. Walsh appeared to be sleeping when Roscoe softly walked into the room.

"Hello, Roscoe," Walsh uttered.

"Hey, Jimmy. How are you feeling?"

"Like Sugar Ray Robinson used my stomach as a punching bag, then Oakland Raiders kicker George Blanda used my guts as a practice tee."

"That good. Huh."

"Am I going to make it, Roscoe?"

"Doc Robinson said that you'll be up and out of here by the end of the week. You know, you were damn lucky."

"Yeah. I don't feel so lucky."

"Vincent Rainwater and Arthur Strong are both dead."

"Dead! How?"

"Fugu."

"But none of us had any."

"You didn't volunteer to try some. Even a small piece?"

"Roscoe, no way! The only ones who tried some were Tinterow and Williams. They kept trying to egg us on, but none of us would."

"Williams told me a couple of hours ago that they informed you all about fugu and that you were excited to try some."

"That's a lie."

"I'm going to have someone come here and get your statement. Then, I'll be having a conversation with Assistant District Attorney Jeffery Harris. We'll soon have these bastards off the streets. Now, you need to get some rest." Roscoe said.

"Thanks, Roscoe."

"I'll stop by tomorrow."

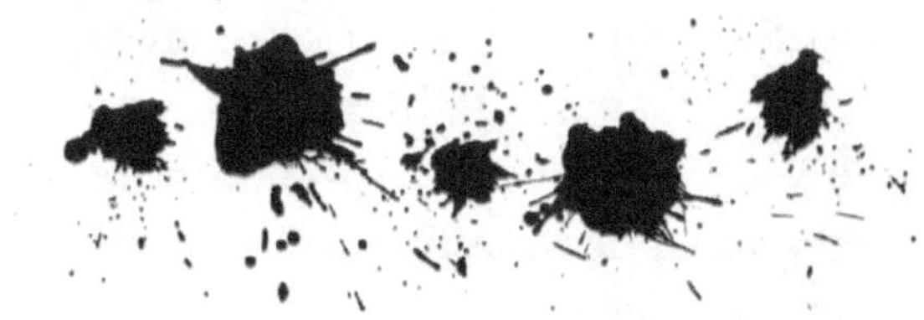

Roscoe had been working with Assistant District Attorney Jeffery Harris, helping him build a case against Tinterow and Williams for the murder of Roger Niles.

Some of the most damning pieces of evidence are the photographs taken at the scene of the blood splatter on the area of the couch where Frank Williams allegedly said that he was sitting. The blood splatter would have been on Williams instead of the sofa. Although Williams did have blood evidence on him, it is consistent with someone who shot the victim.

Other evidence that helps support Roscoe's theory that Williams and Tinterow killed Niles are the inconsistent statements to Roscoe and to Sharon Fiyalka, the Times reporter that Tinterow gave.

Now, he and DA Harris needed to amend their case against Tinterow and Williams to include the murder of Vincent Rainwater and Arthur Strong, as well as an attempted murder of Detective James Walsh.

"Roscoe, I see where Tinterow and Williams made bail."

"You know as well as I do, money is power. The judge had them surrender their passports. But I've alerted all the airports, cruise ships, and the border patrol, both north and south, to be on the alert just in case they get antsy." Roscoe said.

Assistant District Attorney Jeffery Harris told Roscoe to get him all the paperwork and statements, and he would get together with the District Attorney and build new all-inclusive arrest warrants for the murders of Roger Niles as well as the Vincent Rainwater, Arthur Strong killings, and the attempted murder of Detective James Walsh.

"When do you think you might have them, sir?" Roscoe asked.

"I'd say by the end of the week."

"Very good. I can't wait to get these two arrogant assholes off the streets. Pardon my French, sir."

"No need to apologize, Detective Sergeant Brown. I totally understand."

As Detective James Walsh walked into the six 0, he was met with a rousing chorus of cheers and thunderous applause. Captain O'Rourke himself was standing at the station door to greet him. Roscoe walked behind Walsh as a safety precaution. Earlier, Walsh almost fell over from being so weak.

"Welcome home, Detective. It's good to have you back." Captain O'Rourke said stoically. He was shocked to see how weak and frail Walsh looked.

"It's good to be back, sir," Walsh muttered.

"Now, I want you to take it easy for the next couple of days. Just ease back into the job. Understood."

"Yes, sir. Thank you."

Roscoe came up to Walsh, took his arm, and led him to the elevator. When they got to the third floor of the detective squad room, Roscoe brought his partner into his office amongst more cheers and hurrahs.

"Here, have a seat," Roscoe said as he led him to the couch.

"Can I get you anything?" Roscoe asked.

"Roscoe, I'm fine. Quit mothering me.

"Fine! Get your own damn coffee." Roscoe said with a smirk.

While they sat in Roscoe's office, no less than thirty detectives and uniformed cops stopped by to see how Walsh was doing. And that was just in the first hour.

By noon, Roscoe had had it, "Come on. Let's get out of here. This place is like having people come in wanting an audience with the pope.

"Where are we going?" Walsh asked.

"You need something to eat that will stick to them bones. After a week of eating nothing but hospital food.

"Don't tell me. Nathan's Famous."

"Yup. A couple of chili cheese dogs will perk you right up, my boy." Roscoe said with a beam.

They sat on a bench facing the ocean, a warm breeze wafting over them as they polished off two chili dogs each.

Walsh took the last bite of his hot dog, burped, and said, "You know, I actually do feel better. But it will be interesting to see how I feel when this puppy hits my guts."

"See, I told you."

"Roscoe, I was really scared; there was a time when I didn't think I would make it."

Roscoe laughed, "Ah, Hell, kid. I always knew you'd make it."

"Really?"

"Sure. Anyone who can knock off two Nathan's chili cheese dogs like you just did can survive something as toxic as fugu."

Later that afternoon, Walsh and Roscoe were talking in Roscoe's office when Roscoe's phone rang.

BRINNNGGGG BRINNNGGGG BRINNNGGGG

"Detective Brown, Homicide.

Yes, sir.

Yes, sir.

I agree.

Very good, sir.

Yes, sir. Thank you.

All right.

Goodbye."

CLICK

Walsh leaned forward in his chair, "Who was that?"

"Harris," Roscoe replied.

"Assistant District Attorney Jeffery Harris?"

"The one and the same."

"What did he want?"

"He thinks we have enough to charge Tinterow and Williams for the murders of Roger Niles, Vincent Rainwater, Arthur Strong, and the attempted murder of you. He's issuing arrest warrants; he said we should have them within the hour."

Roscoe sat thinking for a while when Walsh asked, "Is there anything the matter?"

"Nothing; I can't wait to see the look on their faces when they see that, one, you're not dead, and two, you're a cop." Roscoe mused.

Walsh stood up and said to Roscoe, "Let's roll."

On their way out, they stopped by O'Rourke's office and told him that the DA had issued warrants for Doctor Gary Tinterow and Frank Williams.

"You guys, be careful. Do you need any backup?" O'Rourke said.

Walsh smiled, "No, sir. I think we're good."

The first stop was to Doctor Tinterow's office. Since it was summer and a Friday afternoon in New York, many offices closed early so the rich could get an early start to head out to the Hamptons or Fire Island. Tinterow's office was one of those. So, they went to his townhouse. He wasn't there.

Both Tinterow's and Williams' bail release was predicated that they were not allowed to leave Manhattan unless given authorization by the courts, for which they hadn't applied. Walsh put out an APB to all the surrounding areas.

They had zero luck finding Frank Williams, either. Roscoe wasn't too concerned that they hadn't found them; they could be out with friends, at a restaurant, or a museum. He knew that sooner or later, the long arm of the law would capture these villains.

On the way back to the station, Roscoe got a call from dispatch; it was Officer Ron Harris.

"Roscoe, I just wanted to let you know we got that Japanese chef Akira Fujimoto sitting in interrogation room two."

"Great. We'll be there shortly." Roscoe replied as he turned to Walsh and said, "Hey, you'll get to see your old pal, Mr. Fujimoto."

"Can't wait." Walsh sneered.

When Walsh and Roscoe walked into the interrogation room, Fujimoto's eye almost bugged out of his head. He turned white as Casper the Ghost and began to shiver.

When they walked in, Officer Harris was sitting in the room, "We nabbed him as he was boarding a plane to Tokyo this morning. I've called for an interpreter; he should be here shortly."

"Did you read him his rights?" Walsh asked.

"I read them in English, but just to be safe, I didn't ask him anything until he had his right read to him in Japanese."

"Good call, Ron. I guess, for now, we sit and wait until the interpreter shows up." Roscoe said.

Two hours passed when the interpreter finally showed up. He was an elderly Japanese American man in his sixties: Mr. Sato, a professor of Japanese studies at NYU.

"Mr. Sato, would you read Mr. Fujimoto his rights," Roscoe said as he handed a laminated card with the Miranda Warning typewritten on it.

Sato took the card and began to read, "*Anata ni wa chinmoku o mamoru kenri ga arimasu. Anata ga iu koto wa subete, hōtei de anata ni taishite shiyō suru koto ga deki, shiyō sa remasu. Anata ni wa bengoshi no kenri ga arimasu. Bengoshi o yatou yoyū ga nai baai wa, bengoshi ga anata ni teikyō sa remasu. Watashi ga anata ni yonda bakari no kenri o rikai shite imasu ka? Korera no kenri o nentō ni oite, watashi ni hanashitai to omoimasu ka?"*

Mr. Fujimoto nodded and said, *"Hai."*

The interpreter looked at Roscoe and said, "Yes."

"Ask him if he wants a lawyer or if he is willing to talk to us."

"Bengoshi ga hoshīdesu ka, soretomo watashitachi ni hanashimasu ka."

"Bengoshi wa imasen. Watashi ga hanashi o shimasu."

"He says, no lawyer. He'll talk to you."

"Ask him where he was Saturday night," Roscoe said.

"Doyōbi no yoru wa dokoni ita no?" Sato asked.

"Watashi wa misutā tintārō no ie ni imashita."

"He says he was at the home of Mr. Tinterow."

"Was he there as the sushi chef?"

"Anata wa sushi shokunin to shite soko ni imashita ka?"

Mr. Fujimoto nodded and said, *"Hai."*

"Yes."

"Did he knowingly serve poisoned fugu to anyone?"

"Doku sa reta fugu o koi ni dareka ni teikyō shimashita ka?"

"Hai."

"Yes," Sato said, looking at Roscoe and Walsh.

"Was it an accident?"

"Jikodeshita ka?"

"*Bangō. Tinterow wa watashi ni sorera no dansei o dokusuru tame ni shiharaimashita.*"

"No. Tinterow paid me to poison those men."

"How much did he pay you?"

"*Kare wa anata ni ikura haratta nodesu ka?*"

"*200 Man-en.*"

"Two million yen."

Walsh and Roscoe looked at Sato and asked, "Two million. What's that in dollars?"

Sato sat there calculating in his head for several minutes, then said, "Twenty thousand American Dollars."

"Ask him if he knows if Frank Williams was involved?"

"*Furankuu~iriamuzu wa kan'yo shimashita ka?*"

"*Hai.*"

"Yes."

"What about the girl, Himari?"

"*Himari-chan wa?*"

"*Bangō.*"

"No."

"Does he know her last name?"

"*Kanojo no sei o shitte imasu ka?*"

"*Takahashi. Himari Takahashi.*"

"Himari Takahashi."

Roscoe thought about his next question.

"Ask him why he did it?"

"*Dōshite?*"

Fujimoto started to weep as he spoke, "*Watashi no musume wa gan de shinikakete imasu. Chiryō wa hijō ni kōkadesu.*"

Sato sat quietly while Fujimoto softly muttered his explanation. He looked at the two detectives and carefully translated, "He said, My daughter is dying of cancer. Treatment is very expensive."

"Tell him we're very sorry. But we are going to arrest him now."

"*Karera wa mōshiwakearimasenga, anata wa taiho sa rete imasu.*"

Fujimoto bowed his head and said, "*Wakarimasu.*"

"He says he understands."

Walsh began to put the handcuffs on the man who tried to murder him, and yet he felt no animosity towards him. His anger was focused on Tinterow and Williams.

Roscoe said, as Walsh cuffed the master fugu chef, "Akira Fujimoto, you are under arrest for the murder of Vincent Rainwater, Arthur Strong, and the attempted murder of James Walsh."

"*Fujimoto Akira, anata wa vu~insento rein'u~ōtā, āsā suto rongu, jēmuzu U~Orushu no satsugai no tsumi de taiho sa remashita.*" Sato executed the translation.

Walsh then led the master fugu chef out of the interrogation room for processing, pictures, and prints before sending him to Rikers Island.

"Mr. Sato, how do you say thank you in Japanese?"

"*Arigatōgozaimashita.*"

"Ah, right. Well, I just want to say thank you for all your help."

Sato gave a short bow, "*Dōitashimashite.* That means you are welcome."

Roscoe returned the bow.

Walsh picked up Roscoe at his apartment a little after eight o'clock the following day and headed over to Chock Full o'Nuts in Manhattan for a bit of breakfast.

"How you feeling?" Roscoe asked his partner.

"Physically, I'm feeling pretty good. But mentally. It was very odd seeing Fujimoto yesterday. I kinda felt bad for the guy."

"No. You felt bad for his daughter. The man tried to kill you. He didn't show any remorse other than his getting caught."

"Yeah, you're right."

"Finished? Ready to go see if the good doctor is in?"

"Can't wait to see the look on his face when he sees the ghost of Detective Walsh."

"Let's go," Roscoe said.

They made their way uptown to 94th Street and Riverside Drive, parked the car, and went to the front door. Walsh rang the doorbell.

DING DONG DING DONG

Walsh was standing behind Roscoe when Tinterow opened the door. His expression was one of disgust and annoyance.

"What! Haven't you harassed and humiliated me enough, Detective Brown!" He sneered.

"Actually, Doctor Tinterow, I just came by to introduce you to my partner, Detective James Walsh."

Walsh stepped out from behind Roscoe, revealing himself to Tinterow, who looked like he had just seen a ghost. And he had.

"Good day, Doctor Tinterow. Mind if we come in?" Walsh asked.

Looking between Walsh and Roscoe, he mumbled, "But I thought. You said. He's not dead!"

Walsh held up the arrest and search warrant, "This is a warrant for your arrest, and a search warrant, to search your home, office, and car. Here." He said as he handed the papers to Tinterow.

Roscoe turned to Walsh and said, "Go out to the car and radio for the CSI boys to get over here."

Walsh headed out to the squad car. While Roscoe was getting ready to place the handcuffs on the doctor, he heard Frank Williams' voice from behind him: "Close and lock the door, Detective Brown."

Roscoe turned to see Williams holding a Smith & Wesson 9mm pointed at him.

Roscoe did as he was told.

"Now, very slowly, take out your gun and place it on the floor.

Again, Roscoe did as he was told.

"Now what?" Roscoe asked.

Walsh noticed that the front door was shut and immediately called in a 10-999 officer needs help. Within seconds, eight police cars came roaring up, lights flashing, sirens blaring.

All the commotion didn't go unnoticed inside Tinterow's townhouse.

Roscoe calmly said, "You must know that they aren't going away. Just hand me the gun, and no one will get hurt."

"Shut up. Just shut up!" Tinterow yelled.

As the police began surrounding the house, Williams cracked the front door and shouted, "Don't anybody try anything, or I'll kill the cop!" He then slammed the door and locked it.

"Let's take him into the den," Tinterow said.

Tinterow led the way into the den. The den was an interior room without any windows; Williams thought it best that they keep the door open so they could hear if anyone tried to break in.

"Sit down, Detective, and don't try any funny stuff. Roscoe did as he was told. He was directed to sit in a chair that was perpendicular to the wooden desk in Doctor Tinterow's office. Williams sat opposite Brown, facing him, so close that their knees were touching. Williams was nervously pointing a Smith & Wesson 9mm at the detective. Dr. Tinterow sat to Roscoe's left behind the desk.

Roscoe noticed that Tinterow had an identical saltwater aquarium to the one in his office. He saw that he had the same species of fish in the tank as well, with the exception of no Tiger Pufferfish.

"Doctor Tinterow, I noticed that this aquarium doesn't have any Tiger Pufferfish in it. Is that because you served them up for dinner Saturday night?"

"You're very observant, Detective Brown. A little too observant for your own good."

"We've already arrested and talked to Fujimoto. He gave us a full confession. He told us how you paid him twenty thousand dollars to poison Rainwater, Strong, and Walsh."

Tinterow said nothing as he opened a desk drawer.

Roscoe, playing for time, asked, "Why Rainwater? I know why you'd want to kill Strong, but why Rainwater."

Williams said, "Because he was working with you."

"Working for me? Who told you that?"

"Amy. She indicated he was working for you to work out a deal."

"Detective Brown, you put us in a very awkward position."

"Gee, I'm sorry, Doc," Roscoe said facetiously.

"If we let you go, we'll probably be arrested and end up in prison. Am I right?"

"That's right."

Tinterow smirked as he began to prepare the lethal dose of Fentanyl.

"You know, Detective Brown, since you're a tad overweight, I'm afraid you're a prime candidate for a heart attack." Tinterow sneered.

"You forgetting four things, Doc. One, there are dozens of cops outside who aren't magically going to disappear. Two, my partner Detective Walsh is alive, no thanks to you, and will step in and see that you both go to prison and possibly die in the gas chamber. Three, you never, and I repeat, never want to be known as a cop killer."

Tinterow instinctively tapped the hypodermic needle to eliminate any air bubbles when he stopped and looked at Roscoe quizzically, beamed, and chuckled, "That's only three. What's number four, Detective Brown?"

Roscoe flashed forward, grabbed Williams' hand holding the revolver, twisted the gun so it was pointing towards Tinterow, and forced Williams' finger to fire four rapid shots, striking the good doctor four times in the torso.

POW POW POW POW

Brown then turned the gun at Williams and fired two shots, hitting him in the right shoulder.

POW POW

Roscoe twisted the gun out of Williams' hand; as he quickly stood up, he pushed Williams back with such force that he toppled the chair over. The wounded man lay on the floor moaning in agony, holding his shoulder, and writhing in pain.

Roscoe went over to check on Tinterow. Tinterow's eyes were fixed on Roscoe as the detective approached to check his pulse. He placed his hand on the doctor's neck. Roscoe had seen too many men close to death; he knew the doctor had only minutes. So, Roscoe leaned down close so Tinterow could hear him. He whispered in the doctor's ear, "Oh, and number four. Don't. Fuck. With. Me."

Tinterow gurgled something unintelligible, rolled his eyes into the back of his head, and died.

The moment the police heard the gunshots, they busted the front and back doors down. They came storming into the den, Walsh leading the charge, where they found Detective Sergeant Roscoe Brown kneeling over a wounded suspect, applying pressure to try and stop the bleeding until the paramedics came.

"Roscoe, you, okay?" Walsh asked.

"You know, Jimmy, I am a little hungry."

"Detective Sergeant Brown, won't you come in, please." Amy Albright Rainwater said invitingly.

"I believe you know my partner, Detective Walsh."

"Yes, of course. I'm so glad to see that you're fine, Detective Walsh."

"Thank you," Walsh said.

From out of the bedroom came a man's voice, "Honey, who is it?"

"It's the police," Amy announced.

The young man entered the living room wearing an old pair of ragged blue jeans, a torn, paint-splattered T-shirt, and bare feet.

"The police?"

"Tony, this is Detective Sergeant Brown and his partner Detective Walsh. Detectives, this is my friend Tony Romeo."

"Mrs. Rainwater, we just stopped by to inform you that we've arrested Frank Williams and the sushi chef Akira Fujimoto. Unfortunately, Doctor Tinterow was killed while resisting arrest."

"Does Mrs. Strong know?" She asked.

"Yes, we just came from there," Roscoe said.

"How is she doing, Detective?"

"She seems to be coping."

"I think I'll go see her."

"That would be nice," Roscoe said with a smile.

"Is that all, Detective?"

"Are you an artist, too, Mr. Romeo?" Roscoe asked.

"Yes, as a matter of fact, I am."

"I look forward to seeing your work."

"Collector, Detective?" Romeo quired.

"Hardly. Not on a Detective Sergeant's salary."

"Stop by the Collingswood Gallery this coming Saturday. I'm having my first one-man show."

"Mmmm, I might just do that," Roscoe said as he and Walsh were going to the door. He stopped, turned, and asked, "Amy, I'm curious. Why did you tell Frank Williams about Vincent helping the police?"

"I didn't." She said, acting shocked.

"Was it because you wanted Vincent out of your life?"

"Absolutely not!"

"You figured that if they thought he was ratting them out, they would get rid of him."

"How dare you!"

"Oh, don't worry, Mrs. Rainwater. I won't be able to prove anything. I checked that Tinterow and Williams don't have any dependents, so not only will you inherit Vincent's wealth and share of the art syndicate, but you'll also get their shares. What's that come to? One hundred million dollars?"

She smiled coyly and said, "More like two hundred million."

"Goodbye, Mrs. Rainwater."

"It's Ms. Albright." She said as she closed the door.

As Roscoe and Walsh walked toward the elevator, Walsh said, "I guess it's true; money is the root of all evil."

"No, my friend, greed is."

EPILOGUE

Frank Williams spent four weeks in Bellevue Hospital recovering from his gunshot wounds before standing trial. His trial lasted thirteen weeks. He was found guilty of the first-degree murder of Roger Niles, Vincent Rainwater, and Arthur Strong, guilty on one count of the attempted murder of Detective James Walsh, one count of kidnapping, and threatening the life of Detective Sergeant Roscoe Brown.

Williams was sentenced to three life sentences plus one year to be served consecutively. He was sent to Attica Prison in upstate New York.

Master Akira Fujimoto, fugu chef, was found guilty of first-degree murder of Vincent Rainwater and Arthur Strong and guilty of the attempted murder of Detective James Walsh. Because of his inability to speak English, a special arrangement with the Japanese government was struck. He was allowed to serve his fifty-five-year sentence at the Fukuoka Detention House in Sawara-ku, Japan.

The widow, Amy Albright Rainwater, became the sole owner of the Rainwater—Tinterow—William's art syndicate's art collection, which is valued at over two hundred million dollars.

Amy married the up-and-coming artist Tony Romeo six days after Vincent Rainwater's funeral.

Detective Sergeant Roscoe Brown and his partner Detective James Walsh received the Medal of Valor from the NYPD. Detective Walsh also received the Purple Shield, awarded to an officer injured or killed in the line of duty. Detective Sergeant Roscoe Brown was awarded the Police Combat Cross, given to a member of the NYPD who has successfully and intelligently performed an act of extraordinary heroism while engaged in personal combat with an armed adversary under circumstances of imminent personal hazard to life.

"I thought I'd find the two of you here." Sharon Fiyalka, the reporter from the New York Times, said.

"Care to join us?" Roscoe asked.

"Hmmm, don't mind if I do." She said as she sat between Roscoe and Walsh on the boardwalk bench outside Nathan's Famous.

"Can I get you something?" Roscoe asked.

Holding up a paper bag, Sharon said, "No thanks, I got a couple of dogs."

"What can we do you for?" Roscoe said.

"You promised me an exclusive, Roscoe."

"So, I did, Ms. Fiyalka. So, I did. How about we return to my office after lunch, where Walsh and I will give you the whole story, gruesome details."

"You know Detective Sergeant Roscoe Brown, facing Tinterow and Williams so soon after their attempt on your partner's life must have been quite a quandary for you."

"No, not really. I've faced bigger dilemmas than that."

"Really, like what?" She asked.

"Well, being an atheist, once I was stuck at a green light behind a car that just sat there with a "Honk if you love Jesus" bumper sticker. Now, that was a dilemma!"

THE END

The Case of the Devil's Tooth

"Hello. I'd like to introduce you to Hounds Tooth Gourmet Canine Cuisine, a new food for your dog.

Hounds Tooth Gourmet Canine Cuisine isn't the average dog food because your dog isn't the average dog.

Hounds Tooth uses only the finest cuts of prime meat from the choicest animals that I personally choose. Our beef is 100% American Angus or Japanese Kobe; our horse meat is selected from only the top Equine stables in the country. Hounds Tooth is filled with the best ingredients and the most refined wheat from Kansas, two-row barley from Montana, and potatoes direct from Idaho. In addition, each can is not only chocked full of goodness but with love.

Hounds Tooth is premium cuisine; of course, the price reflects that, as you might expect. At Hounds Tooth, we make no bones about it, pardon the pun, our carte du jour costs more but isn't your best friend worth it?

We know that Hounds Tooth isn't for everyone or every dog; it's made for the crème de la crème of the genus Canis.

Hounds Tooth Gourmet Canine Cuisine is exclusively made for New York's finest. Available only at the Hounds Tooth Boutique at 2803 West 20th Street, Coney Island.

I'm Louis Tooth Jr., President and owner of Hounds Tooth Gourmet Canine Cuisine, and I approved this ad."

"CUT!" Shouted Miles Sacker, up-and-coming TV commercial director.

"How was that?" Louis Tooth is the on-camera talent and owner of Hounds Tooth Gourmet Canine Cuisine.

"That was beautiful, Louie baby, but let's do one more. This time, try putting a little smile in your voice; you want the people in TV land to like you, am I right? Of course, I am. Now, go back to the number one position."

Cindy, the makeup girl, asked, "How's the shine on his forehead? Does it need a little touch-up?"

Tony, the AD (Assistant Director), asked Miles, "Miles, how's the shine on his forehead? Does it need a little touch-up?"

Miles looked through his $800 Denz Director's Viewfinder and nodded yes.

"Makeup! A little powder on the talent. If you, please."

The DP (Director of Photography) Archie stood up from his seat on the camera dolly and told Billy, the head gaffer, "Billy, put a half scrim on the 2k, will you."

After applying makeup powder on the talent slash client, Cindy asked Tony, "Is that good?"

In turn, Tony asked Miles, "Is that good?"

Miles again looked through the viewfinder and nodded affirmatively.

Here's what you might not know: there is a strict hierarchy regarding filmmaking, especially making TV commercials. Nobody on the crew speaks directly to the Director, with the exception of the AD, DP, head Gaffer (lighting), and head Grip (laborers, go-fers). Everyone else has to go through the AD.

That's because the Director is like the Captain of a ship, the lord and master of the set, the lofty one who brings the banal scripts to life, the creative genius; he and he alone can turn shit into gold.

"Okay, Tony," Miles said.

"Okay! Quiet on set! Camera?" Tony began his ritual.

"Camera ready," Archie replied.

"Sound?" Tony asked.

"Sound ready." Willy, the soundman, said.

"Roll sound!" Tony shouted.

"Rolling." Willy acknowledged.

"Camera!" Tony commanded.

"Speed." The first camera assistant said.

"Slate!" Tony shouted for the 2nd camera assistant to place the camera slate in front of the camera, slap the clapper board, announce the scene, and take the number.

"Hounds Tooth scene 4, take twenty-two." The young assistant said proudly.

"ACTION!" Miles yelled.

After eight hours of shooting what, in reality, should have taken maybe two hours, Tony asked the first assistant to check the gate.

Checking the gate on the camera is checking the part of the camera that sits between the lens and the exposed film, and the checking is being done to see if there are any tiny hairs or strips of film emulsion that may have come off during filming.

"Gate clear."

"Then, ladies and gentlemen, THAT'S A WRAP!" Tony announced.

And with those magic words, the day's shooting was over. The project moved into the capable hands of Frankie Marino, one of New York's premier editors. It's Frankie's incredible knack of editing around a director's minor missteps and major fuckups that has saved so many director's asses, and this one would be no exception.

Miles, Tony, and Frankie gathered in Frankie's editing bay to peek at the dailies the next day. The dailies are the raw footage that was shot the day before.

"Miles, some of these shots don't match; the angles are all wrong. There are gaps in continuity; the sound isn't syncing up. Were you all drunk when you shot this?" Frankie said out of frustration, knowing full well that they were going to rely on him to save this piece of shit.

"Frankie baby, it's a fucking dog food commercial, not Gone With The Wind," Miles said, just wanting to go to the bathroom and snort some more cocaine.

"Miles, what is this, a sixty-second spot? With what I got to work with, you'll be lucky if I can cut a thirty."

"Frankie baby, look, just throw in a couple of title cards for filler, drop on some mega supers, and it's a sixty," Miles said, smiling that shit-eating smile that told everyone that he was stoned out of his mind.

"I ought to just cut the storyboard; then you'll see just what a fucking mess this is."

"Hey, come on, Frankie, baby."

"Don't Frankie baby me; if you want me to save your ass again, it's going to cost you, ya dig?"

"How much?"

"Ten grand above my bid!"

"Ten grand! Are you out of your fucking mind?"

"Fine, get someone else to cut this crap."

"Five grand."

"Ten!"

"Okay, ten. But it better be great."

"This won't ever be great with what you shot, but at least it won't stink up the room."

"When can I see the first rough cut?"

"I'll need three days, so come back Friday afternoon."

"How about seventy-five hundred?"

"Get out!"

Hounds Tooth Gourmet Canine Cuisine owner Louis Tooth Jr. was born and bred in Brooklyn, New York, Coney Island, to be precise. He graduated from Brooklyn College, where he received a Bachelor of Arts Degree in Business and Finance, although, at one point, Louis toyed with the idea of becoming a veterinarian. While growing up, Louis's best friend was the family dog Nero, a pure-bred German Shepherd. Throughout high school and college, he worked as a vet tech in various veterinarian offices. But he discovered that he just didn't have the aptitude for all the science, biology, and anatomy courses needed to become a vet. His strengths were more in marketing, manufacturing, merchandising, and economics.

Because having had dogs all his life, his current dog, Giulia, a four-year-old Italian Spinone bitch, Louis Tooth truly believes that dogs are kinder, gentler, and generally friendlier than people; in fact, Louis Tooth hates people. After growing up and having to withstand the taunts and jeers from hundreds of children making fun of Tooth's name. All through school, they used to call him *the Tooth Fairy, Tooth Booth, Buck Tooth, and Loose Tooth,* to name a few.

That's why he started and built his Hounds Tooth Gourmet Dog Canine Cuisine in Coney Island. Since he couldn't seem to relate to or give a shit about people, he observed that most people, deep down, felt the same way about their fellow man.

But he discovered that just about everybody loves dogs, especially their dogs. He did an informal research experiment. He observed that when a person passed someone on the street who looked needy, the average passerby would do just that—pass by, but if there was a dog who looked needy, almost everyone would stop and try to help the poor pup.

So, after a year and a half of studying the data and careful calculations, Louis Tooth concluded that people suck, and dogs rule. He decided to market to dogs and dog owners. He started a line of gourmet dog food, the Hounds Tooth Gourmet Canine Cuisine Company, and Boutique.

He decided that his dog food would be targeted at the rich; he would be an elite clientele, people willing to pay more for quality for their pets.

Other dog food companies filled their cans with horse meat from horses that pulled milk carts or handsome carriages. Hounds Tooth Gourmet Canine Cuisine filled their cans with thoroughbred horses, ex-Kentucky Derby winners, Dressage champions, and the occasional rodeo bucking bronco champ. And instead of buying his beef from slaughterhouses that would use old, lame, decrepit, and sometimes diseased cattle, Louis would purchase blue ribbon cattle and prize-winning bulls past their stud days.

Tooth found the perfect location for his dog food factory, at the corner of Neptune Avenue and West 20th

Street, right down the street from the Allen Gormely Sanitation Garage.

Of course, he would have loved to open his Boutique in Manhattan on the Upper East Side, but he just couldn't swing it financially, not with what he was paying for the meat.

It had been a week since he shot his TV spot. He couldn't afford an advertising agency, so he wrote and starred in the commercial. Maybe he could afford a big-name actor someday, but he would have to do it for now. He was getting anxious about seeing the final product since he was ready to start running it on TV, locally only.

"Miles? Tooth here; I'm calling to find out the status of my commercial."

"Louie, baby, I was just about to call you. Your spot will be ready this afternoon."

"Excellent, I can't wait."

"Err."

"Is there a problem, Miles?"

"Well, it's the editor, Louie."

"I do hope he's not ill."

"Oh no, it's nothing like that, Louie baby. He says he's had some extra expenses in the editing process."

"Oh?"

"He is asking for an additional $10,000."

"Miles, I believe we had a firm bid, did he not?"

"Well, yeah."

"And can I assume I had no part in causing the overages?"

"Oh no, you were great, Louie baby."

"Well, Miles, then I can't see how it's any of my concern. What time shall I come to your office to view my commercial, Miles baby?"

Louis was shown into the screening room, where he saw Miles, Tony, the AD, and Frankie Marino sitting waiting. When Miles noticed Louis had walked in, he jumped up to greet him.

"Louie baby, you remember Tony, my assistant director? This is Frankie Marino, our editor."

Louis shook Tony and Frankie's hand, "Tony, it's good to see you again, Frankie; it's a pleasure to meet you. I've heard great things about you. I can't wait to see my spot."

Frankie smiled and said, "You're too kind. I hope you'll like the spot. I had to tweak it from the original storyboard, but I think the changes strengthened the spot. I hope you'll agree."

"I'm sure I will."

Miles took charge of the room and asked Louis, "Please have a seat. Now, Louis, what I am going to do is roll the commercial the spots. All right?"

"Yes, very good."

Once everyone was seated, Miles shouted to the man in the projection booth, "Roll 'em!"

The room went dark for a few seconds. Then, the academy leader counted down $10 - 9 - 8 - 7 - 6 - 5 - 4 - 3 - 2$ - a sound sync "beep," and the spot began. That happened two more times. After that, the room went dark again for several seconds before the house lights came on.

"So, Louie baby, thoughts?" Miles asked.

Louis sat quietly for a minute thinking and finally said, "Fabulous. I'm quite impressed; everyone did a great job. Frankie, I agree. I think the changes you made were spot on. Now, what?"

"Well, we'll do the final color and sound mix, then send it off to the networks for airing," Miles said, relieved.

You never know with clients; some can be living dolls and others a living nightmare, and thanks again to Frankie, Miles dodged another bullet.

Miles asked Louis if he'd like to grab some lunch, and when Louis, Miles just knew this day was getting better and better. Lunch with clients was always a chore for Miles, and he sighed with relief when Louis passed.

Outside the studio, they all said their goodbyes. Frankie returned to his editing bay to work on cutting several new Volkswagen spots for the hottest ad agency in town, Doyle Dane Bernbach. Tony went with Miles to score some cocaine, and Louis went to prepare for the throngs of customers he was anticipating once his spots hit the air.

Louis only ran his TV commercial for one month before everyone in New York was all agog and buzzing about the hottest sensation in town, Hounds Tooth Gourmet Dog Canine Cuisine.

The New York Times ran a front-page article about Louis Tooth and his Hounds Tooth Gourmet Canine Cuisine; the New York Post ran a headline, "Canine Cuisine Costs Clumps of Cash!" Louis was invited to all the local morning shows and interviewed on the Howard Stern Show. Louis Tooth had arrived.

The Fine Art of Murder

The Hounds Tooth Gourmet Canine Cuisine Boutique had a storefront resembling some high-end dress shops in upper Manhattan, with a minimalist look. It looked more like a living room than a retail store. There was an overstuffed sofa, a large round coffee table, and two easy wingback chairs with a small side table with six cans of product against one wall. There were beautiful portraits of dogs on the walls. Behind the storefront was the factory, where the meat was cut, processed, and canned to order.

The way it worked was that a client would come in and be seated. Louis would sit across from the owner and discuss their breed of dog, its temperament, whether a pet or a show dog, how old it is, etc., building a thorough dossier.

Once completed, Louis would evaluate the data and recommend a particular canine cuisine, whether horse or beef, and the particular added ingredients, wheat, barley, corn, soy, or other components.

Afterward, the client would decide how many cans they would order at one hundred dollars a can. When the order was completed and paid for, Louis would go back into the factory area, place the order, and have his two butchers begin to cut the meat, mix up the extra ingredients, and then can them.

On average, the monthly dog food bill would be between six and eight thousand dollars, depending on the dog's size.

Soon, Hounds Tooth Gourmet Canine Cuisine became known as the dog food of the rich and famous. Everyone who was anyone was stopping by to order their pup's meals.

There were captains of industry, wizards of Wall Street, movie moguls, Broadway stars, and even a certain ex-first lady, Jackie somebody or other. People were stopping by to order food for their dogs and dropping in to schmooze or invite Louis over for dinner and cocktail parties. He became *"the"* person to be seen socializing with.

When Louis met clients at their homes, he spent more time with their dogs than with them; in fact, he was more interested in the pups than in the people.

There came a time when the business got so popular that people would stop in off the streets to go in the store to gawk and take photos; it got to the point that Louis had to shut his doors and accept clients by appointment only.

The first time it happened was late one day, after 6 pm, when both butchers had left for the day when Alain Robertson, the mega Broadway producer, arrived at the Boutique for an interview as a potential new client. Robertson had decided to bring his Airedale Terrier, the 1966 Westminster Champion Royal Tudor's Wild Irish Rose, to show off to Louis.

Tooth could tell right away that Robertson wasn't the type of client he wanted. The man was abusive to the dog, yelling at it and even striking the poor animal when the dog didn't obey.

"Excuse me, Mr. Robertson, but that isn't any way to treat your pet," Louis said.

"I know what's best for my dog, thank you very much. What he needs is a good thrashing."

"Believe me, Mr. Robertson, what that dog needs is love and patience. I can tell he's fearful of you, and that's why he hesitates to obey."

"Why don't you be a good little shopkeeper, shut your fucking mouth and go scrounge me up some of that damn dog food before I change my mind!"

"I think you should go."

"Fine. Come, Rose."

The dog hid behind Louis, cowering.

"I said, come you damn cur!"

"Mr. Robertson, I must ask you to please leave."

"I'm not going anywhere without that damn dog."

"No, you go, and the dog stays here with me."

"Like Hell! You fucking faggot." Robertson yelled and proceeded to grab Louis around the neck, then started to choke him. He probably would have killed him if it wasn't for Royal Tudor's Wild Irish Rose running up behind his owner and biting him on the ass. Thus, allowing Louis to reach over to the side table, grab a can of the *Kentucky Derby Winners Blend,* and proceeded to continually bash Alain Robertson on the side of the head, leaving several rather large dents in his skull, killing him.

Louis just stood there for a good ten minutes staring down at the dead man, wondering what to do. Should he call the Police? After all, it was self-defense, but would they believe him? What should he do? If nothing else, he figured he'd at least be charged with manslaughter. There's no way he could survive in prison. He barely survived the bullies in high school.

Then, the perfect solution came to him. He went into the factory to make sure Ralph and Jose had gone home. He was there all alone, except for the dead body and Royal

Tudor's Wild Irish Rose, who lay whimpering next to his dead master.

Louis decided to get rid of the body by cutting Mr. Robertson into bite-sized chunks and adding him to the fresh batch of the *Rough 'n Ready Rodeo Blend.*

There are a couple of different machines that they use to make the dog food. There's the chopping machine, the grinding machine, the pulverizing machine, and the packing machine. Poor old Alain Robertson made his way through all of them. He, along with a bronco named Killer McGurk, filled twelve dozen cans of the *Rough 'n Ready Rodeo Blend.*

Louis then called Robertson's house, inquiring if he had left because he told the maid that Mr. Robertson was late for his appointment.

Hazel Atwood, the maid, said, "Mr. Robertson had left a couple of hours ago with Rose. It's not like him to be late."

"Maybe he got hung up in traffic," Louis said.

"But he left over an hour ago."

"Well, I'm sure he just got caught up in traffic. I will be sure to have him call you when he gets here. And if you would be so kind as to telephone me if he happens to return home."

"Of course, Mr. Tooth."

Louis went around the showroom looking for evidence, blood, fingerprints, fibers, and anything that would show he was there.

He did the same in the factory, then scrubbed the floors and walls and wiped down all the equipment. He gathered all of the dead man's personal effects, including his wallet and clothes, and put them into the furnace—

everything except for the jewelry. He made sure every scrap was burnt to a crisp.

He took the jewelry—two gold rings, a gold necklace, a Rolex watch, and a gold engraved bracelet—and walked across Neptune Boulevard. He then strolled along Coney Island Creek and discreetly threw the rings, necklace, watch, and bracelet far out into the water as he walked.

He then waited until three in the morning, drove Robertson's car with Royal Tudor's Wild Irish Rose in the back seat to Coney Island Creek Park, and parked it. He was careful to wear gloves and even brought a small rag with some of Robertson's blood on it to smear around on the inside of the car, hoping that the Police would think that the car was the murder scene.

After leaving the abandoned car, he walked to his house in Seagate, only twelve blocks away. Tooth's house is two blocks south of the Coney Island Lighthouse, on the beach at the edge of Gravesend Bay.

The phone rang at 6 am, waking Roscoe from a deep sleep. He stretched his right arm out and grabbed the phone off the nightstand.

"Hello?"

"Roscoe, it's Jimmy; we got what looks to be a murder."

"Looks to be?"

"Well, there isn't a body, but we have an abandoned car with blood all over the place and what looks to be an expensive show dog in the back seat."

"Where?"

"Coney Island Creek Park."

"Okay, I'll be there in twenty minutes."

Roscoe hung up the phone and rolled out of bed.

"Who was that?" Betty, Roscoe's wife, asked.

"Jimmy, they found a bloody car in Coney Island Creek Park. Try and go back to sleep."

"Nope, I'm awake. I'll fix some coffee while you get dressed."

"Love you."

"Love you, too. Now, go."

Roscoe and Betty are still newlyweds; they've only been married a little over a year. They met eight years ago when Roscoe came in to open a checking account at Maspeth Savings Bank, where Betty worked as a teller. He liked her straight off, and after several visits to the bank, he finally worked up the nerve to ask her out for dinner, and she accepted. She liked him partly because she thought he had a good sense of humor, partially because she thought he was a cute, loveable lug, and partly because her dad and three brothers were all Police Officers, too.

Roscoe had planned to ask Betty to marry him earlier in their relationship, but being a cop, he had seen too many fellow officers leave behind widows. But when he started working homicide and was off the streets, he felt the time was right. Oh, they knew that the job was still dangerous, just not as dangerous.

As Roscoe was getting ready to head out the door, Betty handed him a hot cup of Chock Full of Nuts coffee in his favorite mug, gave him a big newlywed kiss, and said, "I love you. You be careful."

"Love you, too. Talk to you later."

A squad car was downstairs waiting to take him to the crime scene.

"Morning, Sarge."

"Good morning, Harris. What have we got?"

Officer Ron Harris was a rookie just out of the academy assigned to Roscoe and Walsh, his partner, to help in their investigations and to learn the ropes. At 28, Harris graduated top of his class; the department had high hopes for the rookie.

"We have a brand new 1966 Lincoln Town Car with smeared blood all over the front seat and steering wheel, and we have a pedigree dog sitting in the back seat."

"Do we have a name?"

"For the victim or the dog?

"Well, start with the alleged victim first."

"Yes, sir, the car is registered to Alain Robertson of 1056 5th Avenue."

"That, my dear Harris, is the high-rent district, so what's a high roller like that slumming in Coney Island?"

"Maybe he wanted to ride the Cyclone?"

"You're cute."

"Has Robertson's people been notified?"

"Detective Walsh called and spoke to the maid; she said he was supposed to have had an appointment with a dog food company."

"Dog food?"

"Do we know what dog food company?"

"That I don't know, sir."

They pulled up to the scene. There were at least twenty people from the NYPD milling around. Walsh was waiting by the Lincoln, where CSI was going over every inch of the car, inside and out.

As Roscoe approached and said, "Hey, Jimmy, whadda ya got?"

"Well, I think we're looking at murder, although we haven't found the body. I've got divers coming out this morning."

Roscoe walked around the car and looked inside. "Has the photographer been here yet?"

"Yeah, he just left."

"And CSI?"

"Yeah, they left as you were walking up. They said it looked like the insides were wiped clean."

"Anything on the dog?"

"They've taken it back to give it the once over."

"So, who is this Alain Robertson?"

"Big-time Tony-winning Broadway producer. He produced the award-winning hit "Death of a Dream.""

"Oh yeah? Betty wanted to see that, but tickets were out of this world expensive. A hundred bucks a ticket, can you believe that?"

"Ouch."

"So, let's take a ride up to Manhattan and speak to the maid."

Louis woke up in a panic; he was expecting the Police to come knocking on his door any minute. He turned on the television to see if there was anything on about Robertson's murder, but there wasn't. He calmed himself, got dressed, and walked to his store via Coney Island Creek Park.

By the time he reached the park, the Police were loading the Town Car onto a flatbed truck, presumably to take it to the Police car pound. There were just a handful of officers taking down the Police crime scene yellow tape as he was walking by.

"Excuse me, officer, can you tell me what's going on, please?"

"Aw, we just found an abandoned car, is all."

"Oh, thank goodness, I was afraid someone was killed or something."

"No need to worry, Mister, nothing like that."

"Thank goodness. Well, thank you, officer. Have a nice day."

Louis' confidence grew and grew the more he thought about it. He did know that the Police were bound to come and talk to him, but he'd stick to his story. Robertson never showed up for his appointment. And if somebody claimed to have seen his Lincoln parked out front, he'd just tell them that he was probably in the back with the machines on and wouldn't have been able to hear the front door. Besides, the odds of someone remembering something like that would be a million to one, right?

By the time Louis reached his Boutique, there was a car waiting outside, but it wasn't the Police; it was a black stretch limo parked out front, belonging to Ms. Trudy

Winslow, daughter of Walter Winslow, the Texas oil tycoon out of Dallas.

Trudy, who was at least sixty trying to look twenty, was your typical Dallas socialite: blonde, big hair, very shapely, fabulous couture designer clothes, immaculate makeup, but with the face of a horse. Trudy had undergone so many plastic surgeries that you could bounce a quarter off her face.

Louis apologized for having to wait and invited her in. She walked into the boutique carrying a pink-dyed miniature poodle named Snookie.

"Welcome to Hounds Tooth Boutique, Ms. Winslow. How may I be of service?"

"Well, Mr. Tooth."

"Please, call me Louis."

"Well, Louis, I am interested in procuring some of your finest cuisines for my Snookie." She said as she nuzzled the pint-sized pink pup."

"How old is the bitch?"

"I beg your pardon!"

"Snookie, how old is she?"

"Mr. Tooth, I don't approve of such language."

"I'm sorry?"

"Calling my Snookie the B-word."

"Ms. Winslow, you do you that a female dog is called a bitch, and it is by no means a derogatory name."

"Really?"

"I can assure you, Ms. Winslow, that a female dog is referred to as a bitch, and a male dog is called a sire. I have a four-year-old Spinone bitch, named Giulia."

"Oh, Louis, I feel so foolish. I do apologize; can you ever forgive me?"

"Yes, of course. Now, how old is… Snookie?"

"She is two."

"And how much does she weigh?"

"Fifteen pounds."

"Well, I recommend she probably needs four cans a week."

"Fine, I'll start with four cans, and then I'd like four cans every week."

"And you'll be flying in weekly to pick them up?"

"No, Louis, I'd like them shipped to me in Dallas."

"Oh no, Ms. Winslow, we do not ship our gourmet cuisine. One must come in person to obtain our meals."

"But why?"

"We can't have our fare being transported like common freight. You can understand that, can't you, Ms. Winslow? And besides, it essential that you bring in Snookie at least once a month so that I may evaluate if she is worthy of being a customer."

"Don't you mean the other way around?"

"I'm afraid not. You see, not all dogs are Hounds Tooth material, and after a month's trial, we shall rate Snookie's attributes, idiosyncrasies, and value to continue. You do understand?"

"But it's only dog food."

Louis stood abruptly, walked to the door, and said, "Good day, Ms. Winslow."

Trudy started to cry, "Oh, please forgive me, Louis, it's that I am exhausted from my flight this morning; please, please, I beg your forgiveness."

Louis stood there for a moment, basking in the fact that he could have these rich, snooty snobs prostrating before him.

"All right, Ms. Winslow, I quite understand; travel can be exhausting and affect one's judgment."

"Thank you, Louis. Now, do I have to make an appointment to bring Snookie next month?"

"That would be preferable, shall we say, four weeks from today?" Louis said as he wrote the appointment into his Tiffany Day Planner.

"Same time, Louis?"

"Very good if you don't think it would be too early."

"No, it shall be fine."

"Good. Now, let me prepare Snookie's order. I shan't be long." Louis said as he returned to the factory to give Snookie some special Robertson's blend cans.

As Harris pulled up to 1056 5th Avenue, Roscoe said, "Say, Harris, just let me and Walsh out there in front. You find a place to park, and we'll call you when we're ready to go."

"How come I can't go up with you guys?"

"Because we don't want to scare the old lady with a bunch of cops showing up, Walsh is scary enough."

"Funny, very funny," Walsh said, not amused.

Roscoe and Walsh walked under the green awning to where the doorman stood. Roscoe flashed his badge, "Detectives Brown and Walsh here to see Mr. Robertson's maid."

"1801, take the private elevator. The code is pound, one, zero, five, six, five."

"Thank you. Oh, were you working last night?"

"No, I work days. The night doorman, Roger, doesn't come on until five."

"Roger?"

"Roger Cooper."

"Thanks."

They walked to the back of the lobby, where the private elevator was located. The lobby had nicer furniture than Roscoe's apartment: leather sofas, Persian rugs, four Mies Vandero Barcelona chairs, and several paintings that could hang in any art museum in New York.

"Hey, Roscoe, maybe you and Betty should move in here. Whadda think?"

"I think I better start taking bigger bribes if I'm thinking of moving uptown."

When they reached the 18th floor, they stepped out of the elevator to discover that there were only two apartments on the entire floor.

Walsh rang the doorbell.

The door opened to reveal an elderly grey-haired African American woman dressed in a grey maid's uniform, "Won't you please come in?"

"Thank you, ma'am. I'm Detective Sargent Brown, and this is my partner, Detective Walsh."

"Do you have any news on Mr. Robertson?"

"I'm sorry to say not at this time."

Mrs. Atwood led the detectives into the living room, which Roscoe estimated to be the same size as his whole apartment. One wall had windows facing Central Park. The apartment was decorated with antiques and looked to Roscoe to be from the American Revolution era. They sat on a 1770s Chippendale Camelback Sofa with claw and ball feet, estimated to be worth $93,500.

"Would you gentlemen care for some tea?"

"That would be very nice, thank you, Mrs. Atwood."

While the maid left to make some tea, Roscoe and Walsh started to look around. Walsh peeked into cabinet drawers while Roscoe looked through the Connoisseur's Solid Wood U-shaped writing desk; both came up empty.

They were both seated on the sofa when Mrs. Atwood came in from the kitchen with a tray of tea and a plate full of crumpets. She asked each of them how they liked their tea. Roscoe wanted milk and sugar, while Walsh asked for honey.

When Mrs. Atwood finished pouring their tea, she poured a cup for herself and sat across from them on a Queen Anne Walnut Wing Armchair.

"Now, Mrs. Atwood, can you tell me where Mr. Robertson was going last night?"

"He was going to Coney Island's new gourmet dog food company. It's called the Hounds Tooth something or other. I have the phone number written down; it's in the kitchen.

"Well, at a little after seven-thirty when that nice Mr. Tooth called and asked if Mr. Robertson was still coming because he hadn't yet shown up for his appointment with Rose."

"And Rose is Mr. Robertson's dog," Walsh asked.

"That's right, Royal Tudor's Wild Irish Rose."

"And this Mr. Tooth was expecting to meet with Mr. Robertson to discuss dog food?"

"That's right. This Hounds Tooth dog food is supposed to be the greatest thing to happen to dog food since sliced bread, and as we all know, dogs don't eat sliced bread."

"What makes this dog food so good?" Roscoe asked.

"Well, on the TV, they say it's made with the best meats."

"But every dog food says that."

"They use Kobe beef from Japan, ex-Kentucky racehorse winners, big-name horses from the rodeo, stuff like that."

"Really, do you know how a can goes for?" Roscoe asked.

"One hundred dollars."

"For one can?"

"Yes, sir."

Roscoe looked at Walsh in disbelief.

"A hundred bucks a can; I never heard of such a thing," Roscoe said.

"That's what Mr. Robertson said. But he said that nothing's too good for Rose."

"And you never heard from Mr. Robertson after he left?"

"No, sir, I did not."

Detective Walsh leaned forward and asked, "Do you know anyone who would want to harm Mr. Robertson?"

"No, sir. Everyone loved Mr. Robertson, and that's a fact."

Roscoe added, "What about people in the business; you know, disgruntled business partners, actors caring a grudge, or what about lovers? Pardon my asking, but was Mr. Robertson involved with anyone that you were aware of?"

"As far as business associates, there are none that come to mind. As far as romance, I believe he is currently seeing Lorretta Hernandez. I can give you her number, too, if you'd like."

"Would you know if Mr. Robertson had a personal phone book?"

"Yes, I will get you that as well."

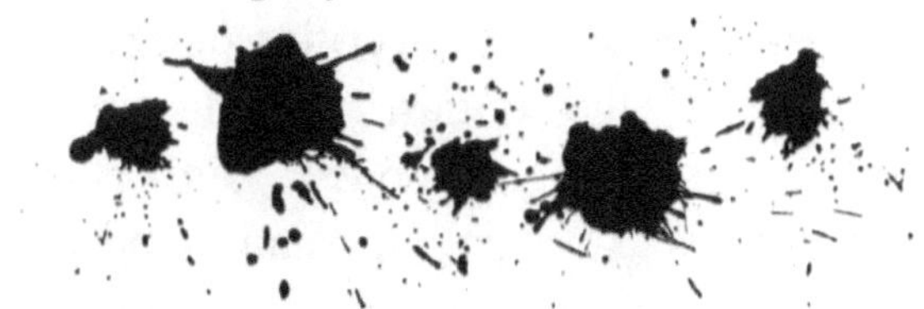

Hounds Tooth Gourmet Canine Cuisine was your basic overnight success. Louis will need to double his production facilities within the next year if sales continue to grow at this rate. He had only been in business for six months, and Wall Street investors were (pardon the pun) hounding him to allow them to be part of his future capitalization and the company's future growth earnings. In other words, they wanted a piece of the doggie pie or canine cuisine, as it were.

Louis had just finished talking to a Mr. Skip Whitehall the third, from the investment firm of Whitehall, Davis, Sanders, Getty, and Rosenbaum, one of the oldest, upper-class, snooty, top-drawer, and overall whitest firms on Wall Street. That is until two years ago when they brought in Jeffery Rosenbaum, a nice Jewish boy who proved to be a killer shark in the field of corporate takeovers.

Of course, not every one of the partners was happy about letting a Hebrew into the firm. Todd Sanders was allegedly heard to have said, "What's next, a Negro?"

Louis was playing it cautiously; he was weary, as he had, after all, had a degree in finance, so he wasn't going to fall into any of the traps set by these fast-talking crooks.

Louis looked at his watch. It was 10 a.m., and he had an appointment for a new client, Hal Shapiro, the hottest new fashion designer taking the world by storm.

He has a new line of women's high-fashion clothes made of used bicycle tires and old farm feed bags. He calls his collection *Velocifeed*. Fashion critics are excited, fervent, and rhapsodic. All the critics, with the exception of Simonetta Trudeau, editor of Vogue, said, "Shapiro's so-called collection weak, appalling, and impotent, a poor attempt by a fashion hack to try and turn crap into couture, and vice versa. Well, not on my watch."

When pushed, the Hounds Tooth doorbell makes the sound of dogs barking to the tune of Elvis Presley's *You Ain't Nothing But A Hound Dog.*

Louis opened the door to find Hal Shapiro standing with his dog Hal Shar-Payo Junior, a two-year-old Shar-Pei.

"Louis? Hi, I'm Hal Shapiro, and this is my best friend, Hal Shar-Payo Junior. Nice to meet you."

"Welcome all; please come in and make yourself comfortable."

Hal and Hal Jr. came in, and both sat on the sofa.

"You don't mind if Hal Jr. sits on the sofa, do you, Louis?"

"Hey, mi casa es su casa."

"Huh?"

"No, I don't mind. Now, Hal, what can I do for you and little Hal?"

"Hal Jr."

"Okay, what can I do for you and Hal Jr?"

"Well, me, Hal Shapiro, am interested in buying some of your yummy Canine Cuisine for Hal Jr. here. So, Louis, who do I have to fuck to make that happen?"

"Hmm, I guess that would be me, Louis Tooth."

Hal jumped up off the sofa, unbuckled his pants, pulled them down, exposing his already erect penis, and said, "All right, let's get it on!"

Louis gazed at the man standing before him, looking rather ridiculous, and began to laugh, "Hal, please put little Hal away, and I'm not talking about the dog. You asked a smart-ass remark, and I answered it."

"What the fuck!"

"Mr. Shapiro, do you or do you not want to continue? I'm a very busy man, as I'm sure you are too."

"Fine!"

"Now, Hal, I need some information about Hal Shar-Payo Junior before proceeding."

You Ain't Nothing But A Hound Dog.

"Excuse me, Hal, the doorbell."

Louis went to the door; when he opened it, there stood two men, definitely not potential clients. Both wore off-the-rack Sears Roebuck grey suits; the older one had a Clark Gable mustache, was slightly chubby, and wore a fedora. The younger one seemed to be in better shape yet average-looking. He reminded Louis a little of the actor Montgomery Clift.

The older one held out a Police badge and said, "Good morning. I'm Detective Sergeant Brown, and this is my partner, Detective Walsh. Are you Mr. Louis Tooth?"

"Yes, I am. Won't you please come in?"

"I'm with a client at the moment. Would you mind waiting in my office, Detectives? I shan't be long."

Louis guided Brown and Walsh to his office, "Please make yourselves comfortable, gentlemen; I'll be right with you."

"Thank you," Roscoe said.

The office was just as sparse as the showroom, with a black tabletop on two chrome workhorses and a black leather office chair behind the desk. For guest's seating, two black and chrome Lesley Black Waiting Room Chairs faced the desk, and behind them was one lone black credenza for files and office supplies; four cans of Hounds Tooth Gourmet Canine Cuisine were sitting on top.

Louis walked back into the showroom where Hal Shapiro was still fuming over his foolishness.

"Mr. Shapiro, Hal, would you mind terribly coming back at another time? I have the Police in my office. It seems that one of my clients is missing, and they're asking everyone he knew for any possible information that might prove helpful. I would appreciate it."

"Oh, all right." Shapiro got up, grabbed the dog leash, and he and Hal Jr. headed towards the door.

"I'll call you later today to reschedule, Hal."

The only response was the slamming of the door.

When Louis entered his office, he found Brown and Walsh talking amongst themselves.

"Sorry to keep you waiting, officers."

"Detectives," Walsh said.

"Oh, I am sorry, I meant no disrespect."

"None taken," Walsh replied.

"Now, Mr. Tooth, we understand that Mr. Alain Robertson was scheduled to meet you here last night; is that correct?"

"Yes, sir, we had an appointment for 6:30, but he never showed up. I called his apartment and spoke to his maid, Mrs. Atwood, asking about him."

"Had you met him before?"

"Yes, but he was supposed to bring his dog, Royal Tudor's Wild Irish Rose, so I could evaluate him."

"Evaluate him?"

"Yes, I evaluate each of our customer's pets to recommend which of my Canine Cuisines would be perfect for each dog."

"I see. Can you tell me when you last saw Mr. Robertson?"

Louis opened his leather-bound desk calendrer book, "Well, now let me see, ah yes, he stopped by here last Wednesday to set a meet and greet with Royal Tudor's Wild Irish Rose."

"Is it normal that people stop by to set up appointments?"

"No, he said he was in the area and thought he'd stop in and look the place over. So, we chatted for a while; then, I gave him a quick tour of the factory."

"Did he say where he was coming from or why he was in the area?"

"No, sir. Has something happened to Mr. Robertson, Detective?"

"We don't know; at the moment, he is missing. This morning, his car and dog were found at Coney Island Creek Park."

"Oh my God. I wish I could help you, Detective."

"Well, here's my card; please call me if you think of anything else," Roscoe said as he and Walsh started to leave.

"I certainly will."

"I hope you don't mind, but I just have to ask. Is it true that your dog food costs a hundred dollars a can?" Roscoe asked.

"That is correct."

"And people pay that?"

"Yes."

"Why?"

"Because Hounds Tooth Gourmet Canine Cuisine is the very best. Do you have a dog, Detective Brown?"

"I do not, but Detective Walsh does."

"What kind of dog is it, Detective Walsh, if you don't mind my asking."

"Aw, Bonzo's just a mutt, a cross between a Chihuahua and an Irish Wolf Hound."

Louis Tooth's eyes got as big as saucers, and then he looked like he had seen a ghost.

"Naw, I'm just kidding you, Mr. Tooth; he's a cross between a Labrador Retriever and a Siberian Husky. I call him a Labsky."

"Whoa, I must say you had me going there. I tell you what: Take these cans of Hounds Tooth Gourmet Canine Cuisine and see if your dog likes them," Louis said as he handed Walsh four cans.

"That's very kind of you, Mr. Tooth."

"My pleasure, Detective. And I would appreciate it if you let me know if there's any news of Mr. Robertson."

"Goodbye, Mr. Tooth."

"Goodbye, Detectives; let me show you out."

"No need, thanks again."

"So, whadda think of Mr. Tooth?" Walsh asked his partner.

"I don't know, he's a little odd, but at the moment, we got no reason to suspect him. But then again, let's not rule him out at the moment. He *was* supposed to meet Robertson, and right now, all we have is his word that they didn't meet.

"Let's get some uniforms out here to canvas this area and the crime scene and see what they can come up with."

Hal Shapiro was walking Hal Jr. across the street from the Hounds Tooth Gourmet Canine Cuisine Boutique, waiting for the Police to leave. He was standing looking in their direction as Hal Jr. decided to take a dump; Roscoe noticed the dog doing his business and observed that the man holding the leash didn't pick it up.

"Damn it!" Roscoe muttered as he pulled a U-turn in the middle of the street and stopped next to Hal Shapiro.

"Hey, buddy, pick that shit up!"

"What?"

"Your dog just shit on the sidewalk; pick it up."

Hal looked down to see the surprise that Hal Jr. had left him. Hal started patting his clothes, looking for something to pick up the steaming pile of feces.

"I'm sorry, officer, but I don't seem to have anything on me to be able to pick it up with," Hal said, smiling.

It was little things like this that irked Roscoe to no end; here's a dog owner walking his dog and doesn't come prepared for the inevitable.

Roscoe looked at Walsh and quipped, "That's it!"

"Roscoe, let it go; just give the guy a citation and forget it," Walsh said, trying to calm his partner down.

"No, this shit stops here." He said as he opened his door.

"You. Get over here."

Hal Shapiro slowly strolled over to Detective Brown, and by now, he was starting to cop an attitude, "Yeah?"

"Pick that shit up now."

"I told you I don't have anything to pick it up with."

"Look, either you pick it up, or I'm hauling your ass to jail. We'll take your dog to the shelter while you try and make bail."

By now, people were starting to gather around and watch the show.

"On what charge?"

"Littering, creating a health hazard, violation of the city leash law, and on the way to the Police station, I'll think of a couple more."

The people were cheering Roscoe on. One elderly man said, "Thank you, officer; I'm tired of stepping in dog shit just because these jerks feel that they're too good to bend over and pick up their dog's mess."

"Yeah."

"Right on!"

Hal turned to the crow and asked, "Does anyone have a plastic bag I might be able to use?"

The elderly man held up a plastic D'Agostino shopping bag that he pulled out of his old leather jacket, "Ten bucks."

"Come on, man."

"Twenty."

"Twenty?"

Vinnie brought out the chili dog and drink for Officer Harris.

"Vinnie, just add it to my tab, will ya?"

"You know, Roscoe, you're the only one in New York that we allow to run a tab. The boss said that he'd appreciate it if you went ahead and settled up; our rent is due soon."

"Ha, Ha, Very funny. You know, Vinnie, you and Walsh ought to team up; you'd be funnier than Abbott and Costello."

"Hey, Sarge, this chili dog is great."

"Told ya so. Don't listen to Walsh; he'll have you eating a steady diet of broccoli, beans, and Brussels sprouts."

After lunch, they drove back over to see Louis Tooth.

You Ain't Nothing But A Hound Dog.

Walsh glanced at Harris, looking around to see where the music came from, "Doorbell," He said.

"Catchy," Harris replied.

The door opened, and Louis Tooth stood in the doorway looking befuddled.

"Detectives?"

Roscoe stepped towards the door, "We have a couple more questions for you, Mr. Tooth. May we come in?"

"Yes, of course. Please come in; let's go into the salon since there's more of you."

Louis led them into the main room, where Louis met with the clients and their dogs.

"Please have a seat," Louis said as he sat on one of the two sofas, leaving the other sofa for his municipal guests to share.

"Now, Detective Brown, how can I help you?"

"We have an eyewitness who claims to have seen Mr. Robertson's car parked outside this building last night around 6 pm."

"Really? Well, like I said, Mr. Robertson wasn't due here until 6:30. At six o'clock, I believe, I was in the back, where the processing machines are. They are very loud, and it is possible that I was back there checking the machines when Mr. Robertson came by. Would you care to see the factory?"

"If it wouldn't be too much of an inconvenience."

"No, not at all. Gentlemen."

Louis was initially nervous, but now he felt this would prove he couldn't have killed Robertson.

The moment he opened the door, the sound was quite overpowering. They saw two male butchers wearing protective headphones cracking, hacking, and whacking bones, hunks of meat, body parts, and organs, and draining blood. The machines had been positioned one next to the other to be an efficient assembly line, going from large hunks and chunks of meat through four machines, finally producing the finished canned product.

"You can see it's very noisy back here!" Louis shouted.

"Mind if we look around!" Roscoe yelled back.

Louis shook his head no.

So, Walsh, Harris, and Roscoe walked around the factory floor. As they looked around, Walsh noticed that Roscoe seemed to have found something; Roscoe gave him a nod, wanting Walsh to distract Louis from observing Roscoe picking something up from the floor.

Walsh approached Louis and asked, "So, how many cans can you produce in a day?"

"Depends, but on average, about a hundred cans," Louis said proudly.

Finally, Roscoe gestured that he had seen enough, so they all returned to the salon.

"Were those men here at 6:30 last night, Mr. Tooth?"

"No, they leave at five. I go back there occasionally after they leave to ensure the machines are properly calibrated. Ralph and Jose are excellent butchers, but I like to check on the equipment personally every week."

"So, you have no one to collaborate your alibi?"

"I'm afraid not, Detective."

"After you finished in the back, did you look outside to see if Robertson was waiting?"

"No, after I finished checking the machines, I went into my office to do some billing; by the time I thought to look at my watch, it was after eight, so I called Robertson's home and spoke to the maid."

"Mrs. Atwood."

"Yes, I believe that was her name."

"Well, I guess that's all for now. If we think of anything else to ask, would it be all right to stop by?

"Sure, anytime, Detective."

It wasn't until they were in the squad car that Walsh asked, "So, what did you find?"

Roscoe held up a shirt button, "It looks like an expensive button, not the type that a butcher or even Mr. Tooth could afford. Harris, let's head back to the station."

Sitting in the front seat, Walsh turned back to Roscoe and said, "When we get back, I'll see Mrs. Atwood and see if she can remember what Robertson was wearing. I'll also check his wardrobe to see if any other shirts have similar buttons."

Roscoe handed the button to Walsh to examine, "I've never seen a button like this. I'll run it down to the lab before I go."

"I'll go and check in with the Captain and give him an update."

"How about me, Sarge?" Harris asked.

"You go with Walsh as backup just in case old Mrs. Atwood gets rowdy."

When they reached the 60th precinct on West 8th Street, Walsh and Harris went to the crime lab while Roscoe went upstairs to Captain O'Rourke.

"Come in," O'Rourke said, responding to the knock on the door.

"Captain, got a minute?" Roscoe asked.

"Ah, Roscoe, come in, come in."

Roscoe sat down across from the Captain's desk.

"Just wanted to keep you up to speed on the possible homicide of Alain Robertson. As you know, his abandoned car and his dog were found in Coney Island Creek Park yesterday morning. There was blood in the car that the lab tells me is a match for Mr. Robertson."

"Suspects?"

"Well, the investigation is still early, but we may have someone of interest. A Mr. Louis Tooth, owner of the Hounds Tooth Gourmet Canine Cuisine company, here on Neptune Avenue."

"Yeah, that's one of the rare Chinese dogs; musta cost you a ton of dough. You can afford it."

Hal looked at Roscoe for some sort of help. Nothing.

"Look, do you want the bag or not?" The old man said as he started to put the bag back into his pocket.

"No, I guess I'll take it."

The people gathered were laughing and cheering as Hal Shapiro gave the old man twenty dollars for a plastic bag.

Hal took the bag and bent down to pick up the pile when the old man said, "Oh, by the way, I think it has a hole in it, so be careful."

Which brought more cheers, jeers, and laughter. Hal silently endured the humiliation, scooped up the feces, and looked at Roscoe, who pointed to a dog refuse station. Hal walked over, deposited the bag into the receptacle, and returned to where Roscoe was waiting. "Okay, okay, everyone, go about your business, the shows over. And as for you, let this be a lesson on being a responsible dog owner. Got it?"

"Got it."

Roscoe walked to the driver's side and got into the car; Walsh turned to him and said, "Feel better?"

"As a matter of fact, I do."

"Good, now let's go solve a murder."

"Yes, dear," Roscoe said sarcastically.

Louis had observed the interaction between the Detectives and Shapiro, and he could tell that Shapiro was pissed, having been embarrassed and humiliated twice in the span of an hour. Then he saw something that outraged him, Shapiro taking his anger out on Hal Junior; he kicked the poor thing. Cruelty towards poor, defenseless animals, especially pure breeds, was where Louis drew the line. Hal Shapiro was a dead man walking.

Louis felt that he got away with murder once; he could do it again. Besides, they can only execute you once. And even if they did catch him, all he needed was one dog person on the jury, and he'd walk out a free man.

Louis would wait until Hal called him to set up another appointment, then he would have him meet him for lunch, lure him to the Boutique, and send Hal the way of Alain Robertson.

He didn't have to wait long; it was half an hour later when the phone rang.

"Did you see what those fucking cops did to me?" Hal ranted.

"No, what happened?" Louis lied.

"It was so humiliating."

"What, did they hit you?"

"I wish. Hal Junior made a little mess on the sidewalk across from your shop, and they made a federal case out of it."

"What did they do?"

"They made me, Hal Shapiro pick up dog poo. Me, who will be showing at fashion week. I wish I had gotten their badge numbers. It was just awful!"

"Listen, just forget about it. How about I take you out for lunch tomorrow, whadda say?"

"Let's see; tomorrow's Saturday. Okay, sure."

"Great, meet me at Gargiulo's. We'll have a nice Italian meal; then I'll take us back to my place to give you a behind-the-scenes tour of the place."

"Super, what time?"

"One-ish?"

"One-ish it is. Thanks, Louis, you're a dear. Bye."

"Bye, Hal, see you tomorrow."

Officer Harris knew where he would find Roscoe and Detective Walsh. Odds were that they were having lunch at the Nathans Famous hotdog stand on Riegelmann Boardwalk. Roscoe and Walsh were sitting on the Boardwalk, enjoying their lunch. It was a picture-perfect day, not too hot and sunny, with a mild breeze blowing in from the Lower Bay.

Roscoe had had lunch there every day for over fifteen years. It's always the same order: two chilidogs, crinkle-cut French fries, and a cup of Joe, black. In fact, on the menu board, you can order that combo just by saying, "I'll have the Roscoe Brown."

Detective Walsh would only allow himself the occasional trip to Nathans; he was still young enough and single to want to watch his weight. Roscoe wasn't fat, just a little, as he would like to say, "jolly."

Detective Sergeant Roscoe Brown was born and raised in Coney Island. He joined the NYPD right out of Queens College, City University of New York. He graduated at the top of his class and majored in Political Science. At one point, he thought of getting into politics, but after talking to a representative from the NYPD on career day, he signed up then and there.

He'd been a cop for twenty-one years, the last fifteen in homicide, and rated as one of the best in the city, partially because of his photographic memory. Roscoe has won dozens of citations and commendations for service above and beyond the call of duty and heroism. He once saved a fellow officer's life at his peril and was wounded. He'd won the respect of his peers and superiors and had been partnered with Jimmy Walsh for the last ten years. They were usually brought in for the strange and special cases, the hard ones and high-profile ones.

"Hey, Jimmy, look who's coming. Officer Harris, want a chili dog?"

"Yeah, thanks."

Roscoe waved his arm to get Vinnie the counterman's attention, "Yo, Vinnie, a chili dog with the works for my friend and a lemonade."

"Hey, thanks, Sarge."

"Sure, got to get you trained right."

"Don't listen to him, Harris; he's just trying to corrupt you." Walsh pleaded.

Roscoe waved dismissively at his partner, "Phooey, What's cooking, rookie?"

"Well, we did a block by block down around Neptune Avenue, and someone, a Mr. Hodgekiss, thinks he remembers seeing a black Town Car parked in front of the dog food store at about 6 pm."

Roscoe looked at Walsh and said, "Woof, woof. I think we need to go back to your supplier's doggie shop and have another chat with Mr. Hounds Tooth."

"Tooth? What an odd name. Well, maybe I should say unusual; odd is a bit derogatory. Nevertheless, what makes him a person of interest?"

"Robertson was supposed to meet with Mr. Tooth last night, but according to Tooth, Robertson never showed. The problem is that we have an eyewitness claiming to have seen the victim's car parked in front of the Hounds Tooth building around the time of their appointment. Tooth claims that he was checking some equipment in the factory at the back of the building and couldn't have heard anyone at the front door due to the noise in the factory."

"And?"

"And, this afternoon, we went back to question Tooth again, and while we were there, I discovered a rather unusual button that I believe may have come from Mr. Robertson. We're having the boys in the lab check it out."

"Any other suspects?"

"Not at the moment, but like I said, it's early."

"Well, it sounds like you got it covered. I appreciate the update. Let me know if things change, Roscoe."

"Will do, chief."

Roscoe headed to the detective's squad rooms and to his office. When he got there, Walsh and Harris were waiting.

"What's up?"

Walsh handed the button to Brown, "Bingo."

"What?"

"It's made of corozo, a 100% natural product consistent with a hard resin. It's referred to as "vegetable ivory." It is known for its unique pattern that, much like a fingerprint, no two buttons are exactly alike."

"Expensive?"

"Well, not super expensive, although it's sold in the higher-end stores, not in Sears or JCPenney's, and places like that."

"Okay, go check out Roberson's wardrobe; then I guess we'll need to see if Tooth has any shirts missing a button like this, or at least does he have any shirts with corozo buttons? That means a search warrant, shit."

"Why shit?" Asked Harris.

"Right now, we're pretty thin on evidence; Hell, we don't even have a body. So, to go ask a Judge for a search warrant might be hard, plus I don't want to tip my hand to Tooth too early." Roscoe explained.

"Well, first things first. Harris and I are off to see Mrs. Atwood." Walsh said.

Louis was standing under the blood-red awning of Gargiulo's Restaurant on 15th Street, just off Mermaid Avenue, waiting for Hal Shapiro.

Unbeknownst to Louis, Gargiulo's fine dining restaurant just happens to be located one block north of Detective Sergeant Roscoe Brown's favorite greasy spoon hotdog stand, Nathan's Famous, which, on most nice days, he walks to from the Police station.

And so, it was that Roscoe was strolling down 15th Street on his way to enjoy the "Roscoe Brown" special when he spied Louis Tooth out of the corner of his detective's eye.

There was a Chinese laundry, an apartment building, and a small Jewish delicatessen on the side of the street where Roscoe was walking. He ducked into the deli to keep an eye on Tooth. A little old Jewish man came over to Roscoe, the deli owner, "Can I help you?"

Roscoe flashed his badge, "Police, I won't be but a few minutes."

"How about a nice corned beef on rye?"

"No thanks."

"Pastrami?"

"No."

"Chop chicken liver?"

"No, I told you, I'm on the job."

"Maybe a nice bowl of matzah ball soup?"

"No."

"Oh, I know; how about a nice black and white cookie?"

"Fine, I'll pick it up on my way out. Now leave me alone."

Roscoe saw a man, who he thought was an obvious homosexual, meet Louis under the restaurant canopy. They shook hands and entered the restaurant.

Hal Shapiro wore a suit made from used bicycle tires and feed bags from his latest collection. Unfortunately for Louis Tooth, the image of that man was one that Detective Sergeant Brown, with his photographic memory, would never forget.

Roscoe started to leave the deli when the old man said, "Don't forget your cookie."

"Right."

Roscoe slipped the cookie into his coat pocket and made his way down to Nathan's.

The hostess greeted Louis and Hal, "Hello, table for two?"

"Yes, and could we have a booth, please?" Louis asked.

They followed the hostess through a maze of tables until she led them to a booth in the back of the restaurant.

"How's this?"

"Perfect, thank you," Louis said.

She handed each a menu, "Enjoy your meals." She said as she walked away.

"So, what's good here?" Hal asked with his head buried in the menu.

"How about we start with some escarole?" Louis suggested.

"Snails?" You're joking, right? Naw, how about some of that fried zucchini?"

Louis smiled and said, "Sure, sounds good."

Louis looked at Hal Shapiro sitting across from him dressed like a poor man's Michelin Man and thought, not only is he a dog abuser, but a no-class cretin.

The tuxedo-clad waiter came to the table and asked, "Good afternoon, gentlemen. My name is Mario, and I'll be taking care of you today. What can I get you to drink?"

"You got beer?"

"Yes, sir."

"I'll have a Bud."

"And for you, sir?"

"I'll have a glass of the Marchese Antinori."

"Very good, sir. I'll go place your order and be back shortly to take your lunch order."

"Hal, I was sorry to hear about your run-in with the Police the other day."

"Yeah, now I understand why people call them pigs. They humiliated me, me Hal Shapiro. It was all that stupid Hal Juniors fault."

"Well, you can't blame Hal Junior; he just did what comes naturally. You know when you got to go, you got to go." Louis tried to make light of a bad situation.

"Damn, dog."

Mario, the waiter, brought the drinks and asked, "Now, what can I get you gentlemen to eat?"

Louis looked at his guest and asked, "Hal, do you know what you want?"

"Yeah, I'll have the spaghettini tomato sauce with two meatballs and two sausages."

"The side is either the meatballs or the sausages, sir."

"So, I want them both," Hal demanded.

"Yes, sir, no problem. And for you?"

Louis looked at Mario, shrugged his shoulders, and ordered, "I'll have the zuppa di pesce."

"Excellent choice. I'll place the orders right away. Would you care for some bread?"

"Yes, please," Louis said.

"Very good; I'll be right back with the bread."

"So, Hal, how is Hal Junior?"

"Oh, he's fine. I have him tethered outside on my terrace."

That's rather cruel, don't you think?"

"No, you've got to teach them who's boss!"

"Well, after lunch, we'll go to the Boutique, and I'll give you the special VIP tour."

"What's so special about it?"

"Ahh, you'll see."

When Detective Walsh found him sitting on the Boardwalk, Roscoe was finishing off the second of his two chilidogs.

"Jimmy! So, what's the good word?"

"Corozo."

"Yeah?"

"All of Robertson's shirts have corozo buttons, all of them," Walsh said, smiling.

"Here, have a seat," Roscoe said as he moved his fedora so Walsh could share the bench.

"That is good news. Guess who I saw over at Gargiulo's on my way here?"

"Well, either Robertson or Tooth and my money is on Tooth."

"Right, you are. He met some nutcase, all dressed in what looked to me to be old bike tires and canvas bags."

"Weird."

"Yeah, he must be some sort of musician, rock star, or artist. I don't know, but he was weird."

"Maybe he's one of those performing artists, doing one of those "happenings?"

"Happenings?"

"Yeah, it's a performance or situation art that so-called artists do that is usually unannounced in advance."

"Have you ever seen one of these happenings?"

"No, I've only read about them."

"Where?"

"In the Times."

"Ah, the Times. Well, excuse me."

"Roscoe, I keep telling you, you should read more than just the Post."

"Hey, I read more than just the Post."

"I don't mean the Daily News."

"Oh yeah, well, I watch Walter Cronkite, so there!"

"I'm proud of you. So, whadda want to do about Tooth?"

"Let's go see if we can get a warrant."

Roscoe finished up the rest of his fries, and they began walking back to the station house.

"Say, I meant to ask you, how did Bonzo like the hundred-dollar dog food?" Roscoe asked.

"He loved them; he scoffed it down in seconds. Now I'm scared."

"Scared? About what?"

"That he won't go back to eating the cheap stuff."

"Walsh, he's a dog! They eat cat shit, for God's sake."

Hal Shapiro lay dead on the factory floor with a meat cleaver stuck so deep into his head that Louis couldn't pull it out, so he just left it there.

Louis lifted his lifeless body onto the butcher's table that resembled the medical examiners' type of autopsy tables. The table had a slight tilt so the blood would run downhill to the drain.

The first thing Louis did was to disrobe the corpse; he placed the rubber and canvas suit in the incinerator along with his underwear and shoes. He decided to wait before turning on the furnace until he was done "canning" Mr. Shapiro due to the smell of rubber burning. Best done at night, he thought.

He used a bone saw to dismember the arms, legs, and head; then, he made several passes of Hal Shapiro's torso through the band saw to enable the parts to fit into the grinding machines.

It wasn't until he had most of the torso turned into ground round that he heard, *You Ain't Nothing But A Hound Dog.*

He looked up at the wall clock at 5:45. He ignored it, thinking whoever it was would go away, but they didn't.

Again, *You Ain't Nothing But A Hound Dog.*

Then came a pounding on the door. Louis quickly removed his rubber vinyl butcher's apron, put on his suit jacket, ran a comb through his hair, and went to answer the door.

"Detective Sergeant Brown, what can I do for you?"

Roscoe stood there along with Detective Walsh and several uniformed Police Officers.

"Mr. Tooth, I have a search warrant for your home and this premises. Please step aside." Roscoe said, holding a folded piece of paper up into the air and then handing it to Louis.

Louis was pushed aside by the onslaught of Police entering the Boutique.

Roscoe tried to open the door to the factory and found that it was locked.

"What is this all about?"

Roscoe didn't answer. Instead, he asked, "Where is the key to the factory door, Mr. Tooth."

Louis feigned, looking for the key, and patted his suit pockets, "I must have left it at home."

"Officer Wilson, break it down."

Officer Tyrone Wilson, a 325-pound African American, played defensive tackle for the New York Giants from 1959 through 1963 and helped the Giants win three consecutive Eastern Division titles. He played alongside Giants greats Y. A. Tittle and Sam Huff until, during the NFL Championship Games against the Chicago Bears, he blew out his knee on the last play of the game, losing to the Bears 14 - 10.

Wilson blew through that door like he did with half the offensive lines he played against. Once inside, everyone stood in stone-cold silence. Human remains still lying on the butcher's table along with Hal Shapiro's two legs and left arm, his right arm sticking out of what Roscoe would later refer to as the "Glop-a-dee Glop Machine."

Roscoe turned to Walsh and said, "Book 'em, and call the ME and CSI; tell them to get down here stat!"

Tooth had been sitting in interrogation room one for two hours before Roscoe and Walsh entered.

The Detectives sat down on the opposite side of a wooden table where Louis Tooth sat.

Roscoe read Louis his Miranda Rights, "Louis Tooth, you have the right to remain silent. Anything you say can and will be used against you in a court of law. You have the right to an attorney. If you cannot afford an attorney, one will be provided for you. Do you understand these rights as I have described them to you?"

"Yes."

"Would you like an attorney?"

"What will happen to Giulia?"

"Who's Giulia?"

"He's my four-year-old Spinone bitch."

"Would you like an attorney, Mr. Tooth?"

"No. If you let me say goodbye to Mona Lisa, I'll tell you everything."

"You want that we should bring your dog, Mona Lisa, here to the Police Station?" Walsh asked.

"Yes, and then I'll tell you everything."

Roscoe looked at Walsh and said to Louis, "Will you excuse us for a minute, Mr. Tooth?"

The Detectives got up and left the room.

Roscoe said, "Go get the dog.

"You sure?"

"Yeah, if it'll help him confess, why not?"

"Okay."

Roscoe returned to the room and sat down, "Mr. Tooth, Detective Walsh is going to get Giulia; in the meantime, is there anything you'd like while you wait?"

"No, thank you."

"Okay, just sit tight. I'll be back shortly."

When Roscoe stepped into the hall, standing outside the interrogation room stood Captain O'Rourke.

"Has he confessed?"

"He's indicated that he will but wants to have his dog in the room."

"What?"

"He said he'll give a full confession if we allow him to see his dog. So, I've sent Walsh to collect the dog and bring her here."

"You don't think he's going to try to claim that the dog is telling him what to do, do you?"

"No, Captain, I think he knows he's going away for a long time and will never see his dog again."

"Okay, but if you think he's heading for an insanity defense, shut it down ASAP."

"Will do, Captain."

"Ah, just curious, what kind of dog does he have?"

"A Spinone."

"Spinone, I thought that was some kind of ice cream."

"You're thinking of spumoni."

"That's what I thought I just said."

"No, Spinone, the dog, is pronounced *spee no nee*, whereas the ice cream is pronounced *spoo moe nee*. See?"

"Spumoni, Spinone, whatever, just so he confesses."

"Yes, sir."

Walsh brought the dog into the interrogation room and let it off its leash; she immediately ran over to Louis and started wagging her tail and licking her master.

After a few minutes, Roscoe said, "Okay, Mr. Tooth, we brought Giulia to see you, so now we'd like to hear about Mr. Roberson and Mr. Shapiro.

"All right."

Roscoe punched the record button on the video camera recorder, "This Detective Sergeant Roscoe Brown, Detective James Walsh, and suspect Louis Tooth; it's Saturday, August 30th, 1966, ten pm.?

Roscoe gestured for Tooth to begin.

"My name is Louis Tooth Jr., and I own Hounds Tooth Gourmet Canine Cuisine."

"Now, Mr. Tooth, would you please tell me what happened to Alain Robertson," Roscoe asked.

"Well, about a week ago, Mr. Robertson came to my boutique to discuss my supplying his dog, Royal Tudor's Wild Irish Rose, with some of my gourmet canine cuisine

"What happened?"

"Everything was going swimmingly when all of a sudden Rose, that's what people call Royal Tudor's Wild Irish Rose for short, anyway Rose was being naughty, nothing egregious, just doing what dogs do when they're curious in new surroundings. But I digress; Robertson got upset and angry; he started yelling at the poor thing and even struck her. Well, sir, I cannot abide violence against an animal, so at first, I tried to calm him down, but the more I did, the more belligerent he got; he put his hands on me and tried to choke me. He would have killed me if it wasn't for Rose. You see, in all the excitement; she bit him on the ass, which allowed me to grab a can of *Kentucky Derby Winners Blend* and whack him in the head. I must have hit him in the temple because he dropped like a stone."

"How many times did you hit him?"

"Not sure, maybe six or seven."

"Why didn't you call the Police after you had hit him? After all, it was self-defense?"

"I was concerned that you might have found out about the others."

"Others? There were others?"

"Oh, my yes."

"How many others?"

"All tolled?"

"Please."

"Over a dozen."

"You've killed over a dozen men?"

"Not just men."

"You've killed women, too?"

"Of course. You see, Detective Brown, I don't believe in discriminating against women. I treat them all equally."

"That's very commendable, Mr. Tooth."

"But, why did you kill them, Mr. Tooth?"

"Because they mistreated their dogs, I mean right in front of me. This aggression will not stand, Detective Brown. They had to die, don't you see?"

"I'm sorry, I don't."

"It was the great Mahatma Gandhi of India who said, *"The greatness of a nation and its moral progress can be judged by the way its animals are treated."*

"But you killed these people, Mr. Tooth."

"Do you know that the word DOG spelled backward is GOD! I think that tells you everything there is to say about the subject."

Louis Tooth Jr. went on to describe in detail the names and circumstances of each of his victims. He was particularly proud that those guilty of cruelty to dogs would end up doing something positive for them, one can at a time.

The newspapers had a field day with the story; there were some outrageous headlines:

"Big Dogs Eat Fat Cats."

"We put a little bit of you in every can."

"You mistreat them, then we feed them, You!"

"Once a meanie, now a weenie."

The trial lasted two and a half weeks. And in the end, Louis Tooth was found guilty of fourteen counts of murder. He was sentenced to 150 years in Attica. He'll be up for parole after 99 years served.

Roscoe took Walsh to Nathan's Famous for a couple of celebratory chili dogs. Sitting out on the Boardwalk, people watching, Roscoe asked, "So, whadda think?"

"I think he's lucky not to have gotten the electric chair."

"Lucky? If it were me, I'd prefer the electric chair to spend the rest of your life in prison."

"Really?"

"You know Jimmy, a female dog is called a bitch, and some say that life's a bitch, but in Attica, poor Louis Tooth is definitely going to be somebody's bitch."

THE END

302

The Case of the Alphabet Killer

Detective Sergeant Roscoe Brown and his wife, Betty, had just sat down in their favorite pizza joint, Totonno's Pizzeria Napolitana. Totonno's happens to be a Coney Island landmark since the 1920s; it also happens to be two blocks from Roscoe's apartment.

Roscoe and Betty are regulars, eating there at least twice a week, and just like with Nathan's Famous, Roscoe is a creature of habit, as his motto is: go with what you know.

"Hey, Antonio, how ya doing?" Roscoe asked Antonio Totonno Pero, the owner and founder.

"Ima good, Roscoe, my friend, and la Bellissima Betty, how are you tonight?"

"We're doing good, and you?"

"Bene molto bene. Hey, don't tell me you want one large pepperoni pizza. Am I right, or am I right?"

"Right, as usual, my friend."

"She's a coming right up."

"Oh, and two Knickerbocker beers."

"I gotta two chilled mugs just for you."

"Antonio, you're the best."

"Grazie."

Halfway through the pizza, Roscoe ordered another round of beers; after all, it was Friday night, and he was due to be off Saturday. Roscoe and Betty sat at the small table, looking out the large plate glass window, watching everyone walking by the pizzeria on a lazy summer evening.

"Can I get you kids anything else?" Antonio asked.

"No, grazie, it was perfetto as usual."

Roscoe paid the check, and on their way out, Betty waved and said, "Grazie arrivederci."

As they approached their apartment building, Roscoe noticed a Police car sitting out front.

"God damnit."

"What's wrong, babe?" Betty asked.

"It's Walsh. Somebody's dead."

Roscoe's partner, Detective James Walsh, got out as they approached the car.

"Hey Betty, how are you?" Walsh asked.

"Fine, it's good to see you, Jimmy," Betty answered.

"I hate to drag him away, but duty calls."

Roscoe kissed Betty and said, "Don't wait up for me, babe; I'll probably be late."

"Sorry, Betty," Walsh said.

"I'm used to it. We'll have to have you over for dinner soon."

"I would like that, thank you."

"Bye, babe," Betty said as she entered the apartment building.

Roscoe got into the back seat, Walsh took shotgun, and rookie Police Officer Ron Harris was behind the wheel.

"Okay, Harris, let's rock and roll."

"Right, Sarge."

Harris put the 1965 green and white Plymouth Fury into drive and punched it. Car 2086 sped off, lights flashing and siren blaring.

"Hey, Harris, turn that siren off; I can't hear myself think." Shouted Roscoe.

"Sorry, Sarge."

"Rookies!"

"I'm sorry."

"It's okay, kid. We were all rookies once ourselves. Maybe next time."

"Thanks, Sarge."

"Now, whadda we got, Walsh?" Roscoe asked.

"Francis Franklin, male, black, forty-three years old, married, father of two girls. He was a mechanic with the Coney Island Metro System; he worked at the Overhaul Shop on Shell Road. He lives at 2770 Amalgamated Warbasse Houses, number 4."

"Yeah. They're those red brick buildings next to the Neptune Avenue F train station."

"Right, that's where he was shot as he was heading home from the train stop. He was shot twice in the head from behind."

"He was shot in the station?"

"No, he had just gotten to the street and was stepping into the adjacent parking lot of the apartments when he was shot."

"Execution style?"

"No, more random-like."

"Anybody see or hear anything?"

"Haven't found anyone yet. The unis are still canvassing the buildings."

When they arrived, Harris parked the car and expected his job to sit and watch the car. He was surprised when Roscoe said, "Come on, rookie, you're not going to learn anything sitting there in the squad car."

"Yes, sir!" Harris said gleefully as he rolled out of old 2086. When he caught up with them, Roscoe and Walsh were half a block from Harris. Roscoe looked at Walsh and said, "Five bucks says he didn't lock the car doors." Before Walsh could reply, they heard Harris say under his breath, "Ah shit." as he turned around and ran back to lock the car doors.

The medical examiner and the folks from the crime lab were still there, finishing up. Roscoe went to see the ME first.

"Hey, Doc. What's the word?" Roscoe asked.

"Well, Roscoe, it appears that Mr. Franklin was fatally wounded by two gunshots to the back of the head; the time of death's approximately 8 pm this evening." Doctor Olsen, the Chief Medical Officer for Coney Island, said.

"Anything else, Doc?"

"Not at the moment. I'll know more after the autopsy."

"Okay, thanks, Doc."

Roscoe wandered over to where Harris, Walsh, and CSI David Bowles were deep in conversation. Bowles spots Roscoe walking his way, "Hey, Roscoe."

"David, what have you got for me?"

"Not much, Roscoe, a couple .9mm casings, possible footprints, and a cigar butt. As you can see, we've cordoned off this grassy area and shut down the stop, which is pissing a lot of people off.

"We're almost done processing the subway stop and will open it up in a couple of hours, but we'll resume searching the grassy area tomorrow morning when it's light. And as usual, we'll have a uniformed officer watching over the area until we return."

"We'll be here sometime in the morning. Thanks, Dave."

Roscoe and the other officers knocked on over a hundred doors and spoke to dozens of people, all of whom said the same thing: I didn't see or hear anything. I don't know nothing.

Roscoe's and Detective Walsh's job was to inform Mrs. Franklin about the tragedy that had befallen her husband of eighteen years. It was, without a doubt, the shittiest part of being a homicide cop.

Roscoe and Walsh approached Mrs. Franklin's apartment, with half the residents standing in the hallway watching.

"People, please, there's nothing to see; return to your apartments. Show a little respect, huh." Roscoe said as Walsh knocked on Franklin's door.

The door creaked open to reveal a young African American girl in her early teens peering out at them.

"Hello, I'm Detective Sergeant Brown, and this is my partner Detective Walsh. Is your mother home?"

The young girl opened the door, "Please come in. I'll go get my mother."

The apartment looked clean and tidy; the furnishings were modest but tasteful. Walsh and Roscoe sat alone on the sofa when Mrs. Franklin entered the living room. Both detectives stood up, and Roscoe removed his fedora.

She sat opposite the sofa in an overstuffed, flowered, upholstered wingback chair. She looked at Roscoe, "What's happened?"

"Mrs. Franklin, I'm Detective Sergeant Roscoe, and this is my partner, Detective James Walsh; there is no easy way to say this: I'm so sorry to tell you that your husband has been found, shot, and killed."

She just sat there staring out the window, not saying a word, not crying, nothing.

"Mrs. Franklin, is there someone you would like us to call?"

"No, thank you." She said, void of emotion.

"Maybe one of your neighbors, perhaps?"

She just shook her head no.

"Mrs. Franklin, I really don't think you should be alone at this time."

"Mr. Roscoe, you don't have to worry about me. I am not alone; I have my Lord Jesus to comfort me," She said as a tear started falling from her cheek.

"Would you like us to talk to your children?"

"No sir, that won't be necessary. I appreciate you all coming by to tell me."

"Well, Mrs. Franklin, is there anyone you can think of who would have wanted to hurt Francis? Anyone at work?"

"Oh, no, sir, my Francis was a good Christian. You go down there to the shop and talk to anyone; they'll tell you Francis was a good Christian man."

"Yes, ma'am, we will. Here's my card; if you need anything or can think of anything, no matter how small, please feel free to call me, all right?"

"Yes, sir, Mr. Roscoe, I surely will."

"Well, don't get up; we'll see ourselves out, and again we're so sorry for your loss."

As they were ready to leave, the young girl standing at the front door whispered, "Is my daddy really dead?"

"I'm sorry, darling," Roscoe said.

"Will you catch the man who did this?"

"You have my word." Detective Walsh answered.

As they were riding back to the station, Roscoe said, "Be careful what you promise, Jimmy. This one's going to be a tough one to solve."

"Hey, I have faith in you, Roscoe."

"Me? You gave her your word."

"Well, I meant our word."

"Thanks a lot."

Captain O'Rourke was getting ready to leave his office when Roscoe and Walsh passed by, heading to their offices.

"Roscoe!"

"Yes, Captain?" Roscoe answered.

"Whadda got on the Franklin murder?"

"Not much; we're going to my office to go over what we have."

"Keep me posted."

"Will do, Captain. Night."

"Good night," O'Rourke said as he turned off the lights in his office.

Walsh and Roscoe settled in to go over the list of evidence and a pile of photos sitting on Roscoe's desk that CSI took earlier at the scene and of Francis Franklin's body.

Officer Harris joined them with all the statements that officers took from neighbors and tenants of the building.

After two hours of pouring over everything they had laid out before them, Roscoe said, "Well, we got jack shit at the moment; let's hope there's something at the scene we may have overlooked. Let's call it a day and get back to it tomorrow."

Roscoe put on his sport coat and signature fedora, nodded to Harris and Walsh, and said, "Officer Harris, would you be so kind as to provide Detective Walsh and me transportation to our humble abodes?"

"Huh?"

"Give us a ride home."

"Sure, Sarge, why didn't you say so."

It was after 2 am when Roscoe crawled into bed.

"How'd it go?" Betty asked, half asleep.

"Go to sleep; it's not for you, baby."

She turned her back to him and whispered, "Come and cuddle with me."

He rolled over and pressed his body next to her warm body; they were a perfect fit. They fell asleep, pressed tightly next to each other, and six hours later, they woke up precisely in the same position. He nuzzled close to her ear and said, "Feeling frisky?"

Betty gave a low moan, "Mmmmm."

Roscoe started to slide his hand under her nightgown top when the phone rang.

"Let it ring." She said, sliding her hand into his pajama bottoms.

"Mmm, okay." He said as he tried to help her take off her nightgown with his left hand while simultaneously trying to remove his pajama bottoms with his right.

They were in the throes of passion when the doorbell rang.

"God damnit!" Roscoe yelled as he jumped out of bed and stomped to the door.

"Yeah? Who the Hell is it!" Roscoe shouted.

"Roscoe, it's me, Walsh. We got another."

"Gimme ten minutes." He said.

Then, looking back into the bedroom and seeing Betty still lying naked on the bed, he said, "Make that fifteen."

"Ulysses Urlacher, male, Caucasian, fifty-three, single, an ER nurse at Coney Island Hospital. He was found this morning at the bus stop at Meucci Square on Avenue U, with two what looks to be 9 mm shots to the back of the head." Walsh said.

"Just like Franklin. What was Urlacher doing at Meucci Square?" Roscoe asked.

"He was going home after his graveyard shift at the hospital."

"Time of death?"

"Well, his shift was over at 4 am, so probably between 4:30 and 5, I'm guessing."

"And, of course, nobody saw anything."

"No, we may have caught a break. The unis spoke to a photographer who was shooting night scenes of Coney Island and thinks he may have gotten a shot of our shooter."

"No shit?"

"Yep, an officer has taken him back to his studio to develop the film."

"Outstanding. Let's go to the scene and talk to the ME; then, we'll head over to talk to the photographer and see how lucky we are."

By the time Roscoe and Walsh got to Meucci Square, the Police had the whole intersection blocked off, making the already cranky New Yorkers even more cranky.

Avenue U and 86th Street is a major intersection in Coney Island; with all the Police cars, ambulances, CSI, and medical examiner vehicles parked, it looked more like a city parking lot than an intersection.

After talking to the ME and the boys from the crime lab, it was evident that there wasn't much physical evidence to be found at the scene.

"Jimmy, why don't you and Harris go to the Overhaul Shop on Shell Road, talk to Franklin's co-workers and boss, and see what you can find out? I'm going to walk over to Urlacher's home and nose around; he only lives a couple of blocks from here."

"Okay," Walsh said.

Looking at his watch, Roscoe said, "Let's meet at that photographer's studio at two."

"Right, we'll see you at two. Come on, Harris."

Roscoe walked east on Avenue U for one block, then turned north on West 11th Street until he got to 2046, a modest red brick two-story house with a coral red handrail out front.

Roscoe walked up the six steps to the front door and rang the doorbell, no answer. He took the keys that the coroner found on Urlacher's body and opened the door.

"Hello! This is the Police. Is there anyone in the house? Please announce yourself."

Nothing.

Roscoe first went upstairs to the master bedroom; the bed was made, and the room was well organized, not what Roscoe had seen in the past from single men. Usually, single men are rather casual, but Mr. Urlacher is quite the opposite.

The rest of the house was the same, very neat and organized. Tastefully decorated, manly but not testosterone-heavy, a rare mixture of macho with just a hint of femininity. Roscoe found no threatening letters or other items that would lead Detective Brown to think Mr. Urlacher was in imminent danger.

He did find a personal phone book and found the number for the victim's mother and father, who lived in Olathe, Kansas. He called and broke the news to Urlacher's father and requested that they plan on coming to New York to identify and claim their son's body. He told him that it was way too early in the investigation for an arrest, but there were several leads that they were following. He lied since they didn't have many leads. They only had the one, a photographer who thought that he might have a photo of the suspect.

By the time Roscoe had finished talking to Urlacher's father, it was 1:30, just enough time to make it to the photographer's studio in lower Manhattan.

The sign on the loft door read James Young, Commercial Photographer. The door was unlocked, so Roscoe went in; the room was cavernous, with polished wooden floors with 20-foot ceilings. One whole wall had floor-to-ceiling windows; on the opposite wall was a small kitchen with a long wooden table surrounded by eight directors' chairs for client meetings. In the middle of the room was a box of thousands of what looked to Roscoe to be dead roaches next to a can of bug spray surrounded by several lights along with a Hasselblad camera mounted on a heavy-duty tripod pointing a very long lens at the insects.

A Police Officer was sitting at the wooden table, looking a bit squeamish.

"You're not looking too good there, Officer Wilson. Not feeling well?" Roscoe asked.

"It's those roaches; they're giving me the creeps. I swear they're not all dead; I've seen some of them move. Nasty little fuckers."

Roscoe walked over to the set-up and watched for a few minutes, "Yup, Wilson, you're right; I see a couple of them moving. Say, where's Mr. Young?"

"He's in the darkroom making some prints."

"Great, have you seen or heard from Detective Walsh?"

"No, sir."

Roscoe pulled a director's chair from the table and sat opposite Officer Wilson. They both sat quietly waiting when they noticed one of the roaches dropped onto the floor and started scurrying across the floor towards them. Wilson jumped up and backed up from the table; Roscoe sat still as the critter got closer and closer, then with lightning speed, Roscoe brought down his size nine wingtip upon the *Periplaneta Americana,* squishing it into nothing more than a gooey glop of ooze on the bottom of Roscoe's shoe.

Detective Walsh and Officer Harris came into the studio as Detective Brown was scrapping the gunk off the bottom of his shoe.

"Hey, Sarge, hey, Wilson," Harris said.

"Greetings, how did it go at the Overhaul Shop?" Roscoe asked.

"From what we could gather, Franklin was a model employee, liked by management and co-workers. Did you find anything at Urlacher's place?"

"Nothing. After this, we'll head over to the hospital and see what they have to say."

"Oh my God, what is this?" Harris shouted when he discovered the box of not-so-dead roaches.

"It's a still life for Death Shot Bug Spray." James Young said as he walked out of his darkroom holding several 8x10 black and white photo prints.

"I hate to tell you, but they ain't all dead." Wilson proclaimed.

"Dead enough," Young replied.

"Not for me," Wilson said.

"Me either." Harris agreed.

"Who gets these?" Young said as he held up the stack of photos.

"That would be me. Mr. Young, I'm Detective Sergeant Brow; this is my partner, Detective Walsh, and that bug lover over there is Officer Harris. How did we do with the photos?"

"Well, I did capture several shots of the man I saw running from the scene; however, I was shooting at a slow shutter speed, so unfortunately, they're all slightly blurred. It happened so fast that I didn't have time to change shutter speeds. I'm sorry, Detective."

Roscoe and the rest looked at the photos, and Young wasn't lying since the shots were slightly blurred. However, it did give them a decent overall visual description of the suspect.

He looked to be about 5 foot 10, maybe 200 pounds, with a short dark haircut, military length and was wearing a grey New York Yankees sweatshirt, baggy khaki pants, and what looked like a pair of black high-top Converse sneakers. There were a couple of shots where they could see the face. Roscoe thought that maybe the Police sketch artist might be able to enhance the face and give it some detail.

"Mr. Young, I want to thank you for your cooperation and fast thinking; most people would have ducked for cover or run away. I think your photographs just might help us catch this guy. Thank you again."

"Thank you, Detective. I'm glad that these might be of some help. Let me know if there's anything else that you need."

"Good afternoon, Mrs. Austin, Coney Island Hospital's Administrator; how may I be of service?"

"Mrs. Austin, I'm Detective Sergeant Brown, and this is my partner, Detective Walsh. We're here about one of your ER nurses, Ulysses Urlacher."

"Ulysses? Is there something wrong? Has something happened to him?"

"I'm afraid I have bad news; Ulysses was found murdered this morning."

"Oh my God." She said as she started to weep.

"We would like to speak to some of his fellow workers if possible?"

"Why, you don't think anyone here had anything to do with such a thing, do you?"

"No, ma'am, but someone might know if there was someone who might have had a problem or grudge against him. It's strictly routine."

"Would it be helpful if I gave you a list of the people who work in the ER, as they all have gone home since their shift is over?"

"Yes, ma'am, that would be most helpful."

She looked through her files and produced a sheet of paper with a list of twenty-eight people assigned to the graveyard shift: doctors, nurses, lab techs, and volunteers.

"Here you are. Is there anything else that I might be able to help you with, Detective Brown?"

"Would you happen to know if he was seeing anyone here at the hospital?"

"I'm sorry, I'm afraid I don't know."

"That's quite all right; thank you for your help."

As they walked out of the hospital, Roscoe said, "Jimmy, why don't you and Harris go and interview the folks on this list while I go back to the office and have a talk with Doctor Olsen and see if we can get a sketch artist down here to work up a drawing of this creep."

"Okay, would you like us to take you back to the station?" Walsh asked.

"Nah, I'll just take a cab; you guys get going. See you back at the station later."

When Roscoe got back to the station, a huddle of detectives and officers was hovering outside Roscoe's office.

"What the Hell's going on!" Roscoe asked.

Detective Conroe turned to Roscoe and said, "Roscoe, who's the doll in your office?"

"Doll? What are you talking about? Everyone get out of my way!"

Roscoe pushed and shoved his way to his office, where he found his sketch artist waiting for him.

"Detective Brown, I'm the sketch artist you requested. My name is Veronica Lennox, but everyone calls me Ronnie." She said as she stood up to shake his hand.

Veronica looked more like a model than an artist; she was five foot eleven, one hundred and ten pounds, with long blonde hair, silky smooth skin, and baby blue eyes.

"I appreciate you coming down to the six oh. I'm Detective Brown; please have a seat."

Roscoe went to his office door, and before he shut it, he said, "Don't you mutts have anything better to do? Because if you don't, you know I *will* find something for you to do, and it won't be pretty!"

He turned to Veronica and said, "I apologize; you would think they never saw a woman before."

"It's quite all right, Detective Brown."

"Roscoe, if I'm going to call you Ronnie, you can call me Roscoe."

"All right, Roscoe."

"Now, Ronnie, I have several photographs of the person we believe to be our suspect; however, the photographer who took the pictures was apparently shooting at a slow shutter speed, whatever that means. So, the images are all slightly blurred. I was hoping that you might use the photos as a reference and make a detailed rendering of the suspect. Does that make any sense?"

"Yes, perfect sense. May I see the photos?" She asked.

Roscoe handed her the stack of black and whites. She looked through them once and then leafed through them again; this time, she seemed to be carefully studying them.

"Whadda think?" Roscoe asked.

"No problem. There's enough detail, and I believe I can give you a pretty good portrait of your suspect. Would you like me to work here?"

"Actually, I think it might be better and less distracting if you might work from your home."

"I won't be distracted working here, Roscoe."

"Yeah, well, it's not you. I'm worried about being distracted, if you know what I mean." He said, nodding his head, indicating all the men standing around outside his door.

"Oh, I see. Well, I should have a reasonable sketch for you first thing in the morning. Would you like me to come by and drop it off?"

"You know, it might be better if you call me, and we could meet somewhere." He said as he handed her his card.

"Very good, well, I guess I'll go home and get started then."

"If you don't mind, I think it might be best if I walk you out to your car."

"Yes, I would appreciate that." She said as she grabbed her purse and briefcase.

As Roscoe slowly opened the door, he could hear the sound of feet scrambling away for his door.

Roscoe allowed Ronnie to take the lead as they made their way downstairs to the parking lot; he was making sure that they weren't being followed by all the men of the six 0.

He escorted her to her bright new orange Porsche 911, where they shook hands, and he waved as she drove away. He quickly turned around to see that all the windows on the station's south side had dozens of men's faces pressed against them.

As he was walking back into the station, he muttered to himself, "Women are right. Men really are pigs."

Doctor Olsen was waiting for Roscoe when he returned to his office as well as CSI's David Bowles. They were sitting next to each other on the old, worn-out leather sofa on the right side of the room. In front of the sofa, acting as a coffee table, was an old lobster trap with a glass top. There were two office chairs facing the sofa; Roscoe plopped down in one of them and asked, "Do either of you gentlemen have anything for me?"

Bowles spoke first, "Not much, I'm afraid. We have confirmed that the same .9mm gun killed both men, but there wasn't any other evidence. Sorry."

"Have you run the gun through the system?"

"Yes, and no matches."

"Doc, anything from a medical standpoint?"

"Sorry, Roscoe, the only thing these two men have in common is that they were both shot from behind, but not execution-style, more like the perpetrator ran up from behind and shot them in the head. The angles suggest that they were both walking; neither the victims nor the shooter was stationary."

There was a brief knock on the door, and before Roscoe could see who was there, he heard Walsh, "Hey Doc, hey Bowles, sorry to interrupt. We talked to everyone who was on the list, but nothing. Roscoe, I'm thinking these are just random shootings."

"I agree, but don't you think it's odd that both victim's first and last names begin with the same letter, Francis Franklin and Ulysses Urlacher, and both were killed on a street that also began with the letters of their names."

"This guy's a real nut."

"Maybe, but he has to do a lot of planning to find someone with their first and last names beginning with the same letters and then to plan on killing them on the street with the same letter; that takes a lot of meticulous calculation."

"So, what's our next move?" Walsh asked.

"Let's go talk to the Captain to see if we can get some help."

"From who?"

"I'm thinking we can get some of the Police trainees from the Police Academy to scour the Coney Island phone book looking for anyone whose first and last names begin with the same letters."

Roscoe turned his attention back to his two guests, "Thank you for coming down to see me; now, if you'll excuse me, we have to go see the Captain."

Jeffery Foster, a 35-year-old recent dropout from the New York City Police Academy, was hunched over the Coney Island phone book, carefully perusing the names listed in the white pages, looking for someone whose first and last names begin with the letter C.

Since he was a kid, Jeffery had always wanted to be a policeman like his dad. Unfortunately, Jeffery was a slacker; his grades were below average, he was slightly overweight, and he thought he would have a leg up on all the competition because his dad was once on the NYPD.

That was really all he knew about his father since Frank Foster left Jeffery and his mother shortly after he was born. Jeffery's mother told him that his father was killed in action so that the young Foster wouldn't grow up with issues. During school, he would brag to the other kids that his old man was a hero, dying in the line of duty.

It wasn't until he attended the Police Academy that he found out that his father wasn't killed in the line of duty but, in reality, had spent the last fifteen years in Attica Prison for killing a black man, whom he claimed pulled a gun on him. After a thorough investigation, it was proven that Officer Foster had planted a gun on the victim. He was convicted of perjury, tampering with evidence, and manslaughter; he was sentenced to twenty-five years to life.

The other cadets were brutal in their taunting and ridiculing him every chance they got. Even some of the instructors took pleasure in mocking him and constantly used obvious innuendoes at his expense until, finally, he attacked a cadet on the firing range, threatening to kill him.

Jeffery only lasted three weeks before being asked to leave. During his exit interview, the officer noted that Jeffery Foster exhibited anger and hostility towards the department. It was the opinion of the officer that the cadet posed a danger to himself and society.

Charles Cunningham was the Vice President and Executive Officer of the Wildlife Conservation Society in partnership with the New York Aquarium, Coney Island.

Charles started with the aquarium twenty years ago and slowly worked his way up the organization. Over the years, Charles had held just about every job, from ticket taker and trainer in the Aquatheater to every job in between until finally management.

Even though Charles Cunningham was by all definition a successful, self-made man, he lived very modestly. He had a small home that he had purchased fifteen years ago on Crawford Avenue, just off the main drag, Coney Island Avenue.

The house was a two-story combination of red brick and stucco with plants and shrubbery on the sides of the driveway, giving it a well-manicured appearance. A very tasteful brass ornate metal fence surrounded the lot, with a carport underneath the house.

It was a quarter to nine in the evening when Charles' black 1965 BMW 2000 CS pulled into the underground carport. He never did see Jeffery wearing all black, hiding behind a large green plastic garbage can. He began to follow him after he locked his pride and joy and started to go upstairs.

As Charles placed his foot onto the first stair, Jeffery fired the first of two gunshots; the second one was slightly off the mark. As Charles began to fall, Jeffery fired his second shot, striking Cunningham in the side of his head, creating a red mist that sprayed blood, bone, and brains onto Jeffery's clothing.

After shooting Charles Cunningham, Jeffery Foster walked towards Coney Island Avenue, where his 1964 white Ford Galaxie was parked. He dropped the shifter on the column into drive and sped off into the night, feeling proud of the evening's accomplishment.

Roscoe and Walsh were in with Captain O'Rourke, explaining their theory of the murders and their request for the cadets at the Police Academy to help scour the Coney Island phone book to look for possible victims. There was a brief knock on the door, and Harris peeked in, "Excuse me, Captain, but there has been another shooting. A Charles Cunningham was gunned down in front of his house on Crawford Avenue."

The Captain pointed to the door and said, "You boys get going; I'll contact the academy to get them started first thing in the morning."

The street where Cunningham's house was had been all cordoned off with Police tape. The ME, Police photographer, and CSI were already there when Roscoe, Walsh, and Harris arrived.

The trio of them walked up to Davis Bowles from CSI, "David, whadda we got?" Roscoe asked.

"The same as the others. We got two .9mm shells, and this time we have another cigar butt; it appears to be the same brand. We'll know more when we get it back to the lab."

"Where did you find it?" Walsh asked.

"We found it behind that garbage can."

"So, our killer was waiting in the dark behind the garbage can for Mr. Cunningham to come home, and he then followed him to the stairs, where he shot him." Roscoe surmised.

"That's what it appears to be. The ME found this one to be slightly different." Bowles said.

"Thanks, Dave," Roscoe said.

Roscoe and Walsh found Doctor Olsen standing by the ambulance.

"Hey, Doc, Bowles says we've got some variety on this one?"

"Yeah, it seems because the victim was up on the first stair when he was shot the first time, he started to fall, so I'm thinking he was falling back towards the shooter, meaning the second shot was more to the side of the head, as the killer was reacting to him falling back."

"And that means what?"

"It means that, unlike the others, this time he got sprayed with the vic's blood and brain matter. Which means that it will be on his clothes, and…"

"And, even if he tries to wash it out, Luminol will still detect deep in the fibers. Thanks, Doc."

"Hey, it's not much, Roscoe, but it's something."

"Any port in a storm, Doc, any port in a storm."

While Roscoe and Walsh went through Cunningham's house looking for anything to tie him with the other two victims, after three hours, they came up empty, as did the uniformed officers canvassing the neighbors. One elderly man whose house is on the corner said that around the time of the murder, he did remember seeing a man dressed in black, running and getting into a white or cream color Ford Galaxie or Ford LTD, then speeding away.

"Well, that's something, maybe," Walsh said.

"We need to go back and ask if anyone remembers a white or cream-colored Ford in and around the area of the shootings," Roscoe stated.

"You mean everyone that we got statements from? That's over sixty, Sarge. Do you know how long that will take?" Harris asked.

"No, but be sure to let me know how long it takes you, Harris," Roscoe said with a smile.

"Me?"

"Well, okay, you can get a couple of fellow officers to help you. Oh, and I want them on my desk by five o'clock tomorrow afternoon."

"Yes, Sarge."

"Five o'clock."

"Got it, five o'clock."

"Okay. Let's call it a night; we'll hit it running first thing tomorrow. Harris, you and some unis will get started on re-interviewing all those who gave statements. Walsh and I will see our sketch artist and then see if CSI and Olsen have anything new to tell us." Roscoe said.

"Yeah, about going to see the sketch artist, do you think I can tag along, huh, can I?" Harris begged.

"She's way out of your league, Harris, my boy."

"She's that hot?" Walsh asked.

"Let me put it this way; she's so hot that having sex with her would probably kill me or at least cripple me for life."

"Yeah, Sarge, but what a way to go." Harris quipped.

"Harris, how much do you make a year?"

"With overtime, about six grand, why?"

"Her watch cost six grand, her orange 911 Porsche cost over eight thousand, son; she doesn't do this for the money; she wants to be an artist and thinks this will be a good experience, understand? I checked; her father is a Wall Street tycoon making millions. You're a cute kid, but you ain't that cute."

The following day at 9 am, Walsh and Brown met with the sketch artist Veronica Lennox at Adelman's Kosher Deli on Kings Highway.

"Why Adelman's?" Walsh asked.

"I feel like having a lox and bagel with cream cheese, so sue me."

"Funny, you don't look Jewish." Mocked Walsh.

"Yeah, well, I'd say you don't look like a "Mick," but you do."

Just as they started throwing verbal jabs, Veronica Lennox walked up to the table.

"Sorry I'm late, Detective Brown, but I had a terrible time finding parking."

"That's quite all right; we just got here ourselves. Ronnie, I'd like you to meet my partner, Detective Walsh."

"It's a pleasure to meet you, Detective Walsh."

"The pleasure is all mine."

"So, Ronnie, how'd we do?" Roscoe asked.

"Well, I looked at all the photos and made a composite from the most prominent features of the subject from each photograph, and here's what I came up with." She said as she handed Roscoe a large brown envelope with a charcoal sketch enclosed.

Roscoe took the envelope, removed the sketch, and held the drawing up so that Walsh could also see.

"Wow, this is fantastic, whadda ya think, Jimmy?"

"You've turned a fuzzy image into focus. That's very impressive, Ms. Lennox."

"Thank you, and it's Ronnie, please."

Roscoe carefully replaced the drawing into the envelope and said, "Ronnie, great job. Can I offer you some breakfast?"

"Gee, you're very kind, but maybe some other time since I have a life drawing class at SVA in an hour."

"SVA?" Roscoe asked.

"School of Visual Arts," Walsh answered.

"Hey, that's right. Are you interested in art, Detective Walsh?"

"Oh yeah, I like most of the masters like Leonardo, Michelangelo, and Rembrandt, but what I love is the contemporary artists Warhol, Picasso, and Pollock."

"Cool. Have you heard that MoMA is having an opening for the exhibit of Frank Stella's new work next week?"

"Yeah, but next week's opening is for members; the following week is for the general public. I can't wait."

"Well, I'm a member, a gift from my father. Would you like to go with me, Detective Walsh, as my guest?"

"That's very kind of you. I would like that very much, under one condition."

"Yeah, what's that?"

"That you call me Jimmy."

"Deal." She said as she opened her handbag, pulled out a business card, and handed it to Walsh.

"Here's my card; give me a call."

Walsh reached inside his coat pocket and handed her his card, saying, "And here's my card. I'll call you tomorrow evening."

"I look forward to it. Well, I got to run. Goodbye Roscoe. Jimmy. Oh, Roscoe, do me a favor and let me know if the sketch was useful."

"Will do, and thanks again, Ronnie. Bye."

They both watched her walk out, as did every man in the Deli. On a scale of one to ten, ten being incredibly beautiful, Veronica Lennox was a twelve.

"Thanks, Roscoe," Walsh said with a grin from ear to ear.

"You owe me big time, Walsh! And you know everyone at the station will hate your guts, don't you?"

"They won't know. I'm not going to tell them."

"Yeah, but I will."

Roscoe and Walsh had just gotten by the squad room to talk to Bowles from CSI when they received a call of a double homicide at 134 Kensington Street.

"Maybe it isn't the same guy," Walsh said.

"Yeah, keep a good thought; maybe it's a different maniac," Roscoe replied sarcastically.

134 Kensington was a well-manicured two-story typical Coney Island brick home. There was a very ornate iron stair railing that extended to enclose the front porch. On the second-story window was a similar ornate iron Juliet balcony, and above the wooden door was an iron arc that echoed the ironwork of the railings.

To the left of the railing and stairs leading to the front door was a small area of evergreen trees and plants, where one of the victims, Ms. Yazmin Youssef, was shot twice in the back of the head.

Laying at the bottom of the front porch steps was Mr. Karl, also shot twice in the back of the head. Kneeling over Kruger was Doctor Olsen examining the body. When he spotted Roscoe, he stood up and said, "Hey, Roscoe, we got to stop meeting like this."

"I'm working on it, Doc."

"Is it our guy?" Walsh asked.

"I would say so, same MO, .9mm shells, and I think Bowles found another cigar butt over there on the sidewalk."

"This is the first time he's killed a woman," Walsh stated.

"There must be a reason for his only killing people whose first and last names begin with the same letters," Roscoe said.

"And killing them on streets with the same letters, too," Walsh added.

An officer was talking to one of the neighbors, leading her over to Roscoe and Walsh.

"Detective, this is Mrs. Mary Whitesides; she lives across the street from our victim. She says she knew the victims and claims to have seen a man leaving the scene shortly after hearing gunshots. He was dressed in black, driving a light-colored car."

"Thank you, officer, Mrs. Whitesides. Can you tell us exactly what you observed, please?" Roscoe asked.

"It was about ten o'clock this morning, and I had just finished watching The Price Is Right when I heard four loud pops. I went over to the front window, and that's when I saw this man all dressed in black running over to this white or cream-colored Ford car and drove away."

"Could you describe the man that you saw?"

"Well, he was of average height, a little on the chubby side, and wearing sunglasses. I couldn't tell you his hair color since he was wearing one of those knit caps on his head."

"Do you think you might be able to recognize him if you saw him again?"

"Hmm, maybe it did happen so fast."

"Did you, by chance, get the license plate number?"

"Not all of it. I only remember NO 89."

"What can you tell us about Ms. Yazmin Youssef and Karl Kruger?"

"They were a lovely couple; she worked at a firm down on Wall Street, and Karl was an Account executive in an advertising agency in Manhattan. They were engaged and planning on getting married in the spring. They've only lived here for less than a year."

"Mrs. Whitesides, thank you; you've been a great help," Roscoe said, shaking her hand.

"Let's get back to the squad room," Roscoe told Walsh.

Back at the station house, Walsh went to see if he could match up a white Ford Galaxie or LTD and the partial license plate number provided by Mrs. Whiteside.

Roscoe had met with CSI Bowles, and he confirmed that the same gun fired all the .9mm slugs and that the cigars were all the same brand and had identical bite marks.

"We're looking at the same guy for all these killings, Roscoe," Bowles stated.

"Great, I'm glad we're not looking at any copycats out there."

Roscoe went back up to his office to wait to hear from Walsh if he had any luck with the DMV. He tacked the sketch onto his cork bulletin board and went to hang up his suit coat and fedora on the coat rack. He walked over to his desk, plopped down in his chair, opened the bottom right drawer of his wooden desk, and pulled out a bottle of Jameson Irish Whiskey with two glasses.

Walsh walked into the office grinning from ear to ear, holding up a piece of teletype paper, and right behind him was Officer Harris.

Walsh tossed the paper onto Roscoe's desk and said, "We got him."

"What's his name?" Roscoe asked.

"His name is..." Walsh was about to disclose the suspect's name when Harris, after looking at the Police sketch, said, "Jeffery Foster."

Both Roscoe and Walsh looked at him, puzzled.

"That's a sketch of Jeffery Foster; he was in my academy class but dropped out after only a couple of weeks. The rumors were that he got the boot because he had anger issues.

"Jeffery Foster is the owner of a white 1965 Ford Galaxie New York, license number NO 8998," Walsh said.

"I think it's time we pay a visit to Mr. Foster, don't you? But, first, let's see if we can get a warrant; let's go see the Captain." Roscoe said as he walked to the coat rack and put on his suit jacket and signature fedora."

"Jeffery Foster?"

"Who wants to know?"

"I'm Detective Sergeant Brown. This is my partner, Detective Walsh, and that, as you may remember, is Officer Ron Harris. I believe you two were in the same class at the Police Academy."

"So, what do you pigs want?"

"Mr. Foster, we have a warrant to search these premises as well as your Ford Galaxie. Please step aside."

"And if I don't?"

"Mr. Foster, do you see those eight other uniformed Police Officers standing behind me?"

"Yeah, I see them."

"If you don't allow us to enter, I will be forced to order those officers to break down your door and place you under arrest for refusing to follow a court order. Do you understand?"

"In that case, pig, won't you please come in and tear apart my home," Foster said as he opened the front door as wide as it would open.

After several hours of rummaging through his house, although they didn't find a weapon or ammunition, they found a black sweater, a black pair of pants, a black watch knit cap, and a box of cigars of the same brand as those found near the crime scenes.

"Mr. Foster, I'm afraid I'm going to insist that you come down to the station house with us. We'd like to ask you some questions."

"Am I under arrest, pig?"

"No, but if you refuse to come with us, I will place you under arrest."

"Fuck you, pig. You want me, arrest me!" Foster said defiantly.

"Harris, would you do the honors?"

As Officer Harris placed the handcuffs on Jeffery Foster, Detective Walsh read him the Miranda Rights, which were enacted for the first time.

"Jeffery Foster, you have the right to remain silent. Anything you say can and will be used against you in a court of law. You have the right to an attorney. If you cannot afford an attorney, one will be provided for you. Do you understand the rights I have just read to you?"

"Yeah, pig, I understand. I ain't no moron!"

"With these rights in mind, do you wish to speak to us?"

"No, I got nothing to say."

As he was being led out of his house, the neighbors were cheering, clapping, and shouting in the street.

"Goodbye to bad rubbish!"

"Lock the bum up and throw away the key."

"Freak!"

"That dirtbag killed my dog. Hope you rot in Hell!"

"Creep!"

Foster didn't return the insults; he just walked stoically to the squad car and sat in the back, looking straight ahead.

Harris took Foster into Interrogation Room Two. Once inside, Foster was handcuffed to the wooden table, where he was seated. Roscoe and Walsh came in and sat down across from the suspect with a folder filled with papers, photos, and Police sketches.

"This interview is being videoed, tape-recorded, and may be given in evidence if your case is brought to trial. We are in interview room number two at the Coney Island Precinct 60. The date is August 18th, 1966, and the time on my watch is 1:46 pm. Detective James Walsh is in attendance. I am Detective Sergeant Roscoe Brown, and the suspect is Jeffery Foster. Mr. Foster, I'll ask you again: do you want an attorney?"

"No," Foster replied.

Roscoe stood up and walked over to a chalkboard mounted on the wall facing the suspect; he picked up a piece of chalk and began to write the victim's names.

Francis Franklin
Ulysses Urlacher
Charles Cunningham
Yazmin Youssef
Karl Kruger

Roscoe placed a typewritten list of the names of each victim in front of Foster, with the date and time that each was shot, "Jeffery, I need you to tell me where you were at the times these people were killed. Can you do that for me?"

Foster sat there staring at Roscoe, smirking. There was a knock on the door, and Officer Harris handed Roscoe a White Pages phonebook and whispered something to Detective Brown.

Roscoe thumbed through the phonebook and wrote two more names on the chalkboard.

Oliver Oates

Ursula Usher

Walsh asked, "Are those people he killed that we haven't found yet?"

"No, these are the names of his next intended victims. Jeffery, this phonebook was found in your basement, and all the victim's names are circled. We also found a key to your safe deposit box, so it's just a matter of time before someone knocks on that door with your .9mm pistol. The noose is tightening, Jeffery. Do you have anything you'd like to say?"

"You still don't see it, do you?" Foster said.

"See what?" Roscoe asked.

"You just don't get it. They booted *me* out of the academy, and somehow, they made you two detectives. It's staring you both right in the face, and you're both too stupid to see it! I'm surprised that you even caught me at all.

And all the time, I'm spelling it out for you. Here unhandcuff, and I'll show you how simple it is, and when I do, you'll see what fools you are."

Walsh took the cuff off Foster; he stood up, grabbed the chalk from Roscoe, proceeded to erase the names on the board, and began rewriting them.

Francis Franklin
Ulysses Urlacher
Charles Cunningham
Karl Kruger
Yazmin Youssef
Oliver Oates
Ursula Usher

He stopped writing and turned to look at the two Detectives to see if they had solved the puzzle.

"You still don't get it; it's right here staring you in the face. What a couple of dummies."

As Foster turned and started to bold and underline certain letters, he began to laugh and said, "Watch!"

<u>F</u>rancis Franklin
<u>U</u>lysses Urlacher
<u>C</u>harles Cunningham
<u>K</u>arl Kruger
<u>Y</u>azmin Youssef
<u>O</u>liver Oates
<u>U</u>rsula Usher

"F•U•C•K Y•O•U. See, see how simple it was. But, no, a couple of New York's finest couldn't figure it out."

"You killed five innocent people because you wanted to prove that you were smarter than the Police?" Walsh asked.

"I bet you're feeling pretty stupid now! And wait until the trial, when I tell the world how the academy rejected someone so smart, someone who could fool their top detectives and make idiots of them. Yeah, just you wait."

"Jeffery, you do know that you're going to prison for the rest of your life unless they send you to the electric chair," Roscoe said.

"No, they won't convict me. They'll be grateful that I exposed the inadequacies of the Police force."

"Jeffery Foster, you're under arrest for murder," Roscoe said.

Roscoe opened the door to the interrogation room and called for Officer Harris.

"Harris, will you be so kind as to escort Mr. Foster to Rikers Island for processing; the charge is five counts of first-degree murder."

"Right, Sarge. Mr. Foster, please turn around and place your hands behind your back."

Walsh and Roscoe stood by as Officer Harris placed the handcuffs on the prisoner. Having locked one hand into the cuffs, Foster twisted around, grabbing Harris' 38 out of his holster and shooting the officer in the right side. Harris had the forethought to grab hold of Foster, giving Walsh and Roscoe time to pull their weapons.

"Drop the weapon, now!" Roscoe shouted.

As Harris started to collapse to the ground, the videotape shows that Foster tried to raise the gun and fire at Detectives Brown and Walsh.

Both Detective Brown and Walsh fired several rounds, striking and killing the prisoner Jeffery Foster.

"How are you feeling, Ron?" Walsh asked.

"I'm okay; I'm sorry about fucking up like that. That was a rookie mistake."

"Harris, you are a rookie. Rookies make mistakes; I bet this is one you won't make again." Roscoe said.

"You got that right, Sarge."

"You know, things could have been worse if you hadn't grabbed hold of him. That gave Walsh and me time to defend ourselves. That was quick thinking."

"How long are they saying you'll be in here?" Walsh asked.

"Probably another three weeks."

"Well, just relax, take care of yourself, and get some rest," Walsh said.

"Come on, Jimmy, let's leave the kid to get some sleep."

"Thanks for stopping by."

"We'll stop by later in the week to check up on ya," Walsh said.

As they were leaving the hospital, Roscoe said, "You know what would really take his mind off of his injury."

"What?" Walsh answered skeptically.

"If you brought Ronnie by to see him."

"Now, why would seeing Ronnie take his mind off his injury?"

"Well, Walsh, someone once said the problem is that God gave man a brain and a penis and only enough blood to run one at a time."

"Got it."

THE END

The Case of the Which Doctor

"Doctor Laveau?"

"Speaking."

"Hi, I'm Donna Dixon; I'm with the law firm of Rabinowitz, Rabinowitz, Rabinowitz, and Fong."

"You're kidding, right?"

"Yeah, we get a lot of that. The reason I'm calling is that your Great Aunt Mary Laveau has recently passed away, and we are executives of her will. We're having the probate process tomorrow morning and hoping you could attend."

"Oh, dear, poor Aunt Mary, I hardly knew her; she lived in New Orleans."

"I'm sorry for your loss. Would ten o'clock be convenient?"

"Yes, of course. Where are you located?"

"1633 Mermaid Avenue, fifth floor. You'll be meeting with Mr. Rabinowitz."

"Why not with Mr. Rabinowitz?"

"He's busy."

"And Mr. Rabinowitz?"

"He's out of town."

"How about…"

"Don't even ask."

"All righty, see you tomorrow at ten."

"Thank you, Doctor."

Doctor Maria Katerina Laveau was born at Charity Hospital in the French Quarter of New Orleans in 1939. Her family has lived in New Orleans for over nine generations; the majority had been brought over as slaves from Senegambia.

Her great, great, great, great grandmother was Marie Laveau, the French Quarter Vodou Queen of the 1880s.

Marie Catherine Laveau was a Louisiana Creole practitioner of Vodou, herbalist, and midwife. She performed many acts of kindness and community service during her lifetime, such as nursing yellow fever patients, posting bail to free women of color, and visiting condemned prisoners to pray with them in their final hours.

Mama Laveau, as she was called, would attend gatherings in Congo Square on Sundays and sell her gris-gris bags, offer spiritual advice, and cast spells in the name of Loa, the spirits of Haitian Vodou.

She would meet with clients at her home. In her backyard, she would hold ceremonies that conjured the spirit of the Li Great Zombi, the deity Damballah Wedo, who would manifest through an albino snake that she called Zombie.

There were a few times when the Police were called to break up Mama Laveau's Vodou ceremonies, but she would always use her juju magic to keep the Police at bay.

Legend has it that a wealthy and influential man's son was on trial for something he was innocent of. He consulted the powerful Marie for help in his son's acquittal. The Vodou Queen went to St. Louis Church and prayed for three days and three nights with three hot peppers in her mouth. The next day, the man's son was acquitted. After that, all of her rivals, and there were many, were subjugated to minor roles in the hierarchy of Vodou royalty.

"Doctor Laveau, welcome. Thank you for coming." Miss Dixon said as she led the doctor to the conference room, where an elderly man was sitting at the head of a large mahogany conference table.

The man rose to greet her as she sat down across from him.

"Doctor Laveau, so good of you to come. My name is Saul Rabinowitz; I am the attorney charged with dispensing your Great Aunt Marie Laveau's last will and testament. Would you care for something to drink, coffee or tea, maybe?"

"Coffee would be nice, thank you."

"Donna, would you mind?"

"Of course, how would you like it?"

"Black will be fine."

With that, Donna Dixon left the conference room, closing the door behind her.

"So, you're a doctor?" Rabinowitz asked.

"Yes, I'm a psychiatrist. I specialize in criminal psychiatry."

"Very impressive."

"Thank you."

"I suppose that you do a lot of work with the Police?"

"Well, at times, but I also work with the defense attorneys, and occasionally I work with the prison systems."

There was a short knock at the door, "I have your coffee, Doctor, and your Chai Matcha tea, Saul."

"Thank you, Donna," Rabinowitz said.

Miss Dixon placed the tray between the attorney and doctor and left the room.

"Now, Doctor, as you know, you are your Great Aunt's only living relative. That makes this very easy. Your Aunt Mary has left you her entire estate worth two hundred and eighty thousand dollars, as well as her home located on St. Ann Street, her household furnishings, and all her worldly possessions."

"I had no idea; thank you, Mr. Rabinowitz."

"Saul, please. I will start the final dispensation, so all I need is your signature on these documents if you don't mind.

"You're a very lucky lady to have such a wonderful aunt. Were you close?"

"Growing up in New Orleans, but once we moved to Coney Island, not so much."

"Well, she must have loved you very much. Now, if there's anything that you might need, please don't hesitate to call me."

"I can't thank you enough, Mr. Rabin...I mean Saul. Thank you again."

She started to open the door when she turned around, "I know it's..."

"Yes?"

"Well, it's just that your firm's name is so unusual, Rabinowitz, Rabinowitz, Rabinowitz, and Fong. Fong?"

"I know we get that all the time. It's a long story, Doctor Laveau."

It took Doctor Laveau six weeks to shore up her Great Aunt Mary's estate affairs in New Orleans. She decided to keep the house on St. Ann Street as a rental property; she left most of the furniture in the house and took mainly her Aunt's mementos and personal items, including several large trunks from the attic. She arranged with a shipping service to drive everything up to her home in Coney Island.

Doctor Laveau had a lovely beachfront home in the Seagate community on 4900 Beach 49th Street. In 1966, Doctor Laveau was the first-ever black homeowner in a progressive gated community. The house was a white two-story stucco with a red roof and sundeck facing Gravesend Bay off the second-floor master bedroom. Behind the house was a small patch of grass for her dog, Dédé, a 50-pound Bearded Collie.

Doctor Laveau had heard the rumors growing up of her mother's ancestry history with Vodou and the Black Arts. But never gave it any credence since she was a modern woman of science. She knew that there is usually a grain of truth in most rumors, but believing in the power of some ancient tribal hocus pocus hoo doo wasn't for someone who was educated and graduated with honors from Princeton.

Over the course of eight weeks, Doctor Laveau slowly incorporated her Great Aunt Mary's possessions in with her own. She decided to store the two large steamer trunks she found in her aunt's attic in the garage until she felt the time was right to go through them properly. At first glance, it looked like a lot of personal mementos, some old clothes, faded photographs of people she didn't recognize, and several books, some printed and some that appeared to be journals. There was also a large black leather valise with small bottles filled with powders, liquids, and strange objects like snake fangs, bird feathers, beaks, petrified lizards, scorpions, and spiders. There were envelopes containing reptile scales, hair of various animals, possibly some human hair, tobacco, and black and white buttons of various sizes.

Doctor Laveau gathered up all items from the trunks to toss into the garbage when she found an envelope addressed to her.

My dear Maria,

If you are reading this, it is because I have passed on to the other side and am with your mother and the rest of our family.

I am leaving you our family's journals of rituals, spells, and incantations to help you in the art of thaumaturgy.

You have always said that you are a woman of reason and science, but isn't science based on the investigation of the unknown and discovery?

I beg you, do not close your mind and dismiss things that you do not yet understand as nonsense or foolishness. Take some time and try to understand what you do not know.

I have written you instructions for a simple Gris-Gris spell. If you follow my directions explicitly, within twenty-four hours, you will instinctively know something has changed; you will experience a feeling of exuberance and enlightenment.

But please weigh your request carefully and be sure that what you are requesting is what you truly want and not something frivolous. You will be amazed. Trust me, Maria.

Protect with light that is pure
Protect through day and night
Protect from harm

Protect from negative energy
This shield cannot be broken
So, mote it be

Your loving Aunt Mary.

Detective Sargent Roscoe Brown and his partner Detective James Walsh had just arrested Ryan Alexander for the murder and beheading his estranged wife's new family. Alexander killed her new husband, mother, and father, two of the three children, and even their dog.

The youngest son suffered a nonlethal head wound and was able to escape while Alexander was busy cutting off the other's heads. Alexander shot them all execution-style after making them lie on the floor.

He was captured while driving over to the new husband's parents' home to attempt to kill them, too.

He claimed that he didn't kill his ex-wife because he wanted her to suffer, having to live the rest of her life in misery and pain for leaving him.

After booking and processing Alexander and sending him off to Rikers Island, Roscoe and Walsh went to Captain O'Rourke's office to fill him in on the bust.

"So, you caught the creep," O'Rourke said.

"Yeah, he seems like he wanted to get caught so he could taunt and torment his ex-wife," Roscoe explained.

"A real sicko," Walsh added.

"I bet his defense lawyer will go for an insanity plea." Roscoe speculated.

"Hey, Roscoe, who's the best shrink that the DA uses to evaluate these scumbags?" O'Rourke asked.

"Doctor Laveau."

"Call DA Gladwell's office and make sure he books her right away. I'd hate to have the defense snag her first."

"He hasn't been assigned a PD yet," Walsh said.

"Even better. Boy, I'd love to see this creep get a date with Old Sparky." The Captain expressed.

"Will do, Captain. We'll keep you posted." Roscoe said as he and Walsh were leaving.

"Say, how's the boy?" The Captain asked.

"The Doc says he'll be okay physically, but mentally who knows. Seeing your whole family gunned down like that. It really has to mess with your head. He's probably facing years and years of therapy. Who knows." Roscoe said.

"Well, keep a good thought."

"Yeah, that's all we can do."

"Thanks, Roscoe; you guys did a great job."

"Thank you, Captain."

Doctor Laveau's dog, Dédé, was diagnosed with cancer and had been given only months to live. On Monday, she was scheduled to bring Dédé to the vet for an examination, which was in two days. She decided to try her Aunt Mary's Gris-Gris for Dédé.

Doctor Laveau made a small canvas bag about the size of a matchbox, placed some of Dédé's hair inside, then wrote a verse from the Bible and put it in the bag along with her dog's tag that had its name inscribed on it, plus a cut from Dédé's favorite squeaky toy. Doctor Laveau then tied it around the dog's neck, and over the weekend, she tried to have only positive thoughts about Dédé.

Doctor Laveau brought Dédé to the vet's office at 10 am Monday as scheduled. They sat patiently waiting their turn alongside a woman with three ferrets in a carrying case, a man with a miniature poodle, two spinster-looking women, each with two cats, and a young boy holding a pygmy boa constrictor named JoJo.

After an hour, the vet tech called out, "Doctor Laveau. Please come through."

She came up and walked Dédé into the exam room where Doctor Young was waiting, smiling.

"Hello, Doctor Laveau, how's Dédé doing? She seems playful."

"Her energy is good, as is her appetite."

"Good. Good." Doctor Young said as she examined the dog, listening to her heart and breathing, then looking into her ears, eyes, and teeth.

"She seems good, but we'll take some blood to really see what the story is. I know she seems healthy, but a dog's energy often spikes before a crash happens. The blood test will tell the tale." She stated as she took a syringe and withdrew a vile of blood. Dédé didn't react at all; she just sat upright with a very regal look on her face.

"If you would care to wait in the waiting room, we'll have the results for you shortly, Doctor Laveau."

"Thank you, Doctor Young; come on, Dédé." Doctor Laveau said as she led Dédé out into the waiting room, where they found themselves to be the only ones there.

Dédé plopped down at Doctor Laveau's feet, closed her eyes, and was sound asleep, snoring within seconds.

Laveau was trying to keep those positive thoughts while waiting for the blood test results.

"Doctor Laveau." Doctor Young said as she entered the waiting area.

"I don't know how to say this; I've never seen anything like it before. Dédé blood work shows no sign of cancer at all. I can't explain it, but she is cancer-free. This one for the books, I even ran the test twice just to be sure."

"Totally free?"

"Yes, she had had stage four liver cancer two weeks ago, but now. I don't really believe in miracles, but this comes pretty darn close."

"Oh, thank you, Doctor."

"Don't thank me; I didn't do anything. I would suggest that you bring her back in for a checkup in a month."

"Gris-Gris!" Doctor Laveau said under her breath.

"I beg your pardon?" Doctor Young asked.

"Oh, nothing."

Two months after the "*Miracle of Gris-Gris,*" Ryan Alexander sat across from Doctor Laveau in one of Riker Island's medical examination rooms, a prison guard standing watch outside.

"Mr. Alexander, do you know why you're here?"

"Yeah, I got caught."

"For?"

"Oh, I killed my ex-wife's new husband, her mother and father, their three children, and even their dog."

"Well, one of the children didn't die; they say he will make a full recovery."

"Well, whoopty freakin do. Do I look like I give a shit, Doc?"

"So, you have no remorse for killing all those people?"

"No."

"Not even the children?"

"I could give a shit about those snot-nosed brats of hers. She left me, so fuck her. I'm glad that she's suffering. Bitch."

"Mr. Alexander, let me ask you this. Can you tell me what your first memory was?"

"What? You mean as a kid?"

"Yes, can you remember what your very first memory was?"

"My Dad coming home drunk when I was five or six and punching my mother in the face because his dinner was cold."

"Tell me about your parents."

"We were dirt poor. My old man was a janitor; he spent eight hours a day cleaning toilets and urinals, he'd come home smelling like piss. My mother was pathetic; she never stood up to him, always cowering. He'd beat the shit out of me and my brother for no reason until, one day, my brother, who was four years older than me, took a Louisville Slugger and bashed his brains in. He was twelve at the time; he was arrested and spent four years in juvie."

"So, what happened to you and your mother after your father was killed and your brother went away?"

"My mother started whoring, bringing home men, one after another. Sometimes two or three a night."

"Where would you be when she brought home these men?"

"We lived in a one-room flat, so most nights I slept hiding in the closet."

"Were you ever sexually assaulted?"

"Sometimes, when she would bring two men to the flat at one time, she'd offer me up as an appetizer to the one waiting."

"Did that happen a lot?"

"Yeah, it did, until one night, some drunk old bastard was trying to force me to blow him. I got hold of a butcher knife and cut his dick off. I ran out of the building, down the street holding it, and eventually fed it to some dog in an alley."

"What happened?"

"I was sent to foster homes for the next eight years."

"And your mother?"

"Some john choked her to death, claimed she tried to rob him."

"How did you feel about that?"

"Good riddance to bad garbage."

"Really, your mother?"

"Just because you give birth don't make you a mother."

There was a long period of silence before Doctor Laveau asked the next question, all the while scribbling notes in her notebook.

"Mr. Alexander, what steps did you take to hide these murders?"

"None."

"Were you content in your actions, or were you nervous?"

"It felt so good. I felt, and still do, proud."

"Mr. Alexander, could you describe yourself to me?"

"I'm an easy-going guy; just don't fuck with me." He said as he finished his cigarette, dropped it on the floor, and then stomped on it.

"Thank you, Mr. Alexander; I think I've heard enough."

Alexander leaned over the table, grabbed her shirt collar, and said, "Listen up, Doc. If you don't tell the court I'm not fit to stand trial due to mental incompetence, my brother will visit you one night with his Louisville Slugger. Maybe not this week or next, maybe not for months, but he will come to visit. You dig, bitch?"

Doctor Laveau didn't reply; she stood up and signaled the guard to enter. The guard opened the door and asked, "Are you done?"

"There is just one more thing I need before Mr. Alexander is dismissed. I need a small snip of his hair."

"Say what!" The guard uttered.

"You see, officer, I take a small cutting sample of his hair and do a spectral analysis to determine the magnitude of his eigenvalues."

The guard stood motionless and looking perplexed for a few seconds before shouting, "Okay, you heard the doctor stand up and turn around facing the wall."

With the prisoner's back to the wall, Doctor Laveau took a pair of children's plastic scissors, cut a large clipping of hair, and put it in an envelope.

"Thank you, officer, that's all I need. You may take Mr. Alexander back to his cell."

The guard gave Alexander a push towards the door, "Let's go."

Once they had left, she gathered up her notebook and purse, bent down, picked up the cigarette butt, placed it in another envelope, and headed back to her office at 3119 Coney Island Avenue, second floor, to fill out her report on Ryan Alexander.

"District Attorney Gladwell's office, how may I direct your call?"

"Good afternoon, this is Doctor Laveau. Would you please let Mr. Gladwell know that I have completed the psychiatric analysis report on Mr. Ryan Alexander."

"Of course, Doctor Laveau."

"Thank you."

When Doctor Laveau got home later that evening, after walking her dog, Dédé, she took a lump of natural beeswax the size of her palm and laid it flat in front of her. Using a straight pin, she pricked her finger and let 14 drops of her blood fall onto the wax; she then began to knead the wax with her blood.

Doctor Laveau then started to model the wax into the shape of a human figure, a human figure that resembled Ryan Alexander. After having shaped the wax, she took a large piece of raw burlap and began to cut out two shapes of a crude human figure. She sewed the two pieces together with the wax form inside before sewing the two pieces together. She then took the hair clippings from Alexander and the cigarette butt, placed them inside the burlap, and finished sewing the burlap completely shut.

Two buttons were sewn onto the head of the figure: one large black button and a smaller white button.

When the doll was ready, she applied some blood on the doll's forehead, chest, and belly while chanting, "I name you Ryan Alexander. You are now him!"

Doctor Laveau lit three black candles; she put a photo of Alexander on the doll.

"You are the black candle I want to die, Ryan Alexander; you are the spirit of my enemy should die spiritus of death. I call you to take this life as a blow my breath with angers."

She held the doll over the candles and continued, "Spiritus of death, take away this persona life after I blow out this candle."

Doctor Laveau leaned over the candles and blew two of them out, still holding the doll over the remaining burning black candle. She took two Vodou spirit pins and stuck one into the doll's head and one into the doll's heart while chanting,

"I here call upon Goddess Hecate, the Powerful
Spirit of death,
I ask your help to kill my enemies.
Appear to me now, show yourself!
Kill Ryan Alexander.
By the power of you full moon tonight.
I swear these words until they die. I swear they die.
Until the candles light gone!
This is my will, so mote it be!"

The day after she constructed Alexander's Vodou doll, listening to the radio while sitting in her living room, reading the novel Blood of the Beast, she was startled to hear the lead story.

"Good evening, and welcome to WJM's six o'clock news; I'm Biff Bradley with breaking news. Ryan Alexander, the suspected mass murderer of his ex-wife's family, was found dead in his prison cell this morning. We're awaiting the official coroner's report, but sources tell WJM that it doesn't seem to be a homicide; it looks like it was possibly a heart attack or stroke. Mr. Alexander was forty-eight years old.

We go live to Justin Trice, who is at Rikers Island with more...."

"Roscoe, I want you and Walsh to run up to Rikers Island and see what you can find out about Alexander's sudden death; see if there was any possibility of foul play."

"Captain, you know this isn't our jurisdiction."

"I've already spoken to the folks at Rikers; you and Walsh will be primarily backup."

"Got it."

"Let me know what you find."

"Will do, Captain."

Officer Ron Harris drove the usual one hour and thirty-minute drive from the 60th Precinct to Rikers Island in under an hour; he timed all the stoplights just right. Harris instantly became a legend in Six O.

Walsh riding shotgun and Roscoe sitting in the back seat would authenticate the record to all the nonbelievers back at the station.

Rikers Island is home to one of the world's largest correctional and mental institutions and has the nickname "the Tombs."

Once on the island, Roscoe and party went to the Eric M. Taylor Correctional Center and met with Warden Britton. The Eric M. Taylor Correctional Center houses male adolescents and adults awaiting trial.

As they entered the correctional facility, Warden Britton was waiting for them.

"Detective Sargent Brown, I'm Warden Britton."

"Pleased to meet you. This is Detective Walsh and Officer Harris."

"Gentlemen. Please follow me." Warden Britton said as he turned and led them down the hallway, through several locked metal doors, then down into the basement, where the covered body of Ryan Alexander lay resting on an ambulance gurney.

Warden Britton pulled the sheet back, exposing the naked body of Mr. Alexander.

"As you can see, there aren't any noticeable blunt force marks, no distinctive contusions, no stab wounds, nothing visible. We're sending the body down to Doctor Olsen at the ME's office this afternoon so that he can conduct a proper autopsy. Would you care to examine the body closer, Detective Brown?"

"Thank you, Warden."

Roscoe and Walsh began to examine Alexander, particularly for needle punctures. But they saw none. One thing that they did notice was that there was an irregularity in his haircut. It looked as if someone took a pair of scissors and randomly cut a chunk of hair from the back of his head.

Roscoe looked at Walsh, then to the Warden, "Did any of your men do this?" Roscoe said, indicating the hair loss.

"I noticed that too. It appears that Doctor Laveau did that when she met with the prisoners at the end of her psychological evaluation the day before yesterday."

"Did she give a reason?"

"The officer said she told him it was for some sort of spectral analysis. Alexander didn't seem to mind, so the guard permitted it. Would you like to speak to Officer Ryerson?"

"No, I don't think that will be necessary."

"Will there be anything else, Detective?"

"No, Warden Britton. I think we're good. Thank you for your time."

"Very well, let me show you, gentlemen, out."

"Doctor Laveau, there are two Police Officers here who like a few minutes of your time."

"Please send them in, Sarah."

Doctor Laveau's receptionist hung up the phone, pointed towards the doctor's door, and said, "You may go in."

"Thank you," Roscoe responded.

When Roscoe and Detective Walsh entered Doctor Laveau's office, she was standing behind her desk. She gestured to the two chairs in front of her desk and said, "Won't you please have a seat?"

Roscoe removed his fedora as he sat down, "Thank you for seeing us, Doctor Laveau. I'm Detective Sargent Brown, and this is my partner, Detective Walsh. We're here about Ryan Alexander."

"Oh?"

"We understand that you met with Alexander at Rikers Island to conduct a psychiatric evaluation."

"Yes, that's right."

"May I ask if you have formed any conclusions?"

"Well, I haven't completed my findings, as I stopped since I heard he died."

"I understand, but is there anything you could tell us?"

"Sure, but these are just preliminary impressions at this point. It isn't evil that drives people to kill. Killers are driven by devastating histories of trauma."

"Did Alexander have a traumatic childhood?"

"Extremely."

"Doctor Laveau, can you give a quick snapshot of Ryan Alexander? This is strictly off the record."

"Well, Mr. Alexander suffered from alcoholism, depression, an antisocial personality disorder with obsessive-compulsive and sadistic components."

"Wow, the guy was a real mess," Walsh said.

"Was the guy legally insane?" Roscoe asked.

"Not in my opinion, Detective."

"Thank you, Doctor Laveau; I believe that's all."

"Detective Brown, why the interest? I heard that they believe that he died from a heart attack."

"It's just my routine; I hate loose ends. Oh, by the way, may I ask about the hair sample you took from Alexander for spectral analysis? Is that right?"

Doctor Laveau knew that the spectral analysis might come up, "No, not spectral analysis, I said species analysis. You see, Detective Brown, it's just a theory I'm researching. I'm looking to see if any mineral imbalances in the subject's DNA might have any correlation to that part of the brain that triggers anger and motivates us to act."

"DNA?" Walsh queried.

"Deoxyribonucleic acid is the molecules that are the building blocks of every living thing. Am I right, Doctor?"

"Very good, Detective Brown, very impressive."

"I can thank my wife; she subscribes to Scientific American."

"Is there anything else I can help you with?"

"Can't think of anything. If we do, would it be all right to talk again?"

"Of course, any time."

"Deoxyribonnucleic acid! Really?" Walsh ragged.

"Gee, I thought everyone knew that."

"Bite me, Roscoe."

"Now see, that's what one would expect from a philistine."

"Hey, I got your philistine right here, Detective Sargent Brown!"

"So, what did you think of Doctor Laveau's hair analysis mumbo jumbo?"

"I think she was trying to dazzle us with scientific bullshit."

"I got the same feeling, but let's go have a chat with Doctor Olsen."

When they got into the car, Roscoe asked Officer Harris, "Hey, Harris, have you ever heard of DNA?"

"Yeah, ain't that the Democrat's political organization or something like that?"

"No, that's the DNC."

"Oh, well, what is DNA, Sarge?"

"Tell 'em, Walsh."

"It's the building blocks of every living thing."

"Oh yeah, I got some of them for my kid. He loves his blocks."

Roscoe slipped his fedora over his eyes as if he were sleeping and said softly to himself, "I'm surrounded by Neanderthals."

Harris drove them to the coroner's office on Winthrop Street in East Flatbush. Doctor Olsen was performing the autopsy on Ryan Alexander when they arrived; Olsen had just removed the top of the skull when Officer Harris entered the room. The sight of Alexander split open like a roast chicken combined with the overpowering stench of formaldehyde caused Officer Harris to upchuck his Burger King double Whopper, large order of fries, and strawberry shake all over his spit-shined shoes.

As Harris was making his way to the bathroom to regain his composure, he could hear Roscoe, Walsh, and Doctor Olsen having a good laugh at his expense. And it wouldn't be long before it was all over the Precinct how the rookie tossed his cookies at his first autopsy.

By the time Harris returned to the dissection room, the autopsy was over, Alexander's body was covered with a white sheet, and Doctor Olsen was absent. Roscoe noticed him enter the room and said, "Feeling better? Hey, Harris, don't sweat it; we all do it the first time."

"Yeah, it stays with us, so don't worry about it," Walsh added.

"Thanks, guys."

Doctor Olsen returned to the room, "Roscoe, it's the darndest thing; I haven't seen one like this ever."

"What happened, Doc?"

"Alexander died of simultaneously having a stroke and coronary at the exact same time."

"Far out, man!" Harris said.

"The odds of something like this happening are astronomical, probably in the billions to one, and the weird thing is that he was in excellent health," Olsen stated.

"So, whadda ya think, Doc? Just a freak of nature?" Roscoe asked.

"You know me, Roscoe, I'm a man of science, but even I am baffled with this one."

"Say, Doc, on a different subject. Have you ever heard of something called species hair analysis? We were talking to Doctor Laveau, the psychiatrist for the DA, who said that she's doing some kind of research to see if any mineral imbalances in people's DNA might have some correlation that could affect that part of the brain that triggers anger and motivates us to act. She claims that's why she took a cut of Alexander's hair the other day at Rikers during her evaluation."

"Species hair analysis? That's a new one on me; it sounds a bit fishy but let me ask around."

"Thanks, Doc."

Doctor Laveau was in her office when Sarah, her receptionist, buzzed her, "Doctor Laveau, the district attorney on line one."

"Thank you, Sarah."

"Hello?"

"Doctor Laveau, good afternoon; this is Thomas Gladwell; how are you?"

"I'm doing well, and yourself?"

"Not well; I have some disturbing news. Roger Everhart is being released tomorrow."

"Why, what happened?"

"It appears that his attorneys convinced the Judge that the Police didn't have probable cause to enter his house, so the Judge has thrown out all the evidence seized in Mr. Everhart's home. I'm sorry; I know you put a lot of time and effort into this case."

"When did you say he was being released?"

"Tomorrow afternoon."

"Is there any way I could see him before he's released?"

"I'm afraid that his attorneys would object. Why do you want to see him?"

"It's for a research project that I'm conducting. It would have nothing to do with his trial; nothing that we would discuss would be used in any way in court."

"Well, I have no objections if they don't; I don't think they'll allow it but go ahead if you like."

"Thank you, I appreciate it. Goodbye."
Goodbye, Doctor Laveau, good luck."

Roger Everhart was arrested for torturing and killing eleven people. Mr. Everhart was convinced that aliens from outer space had landed on Earth and had begun occupying the bodies of Manhattan's homeless people while they were asleep.

Everhart would cruise the areas where the homeless were camped out or sleeping in doorways, and he would invite them to his home for a home-cooked dinner and an opportunity to bathe and a change of new clothes.

After they showered, he would offer them dinner, which he had drugged. Once they had passed out, Everhart would take them down to the basement, where he would strip them naked, then strap them to a gurney, where he would conduct experiments to see if they had indeed been possessed.

His first test was to inject vinegar into their eyes with a syringe to see if their eyes would become reptilian. He would then make a V-shaped cut on their breast to see what color the blood was, and finally, he would rectally insert a six-inch metal rod connected to an electric outlet. If the victim didn't confess that they were an alien, Everhart would turn on the electricity, thereby electrocuting them. If they did confess, he would also electrocute them.

He was eventually apprehended when one of the homeless people wasn't completely drugged and had enough strength to overpower Mr. Everhart and called the Police.

Mr. Everhart was arrested on assault charges, made bail, and was released. It wasn't until two days later that the Police from the twelfth precinct failed to execute a proper search warrant, and all the evidence of the murders was inadmissible; it boiled down to a couple of overzealous detectives blowing the case.

Everhart was about to be released on bond, and the police had to try to build a case without vital evidence.

The Police were outraged, the people were outraged, and Doctor Laveau was outraged.

It was Doctor Laveau's diagnosis that Roger Everhart while being both a psychopath and sociopath, was legally sane and should stand trial. So, she was shocked when his defense team granted her request to visit Everhart in jail. There were a couple of stipulations: one of her attorneys must be present, she wasn't allowed to discuss the case, and she was permitted only to interview him regarding her research.

Doctor Laveau found Roger Everhart and his attorney, Lisa Wernersbach, sitting in an interrogation room in the solitary confinement unit at Rikers Island, commonly referred to as the "Bing."

Ms. Wernersbach came out of the room when she saw Doctor Laveau approaching. She greeted Doctor Laveau, "Good morning, Doctor Laveau; I'm Lisa Wernersbach, Mr. Everhart's attorney."

"It's a pleasure, Ms. Wernersbach. I really appreciate you allowing me to speak with Mr. Everhart."

"Before I allow you to see Mr. Everhart, you know you are not permitted to speak or mention anything about his case."

"Yes, my interest in speaking to him is for my research, to see if there are any mineral imbalances in people's DNA that might have some correlation that would affect that part of their brain that triggers anger and motivates them to act. All my questions will be of a general nature. There is one thing if you and Mr. Everhart wouldn't object: I would like to have a small clipping sample of his hair."

"His hair?"

"Again, this is for my analysis only. I have a signed affidavit attesting to the fact that I will share my findings with the Police or any governmental authorities." She said, handing Wernersbach the affidavit.

"Okay, let's ask Mr. Everhart if he will consent."

The interview lasted over an hour, and at the end, Roger Everhart did consent to allow Doctor Laveau to take a small clipping of his hair. The majority of the questions that Doctor Laveau asked Everhart were the type of questions that a first-year medical student would ask. Of course, the questions were just a ruse to placate Ms. Wernersbach since all Doctor Laveau was interested in was gathering a sample of the psycho's hair.

During the interview, she noticed that Everhart was chewing gum. When the interview ended, he took the gum out of his mouth and defiantly stuck it under the table before returning to his cell.

"Doctor Laveau, is there anything else?" Ms. Wernersbach asked.

"No, thank you and Mr. Everhart again for helping me with my research. Good luck to you, Mr. Everhart."

Just before he left the room, he turned and stared at her, "Are you an alien, Doctor?"

"No, Mr. Everhart. I was born on Earth." Doctor Laveau said, smiling.

Doctor Laveau went home and began to mold the wax into the shape of another human figure resembling Roger Everhart. Once she shaped the wax, she took a large piece of raw burlap and began to cut out two shapes of a crude human figure. She again sewed the two pieces together with the wax form inside, then took the hair clippings from Everhart and the chewing gum that she retrieved from under the desk and placed them inside the burlap. She then finished sewing the burlap completely shut.

Doctor Laveau sewed two buttons onto the head of the figure, one large black button and a smaller white button like the one for Alexander.

When the doll was ready, she applied some blood on the doll's forehead, chest, and belly while chanting, "I name you Roger Everhart. You are now him!"

She lit three new black candles and placed an Everhart photo on the doll.

"You are the black candle I want you to suffer, Roger Everhart; you are the spirit of my enemy and should die a long and lingering spiritus of death. I call you to take this life as a blow my breath with anger."

She held the doll over the candles and continued, "Spiritus of death, take away this persona life after I blow out this candle."

Doctor Laveau held the doll over the candles and blew out two. While still holding the doll over the remaining burning black candle, she took two Vodou spirit pins and stuck them into the doll's lower back and in his mouth while chanting,

"I here call upon Goddess Hecate, the Powerful
Spirit of death,
I ask your help to kill my enemies.
Appear to me now, show yourself!
Kill Roger Everhart.
By the power of your full moon tonight.
I swear these words until they die. I swear they die.
Until the candles light gone!
This is my will, so mote it be!"

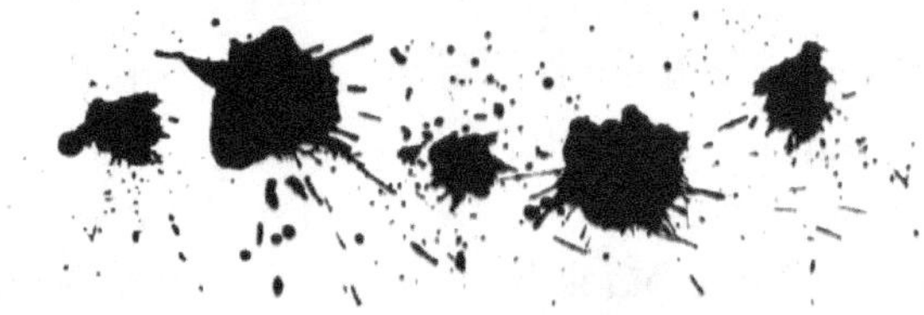

Two days after constructing Everhart's Vodou doll, Doctor Laveau was listening to the radio in her car driving home from work,

"Good evening, and welcome to WJM's six o'clock news. I'm Biff Bradley with breaking news. Roger Everhart, the suspected mass murderer of eleven people, was found in his home paralyzed from the waist down this morning. The Police have released a statement that no foul play is suspected at this time, although they are not ruling out the possibility.

Sources tell WJM that Mr. Everhart was found this morning by one of his attorneys, Ms. Wernersbach, who said she tried to reach him by phone to no avail, so she stopped by his home. Looking through the living room window, she saw what she thought was a person lying on the floor. She then called 911.

Ms. Wernsbach told WJM that it appears that he is also unable to speak.

Mr. Everhart was suspected of killing eleven people, claiming that they were aliens from outer space. He was recently released from custody through a Police procedural error in obtaining a search warrant.

We go live to Justin Trice, who is at Bellevue Hospital with more...."

Captain O'Rourke called Roscoe and Detective Walsh into his office, "What the Hell's going on Roscoe first Alexander died mysteriously, and now Everhart is struck down, paralyzed, and mute. Something fishy is going on here."

"I agree, sir, it's odd. Do you think something might be happening at Rikers, maybe some kind of virus or bacteria?"

"I guess it's possible; I'll call the Board of Health and see what they have to say. Meanwhile, Roscoe, why don't you and Walsh look into their cases and see if anything jumps out at you."

"You got it, Captain."

Roscoe and Walsh went downstairs to the detective's squad room to review the Everhart and Alexander files. It took most of the morning before they noticed something both cases had in common… Doctor Laveau.

Both Ryan Alexander and Roger Everhart had meetings with Doctor Laveau days before they were struck down. Roscoe was about to call the Captain when he got a call from Doctor Olsen, the ME.

"Roscoe, this is Doctor Olsen."

"Hold on, Doc, I'm putting you on speaker. I got Jimmy with me; go ahead."

"I just wanted to alert you that Roger Everhart has died this morning. I got a call from Bellevue Hospital saying that he had died."

"Do they know from what?" Walsh asked.

"No, not yet. They said that he suffered from severe convulsions at the end. It was an excruciatingly painful death, I'm told."

"Well, I can't say the bastard didn't deserve it," Roscoe said.

"Oh, Roscoe, by the way. I checked with some of my colleagues, and none of them have ever heard of species hair analysis. Now, that's not to say that this Doctor Laveau might not be on to something, you know, weirder things have happened, but everyone I've spoken with said that it sounds like a bunch of hooey."

"Doc, can you think of any reason why she would be taking a clipping of hair?"

"As I said, Roscoe, not unless she's on to something unique."

"Okay, thanks, Doc. I appreciate it."

"Shall we go tell the Captain?" Walsh asked.

"Right after we go over to Nathan's Famous for a couple of dogs, my treat."

"Roscoe, you've eaten at Nathan's every day this week. Don't you ever get tired of eating hot dogs?"

"No."

"Say, why don't we try that little Japanese restaurant over on Brighton Beach Avenue? I hear it's delicious."

"Are you seriously considering eating fish heads and rice, Walsh?"

'It's not fish heads. It's called sushi. Sushi is vinegared rice, usually with some sugar and salt, with a piece of seafood on top. Sometimes it's a piece of raw fish, but you can get it with some cooked shrimp and even smoked salmon."

"Agh! Gag me with a spoon."

"Well, at least it doesn't have rat turds in it like hot dogs."

"Hey! Nathan's Famous don't have rat shit in them; maybe some of them low-quality dogs do, but not my Nathans. So, you go ahead and eat your vinegary fish guts. I'm heading over to Nathan's for some real American food. See you back here in about an hour."

"Your loss."

"See ya later."

"Sayōnara."

Doctor Laveau was walking down near the Boardwalk when she walked past Deno's Wonder Wheel Amusement Park on West 12th Street to Surf Avenue.

Several small vendors were using a vacant lot selling souvenirs, and a woman in the back was dressed like a gypsy sitting at a small card table. She had a large black raven perched on a wooden stand next to her, and there was a handwritten sign, "Gypsy Joan. Psychic Readings & Fortunes told."

Gypsy Joan offered all the standard arts, Palm Readings, Tarot Cards, Candle Readings, and Crystal Ball readings, but she also did specialty spiritual consultations using more mystical forms and methods.

Gypsy Joan performs Cleromancy, a form of sortition, the casting of animal bones; Alectormancy, the observation of a rooster pecking at grain; and Extispicy, the reading of the entrails of animals.

The gypsy woman was sitting behind a round table covered with a black tablecloth embroidered with golden skulls. In the middle of the table was a crystal ball surrounded by three black candles.

Gypsy Joan was a woman in her late sixties, but she looked like she was in her fifties, with hazel eyes and blond, gray hair. She wore a traditional multicolor headscarf and two oversized gold hoop earrings.

As Doctor Laveau approached the gypsy woman, who was in deep concentration reading tarot cards, she looked up and said reluctantly, "Have a seat, Vodou woman."

Doctor Laveau stood in front of the gypsy in shock, "What did you say?"

"You are a Vodou queen, are you not?"

"You… How… How… What makes you say that?"

"I am not a charlatan, Doctor. I am a descendant of twelve generations of pure Hungarian gypsy blood. We came to this country to escape the Nazis in the 1930s, but our powers of necromancy and divination remain as powerful as ever."

"That's amazing."

"What is it you wish to know, Doctor."

"How did you know that I'm a doctor?"

"You are not here to ask such trivial questions." The gypsy said as she gazed into her crystal ball.

"You are here because you are deeply troubled. One part of you is good; you help people, but recently, since you have gained your Vodou powers, you have been tempted and drawn into the Black Arts, am I right?"

"Yes. I'm very troubled and conflicted."

Still looking into the crystal ball and not at Doctor Laveau, the gypsy said, "I can see that even though you are a good person, you see pure evil, and you feel that you must act."

"It's true. I see evil every day. It's gotten to the point where I feel I can no longer idly stand by, not when I have the power to intercede. I guess I want to know how it will all end?"

"Death comes to us all, Doctor."

"I guess I'd just like to know when."

"If you really want to know, I will tell you. But knowing will not change the future. You will die when you die; nothing you do will alter your destiny. Every decision you make, even after you know everything, is preordained. In this, you are powerless."

Doctor Laveau sat motionless for several minutes, staring off into nothingness. She slowly returned to being in the moment and said, "Thank you, gypsy woman."

Doctor Laveau stood from the chair, reached into her purse, handed Gypsy Joan two one-hundred-dollar bills, and walked away.

As she walked fifty feet from the gypsy's table to the street, she turned around and discovered that the gypsy was gone. The table, the chairs, the sign, everything, gone as if she had never existed. When Doctor Laveau reached the corner of West 12th and Surf Avenue, a large black raven sat atop the stop sign.

"Thank you, Gypsy Joan," Laveau whispered.

"Cacaw, Cacaw."

Over the next six months, there were eight more unexplained deaths at Rikers Island, and every one of them had but one thing in common: Doctor Laveau.

"Captain, there just has to be a connection. Doctor Laveau is the one common thread that runs through every one of the deaths. I don't know how, but somehow, she's part of these deaths." Roscoe said.

"I've already spoken to DA Gladwell; he's talking to Judge Parker, and hopefully, we'll get a warrant for her office and home. I know I don't have to mention this to you and Walsh, but there can be no invasion of any doctor-client privilege, so tread carefully." Captain O'Rourke stated.

"Yes, sir."

O'Rourke, Walsh, and Roscoe sat silently in the Captain's office, waiting to hear from Gladwell.

"Captain O'Rourke, you have a call on line one. It's the DA's office." A voice from O'Rourke's intercom broke the pregnant pause in the room.

"O'Rourke here.

Yes sir.

Uh-huh.

Got it.

I understand.

Thank you, goodbye."

The Captain hung up the phone, turned to the two detectives, and said, "Okay, you got the warrant. Gladwell wants me to reiterate that you are to err on the side of caution when it comes to the sanctity of doctor-client privilege. If you have any doubts or questions, stop and wait for clarification from the DA's office, understood?"

"Got it," Roscoe said as he and Walsh left O'Rourke's office.

"How about you take her office, and I'll scope out her home."

"I'll call you if we find anything, Roscoe."

"I'll do the same."

Roscoe rang Doctor Laveau's doorbell at her home. He was accompanied by six uniformed Police Officers, two of them women.

There was the barking of a dog, and a few moments later, Doctor Laveau came to the door.

She seemed surprised to see so many Police Officers on her doorstep.

"Yes?"

"Doctor Laveau?"

"Yes, I am Doctor Laveau; how may I help you?"

"I am Detective Sergeant Brown, and I have a warrant to search these premises."

"Well, if you have a search warrant, I guess you're going to come in."

"If you would please stay with Officer Adele in the living room with your dog while we execute the warrant. I suggest that you might want to call your attorney, Doctor."

It took less than an hour before they came across ten Vodou dolls with voodoo pins still stuck in them displayed in a glass-covered cabinet, each one labeled with the name of the victim in what looked to be a library/study. There were hundreds of standard medical books on built-in bookcases within the room and dozens of books on Vodou, the occult, and the Black Arts.

Roscoe had Doctor Laveau brought up to the library, "Doctor Laveau, can you tell me what these dolls are?"

"They are Vodou dolls, Detective Brown."

"And their purpose?"

"To cast a spell or curse upon the subject."

"And did you cast a spell or curse upon Ryan Alexander with this doll?"

"I did."

"And the result?"

"He died."

"Doctor Laveau, are you saying that you killed Ryan Alexander?"

"No, I didn't say that. I said that I cast a curse on Mr. Alexander, and he died."

"Oh boy. Doctor Laveau, would you mind if I use your phone?"

"Not at all, Detective."

"Thank you, Doctor. Officer Adele, would you mind escorting Doctor Laveau back into the living room?"

Roscoe called Detective Walsh to have him meet him at Doctor Laveau's home; then he dialed the precinct.

"Hello, Captain, Roscoe here. I need you to come to Doctor Laveau's. It's 4900 Beach 49th Street, and you better bring Gladwell, too. You ain't going to believe this one."

Roscoe and Walsh were waiting upstairs when a uniformed officer brought the Captain and the DA into the library.

Roscoe had laid out all ten Vodou dolls on a long wooden table. Placed next to each doll was the name of the ten men who had died after meeting with Doctor Laveau at Rikers Island.

"What is all this, Detective Brown?" Gladwell asked.

"These are Vodou dolls Doctor Laveau made of the ten men she met at Rikers Island."

"You brought us out at this time of night to look at some hoodoo dolls!"

"Mr. Gladwell, Captain, these are Black Magic Vodou dolls, and according to Doctor Laveau, she made these dolls with the express purpose of placing a death curse on each of these men, who subsequently died. She freely admits it."

"You're not seriously telling us that Doctor Laveau killed these men with a curse. Is that what you're telling us, Detective? If this is the best you've got, Detective Brown, maybe you should see someone at CIT." Gladwell demanded.

"Look, I know it sounds crazy, I'll admit it. But we have ten men who all died at Rikers Island, every one of whom died unexpectedly and inexplicably. Every one of them last met with Doctor Laveau.

Now, I'm just a detective, but I have a suspect who freely admits to meeting with the victims, who freely admits to taking samples of each hair, and who freely admits to constructing these dolls and placing a death curse on them.

What you do with this information is for you to decide, District Attorney Gladwell. You can hold her, charge her, or free her; I really don't give a rat's ass! But don't you ever, ever question my detective abilities or my mental competency, you got that!" Roscoe snarled.

"I'm sorry, Detective Brown. I apologize for my regrettable remarks. It's just that this is something beyond the norm.

You're right; I think it might be best if we hold her so we can ascertain more information." Gladwell said apologetically.

"I'll go and have Officer Adele take her to the station for questioning," Roscoe said as he left the room.

Captain O'Rourke turned to Gladwell, "Not cool, Roger."

"I'm sorry, Sean, but you must admit how ludicrous this sounds?"

"That doesn't give you any excuse to kill the messenger."

"Come on, Sean. Death by Vodou!"

"There are more things in heaven and earth."

"Ecclesiastes?"

"Shakespeare," O'Rourke said.

Doctor Laveau sat stoically in the interrogation room, waiting for her inquisitors. She didn't have to wait long. Detectives Brown and Walsh entered the room along with District Attorney Gladwell, and a court stenographer sat across from the doctor. Roscoe said, "Doctor Laveau, at the present time, you are not under arrest; however if you should want a lawyer present, that is your prerogative."

"No, I'm fine."

"Very good; before we get started, Doctor Laveau, I am Detective Sergeant Brown; this is Detective Walsh, and sitting next to him is District Attorney Gladwell. And that lady sitting over there is a court stenographer making a record of this conversation, do you understand?"

"Yes."

"Now, doctor, I am holding what you call a Vodou doll that you said you constructed to cast a death spell on Ryan Alexander. Is that correct?"

"Yes, I took a sample of Mr. Alexander's hair and a cigarette butt that he had been smoking, and I constructed a doll in his likeness, incorporating the cigarette and hair into the doll figure before sewing it up."

"And you did the same with the other nine men that you had psychic evaluation meetings with at Rikers Island, is that correct?"

"Yes, I managed to get hair samples from each man, along with some other items that they had touched or owned, so that I could put them into their doll."

'What did you do after you had made the doll of the men?"

"I performed a Vodou ritual, a Black Arts ritual to put a death curse on them. After I performed the ceremony, I chanted a death incantation, naming my victim. I took the pins you see in the doll and placed them in the body where I wanted the curse to affect death.

For Mr. Alexander, I put a pin in his heart and one in the head, which would cause him to die from a heart attack or a stroke. As it turned out, he had both a heart attack and a stroke."

"But Mr. Everhart didn't die right away, did he?"

"No, that's because I wanted him to suffer, so I didn't insert the Vodou pin in all the way until two days later when he did die.

Detective Brown, if you scrutinize the other dolls, you'll see that the position of the pins will all coincide with how each man died." Doctor Laveau said calmly and methodically, without emotion.

District Attorney Gladwell leaned forward and said, "With all due respect, Doctor Laveau, you expect me to believe that in this day and age, in 1966, you murdered these men with Black Magic?"

"How do *you* explain their deaths, Mr. Gladwell?"

"Well, not by a bunch of hoodoo, hocus pocus bullshit that some self-proclaimed witch doctor claims to have magical powers, that's for damn sure, Doctor."

"Does that mean you're not charging me with a crime?"

Gladwell looked at Brown and Walsh like a deer in the headlights, then turned to Doctor Laveau and said, "No, you may go."

Doctor Laveau stood up and reached out her hand to Roscoe, "May I have the doll?"

Roscoe glanced over to Gladwell, "Are you sure?"

"Give her back the fucking doll, Detective Brown."

Roscoe handed the doll to Doctor Laveau, "Thank you, Doctor Laveau; you have to know that your days as a criminal psychiatrist in New York are effectively over."

"Yes, Detective, I know. I've decided to move back to New Orleans, where my great aunt has left me some property."

On her way out of the interrogation room, Doctor Laveau stopped short of the door; she turned around and said, "Mr. Gladwell."

He turned to face her, "Yes?"

Doctor Laveau raised her right hand to cover her mouth; she mumbled something and pointed her left hand at the DA.

Gladwell started to say something, but nothing came out. He jumped up from his seat and tried again to speak; again, no sound emerged. Sweat began to pour down his face. A look of panic and desperation fell across his face.

"Doctor, please!" Roscoe said.

Doctor Laveau touched her mouth again, uttered something, snapped her fingers, and walked out the door.

Gladwell gasped and finally spoke, "Jesus Christ, Roscoe! What the Hell was that?"

"Oh, just a bunch of hoodoo, hocus pocus bullshit."

The following day, the New York Post ran the headline, *"Voodoo Queen Kills Cons."*

The story went on to describe how Doctor Laveau, a criminal psychiatrist, was brought in for questioning to the 60th Precinct after admitting that she placed voodoo curses on ten men being held at Rikers Island whom she had interviewed and who all later mysteriously died. She was later released but remains a person of interest.

Doctor Laveau met with Roscoe and Detective Walsh at the Six O two days after her initial interrogation with DA Gladwell.

"Doctor Laveau, thank you for coming."

"What can I do you, Detective Brown."

"Doctor Laveau, I've spoken with the District Attorney's office."

"Yes?"

"They've officially decided not to press charges."

"Why is that, Detective Brown?"

"Gladwell doesn't want to go through a public trial prosecuting a witch doctor. You see, there are just too many religious voters, and Gladwell feels that it's a no-win situation for him."

"What do you think, Detective Brown?"

"Doctor Laveau, I'm just a cop; I go where the evidence takes me. I've seen people killed every way imaginable and in a lot of unimaginable ways as well. Over the years, I've learned never to rule anything out.

I believe you killed those men, Doctor. But believing that you did it and proving that you did it are two different things.

"So, what will you do now?"

"Like I said, I'm moving back to New Orleans with my dog Dédé. Goodbye, Detective Brown, Detective Walsh, thank you."

Doctor Laveau shook their hands and left. Captain O'Rourke came in after she had gone.

"Roscoe, do you think she actually killed those ten men with voodoo?" O'Rourke asked.

"Oh, I don't know, Captain, but it will be interesting to see which doctor she chooses to be."

"What do you think, Walsh?" O'Rourke asked.

"I don't know Captain; she's very convincing, and that thing she did with Gladwell, pretty spooky."

"Hey, Walsh, knock, knock," Roscoe said.

"I don't want to!"

"Come on. Knock, knock."

"Who's there?" Walsh asked skeptically.

"Voodoo."

"Voodoo, who?"

"Voodoo, you think you are asking all these questions?"

"Cute."

THE END

The Case of Our Lady of the Bone Yard

Detective Roscoe Brown and Betty were sitting on the sofa watching Gunsmoke when Betty said, "Roscoe, I feel like going to Mass tomorrow."

"Uh, okay."

"Will you come with me?"

"Aw, Betty, but the Giants are playing the Eagles tomorrow."

"Please?"

"Oh, all right, but if we have to, let's go to the early Mass. Okay? The kickoff is at noon."

Si iniquitátes observáveris, Dómine, Dómine, quis sustinébit? quia apud te propitiátio est, Deus Israël. De profúndis clamávi ad te, Dómine: Dómine, exáudi vocem meam. Glória Patri et Fílio et Spíritui Sancto, sicut erat in princípio, et nunc, et semper, et in sǽcula sæculórum. Amen. Si iniquitátes observáveris, Dómine, Dómine, quis sustinébit? quia apud te propitiátio est, Deus Israël.

Roscoe felt that if he had to sit through Mass, he'd prefer it to be in Latin. He wasn't really a Catholic, but he converted when he married Betty. Roscoe thought of himself as a spiritual person, but he never felt he needed an organized religion to proselytize to him.

When the Priest was conducting Mass in Latin, Roscoe's eyes would glaze over, and for an hour, he would transport himself into his own little world somewhere far, far away. He would linger there until Betty would nudge him in the ribs for him to return to the present.

Qui vivis et regnas, cum Deo Patre in unitáte Spíritus Sancti, Deus, per ómnia sǽcula sæculórum.

Amen.

As they walked out of Our Lady of Solace, Betty asked, "Roscoe, do you get anything out of these services?"

"Sure, I do, Betty."

"What?"

"An hour of serenity."

"But you don't really pay attention or truly understand what's happening."

"True, but just spending that peaceful and reverent time in such a spiritual place gives me peace, especially when I'm with you."

Betty smiled and replied, "You're such a lair, but thank you."

The Priest, Father McDonnell, approached them as they were just outside.

"Roscoe, could I have a moment of your time, please?"

"Shit," Roscoe uttered under his breath to Betty.

"Roscoe, I believe I might have a matter requiring the Police."

"Really, Father?"

"Well, we were having some construction work done behind the Our Lady of Solace Rectory, and this morning, some members of the construction crew believe that they may have found some human remains, some bones."

"Betty, why don't you go on home, and I'll be there as soon as I check this out," Roscoe said.

"I don't mind waiting."

"No, you go on; I don't know how long I'll be," Roscoe said as he kissed her.

"If you'd just follow me." Father McDonnell said as he led the way.

Roscoe followed Father McDonnell past the Convent of the Holy Names of Jesus and Mary, turning left into the driveway of the Rectory to the back of the building where a large hole had been dug.

Several construction workers were standing around the rectangular-shaped, three-foot-deep crater. Down at the bottom were cloth fragments and definite human remains.

Roscoe turned to Father McDonnell and said, "Father, this is now a crime scene; nobody touches anything. Can I use your phone?"

"Yes, of course."

Within twenty minutes, the Our Lady of Solace Rectory was swarming with Police, folks from the crime lab, Police photographers, and the coroner.

Detective James Walsh, Roscoe's partner, arrived shortly after the coroner.

"Hey, Jimmy, sorry to ruin your weekend," Roscoe said.

"You actually did me a favor; I was sitting on the 40-yard line at Yankee Stadium watching the Giants getting their asses handed to them by Philadelphia."

"In that case, you're welcome."

"Whadda we got?"

"The construction workers found the remains of a body in that hole."

"Do we know if it's male or female?"

"Should know soon; Doc Olsen is down there now."

Father McDonnell approached them, "Roscoe, what's happening?"

"Still waiting to hear from the medical examiner. Oh, Father McDonnell, this is my partner, Detective Walsh."

"It's nice to meet you, Detective Walsh. I just wish it could have been under more pleasant circumstances."

"Nice to meet you, too, Father McDonnell."

"Hey, Roscoe!" A voice from down in the crater bellowed.

Roscoe looked at the Priest and said, "Excuse me, Father."

Roscoe and Walsh walked to the excavation site to see Doctor Olsen kneel beside the skeleton. "So, Roscoe, it appears to be the remains of a young woman. I'd say probably between 16 and 20 years old."

"Can you tell the cause of death, Doc?"

"Yeah, it looks like blunt force trauma to the back of the skull. It's definitely murder."

"Can you tell me how long he's been buried?"

"I can't say until I get her back to the lab."

"Thanks, Doc," Roscoe said.

Roscoe went over to where Father McDonnell was standing.

"I'm sorry, Father, it appears to be the remains of a young woman, around 16 to 20 years old, and it looks like she was murdered."

"Oh, dear God. That poor child. What happens now?"

"Well, this area will be closed off as a crime scene until the crime lab gives the all-clear. Until then, I need you to keep everyone away from this area so as not to contaminate any evidence."

"Yes, of course. Any idea how long that might be?"

"Sorry, Father, I haven't a clue. But it shouldn't be longer than a couple of days."

"Well, I thank you, Roscoe. Please keep me up to date. Now, if you'll excuse me, I must alert the Archdiocese."

As Father McDonnell walked away, Roscoe said, "Come on, Jimmy, let's head back to the squad room and check the missing persons for missing girls over the last ten years. We'll wait to hear from the Doc."

"Roscoe, are you thinking what I'm thinking?"

"Yep. I got a bad feeling about this, Jimmy."

"Me too, Roscoe. Me too."

Roscoe and Walsh started looking for children through all the missing person reports going back ten years until they got confirmation from the ME. They decided to look for missing girls and cross-reference them with families in the Our Lady of Solace Church area.

Roscoe looked at his watch and said, "Hey, Jimmy, let's call it a day; it's five o'clock. We'll pick it up first thing in the morning."

"Okay, how many do you have?"

"I have six, you?"

"Four."

"You have dinner plans? Want to come over?"

"Thanks, but I'm supposed to get together with Veronica."

"Yeah, that's better than having dinner with an old married couple. You kids go out and have fun."

"Kids, Roscoe, you're only five years older than me. Kids!"

When Roscoe got home that evening, Betty was putting dinner on the table. She had made one of his favorite meals: meatloaf, mashed potatoes, and broccoli.

"Hey, babe, smells good. Meatloaf?" Roscoe said as he entered the apartment. He hung up his overcoat and trademark fedora on the coat rack just inside the front door.

"Hi, honey; sorry about making you go to Mass this morning." She said as she put her arms around his neck and gave him a big kiss.

"So, were they human remains?" She asked.

"I'm afraid so, and they appear to be that of a young woman."

"Oh, Roscoe, how terrible."

"We're waiting to hear back from the ME tomorrow for more information."

"Say, why don't we eat in front of the TV tonight."

"Really?"

"Sure, I saw that on the Ed Sullivan Show, there's going to be your favorite Robert Goulet, Louie Armstrong, that rock and roll band the Rolling Stones, and Red Skelton."

"Ooh, Robert Goulet and Red Skelton, great."

They spent the evening keeping things light. Betty knew that the murder of the young always weighed heavy on Roscoe, so after Ed Sullivan, they watched the Smothers

Brothers' show Candid Camera, then went to bed early and made love.

"Doctor Olsen called this morning; she said they're sending out the girl's dental records to see if they can get a match. He said that he thinks the body has been there for at least ten to twelve years." Walsh told Roscoe as he strolled into the squad room.

"Find any more missing person reports that might be our girl?" Roscoe asked.

"I narrowed it down to three with the new timeline from the Doc.

There's Melissa Roberts, sixteen. She was reported missing six years ago; she and her family have attended Our Lady of Solace for over ten years.

Then there's Sally Beechwood, eighteen. She was reported missing ten years ago by her aunt and uncle. They were her legal custodians since her parents were killed in a car crash. They've been attending Our Lady of Solace for over ten years.

And finally, we have Diane Harris, also eighteen. She was reported missing eight years ago by her mother. She's a single mother; the husband abandoned them when Diane was four. They aren't regulars at Our Lady of Solace; they are more like the holiday faithful. "

"So, who do you want to start with?"

"Start with the one who's been missing the longest, Sally Beechwood."

"Okay, you check the girls out, and I'm going to do some nosing around Our Lady of Solace. Hate to say it, but most Churches have plenty of, forgive the pun, skeletons buried in their closets."

"Ouch."

"Hey, give me a break."

"So, you go to Our Lady of Solace. Have you heard any rumors of bad behavior?"

"Walsh, you know I only go there because Betty makes me go, Hell I'm not even Catholic. I guess she's probably a good place to start since she's been going there since she was a kid."

As Walsh was heading out to interview the missing girls' families, Roscoe's phone rang.

"Hold on, Jimmy, this might be important," Roscoe said as he put it on the intercom.

"Roscoe here."

"Roscoe, this is David Bowles over at the crime lab."

"Oh, hey, Dave. What's up?"

"Well, not good news."

"What?"

"We found more bones in the hole behind the Rectory."

"Holy shit! How many?"

"At least two more bodies."

"Did you call Olsen?"

"Yeah, he's on his way."

"Me and Walsh are leaving now."

"Okay, we'll see ya soon."

Father McDonnell went to the Diocese of Brooklyn to report the tragic news and spoke to Bishop Guido Bergamaschi, Bishop of Brooklyn.

He approached the Bishop, kneeled, kissed his ring, and said, "Your Excellency Bergamaschi, I have some distressing news."

"What is it, Father McDonnell?"

"While men were working on the Rectory, they have uncovered human remains."

"Could they be relics, Father McDonnell?"

"Doubtful, Your Excellency, the Police believe them to be the remains of a young woman."

"Pity. Do they think foul play was involved?"

"Yes, Excellency. I heard there was evidence of blunt force trauma."

"Oh, dear. Well, you must, of course, give them your full cooperation, Father McDonnell, and you will keep me apprised of any developments."

"Of course, Your Excellency."

"Father McDonnell, I must inform the Archbishop of this terrible situation."

"Yes, Your Excellency."

"Have you told anyone about this?"

"No, Your Excellency."

"So, as far as you know, the media is unaware of these findings?"

"As far as I know, Your Excellency. I have not spoken to anyone about this."

"Very good; if anyone does contact you, refer them to my office, do you understand?"

"Yes, Your Excellency."

"Tragedies like this have to be handled delicately; we don't want any bad press for the Church."

"Yes, Your Excellency."

"Father McDonnell, refresh my memory; how long have you been at Our Lady of Solace?"

"Six years, Your Excellency."

"Well, Father McDonnell, thank you for bringing this to my attention."

"Yes, Your Excellency. Thank you, Your Excellency." Father McDonnell said as he stood awkwardly waiting to be dismissed.

"You may go now, Father McDonnell."

"Thank you, Your Excellency."

Doctor Olsen had just climbed out of the crater when Roscoe and Detective Walsh arrived.

"Roscoe, it looks like we have two more, similar to the first, blunt force trauma to the head. These two look to be about the same age. Oh, and the crime lab found this." Olsen said as he handed Roscoe a small statuette of Jesus carrying a lamb encased in a plastic evidence bag.

Roscoe called David Bowles from CSI, who was still looking for evidence down in the hole, "Hey, Dave when you get a free minute, could you come here?"

"Be right there, Roscoe."

"I think there still might be viable fingerprints on it, Roscoe?" Detective Walsh asked.

"That's what I want to ask Bowles," Roscoe answered.

Doctor Olsen patted Roscoe and Walsh on the back as he headed to his car. "I'll phone you boys after I reach my conclusions."

"See ya, Doc," Walsh said.

David Bowles climbed the ladder out of the hole holding two plastic bags. "Here you go. We found these, too."

Roscoe held the bags up; he saw that they were two gold chains, each with a gold medallion attached. Father McDonnell, standing nearby, saw that Roscoe was trying to figure out what he was holding and asked, "Roscoe, may I be of some help?"

Roscoe handed the two bags to McDonnell, "I know They are saints, but I don't know who. Can you tell, Father?"

Father McDonnell examined them and said, "One is Saint Agnes, the patron saint of girls, and the other is Saint Francis de Sales, the patron saint of writers and journalists."

"Thanks, Father McDonnell, that could be a big help in identifying who these poor girls are."

Roscoe took back the plastic bags containing the medallions and went back to confer with David Bowles. "Dave, how likely will you be able to pull any fingerprints from the statuette of Jesus and the lamb?"

"To be honest, slim to none. But we'll try."

"Have the photographer whip me up some photos of all this so we can start to try to identify these girls."

"Will do. You should have them in a couple of hours."

Roscoe noticed that Father McDonnell was starting to walk back into the Church.

"Father McDonnell, could you get the names of all the staff and employees of Our Lady of Solace for the past ten years?"

"You don't actually suspect anyone from Our Lady of Solace could have had anything to do with these horrific crimes, do you?"

"Father, it's routine Police procedure, and at this point, I suspect everyone; I'm sorry."

"I understand, Roscoe. I'll have my secretary get you those names, even the members of the clergy?"

"I'm afraid so, Father, even clergy."

"Saints alive!"

Officer Ron Harris drove Detective Walsh and Roscoe to 2811 West 16th Street, just a few blocks from Our Lady of Solace. An all-blonde brick two-story house amongst several apartment buildings on both sides of the street.

While Officer Harris waited in the car, Roscoe and Walsh went to the front door. Roscoe rang the doorbell, took out his ID badge, and held it up when the door opened.

A woman in her forties answered the door. She was dressed in a floral housecoat, no makeup, and hair in curlers. Roscoe could tell she was probably an absolute stunner when she was younger, but twenty-some years of marriage and a couple of kids had taken its toll.

"Mrs. Roberts?" Roscoe asked.

"Yes?"

"Mrs. Roberts, I'm Detective Sergeant Brown, and this is my partner, Detective Walsh. May we come in?" Roscoe said, holding up his ID badge.

Mrs. Roberts clearly looked embarrassed about how she was dressed, "Yes, please come in. You'll have to forgive the way I'm dressed; I was getting the children off to school."

"No need to apologize, Mrs. Roberts," Roscoe said as he removed his fedora.

"You're here about Melissa. Please come in. Have you found her?" She said as she dropped down on the sofa; her eyes started tearing up.

"Mrs. Roberts, could you tell us if Melissa wore a medallion of a Catholic saint?"

"Catholic medallion? Yes, she always wore a gold necklace with Saint Francis. You see, our Melissa loves animals and wants to be a veterinarian when she grows up. Why?"

"We found the remains of three girls, and amongst the remains, there were two gold necklaces with saint's medallions and one gold necklace with nothing attached."

"So, my Melissa wasn't one of the bodies you found. So, she still might be alive!"

"We can't say that for sure. We still have to check dental records. If you don't mind, could you give us the name of Melissa's dentist so we can eliminate the possibility that your daughter was one of these girls?"

"Doctor Tripp, over on Mermaid Avenue."

"Mrs. Roberts, do you have a photograph of Melissa that we might borrow? We promise to return it to you." Walsh asked.

She walked to the fireplace and took a framed photograph of a beautiful, smiling sixteen-year-old girl off the mantle; she kissed it and handed it to Detective Walsh. The girl had braces and was wearing a gold necklace with a Saint Francis medallion.

"Thank you, we'll take good care of it," He said.

"Mrs. Roberts, we're sorry to have disturbed you. We will be in touch as soon as we know anything." Roscoe said as he handed her one of his cards.

"How'd it go?" Harris asked.

"She might be one of them; we'll have to wait to hear back from the dental records," Walsh said.

"Where to now, Sarge?" Harris asked, looking in the rearview.

"Let's go see Sally Beechwood's aunt and uncle. Where do they live, Jimmy?"

Walsh looked up the address in the folder, "Aw shit." Walsh sighed.

"What's the matter?" Harris asked.

"They live in Luna Park."

"What's wrong with that?"

"Go ahead and tell him, Roscoe."

"Walsh is just upset that since we'll only be two blocks away from the world's greatest hot dog stand, that we'll be dining at Nathan's Famous, and of course we will," Roscoe said with a big shit-eating grin on his face.

"Come on. Roscoe. Don't you ever get tired of having the same thing for lunch nearly every single day? Can't we eat somewhere else?" Walsh pleaded.

Roscoe sat in the backseat smiling with his arms crossed his chest and said, "No and no."

"Mr. Beechwood, I'm Detective Sergeant Brown, and this is my partner, Detective Walsh. May we come in?"

"Sure, sure, sure, come on in. What's this all about, officer? I thought I paid that parking ticket."

"No, Mr. Beechwood, we're here about Sally."

"Sally? Have you found her? Where is she? Is she all right?"

"That's what we're trying to ascertain. Mr. Beechwood. Do you know if Sally wore a Catholic saint's medallion necklace?"

"Why yes, she wore a medallion of Saint Agnes. My wife, Sally's aunt, gave it to her for her sixteenth birthday."

"Mr. Beechwood, we found the remains of a young woman two days ago, and there was a medallion of Saint Agnes. I have a photograph of it I'd like to show you." Roscoe said as he handed Beechwood the close-up photo of the medallion.

Beechwood stared at the photo for a few minutes; his shoulders dropped, then his whole body's posture slumped. "Yes, it's hers. Where was she?" He asked.

"Some workers found her remains behind the Rectory at Our Lady of Solace."

"Our Lady of Solace?"

"Yes, sir."

"That son of a bitch!"

"Who?"

"Father Byrne. Father Michael Byrne."

"And why would you say that he might have had something to do with Sally's murder?"

"I told you people ten years ago that you should have checked him out. There were several complaints made about his misconduct with young girls, complaints to the Church and even to the Archbishop, and nothing was ever done until he was transferred, or whatever they call it, to another Parrish. I heard that he's over in Rome now working in the Vatican. Can you believe it? They promoted the bastard."

"Well, Mr. Beechwood, I can promise you that we will personally look into these allegations against Father Byrne," Roscoe said as he handed him his business card.

"Please call me if you can think of anything else, Mr. Beechwood. We appreciate your time." Roscoe said as he and Walsh left the apartment.

While waiting for the elevator, Walsh asked, "So, whadda ya think? A Priest?"

"Hey, contrary to popular belief, Priests are human too. After lunch, let's see what Diane Harris's parents have to say."

"Mr. and Mrs. Harris, I'm Detective Sergeant Brown, and this is my partner, Detective Walsh; we're here regarding your missing daughter, Diane. May we come in?"

The Harris' lived in the affluent Manhattan Beach area on the east side of Coney Island. Their single-story brick home on Shore Boulevard had a magnificent view of Sheepshead Bay, where all the sailboats and yachts from the Sheepshead Bay Yacht Club were moored.

Roscoe and Walsh were invited into the living room.

"Please have a seat, Detectives." Mr. Harris said as he and his wife sat across from them on facing sofas.

"Have you found our baby?" Mrs. Harris asked.

Roscoe leaned forward and handed Mr. Harris the photograph of the Saint Francis de Sales medallion. "Do you recognize this medallion?"

"Yes, it's Saint Francis de Sales, the patron saint of writers. Our Diane had been accepted to NYU on a writing scholarship."

"What Church do you attend, Mrs. Harris?"

"We used to attend Our Lady of Solace."

"Used to? Why did you stop?"

"We found, or I should say, I found, no solace given by the Church or the clergy to our grief. Particularly from Father Michael Byrne, who was the Priest at the time." Mr. Harris said.

"Detective Brown, have you found our Diane?" Mrs. Harris begged.

"It appears we have the remains of three young women who were uncovered behind the Rectory at Our Lady of Solace two days ago. This necklace was found at the scene, but we're still checking dental records before making a positive ID."

"I want to know how she died?" Mr. Harris demanded.

"According to the medical examiner, all the girls were killed by a blow to the head."

"Did she suffer, Detective?"

"No, ma'am, I don't believe she did." Roscoe lied.

"Thank God." Mrs. Harris uttered.

"Was Diane involved in activities in the Church?"

"She wrote for the Church bulletin."

"Do you know who she worked with on the bulletin?"

"Mrs. Doyle, Father Byrne's secretary, Mrs. Falaeye who was in charge of the altar servers at the time, Mr. Delvecchio, head of the Church choir, and of course Father Byrne."

"What did you think of Father Byrne?"

"He was in his fifties, good-looking, and very charismatic." Mrs. Harris said.

"I found him to be a little too touchy-feely with women, especially girls around Diane's age." Mr. Harris stated.

"Were there ever any formal complaints made against the Priest that you were aware of?"

"Nothing official that I heard of, but there were grumblings and rumors for a while, and then BOOM, he was gone. The next thing we heard was that he had been sent to Rome to work in the Vatican." Mr. Harris said.

Mrs. Harris implored, "Detective Brown, please, do you think Father Byrne might have done this to our baby?"

"Mr. and Mrs. Harris, I don't know. I'm just trying to cover all the bases and to find the truth. I promise you this: we will do our best to find out who did this and bring them to justice, no matter who they are."

"Your Excellency, Bishop Guido Bergamaschi is here to see you." Bishop Alexander announced.

Archbishop Gisotti, the Archbishop of Brooklyn, stood and held out his hand as Bishop Bergamaschi approached. Bergamaschi took the Archbishop's hand, bowed, and kissed the Archbishop's ring, saying, "Your Excellency."

"Bishop Bergamaschi, is it true that the Police have found the remains of three young women behind the Rectory of Our Lady of Solace?"

"It is true, Your Excellency. It is most distressing."

"I can imagine, Guido. How are the parishioners handling this news?"

"I have been getting dozens of calls; people are scared. I've made a public statement in our Church bulletin to alleviate people's fears. I hoped the Archdiocese might release a statement, Your Excellency."

"That is a matter that I will address with Cardinal Wahren."

"Thank you, Your Excellency."

"Bishop Bergamaschi, have there been any speculation of who might have perpetrated such a heinous crime?"

"None that I have heard of, Your Excellency."

"You will let me know if you hear of anything, won't you, Bishop Bergamaschi."

"Yes, Your Excellency."

"You may go."

"And the Cardinal, Your Excellency?"

"All in good time, Bishop Bergamaschi. All in good time."

Captain O'Rourke sat looking gobsmacked after Roscoe and Walsh told the tale of the three dead girls found at Our Lady of Solace.

"Are you telling me that, at the moment, your prime suspect is a killer Priest?"

"Well, I wouldn't say, prime suspect, Captain, but a suspect," Roscoe said, trying to take the edge off the concept that a Catholic Priest might be involved in the murder of three young women.

"Who else are you looking at?" O'Rourke asked.

"We should be getting a list of everyone who either worked or volunteered at Our Lady of Solace over the past ten years and the names of all regular parishioners."

"Have you mentioned your suspicions of this Priest Byrne to anyone?"

"Of course not, Captain."

"Good, because unless you got some pretty definitive proof, this goes no further than me, understand?"

"Yes, sir."

Walsh and Roscoe headed to the Detective's squad room to Roscoe's office. When they arrived, there was an envelope from Father Donnell with two lists, workers and volunteers, and a separate list of the parishioners.

"Who do you want, workers or parishioners? You're choice." Roscoe offered Walsh.

"I'll take workers; you can have the congregation."

"Okay, I'll start with Betty; she's been going there forever. I'll see what she has to say about Father Byrne.

Why don't you take Harris with you? It might speed things up."

Roscoe left the precinct and drove to the Maspeth Savings Bank on Fresh Pond Road in Ridgewood, where Betty worked. He stood in line like all the other customers, allowing others to get in front of him to be sure to be called upon by Betty.

"Next!" she said.

Roscoe strolled up to her window.

"May I help you, sir?" She asked.

"Yes, Miss."

"That's Mrs., Mrs. Brown."

"Oh, excuse me. Mrs. Brown, I think that you're the prettiest teller here. Do you think your husband would mind if I took you to lunch?"

"Well, I don't know since he's jealous and a cop."

"A cop, huh?"

"But you're so darn cute, and I guess it will be okay."

"What happens if he finds out?'

"Oh, he'll just kill ya."

"Seems fair."

"Roscoe, what are you doing here?"

"I want to have lunch with you."

"But I brought my lunch."

"That's okay; bring it along."

"Well, I get off for lunch in fifteen minutes." She said, looking at her watch.

"I'll be in the car."

Twenty minutes later, Betty walked out of the bank to see Roscoe leaning against a black and white patrol car.

"Oh, so this is official Police business, and here I thought you wanted to go fool around." She said.

"Why can't we do both?"

"You know I only have an hour."

"So, I'll run the siren; come on."

They made the seventeen miles to their apartment in under twelve minutes. On their way to their apartment, they split Betty's lunch between them: a ham and cheese sandwich, a small bag of chips, and a bottle of Dr. Pepper.

They started undressing the minute the front door closed; by the time they reached the bedroom, they were both completely naked.

"Let's not rush." She purred.

"No, I want to last forever." He whispered.

Lying spent and intertwined, ebbing in and out of sleep, Roscoe catches a glance at the clock radio.

"Hey, Babe, it's a quarter after one."

"Mmmm, that's nice," Betty said before total realization kicks in.

"Roscoe, I'm late! Let's go."

Roscoe grabs her arm as she tries to spring from the bed.

"Come on, Betty, just another few minutes."

"No, let's go. I'm in trouble enough already."

"How about..."

"No!"

On the way back to the bank, siren blaring, Roscoe asks, "Hey Betty, how well did you know Father Byrne?"

"Father Byrne? Why?"

"Did you ever hear any rumors about his behavior around young women?"

"Oh, there were some rumors that he was a bit of a flirt. But we just thought that since he was so good-looking and charismatic, most people attributed such gossip to young girl's infatuation."

"Did he ever flirt with you?"

"No, I was in my early twenties when he came to the Church. I believe that he was at Our Lady of the Solace for ten years, and then he got picked to go to the Vatican.

Why all the questions about Father Byrne?"

"His name comes up from a couple of the victim's parents."

"You don't think Father Byrne had anything to do with the killing of those girls, do you, Roscoe?"

"Well, here we are, and you're only twenty minutes late. If Mr. Wetherbee says something, tell him it was official Police business."

"More like monkey business."

Three days after the official investigation began, Walsh, Officer Harris, and Roscoe went over all of their interviews when Roscoe's phone rang, "Hello."

"Hey, Roscoe, it's Bowles in the crime lab. I got some surprisingly good news for you. We were able to lift a thumbprint from that statuette of the Jesus found in the pit with the girl's remains."

"Any matches?"

"Nothing yet, but we haven't heard back from the FBI databank, but we should hear something in a day or two."

"Thanks, Dave. Let me know if you hear anything. You guys rock."

"Talk soon."

"What?" Walsh asked.

"The lab was able to pick up a thumbprint from the statuette but hasn't matched it yet. Hopefully, we'll get lucky and match something from the FBI's records."

"What did you learn about Father Byrne from the Church's parishioners?" Walsh inquired.

"As it turns out, there were a lot of rumors about Father Byrne, nothing concrete. But as the saying goes, there's usually a grain of truth in every rumor.

I need to go and talk to Bishop Guido Bergamaschi, the Bishop of Brooklyn, after I talk it over with the Captain.

How about you guys come up with anything?"

"Yeah, we discovered that over the past ten years, the Church has no less than six ex-cons working there: two bank robbers, two B & E's, an arsonist, and a loan shark. But no one was convicted of a violent crime. None of them matched the fingerprint found on the statuette, and none of them worked there long enough to cover the timeline of all three victims." Walsh said.

"How about any of the workers or contractors?"

"The same problem, Sarge, none of the contractors or workers fit the timeline of working at the Church at the time of the three murders. Although they have had the same handyman at the Church for over twenty years, Charles Hamilton, who at the time of the murders would have been in his sixties." Officer Harris added.

"Yeah, I know Charley. During World War II, he was a Catholic Deacon in Warsaw and was captured and held in the Priest Barracks in Dachau Concentration Camp."

"Weren't only Jews and gypsies sent to those death camps?" Harris asked.

"Dachau held Jews, gypsies, Jehovah's Witnesses, criminals, homosexuals, and Catholic Priests. Over half of the twenty-seven hundred Priests held in Dachau were killed." Roscoe said.

Walsh softly uttered, "I guess we can cross Charles Hamilton off our suspect list."

"Harris, how about you start writing up your report on your interviews while Walsh and I go talk with the Captain."

"Right, Sarge."

"You ready, Jimmy?"

"No. Roscoe, are you sure you really want to do this? You're basically accusing a Catholic Priest of murder, of triple murder."

"Jimmy, we gotta go where the evidence takes us."

"No matter where?"

"No matter where."

"Detective Brown, are you out of your fucking mind, a Catholic Priest!" O'Rourke shouted.

"Look, Captain, just listen to my thinking. I'm not advocating that we arrest him… yet. I just think we need to talk to him, if nothing else, to clear him as a suspect."

"Roscoe, this better be damn airtight."

Roscoe spent the next two hours going over the evidence, timeline, and forensics. All the while, Captain O'Rourke sat stoic, not showing any emotion; finally, he said, "Kinda weak; I doubt if the DA would feel comfortable going forward with what you have now. You don't even know if the fingerprint found on the statuette is Father Byrne's."

"I know; that's why I want to go to Rome and meet with Father Byrne."

"Whoa, whoa, whoa. I'm not authorizing you to go off to Rome on a hunch, Whadda you crazy! You haven't even talked to the Bishop yet."

"You're right, Captain. That's a good idea. I'll arrange to meet with the Bishop tomorrow."

"That's better; go see what light Bishop Bergamaschi might be able to shed on Father Byrne."

"Thanks, Captain."

As Roscoe and Walsh headed back down to the Detective squad room, Walsh turned to Roscoe and said, "You are the man!"

"What do you mean?" Roscoe feigning modesty.

"You knew the Captain wouldn't want you to see Bishop Bergamaschi, so you played the Rome card very cunningly. I am truly learning from the master."

"Come, grasshopper; you have much to learn."

"Bishop Bergamaschi, I can't thank you enough for meeting with us," Roscoe said as he removed his hat as he and Detective Walsh entered the Diocese.

"I'm glad to meet with you, although I don't know what possible assistance I might be able to add to your investigation, Detective Brown."

"Well, Your Excellency, as I'm sure you know, the remains of three young women were found behind the Rectory at Our Lady of Solace a week ago. Detective Walsh and I are doing our due diligence by inquiring about all members of the clergy that were at Our Lady of Solace during the time of the murders so that we can eliminate them as suspects."

"Surely, you cannot suspect any member of the Holy Order would be involved in such a heinous crime, Detective."

"Of course not, Your Excellency, but it is necessary that we eliminate the innocent as soon as possible so as not to have them muddy the investigation waters; you can understand that."

Bishop Bergamaschi sighed deeply, "What would you like to know?"

"We just need the names of all the clergy assigned to Our Lady of Solace from March 1954 to November 1966. We already have the names of all the contractors, workers, volunteers, and parishioners we will be going through. We just need to know the names of the clergy, Your Excellency."

"Very well; I will have my secretary send you a list."

"Here's my card, Your Excellency, with my phone and fax numbers. We really appreciate your help and thank you again."

Once the two detectives were gone, Bishop Bergamaschi walked over to the phone sitting on his large oak desk and placed a call to Archbishop Gisotti's office.

"Hello, this is Bishop Bergamaschi. I need to speak with His Grace; it's a matter of some urgency."

The voice on the other end of the phone said, "His Grace is unavailable at the moment. I will let him know you called."

"Please tell him it's of the utmost importance."

"Yes, Your Excellency, I will."

Roscoe and Walsh were sitting in O'Rourke's office listening in on a phone call from the New York City Police Commissioner Raymond Kelly, "Do I make myself perfectly clear, Captain, you tell your men to stay clear of anything having to do with the Catholic Diocese and this Father Byrne. This comes straight from Mayor Wagner; do you understand me, Captain?"

"Yes, sir. I'll tell them."

O'Rourke hung up and said, "Well, you heard him stay away from the Church. Got it?"

Roscoe squirmed in his seat for a minute as if he had something to say.

"What!" O'Rourke barked.

"It's just that… well, you're not going to like what I have to say, sir."

"Go on, damn it. What is it."

"We just got word from the lab that they were indeed able to identify the fingerprint on the statuette found in the pit where the girl's remains were found, and it was that of Michael Byrne, Father Michael Byrne. They matched it from his fingerprints when he served in the navy."

"Jesus Christ! Are they sure it couldn't be a mistake?"

"No sir, they were positive."

"Fuck me."

"What do you want us to do, sir?"

"Give me everything you have on this case and stay put. I'm going to have to take this up with the brass. Sit tight, and don't do anything until you hear from me."

"Yes, sir."

"And close the door on your way out, if you would."

Roscoe and Walsh went down to his office to get the files on the three victims to bring to the Captain.

"Well, that went well." Walsh quipped.

"Yeah, couldn't have gone better."

"Onorevoli colleghi, in preparazione all'atterraggio, assicurarsi che le cinture di sicurezza siano allacciate e che i sedili siano in posizione verticale.

Ladies and gentlemen, in preparation for landing, please make sure your seat belts are fastened and your seats are in the upright position.

We shall be landing at Leonardo da Vinci International Airport in ten minutes.

Tra dieci minuti atterreremo all'aeroporto Internazionale di Leonardo da Vinci."

Roscoe and Detective Walsh buckled their seatbelts and raised their seatbacks. It had been a rock 'em sock 'em bumpy flight even before they got on the airplane. This whole investigation had everyone on edge, everyone from

Governor Rockefeller, Mayor Wagner, Commissioner Kelly, and the entire Catholic Church all the way up to Pope John Paul VI.

Once Roscoe and Walsh had cleared customs, they were met by the secretary of the Vatican Emissary to the United States. "Detectives Brown and Walsh, benvenuti a Roma, I am His Eminence, Cardinal Sarducci's secretary, Luigi Stallone. Please follow me to the car waiting outside."

Outside sat a silver and black Rolls Royce Silver Shadow. Luigi opened the door to reveal Cardinal Vito Sarducci seated in the back seat. Cardinal Sarducci was a paunchy, doughy sixty-eight-year-old man with snow-white hair and blue eyes behind a pair of gold wire frame glasses. He seemed to be a man of good cheer, beaming with a contagious smile and an infectious laugh.

"Detectives, please come in; I won't bite." He said, laughing.

Not exactly the reception Roscoe and Walsh were expecting. They thought they would be met with scorn and skepticism.

Roscoe said, "Your Eminence, I am Detective Sergeant Roscoe Brown, and this is my partner, Detective James Walsh; it's an honor to meet you, sir."

"Gentlemen, I want to assure you that I understand the circumstances of your trip and will provide you with any assistance that you might need.

Speaking for His Holiness, we want to assure you that we have nothing to hide, nor would we try to cover up any wrongdoing."

"Thank you, Your Eminence. We are here just to gather some information to fill in some details and get answers to help us solve our case, so we're not there to make accusations."

"Grazie."

"Your Eminence, you should know that I am a man who plays strictly by the book. I do not prejudge or jump to conclusions. I am a man who follows the evidence wherever it takes me, but no man is above the law."

"I understand, and I respect your honesty and candor."

"Grazie, Your Eminence."

"Detective Walsh, you do not say much."

"I guess you could say that I am the silent partner."

"Walsh? Are you Catholic, my son?"

"No, sir. My mother is Jewish, and my father was raised Catholic but never practiced after the Church refused to recognize the marriage. I consider myself to be half Catholic and half Jewish."

"Which half of you is Jewish?"

"The bottom half," Walsh said with a grin.

Cardinal Sarducci sat there for a second before getting the joke. Once he did, he gave out a big laugh, "The bottom half, Ha! That's a good one; I'll have to remember that. The bottom half."

Cardinal Sarducci took Roscoe and Walsh to check in at Hotel Alimandi Vaticano, centrally located just a couple hundred meters from St. Peter's Square.

"I'm sure you fellas could use a couple of hours rest to try and acclimate to the time change. It's nine o'clock in the morning, so how about I send a car to pick you up for lunch, let's say two o'clock?"

"That sounds wonderful, Your Eminence. We look forward to seeing you then. Grazie."

"Grazie, Your Eminence," Walsh added with a wave goodbye.

They checked into their room, a double suite on the third floor with access to the terrace, which has a view of the entrance to the Vatican museums.

They stood on the terrace and marveled at the grandeur of it all.

"Roscoe, can you believe that some of these buildings were standing before Christ walked on earth?"

"I know; it's all so humbling."

"Well, I'm knackered. I don't know about you, but I'm going to grab 40 winks. See you later, Roscoe."

"I'm too wired. I'm going to take a short walk to unwind. I'll see ya later."

Roscoe went downstairs and walked out of the lobby and onto Viale Vaticano. He turned left and walked half a block to a small café, the Caffè Vaticano, where he ordered an espresso and a cannoli. He sat outside and watched all the tourists passing by on parade. It was easy to pick out the American tourists since the men usually wore baggy plaid shorts, bright-colored shirts, black knee-high socks with wingtips, and sported a 35mm camera around their neck. The women wore a floral dress, sunglasses, a large floppy hat, a satchel-style handbag, and open-toed sandals.

He noticed a group of gypsy women with a large gaggle of children who stood outside the Vatican Museum begging for money from tourists. Many of the children were very aggressive, roaming in packs like wolves, rushing the tourists, surrounding them, and some sticking their hands into the men's pockets for loose change or even grabbing their wallets. One woman gypsy would distract a lady tourist while another would try to open her handbag; all the while, a Carabinieri stood by and did nothing. It kind of reminded Roscoe of the Coney Island Boardwalk back in the day before his time on the force.

A small group of gypsy children started to approach him, sitting outside the café. As they got closer, he reached into his coat pocket and flashed his Detective's gold badge. That's all it took for them to run back to the safety of stealing from the tourists.

Even after the espresso, the jet lag hit him fast and hard. He made his way back to the hotel, took the elevator up to the third floor, got to his room, and managed to get his fedora, sports coat, and shoes off before crashing face down on the bed.

Walsh's voice slowly crept through the thick, hazy fog of deep sleep. As hard as he tried, he couldn't lose it. Walsh kept repeating the same monologue over and over, "Hey, Roscoe, wake up, man, it's one o'clock; we got to get going."

"Hey, Roscoe, wake up, man, it's one o'clock; we got to get going."

"Hey, Roscoe, wake up, man, it's one o'clock; we got to get going."

Finally, Roscoe opened one eye to see his partner standing beside the bed, dressed and ready to go. He propped himself up onto his elbows, slowly prying himself off the bed. He noticed that there was a large wet drool spot on the sheet where his head had been.

"I hope it dries before the maid comes in; it could prove slightly embarrassing," Roscoe said, half-joking.

At precisely two o'clock, the Rolls pulled up to the hotel entrance, and Luigi Stallone, Cardinal Sarducci's secretary, got out of the front passenger's seat and greeted Roscoe and Walsh.

"Gentiluomini, I hope you both had a good rest?"

"Yes, thank you," Roscoe answered.

Luigi opened the Roll's back door and said, "If you please."

Their journey lasted all of six minutes; they arrived at the Apostolic Palace, the residence of the Pope and Cardinals. Outside, on one of the third-floor windows, was the insignia of the papacy, the image of two Crossed Keys, one gold and one silver, bound with a red cord indicating the Pope's residence.

Two of the Pontifical Swiss Guards stood at attention just inside the lobby. They appeared to be more ceremonial than for actual protection.

Further in the lobby, two concierges were working behind a reception-style counter made of mahogany. They acknowledged Luigi with a slight nod of the head.

The lobby was as grand as any of the finest hotels anywhere, with marble floors, mahogany paneling, artwork, and ceiling frescos that would be the envy of any museum in the world.

They went to the elevator, where the elevator operator, wearing a military-style uniform, greeted them, "Buona giornata."

"Primo piano, per favore." Luigi said as they entered the elevator.

The elevator ride took almost as long as the ride from the hotel up to the first floor.

Luigi smiled and said, "You'll have to pardon the slowness of the elevator, as it is quite old, but luckily, it is very seldom that anyone is in a hurry."

When the elevator door opened, the hallway appeared very austere, with none of the luxury and trappings of the lobby. There were off-white walls, a conservative pattern carpeting, and dark wooden doors with a number and letter painted in gold, 4B.

Luigi knocked softly on the door; moments later, Cardinal Sarducci answered, "Ah, Detectives, come in, come in."

When they entered the apartment, Father Byrne was sitting on the sofa. He stood up and approached Roscoe and Walsh.

"Hello, I'm Father Michael Byrnes. I hope I can help you in any way I can." He said as he shook both of their hands.

"Please have a seat, Detectives." Cardinal Sarducci said, gesturing to the two chairs opposite the sofa.

Turning to Luigi, he said, "Luigi, would you be so kind as to take Detective Brown's hat, please."

Roscoe removed his hat and handed it to the Cardinal's secretary, then he and Walsh took their seats.

Sarducci smiled and said, "I thought we could meet first, then sit down for lunch, if that's agreeable to you, Detectives?"

"That would be fine," Roscoe said.

On the flight over, Roscoe suggested that Walsh take the lead in questioning Father Byrne. Roscoe figured it would be good for Walsh to get some experience as lead Detective. He noticed that his junior had a softer approach to interrogation that might better suit this situation.

Walsh placed a brown leather briefcase on the coffee table in front of him but didn't open it.

He started by asking, "Father Byrne, what years were you at Our Lady of Solace?"

"I believe I was assigned to Our Lady of Solace in 1951, and I left in 1961 when I went to Catholic University to study canon law. Once I graduated in 1966, I was sent here to work in the Vatican, and I've been here since."

Walsh unlatched the briefcase and opened the lid. He removed three color photographs and placed the three photographs on the coffee table in front of Cardinal Sarducci and Father Byrne; each of the photos was one of the three murdered girls, Melissa Roberts, Sally Beechwood, and Diane Harris.

"Do you recognize any of these three girls, Father Byrne?"

"It was so long ago."

"Take your time."

The Priest picked up each photograph and appeared to study each one carefully.

"They look familiar, but I can't place a name to any of them."

Walsh pointed to the one to the right of Father Byrne. "That's Melissa Roberts; she was sixteen. This is Sally Beechwood, and this is Diane Harris, also eighteen. Does that help?" Walsh asked.

Byrne stared at them with no sign of emotion, looked at Walsh and Roscoe, and shook his head, "No, I'm afraid not, sorry."

Detective Walsh reached into the briefcase, took the evidence bag containing the statuette of Jesus carrying the lamb, and set it on the table.

"Do you recognize this, Father Byrne?"

Father Byrne reached for the bag, "May I?"

"Yes, but please do not open the bag."

The Father looked at it from every angle and said, "Well, I recognize the statuette as that of our Savior Jesus Christ holding a lamb, but I cannot say that I recognize it to be a particular statuette."

"It was found in a pit where the remains of these three girls were also found behind the Rectory of Our Lady of Solace."

"I see."

"Can you explain why your fingerprints are on this statuette, Father Byrne? The statuette that was found where the bodies of three murder girls were found."

The Cardinal's body stiffened; the once jovial smile was gone. He looked wearily at the Priest sitting next to him.

Father Byrne reached into his cassock pocket and removed a pair of rosary beads that he began to handle as if praying.

"No, I can't explain how or why my fingerprints would be on the statuette unless I had given it to one of these girls, and she had it with her when she was killed.

Oh, wait, now that I think about it, it's starting to come back to me. I believe that I gave the statuette to this girl here," he said as he pointed to the photograph of Melissa Roberts." Father Byrne continued to fidget with his rosary.

Roscoe, although never really used the rosary, he observed Betty using them dozens of times while she sat at Church. He noticed something different from Betty's rosaries and Father Byrne's.

"Father Byrne, might I see your rosary beads?" Roscoe asked.

"They're just rosary beads."

"I know. But there's something special for me as a Catholic to hold a Priest's rosary who works in the Vatican, please. I'll give them right back." Roscoe glanced at the Cardinal for a little help.

"Father Byrne?" The Cardinal pushed.

"All right, here."

Roscoe looked at the rosary. It was basically just like Betty's with one exception: Father Byrne's rosary had a small medallion of Saint Francis, where the 'Our Father' bead should be.

"Father Byrne, you know it's a funny thing. Melissa Roberts always wore a Saint Francis medallion on a gold necklace. We found her gold necklace in the pit, but the Saint Francis medallion was missing, and here on your rosary, you have a Saint Francis medallion. I find that to be an odd coincidence, don't you, Father Byrne?" Roscoe asked.

Before Father Byrne could say anything, Cardinal Sarducci stood up and said, "Father Byrne, I need to speak to you. Now!"

Father Byrne got up off the sofa and followed the Cardinal out of the living room and into another room, closing the door behind them.

They had walked into the Cardinal's office den. Before Cardinal Sarducci could speak, Father Byrne dropped to his knees and said, "Your Eminence, hear my confession."

Cardinal sat in his desk chair while Father Byrne knelt next to him. Sarducci was facing away from the Priest,

"Bless me, Father, for I have sinned. My last confession was…"

Roscoe and Walsh waited patiently for the Cardinal and Father Byrne to return to the living room. They sat there for over an hour when the door finally opened, and the two clergies emerged. Roscoe and Walsh stood as the Cardinal led Father Byrne back into the room.

"Please, gentlemen, be seated. What is it that you want?" The Cardinal said.

Roscoe leaned forward, looking at Father Byrne, and said, "I want the truth, Father. Did you have anything to do with the deaths of these three young girls?"

"No, I did not."

The look on the Cardinal's face told otherwise.

"Do you have any knowledge of anyone who did?"

"No, I do not."

Roscoe looked at the Cardinal, who gave a half-smile and said, "I'm sorry, my son, I cannot break the seal of confession."

"Father Byrne, I want to inform you that I am going to report all of the evidence, my findings, and our conversation to the New York District Attorney's office. As to what action he decides to take, I cannot say, but if I were you, I'd get a good lawyer."

"Detective Brown, may I have my rosary back?" Father Byrne said, holding his hand out.

"No, Father, you may not; it's evidence."

As Roscoe and Walsh stood up, Luigi brought Roscoe's hat to him. Roscoe smiled and said, "Grazie."

The Cardinal and Father Byrne stayed seated; when Roscoe reached the door, he turned to Father Byrne and said, "You might think you're untouchable, but you just might want to look up Father Hans Schmidt. Your Eminence."

Luigi walked them to the elevator and out of the palace.

"Good day, Detectives."

"Good day and thank you. Luigi." Roscoe said.

As they were walking back to the hotel, Walsh asked, "Who is Father Hans Schmidt?"

"Hans Schmidt was a German Roman Catholic Priest convicted of murder, and the only Priest ever to be executed in the United States, at Sing."

"No kidding?"

"I kid you not."

Back at the hotel, Roscoe called the New York DA's office and spoke to DA Hanson. Roscoe relayed all the evidence that he had and spelled out the case against Father Michael Byrne.

"Sounds like a solid case, Detective. And where is Father Byrne at the moment?"

"He's currently attached to the Vatican as a canon lawyer."

"Ouch, that could be a major obstacle. You see, Detective Brown, the Vatican doesn't have any extradition treaties, so unless they want to, they don't have to turn him over for prosecution. I'll talk to the State Department and see what, if anything, they can do."

"Okay, we'll sit tight until we hear from you."

"What did the DA say?" Walsh asked.

"He said the Vatican doesn't have any extradition treaties, so as long as he stays inside the Vatican, he's safe."

Roscoe grabbed his hat, "Come on, Jimmy, let's go see the Cardinal."

They walked back to the Apostolic Palace. After entering the lobby, they made their way to the concierge desk. Roscoe presented his Gold Shield and said, Detective Brown and Walsh, to see His Eminence, Cardinal Sarducci, please."

"Un momento, per favore."

The concierge picked up the phone and dialed a four-digit number. When the person on the other end answered, the concierge slightly turned away from Roscoe and Walsh and spoke in a half-whisper, "Eminenza, ci sono due investigatori americani che desiderano vederti."

Roscoe could hear a mumbling on the other end but couldn't make sense of it.

"Si, li invierò. Si, grazie Emininenza." The concierge hung up the phone, smiled at Roscoe, and gestured toward the elevator, "His Eminence will see you now."

This time, the elevator ride seemed even slower than the last time. When they stepped out of the elevator, Luigi was waiting for them. He didn't speak as he led them to the Cardinal's apartment. The door was slightly ajar when they entered, and they noticed Cardinal Sarducci sitting on the sofa alone.

He spread his arms in an inviting gesture and said, "Detectives, please sit."

Luigi once again took Roscoe's hat, bowed to the Cardinal, and left the room. Roscoe went to where Sarducci was sitting, bowed, and kissed the Cardinal's ring.

"Thank you for seeing us, Your Eminence."

The Cardinal smiled and asked, "Now, what is it that you want, my son?"

"Michael David Byrnes, you're under arrest for the murders of Melissa Roberts, Sally Beechwood, and Diane Harris.

You have the right to remain silent. Anything you say can and will be used against you in a court of law. You have the right to an attorney. If you cannot afford an attorney, one will be provided for you. Do you understand these rights as

I have described them to you?" Roscoe said to Father Byrne as he stepped off Pan Am flight 760 from Rome to Kennedy Airport.

"Detective Brown, you have no right to arrest me. I am a Vatican emissary."

"That grants you immunity so long as you remain with the Vatican walls; once you step outside the sanctity of the Vatican, you're no longer covered by immunity, Father," Roscoe said as he placed handcuffs on the Priest.

"You know, Father, maybe you should have taken a couple of criminal law classes as an elective and not be so focused on canon law," Walsh added.

Several of New York's newspapers had a field day with such a bombastic story. The headlines read, "Beauties and the Priest," "The Priest from Hell," "Coney Island Killer Priest," "Holy Hell," and "Death at Our Lady of the Bone Yard."

The Church condemned his actions in a written statement from the Archdiocese of New York, but no interviews were given.

The trial was expected to last six weeks, but the DA cut a deal with Michael Byrne in exchange for taking the death penalty off the table. The Church was instrumental in brokering the plea agreement. The official reason was that the Church acted on behalf of the families so they wouldn't have to endure the pain and agony of a trial. But the official unofficial reason was to avoid any undue embarrassment to the Church.

Michael David Byrne was sentenced to three consecutive life sentences plus a day and sent to Sing Prison in upstate New York outside the city of Ossining.

"Roscoe?"

"Yeah, Babe."

"Any interest in going with me to Mass tomorrow?"

"Tomorrow?"

"Yeah, I think it might do you some good."

"You know, Betty, I'm kinda Catholicismed out for a while."

"Roscoe, Catholicismed is not a word."

"It might not be in the dictionary, but it's definitely a thing; besides, Jimmy's got us some great tickets for the Giants' game this Sunday."

"Are you sure?"

"Oh, okay, Roscoe, well, I'll have Father McDonnell say a prayer for you."

"Oh, don't worry about me, Babe; it's the Giants who could really use his prayers."

THE END

426

The Case of the Killer Clown Killer

Detective Sergeant Roscoe Brown was sitting on a bench on the Coney Island Boardwalk as usual, eating what he always eats for lunch. Two chili cheese dogs and an order of fries from Nathan's Famous when he noticed a group of clowns on bicycles heading his way.

Normally, a group of clowns riding bicycles on the Boardwalk wouldn't give Roscoe pause since it is, after all, the Coney Island Boardwalk. The Boardwalk has been the home of The World Circus Freak Show, The Steeplechase Circus Big Show, Hubert's Museum, the Strand Museum, the Wonderland Circus Side Show, and the Coney Island Circus Sideshow. All have been home to such world-famous freaks as The Lion-faced Man, Violetta, the Limbless Woman, Jean Carroll, the Tattooed Lady, Zip, the Pinhead, The Four-Legged Woman, Sealo, the Seal Boy, and Rubber Nelson, the man who bounces like a ball. Of course, these are just a few because the list is endless.

But these clowns were unlike any clowns Roscoe had ever seen. Clowns usually have the appearance to make kids of all ages smile and laugh, but these clowns were painted with evil and scary faces. Their faces were painted using black and white with a touch of red to represent blood.

They seemed to be riding their bicycles as if to terrorize the people strolling on the Boardwalk, and they were laughing and throwing leaflets at the people.

Roscoe was never a big fan of clowns, but when these clowns interrupted his chili dog lunch, they went too far. As the lead clown approached Roscoe, he stood up, walked to the center of the Boardwalk, and flashed his badge.

"Hold it right there, clown."

"What's the problem, officer?" The clown said as the others came to a halt behind him.

"What's the problem? You and these other clowns were riding erratically, endangering the safety of the pedestrians, littering, and, on top of that, you interrupted my lunch. My chili dog is getting cold. I don't like a cold chili dog."

"I'm sorry, officer, but we're just out promoting the circus, Cirque de Clowns Tueurs, the Circus of Killer Clowns."

"Killer Clown Circus?"

"Yeah, it's more of a circus for adults, not really for kids. We have a really bizarre freak show, and all the acts are kinda gruesome. Here's a couple of free passes; it's really groovy. Although, unless your lady friend is into the macabre, gross, and horrific, you might want to go with a buddy. And I am sorry about your wiener getting cold."

"It's a chili dog, smart ass. Now, you clowns ride more responsibly and stop throwing those leaflets around. You can hand them out, but no throwing them. Got it?"

"Got it. Hope to see you at the show, officer."

"It's Detective Sergeant."

"My apologies; hope to see you at the show, Detective Sergeant." He said as he and the other clowns headed down to the opposite end of the Boardwalk.

Roscoe returned to his chili dog sitting on the bench where he had left it. He picked it up and took a bite, cold.

"I hate clowns." He muttered to himself.

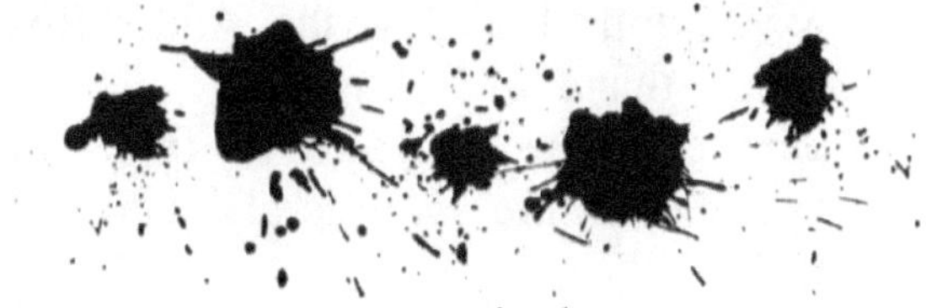

"You sure?" Roscoe asked.

Betty smiled, "Yes, it's really nothing I want to go see. So, you and Jimmy go and have fun."

Roscoe grabbed her, brought her close, and kissed her, "Hey, as Ralph Kramden used to say, "Baby, you're the greatest."

Roscoe walked to the wall phone and called his partner, Detective Jimmy Walsh.

"Hey, Jimmy. Just talked to Betty, and she says she has zero interest in seeing the Killer Clown Circus, so what do you say we go over tomorrow after work? Okay, see you in the morning. Bye."

As Roscoe and Walsh entered the big top, he heard someone shout, "Hey, pig!"

He turned around and saw the clown who gave him the tickets. The clown smiled, "Hey, no offense, man, it's all part of the show. You know, Killer Clowns, we gotta look antisocial."

He held out his hand, "I'm Grouchy."

Roscoe shook the black spiked gloved hand and said, "I'm Detective Sergeant Brown, and this is my partner, Detective Walsh, and I'm not too happy myself."

"No, my clown name is Grouchy. I'm Kevin Cohen."

"A Jewish Clown?" Walsh asked, surprised.

"Funny you don't look Jewish." Added Roscoe.

"Yeah, I get that a lot."

A booming voice came over the loudspeaker, "Ladies and Gentlemen, the show is about to start. Please take your seats."

"Well, look, I got to go; the show is about to start. Hope you enjoy the show."

Roscoe said, "Well, break a leg."

"Oh, I will; that's part of my act."

Grouchy, the clown shook the Detective's hands before he ducked behind a black tent flap painted with a messy hand-painted white skull and crossed bones.

Walsh and Roscoe looked at each other in disbelief.

Roscoe blinked his eyes several times to regain his composure, "That there is a very strange young man, don't you think?"

"Strange is a word, weird, bizarre, and whacked-out our others that come to mind."

"Well, come on, the show is about to start, and I'm thinking we don't want to miss a minute of it."

Roscoe removed his fedora as they continued into the tent and proceeded to find their seats, front row center. They weren't sure if that was a good thing or not.

The Ringmaster walked out into the center of the ring. He was dressed in tails and a top hat like the vampire character out of an old Bela Lugosi Dracula film. He had on white makeup with a small trail of what looked to be blood dripping from the left side of his mouth. He held up his hands for silence before he spoke.

"Welcome, ladies and gentlemen and children of the night. I am Rowdy the Ringmaster, and I promise you a circus like you've never seen before. Here, there is no laughter and joy, only screams and terror. We don't promise you memories, only nightmares. Our show isn't for the faint of heart; if you're scared, squeamish, or shock easy, I suggest you leave now. Because once the show starts, the doors will be locked from the outside, so there will be no escape."

He looked around and saw no one was leaving, "So be it, you have been warned."

As he started to walk away, a hatchet came flying out of the darkness and struck the ringmaster square in the back; he gave out a scream and fell to the ground. All the lights went out, and the entire room was in blackness. There were people in the audience screaming, men and women. But before things got too out of hand, a spotlight from above shone into the audience, swinging from one side to the other and finally landing on Grouchy, the clown Roscoe and Walsh had met earlier.

He was standing next to the body of the Ringmaster, holding a hatchet, smiling. He took the hatchet and threw it at a large pole holding up part of the tent. The hatchet hit the pole with a thunderous thud.

"Hey, don't nobody move! Stick around; the fun is just getting started. But first, we got to get rid of this clown, heh, heh, heh."

Grouchy signaled to some clowns standing off to the side of the ring for them to join him. The spotlight swung over to where they were; as soon as they were in the light, they began to run to the center of the ring to join Grouchy, dragging a giant woodchipper with them.

The clowns placed the woodchipper next to the lifeless body of the Ringmaster. Grouchy walked over to the Ringmaster, pointed to two of the clowns, and said, "Hey, Cheeky, Itchy, let's give old Rowdy a true Killer Clown sendoff."

As the Itchy and Cheeky picked up the Ringmaster's body, Grouchy turned on the woodchipper.

"Ladies and gentlemen, old Rowdy was a real chip off the old block. You'll see, wocka, wocka!" Grouchy said, laughing.

He turned the woodchipper so it faced the audience. Seconds later, what sounded like meat and bones were being pulverized. Then, something wet started flying out of the chipper into the audience.

People started freaking out and jumping out of their seats until they realized that it was just wet confetti spewing out of the chipper. The shrieks turned into nervous giggles, then laughter.

Rowdy, the Ringmaster, suddenly appeared from the right side of the ring, waving to the people.

"Hey, everybody, did you miss me?" Rowdy shouted.

The crowd erupted into applause and cheers; Roscoe looked at Walsh. Both were drenched in wet confetti and started to laugh, "I bet that clown Grouchy put us upfront, so we'd be sure to get good and soaked." Walsh said.

"Did I ever tell you; I hate clowns," Roscoe said.

There were several equally gruesome acts involving dismemberments, disembowelments, and decapitations, followed by a parade of assorted freaks. The grand finale was when the clown named Decay would catch a .357 magnum slug while holding a deck of cards in front of his mouth. The gun was going to be fired by Pogo, the clown from the other side of the center ring. The bullet would break the pane of glass between Pogo and Decay.

Rowdy the Ringmaster walked into the center of the ring and faced the audience. He held the large handgun in the air and said, "Ladies and gentlemen, I have been informed that there is one of New York City's finest in the audience. Would Detective Sergeant Brown please identify yourself?"

Roscoe reluctantly held up his hand.

"Ladies and gentlemen, can we have a big Killer Clown round of applause for Detective Sergeant Brown? Detective Brown, could I impose on you to come up here with me to inspect this weapon?"

As Roscoe stood up and headed on to the stage, he gave Walsh a pleading look for some sort of help, but none came.

"Detective Brown, I want you to inspect these to make sure that it is the real deal," Rowdy said as he handed Roscoe the gun and bullet.

Roscoe took them, inspected them thoroughly, and proclaimed them to be a real .357 magnum handgun and what appeared to be a real bullet.

"Thank you, Detective Brown, you may be seated. Please a round of applause for Detective Brown, ladies, and gentlemen."

Rowdy handed the gun and bullet to Pogo, the clown. Pogo then placed the single .357 bullet into the chamber, closed up the cylinder, cocked the hammer, and walked to his position opposite Decay, who was holding the deck of cards in front of his face.

"Ladies and gentlemen, on the count of three, Pogo will fire his pistol at Decay, the bullet will shatter this pane of tempered glass, then penetrate the deck of cards that Decay is holding in front of his face. Decay will then catch the bullet between his teeth. Are you ready, Pogo?"

Pogo nodded and raised the gun at Decay.

"Are you ready, Decay?"

Decay said, "Ready."

"On three. One… two… three."

There came a thunderous *Ka-Boom* that vibrated throughout the entire room. The pane of glass shattered, the deck of cards flew up, scattering into the air, and the back of Decay's head, and most of his brains splattered all over the side of the tent behind him.

Everyone, sat in stunned silence, not quite sure if this was some sort of illusion like all the other gags and tricks, everyone except Roscoe and Walsh.

Both Detectives jumped up onto the stage and went to the fatally wounded clown. While Walsh inspected the dead clown, Roscoe stood up and announced, "Everyone please stay in your seats. This is now a crime scene. No one is allowed to leave until you have been interviewed by the NYPD."

He turned to Rowdy and ordered, "Call the Police now!"

Roscoe and Walsh interviewed the entire circus staff, the clowns, the freaks, and all the worker bees who toil behind the scenes. A couple of uniformed officers interviewed all hundred and twenty paid customers.

Roscoe started with Kevin Cohen, *aka* Grouchy.

"So, Kevin, can you tell me who has access to the .357?"

"Well, usually, Rowdy keeps it in the prop room behind the stage with all the other props."

"Who had access to the prop room?"

"Anyone and everyone in the company, there's no lock on the door. It's kept unlocked in case someone needs a prop."

"Perfect."

While Roscoe was interviewing Grouchy, Walsh was talking to Rowdy, the Ringmaster.

"What's your real name?" Walsh asked.

"Ronald McGovern."

"So, Ronald, whose gun is it?"

"It belongs to the company, but it's registered to the circus owner, Arthur Garbett."

"I'll need his contact info; in fact, I'll need the contact information for everyone who works for the circus, and not just the performers."

"I don't have that information; you'll have to talk to Margret Mann. She's the office manager. When she's not on the midway as the bearded lady, you'll find her in her office upstairs, second floor. You can't miss it; her name is on the door, in all caps."

After Roscoe and Walsh finished interviewing all the staff, either the on-stage actors or the behind-the-scenes production crew, they headed to see Margret Mann.

Rowdy was right; you couldn't miss her office at the end of the hall. You could read her name on the door from the other end of the corridor. There, in Futura Extra Bold Condensed type, painted all caps in gold, was the name MS. MANN.

They knocked on the door.

"Yeah, who is it?" A gruff voice from the other side of the door bellowed.

"Police." Walsh acknowledged.

"Come in!"

Roscoe and Walsh walked in and were surprised to see a woman wearing a flowered moo-moo weighing at least 300 pounds. She had jet black hair pulled back into a ponytail, sporting a full beard, and smoking a cigar. She had stacks of cash piled up on her desk, and she was punching number keys on an olive-drab industrial Burroughs adding machine like a whirling dervish.

"Cops, huh? Whadda yous guys, Bunko? Listen, pal; my books are clean!" She said, not bothering to look up while adding the count from the evening's gate receipts.

"No, Ma'am, we're not Bunko; we're Homicide. I'm Detective Sergeant Brown, and this is my partner, Detective Walsh."

"Homicide!"

"Yes, ma'am, during tonight's performance, one of the clowns was shot to death."

"Who? It wasn't Pogo, was it?"

"No, it was the clown named Decay."

"Oh, him, he's trash. No great loss."

"Excuse me?"

"He wasn't true circus folk; he and the rest of the freaks are all carney trash."

"Carney trash?"

"Yeah, they were all working on the carnival circuits before Mr. Garbett hired them on. Why, I'll never know."

"So, you don't like these folks from the carnivals."

"Hey, we run a class show here, not like them ragbag carneys. All they care about is stiffing the Alvin's."

"Alvin's?"

"Alvin's, you know, rubes. bumpkins, clodhoppers, dolts, hayseeds, hicks, blockheads…"

"Yeah, yeah, I get the picture. Why do you think Mr. Garbett hired them?"

"Cause he has a big heart. I guess he felt sorry for them, schlepping all over the country just to be exploited and taken advantage of by every crooked promoter, grubstaker, five-percenter, four-flusher, stank right hood rat…"

"Got it. So, he thought it would be better if they could be in just one place to be exploited and taken advantage of."

"Yeah, exactly; see, I told ya, a big heart."

"Would you happen to know what Decay's real name was?" Walsh asked.

"Max Wojciehowicz."

"Could you spell that for me, please?"

"Wojciehowicz, you spell it just like it sounds. W O J C I E H O W I C Z. Wojciehowicz."

"Do you have an address for Mr. Wojce… Do you have an address for Max?

"155 Kings Highway."

"Hmm, right here in Coney Island."

"Apartment 2C."

"Was he married?"

"No, but he lives, or I should say he lived with his boyfriend. If you know what I mean, and I think you do. Queer, ponce, faggot, poof, fairy, rump ranger, a friend of Dorothy…"

"Okay, okay, so Max was homosexual," Roscoe said.

"Flaming. A real drama queen."

"Would you know his partner's name?"

"Hell no, I'm no snoop!"

"Right. Ms. Mann, any idea who might have wanted Max dead?"

"Tell me someone who didn't."

"If he was so hated, why did they keep him on?"

"Because he was the only one who would do the bullet catch."

"Really?"

"Would you, especially now?"

"No, probably not."

"Well, at least poor old Wojciehowicz finally did something good for the company."

"What's that?"

"Getting his head blown off is going to do boffo at the box office. We're going to sell out for the next six months."

"Ms. Mann, I'm afraid you don't understand; until we're finished investigating Max's death, you're closed down. This is now a crime scene."

"Are you shitting me!"

"I'm afraid not."

"Fucking carney trash!"

"Well, thank you for your time, Ms. Mann. Here's my card. If you think of anything else, please do call." Roscoe said as he and Walsh were heading toward the door; from her, they heard, "Be sure to shut the door!"

As they made their way to the stairs to meet with the boys from the crime lab, Roscoe said, "Pleasant enough sort of lady, don't you think?"

"I wish I could grow a beard like that," Walsh said.

From behind the closed door of Ms. Mann, they heard, "You ain't got the balls to grow a bread like this, copper!"

Standing over Max Wojciehowicz's body was Doctor Olsen, the Chief Medical Officer for Coney Island, and CSI lead officer David Bowles, examining the .357 in a plastic evidence bag.

"Hey, Doc. Hey Dave, got anything?" Roscoe asked.

"Besides a clown with the back of his head blown off?" Olsen snarked.

Bowles held up the gun, "It's the real deal, and the casing in the cylinder is real, too."

"I know. I examined them both before the gun was fired." Roscoe admitted.

"Why would anyone try something as stupid as trying to catch a bullet in their mouth is beyond me." Doctor Olsen uttered.

"It's a trick, Doc. They swap the real bullet out and replace it with a wax bullet. You see, the spray from the wax bullet has enough force to break the glass. The guy supposedly catching the bullet has the real .357 bullet already hidden in his mouth, so when the gun is fired, it looks real, but in fact, harmless." Walsh explained.

"Except this time," Roscoe added.

"Well, I'll take the gun down for prints, and maybe we'll find someone other than Detective Roscoe Brown's fingerprints on the murder weapon." David Bowles said sarcastically.

"Not funny, Bowles." Roscoe snapped back.

It was after midnight when Walsh and Roscoe drove over to 155 Kings Highway to inform Max Wojciehowicz's partner that his lover had been killed. Apartment 2C was above the Chinese restaurant located on the street level.

155 was a walk-up with no elevator. As they climbed the stairs, they heard music coming from apartment 2C; they could hear voices.

Roscoe knocked on the door several times before the music stopped, and a voice from behind the door asked, "Who is it?"

"Police."

Roscoe and Walsh could hear muffled voices speaking rapidly. Roscoe knocked again.

"Police, I need you to open the door."

The voice asked, "I'd like to see some ID."

Roscoe held his ID and badge up to the peephole, "Here you go."

A few seconds later, they heard the door locks being unlocked. The door opened about three inches with the door chain still attached. A good-looking man, who appeared to be Hispanic, peeked out and again asked, "May I see your identification again, please."

"Sure," Roscoe said, holding up his ID and badge again. "I'm Detective Sergeant Brown, and this is my partner, Detective Walsh. May we come in, please?"

"Is this about the music? I turned it off."

"No, it isn't about the music; it's about Max Wojciehowicz."

The door closed, and they heard the safety chain being slid off the track. The door opened. "Come in." said a short Hispanic-looking man who looked to be in his early thirties.

Roscoe and Walsh could see that the man had been crying.

"May I ask, who are you?" Roscoe asked.

"I am Juan Perez. What is this about Detective?"

"Mr. Perez, might you have some form of identification we could see."

The young man pulled his wallet from his back pocket and produced a Puerto Rican driver's license.

"Mr. Perez, whose apartment is this?"

"I share it with a friend."

"Max Wojciehowicz?"

"Yes."

"Mr. Perez, who else is in the apartment with you?"

"Nobody."

"We distinctly heard voices when we came to the door."

Juan stood silent for a minute, then said, "Better come on out."

The bedroom door opened, and Kevin Cohen, aka Grouchy, stepped out.

Roscoe slid his fedora up and back on his head, looked at Grouchy, and said, "What the hell is going on!"

"I just came by to break the news about Max," Grouchy explained.

"And from the sound of the music and the laughter, it looks like he took the news pretty well."

"I can explain," Juan said as he broke down sobbing.

"I'm sure you can. I think it best if we all go down to the station. You can do your explaining there; you too, Grouchy, grab your coat."

When they got to the six 0, Roscoe took Grouchy to interrogation room 1, and Walsh took Juan to room 2.

"Would you like something to drink?" Walsh asked.

"No. Why am I here."

"You were friends with Max?"

"We were more than friends; we loved each other."

"Did you know that Max was killed tonight?"

"Yeah, Kevin came over and told me."

"Are you and Kevin involved romantically?"

"No, we're just friends, that's all."

"You see, the reason I'm asking is that when Detective Brown and myself came to your apartment this evening, it sounded like you were having a party, like you were celebrating, with all the music and laughing because

It just seems a little odd that you were having such a good time hours after your lover's brains were blown out. So, you can see how it might seem a little suspicious to us that you and Kevin were yucking it up instead of mourning, know what I mean?"

"We weren't having a party. We just remembered the good times we had with Max. That's all, man. I was playing some of Max's and my favorite songs; Kevin and I remembered all the good and fun times we had. I believe Max would have wanted us to remember him laughing and not crying."

"Did Kevin have anything to do with Max's death, Juan?"

"No."

"Did you?"

"No, man, I loved him. I would never do anything to hurt Max. You got to believe me."

With that, Juan broke down and started bawling like a baby.

Over in interrogation room one, Roscoe was having a go with Kevin.

"Am I under arrest, man?"

"No. Why should you be?"

"Hey, I didn't do nothing. The person you really should be talking to is Pogo."

"Why?"

"I heard him bragging to Bruiser after the killing that there was going to be a little something extra in his paycheck this week for a job well done."

"And you think he was talking about killing Max? Why didn't you say something when we interviewed you earlier?"

"Are you kidding? Pago's a monster; he bullies all the other clowns around like he owns the joint and gets away with it."

"Isn't there anyone to complain to, Ms. Mann?"

"No way, she and Pogo are an item. With her, Pogo can do no wrong, and if you try and lodge a formal complaint, you'll catch shit from both ends."

"Why would Ms. Mann want Max dead?"

"Well, for one thing, he's a carney, and the other is that Max was a Jew, a Polish Jew."

"Ms. Mann don't like Jews?"

"Mann is her married name; her maiden name was Schultheiss, Greta Schultheiss. Her old man was a big mucky-muck in the Gestapo, nicknamed the Jew Hunter. He was found guilty of multiple war crimes and was hung with all the other Nazis at Nuremberg.

She married an American GI, Major Marshal Mann, after the war. Of course, that was before her congenital general hypertrichosis kicked in. Since there wasn't a cure for the disease, she became the bearded lady. Back in the day, I heard she was quite beautiful. The story is that once her husband found out about the disease, he wanted out of the marriage."

"Did they split up?"

"Oh, they split up all right. A couple of months later, Mann was found floating face down in Gravesend Bay, his throat slit from ear to ear. He'd been bobbing in the bay for several weeks, and with all the fish munching on him, there wasn't much evidence left to go on, except they said her husband's death was a murder. Apparently, she had an airtight alibi."

"Remind me again, what's Pogo's real name."

"He tells everyone it's Matt Miller, but I saw a German photo ID card with the name Mattäus Müller. The card said Schutzstaffel N.S.D.A.P. on the top with a government stamp and the SS logo. I'm sure he's a fucking Nazi too."

Roscoe stood up and said, "I have to step out for a few minutes. Can I get you something to drink, Kevin?"

"I could use a cup of Joe."

"Sit tight; I'll be right back."

When Roscoe stepped out of the interrogation room, Walsh was standing there waiting for him.

"So, what do you think?" Roscoe asked.

Walsh shook his head, "Juan's no killer. Grouchy?"

"No, and I suggest we take another look at Pogo and Ms. Mann. I think we're dealing with a couple of anti-Semitics."

"Really? Matt Miller and Greta Mann?"

"Their real names are Mattäus Müller and Greta Schultheiss. I think we should talk to somebody at the Anti-Defamation League tomorrow and see if they have any information on Mattäus and Greta."

"So, I guess we should cut Kevin and Juan loose."

"Yeah, call downstairs and have a uni drive them home. Then let's meet back here tomorrow morning."

"Sounds good. See you in the a.m."

"Yeah, but not too a.m., if you catch my drift."
"I read you loud and clear."

Roscoe got to the precinct a little before seven the following day. On the way to the station, he stopped off at Nathan's Famous for a cup of coffee to go; while there, he was tempted to grab a chilidog as an eye-opener, so he did.

As Walsh walked toward Roscoe's office, he could smell the pungent odor of garlic, onions, cumin, and chili peppers, smothering the steamed link sausage that had been soaked in wiener water. He loudly said, "Roscoe, really you are one sick puppy, eating a chilidog at 7:30 in the morning. You are truly mental, my friend."

"Hey, you wanna bite?"

"Thanks, but no thanks, I've already eaten breakfast. I ate something that you would consider weird for breakfast: eggs and bacon."

"Say, that is weird. You ready?"

"Yeah, Harris is waiting downstairs with the car."

"Let's roll."

The Anti-Defamation League was located in midtown Manhattan near Grand Central Station. The ride from Coney Island, with traffic, took over two hours. A seven-car pile-up had caused a major shutdown leading up to the Brooklyn Battery Tunnel.

It gave Roscoe time to read the front-page story in the Daily Herald, "Killer Cult Clown Killed." According to the article, Max Wojciehowicz, aka Decay, the clown, was the leader of a clown cult that preyed upon children and used animals in ritual sacrifices.

"Wow, did you read this? What a load of crap." Roscoe said.

"And yet people will eat it up." Officer Harris said.

"With a spoon," Walsh added.

"These people don't even get off their asses to investigate; they just make this shit up."

"People want sensationalism. The more outrageous the story, the more papers they sell. If it bleeds, it leads." Walsh noted.

The Anti-Defamation League was on the third floor of 605 3rd Avenue in the Murray Hill neighborhood of Midtown Manhattan. Their offices were relatively modest, a small reception area with few offices and a bunch of cubicles.

When Walsh and Roscoe stepped off the elevator, they were greeted by an attractive young woman, "Good morning, may I help you?"

"Good morning, I'm Detective Sergeant Brown, and this is my partner, Detective Walsh. We'd like to speak with someone about obtaining information about possible Nazis living here in New York."

"I'm sorry, Detective, but we wouldn't have that sort of information. For that, you'd have to go to the offices of the National Archives down at One Bowling Green. I'm sorry."

"That's all right; we appreciate your help."

The National Archives offices were in the Alexander Hamilton U.S. Customs House, third floor, room 328.

The office seemed like a library, with people sitting at large wooden tables reading books, going through documents, and doing research. Roscoe and Walsh walked to the back of the cavernous room to where the information desk was located and again asked to speak with someone about obtaining information about possible Nazis in New York.

The man behind the desk asked them to wait and said he would see if he could get someone to help them. Moments later, the man appeared and said for them to follow him. He led them through a maze of twelve-foot-tall book stacks to a small office in the back of the building. An elderly man with snowy white hair and a mustache sat, wearing black rim glasses with Coke bottle lenses. He was dressed in a tweed jacket, white button-down shirt, and red polka dot bowtie and sat behind a large stack of books.

He smiled and stood up, saying, "Please, have a seat. I'm Professor Theodore Remer; how may I assist you?"

"Professor Remer, I'm Detective Sergeant Brown, and this is my partner, Detective Walsh. We'd like some information about possible Nazis living here in New York."

"Oh, it's more than possible, Detectives. There are hundreds of Nazis living in and around the New York City area."

"Doesn't the government know?"

"Know? After the war, American Intelligence officials created a "safe haven" in the U.S. for Nazis and their collaborators."

"What!"

"Sure, anyone that the government thought could help us either help us win the space race or help fight the Commies, we overlooked their past war crimes and allowed them entrance."

"That's insane."

"You've heard of Wernher Von Braun?"

"Yeah, he works for NASA."

"He helped develop the German V-2 "Buzz Bomb" that killed hundreds of civilians in England. His underground factory was near the central German town of Nordhausen. Prisoners from Dora-Mittelbau concentration camp dug the underground facilities and tunnels. Over 60,000 prisoners lived, worked, and died working to build the factory. Most died from disease or malnutrition; some were worked to death, while others were hanged publicly as an example to the other workers. The death rate was so high they built crematoriums."

"Von Braun was part of that?"

"Well, old Wernher was a good little Nazi until a year before the war ended when it looked like Germany was going to lose the war. He admitted that he had been through the tunnels and the abysmal prisoner's sleeping quarters. So, he had to be fully aware of the horrific conditions and treatment those men were subjected to."

"And he did nothing."

"He did nothing, as so many did after the war. "*I was just following orders.*" "*What could I do?*" "*If I objected, they would have shot me and just replaced me with someone else.*" The typical Nazi response."

"Amazing."

"Well, I bet you didn't come here to hear me ramble on about Wernher Von Braun. What can I do for you, Detective?"

"Professor, we're investigating a murder, and we have reason to believe that our suspects maybe have been Nazis."

"Do you have their names?"

"Greta Mann, whose maiden name was Greta Schultheiss, and Matt Miller, who we think is Mattäus Müller."

"I know those names quite well. Greta Schultheiss was the belle of Berlin at one point. Her father, Franz Schultheiss, who was the number three man in the Gestapo, was extremely close to Adolf Hitler. There were rumors that before Hitler was involved with Eva Braun, he had a brief affair with Greta.

I had heard that she married Major Mann, U.S. Army, after the war; as she was not officially a member of the Nazi Party, the marriage wasn't objected to by the Army. She's known to be a raging anti-Semite and bigot but hasn't had any political affiliations with organized neo-Nazi groups that we know of.

Now, Mattäus Müller was an SS guard at Mauthausen Concentration Camp in Austria. Mauthausen was referred to by its nickname Knochenmühle – the bone grinder. Its whole purpose was extermination through labor; they literally worked the people to death.

There was a rock quarry at the base of the "Stairs of Death." Prisoners were forced to carry hundred-pound rough-hewn stones up the 186 stairs, one prisoner behind the other. Often, a prisoner in the front of the line would collapse, knocking down the person behind him, who would, in turn, fall back on the next prisoner, and so on.

The SS guards would sometimes force the exhausted prisoners from hours of hard labor to race up the stairs carrying the large blocks of stone. Those who survived would be lined up at the edge of a cliff known as "The Parachutists Wall." They would have the choice of either being shot or pushing the prisoner in front of him off the cliff.

Later on, in the war, there were some American POWs sent to Mauthausen, and they suffered the same fate as all the other prisoners. Mattäus Müller was known to be one of the cruelest of all the SS guards.

You say that you suspect Greta Schultheiss and Mattäus Müller to be suspects in a murder?"

Walsh and Roscoe sat in silence for a few seconds, stunned by the story of the cruelty that occurred at Mauthausen.

"You know, Professor, we've heard stories about the holocaust, but it still seems so hard to believe that people could do those kinds of things to another human being," Walsh said.

"Detective Walsh, you have to remember that mankind has only crawled down from the trees in the last 10,000 years. We're still basically animals."

Roscoe came around from deep in thought, then said, "Schultheiss and Müller are suspected of killing a Polish Jew who worked in a circus over in Coney Island, where the both of them work as well."

"Well, I can give you some copies of their Nazi ID cards that will have their photographs attached. Would that be of any help?"

"Extremely."

"Sit tight, and I'll be right back." Professor Remer said as he left the room.

Roscoe turned to Walsh, "Fucking Nazis."

"Detective, why have you brought me down here? Am I under arrest? If so, I want my attorney." Miller demanded."

"Mr. Miller, you are not under arrest; we're just doing our jobs, trying to find out what happened," Roscoe said.

"So, I am free to go any time?"

"Yes, of course. We're re-interviewing everyone to see if there's anything that we may have missed. You understand."

"You're talking to everyone again? But why here?"

"We find it easier, as there aren't any distractions, and sometimes people feel freer to speak."

"Okay, what is it you want to know?"

Roscoe opened his file folder and showed Miller a photo of the .357 pistol.

"Is this the gun you used in the bullet catch trick on the night in question?" Roscoe asked.

Miller picked up the photo and examined it, "Yes, it's the gun."

"How can you be sure?"

He pointed to a small engraving of two letters, KC.

"See that, that's for Killer Clown."

Roscoe produced a photo of a box of .357 ammo.

"Do you recognize this?"

"Yeah, that's a box of live .357 bullets; see the KC written on the top of the box?"

"Why use live ammunition in the trick?'

"Well, to make the audience think the trick is real."

"As you know, I examined the gun and the bullet, and I saw you place the bullet into the chamber of the gun."

"What you didn't see was that I switched the bullet that you looked at with a wax bullet, or what I believed was a wax bullet."

Roscoe showed Miller a photo of a box of wax .357 bullets that looked identical to the box of live ammunition.

"Do you recognize this?"

"Yes, that's the box of wax bullets we use; see the KC there?"

"So, who gets the props for the trick?"

"Either me or Rowdy."

"And who got the props that night?"

"It was me; I distinctly remember taking one bullet from each box."

"Could you have mistakenly mixed up the bullets?"

"No, I always put the live round into the chamber and conceal the wax bullet up my sleeve like I've done every night for three years."

"Then what do you think happened?"

"Maybe somebody switched some of the live bullets with the wax ones."

"Well, we are having both boxes checked for fingerprints, and if anyone's prints other than yours and Rowdy's are on those boxes, we'll know."

"Have you guys talked to Rowdy yet?"

"As a matter of fact, my partner, Detective Walsh, is interviewing him as we speak. Any idea who might have wanted Max dead?" Roscoe lied; Walsh was in interrogation room two interviewing Greta Schultheiss.

"How would I know?"

"Come on, Matt, the circus is like a small town; everyone knows everybody else's business. Who likes who, and who hates who."

"I have to ask you. Matt, did you have anything to do with the death of Max Wojciehowicz?"

"No way."

"Do you know Danny Sullivan?"

"Bruiser? Yeah, we worked together at the circus. You don't think he had anything to do with this, do you?"

"Do you?"

"No."

"Did you have a conversation with Danny Sullivan after the killing in which you bragged to him that there would be a little something extra in your paycheck for a job well done? If so, what did you mean by that?"

"That's a damn lie. I never said that."

Roscoe lied again, "Really? We talked to Danny, and he said you did."

"He's a damn liar!"

"How long have you been involved with Greta Mann?"

"What?"

"I'm sorry, I mean Greta Schultheiss?"

"That's it! I'm done here. I want to leave now!"

"Sure, but before you go, I'd like you to meet someone."

There was a knock on the interrogation door, and two men dressed in dark blue suits walked in. One man was thin, tall, and young; the other was short, chubby, and middle-aged. The young man held out his identification card and badge and introduced himself as Special Agent Gladwell with the U.S. Justice Department. The older man said nothing as he reached behind his back and produced a pair of handcuffs.

Agent Gladwell said, "Stand up. Mattäus Müller, you are under arrest for war crimes against humanity and will be held without bond."

"You're making a mistake; my name is Matt Miller! I was never a Nazi."

Agent Gladwell looked at Roscoe, "It's amazing; we haven't met one German who was a Nazi, knew a Nazi, or even heard of Adolf Hitler. Cuff him, Jerry."

Down in interrogation room two, Walsh was interviewing Greta Schultheiss.

"Ms. Mann, Can you think of anyone who would want to kill Max Wojciehowicz?"

"No."

"You didn't like him, did you?"

"I told you he was carney trash."

"So, the fact that he was a Polish Jew didn't mean anything to you?"

"I couldn't have cared less."

"Really? Can I ask what your father's nickname was in the war?"

"I don't remember."

"Wasn't it the Jew Hunter?"

'Were you a member of the Nazi Party, Ms. Schultheiss?"

"My name is Greta Mann, and no, I was never a member of the Nazi Party."

"Is it true that you dated Adolf Hitler?"

"That was a long time ago."

"Well, I can't image Hitler ever being with anyone who didn't share his beliefs. Like his views on Jews."

"He never brought it up."

"Did you share his views about the Jews, Ms. Schultheiss?"

"No."

"So, you just hated Max Wojciehowicz just because he was Carney trash; the fact that he was a Polish Jew didn't come into it?"

"So, you like Jews."

"Some of my best friends are Jewish."

"Name one."

She sat silent, trying to think of a name.

"How about Kevin Cohen?"

"Grouchy? Yeah, Kevin, he's one of my friends."

"You said best friends. Is he one of your best friends?"

"I think so."

"Well, we've spoken to Kevin, and it's funny, according to him, you're, in fact, not best friends or even friends. He has nothing good to say about you."

"That fucking little kike!"

"Kike, is that a term of endearment?"

"Fuck you!"

"Is Mattäus Müller a best friend of yours?"

"Yes, he is."

"Mattäus Müller, the SS guard from Mauthausen, is your best friend?"

Realizing that she let her anger trip her up, Schultheiss tried to walk back her previous statements.

"I meant to say Matt Miller. I do not know anyone named Mattäus Müller."

Walsh thought he'd try a little trickery, "If you'll excuse me for a minute, I'll be right back, Ms. Schultheiss."

"That's Ms. Mann."

Walsh stepped outside and went to take a pee and get a cup of coffee. He was gone fifteen minutes before going back inside.

"It's interesting that you say that you don't know Mattäus Müller, as he's down the hall talking to Detective Brown and a couple of U.S. Justice agents. He claims that it was you who wanted and planned how to eliminate that filthy Jew, Wojciehowicz. I think he's hoping that by cooperating, they won't send him back to stand war crimes trial."

"Dieser dreckige Schweinehund!"

"I beg your pardon?"

"I would have thought that as a member of Germany's elite, he would have more honor than to betray his loyalty."

"Mattäus Müller." Walsh said.

"Yes, Mattäus Müller was an SS guard at Mauthausen Concentration Camp. He served our country with distinction. Before joining the circus, Mattäus had undergone facial plastic surgery to alter his features so he wouldn't be recognized.

Everything was going well until that pig Jew Wojciehowicz joined the circus. One day, when changing into their costumes, Mattäus noticed that Wojciehowicz had an identity tattoo given to all concentration prisoners. He knew the number sequence for the prisoners assigned to Mauthausen; although he didn't remember him, he felt he couldn't take the chance of this Jew recognizing him. So, he had to be eliminated. It would be no great loss. We exterminated six million of the vermin; what's one more or less, am I right?"

Mattäus Müller was extradited to Poland, where he stood trial and was found guilty of war crimes and crimes against humanity. As he was being led to the gallows crying, he wet himself from fear; so much for the master race.

Greta Schultheiss Mann was convicted of accessory to first-degree murder and sent to spend the rest of her life in Bedford Hills Correctional Facility for Women. After only one week, she was stabbed and killed. Rumors say that a group of Jewish prisoners attacked her in the shower after cutting off all of her hair, even her beard.

    Roscoe and Walsh were sitting in Roscoe's office when Roscoe got a call from the District Attorney's office alerting Roscoe of Schultheiss's murder. Roscoe listened intently; he looked at Walsh, smiled, and said, "Thanks for letting me know. Goodbye."

"Who was that?" Walsh asked.

"It was the DA's office; Greta Schultheiss was found in the women's shower, stabbed to death."

"Aw, that's a shame." Walsh feigned sorrow.

"Well, I guess she did Nazi that coming."

"Roscoe, that's cold."

THE END

The Case of the Cyclone Psycho

Detective Walsh and his lady friend Veronica Lennox, a Police sketch artist, were enjoying a leisurely stroll along the Riegelmann Boardwalk, better known as the Coney Island Boardwalk, early Sunday morning while watching the sunrise.

All the tourist shops and restaurants were closed, so they had the entire Boardwalk to themselves. There was a fine, cool mist in the air, a light salty breeze blowing in from the Atlantic, and a tiny sliver of sun peeking up off in the horizon.

They stopped and faced the sun rising slowly, turning the low-lying clouds off in the distance to a fire engine red.

Standing behind Veronica, arms around her waist and head on her right shoulder, Walsh whispered in her ear, "Red sky in the morning, sailor take warning."

Jokingly mocking him, Veronica said, "Jimmy, you're such a romantic."

"What do you say we go back to my place and have breakfast in bed?"

Veronica was about to turn around when she spotted something odd on the water's edge, "Look, Jimmy, is that a dead seal that's washed up on the beach?"

Walsh stared at the object briefly, "That's no seal, babe. That's a man. Go find a phone and call the station. I'm going down there and fish him out."

"You be careful." She said as she went to find a payphone.

"Shit, there goes breakfast in bed," Walsh mumbled to himself.

By the time Roscoe arrived, the Police had cordoned off the area. Doctor Olsen, the ME, and his team were there, as were David Bowles and his CSI people.

Detective Walsh, Roscoe's partner, was standing off to the right of the deceased as Doc Olsen was examining the body.

"Hey, Jimmy, what's up?" Roscoe said.

"We got a floater. I was walking on the Boardwalk early this morning with Veronica when we spotted the body washed up on the beach."

"Veronica, huh? Where is she?" He said, looking around.

"I sent her home; she doesn't need to be here. I'm sorry to bring you out."

Roscoe looked at the sky and said, "Ah, it's a beautiful day for the beach. Do we know who he is?"

"He didn't have any ID on him, so once the Doc's done, we'll get some prints, and hopefully, he's in the system."

"Have Dave and his boys gotten anything to go on?"

"Nothing yet; they're still looking around."

Roscoe walked over to where the medical examiner was examining the body of a male Caucasian, who looked to Roscoe to be late twenties, with long blond hair, surfer cut, weighing about 185, six feet tall, and naked as a BluJay.

"Whadda think Doc, drowning?"

"Won't know until I get him on the table, Roscoe. But there seems to be several unusual contusions and look at this." Olsen said as he turned the man over.

"Where's his dick?" Roscoe asked.

"Shark," Walsh said.

"No, it looks to have been cut off with something sharp, a knife or some other blade."

"How long has he been in the water?" Walsh asked.

"Just a guess at this point, but I'd say at least two, maybe three days."

Roscoe turned to Walsh and said, "You found him; he's all yours. It's your case; I'm going to Nathan's for a chilidog. Let me know if you need my help."

Detective Walsh had just sat down at his desk when the phone rang.

"Detective Walsh, sixtieth precinct."

"Walsh, this is Doctor Olsen; I got the report on the John Doe. I think you might want to come down here. We got a weird one."

"Okay, Doc, I'll be right down."

Walsh thought about grabbing Roscoe on his way to see the medical examiner but decided to wait and see what the Doc had to say first.

When he got there, Roscoe was sitting outside in the waiting room.

"Hey, Roscoe, what are you doing here? Did Doctor Olsen call you, too?"

"No, I'm here on another case, infanticide."

"Oh, God."

Doctor Olson was performing an autopsy on an eleven-month-old baby whose father shook it so hard and for so long that he turned his baby's brain into cerebral succotash.

"Yeah, the father comes home drunk, the mother's stoned out of her freaking mind, the baby won't stop crying. So instead of comforting and holding the poor thing, Dad decides to shake it like a human maraca until the baby goes quiet."

"Jesus."

"I got both mom and dad upstairs in custody. They're sitting up there right now, blaming each other, thinking of how they can save their own ass. Hell, you need a fucking license to own a dog in New York, but any two dumbasses can spawn a child."

Doctor Olsen stuck his head out from the lab, "Hey Roscoe, here's the report on baby Hernández. If it's not murder, it's manslaughter for sure."

"Thanks, Doc," Roscoe said as he took the folder of the dead baby from the ME.

"Walsh, you need to see this; come on in." The medical examiner said, holding the lab door open.

Walsh glanced at Roscoe, "Mind taking a look?"

"No, I'm fine letting the parents of the year stew for a while."

As they entered the morgue, one of the assistants was placing baby Hernández's body into one of the cold chambers where they keep the cadavers. They walked back further into the morgue, past six porcelain autopsy tables, all containing an occupant, to where the body of the 'surfer boy' lay. A sheet covered his body; only the back of his head was uncovered. Olsen took hold of the sheet and peeled it back to reveal the victim's severed penis stuffed into his rectum.

"It was done while he was still awake. See this small needle mark on his right forearm; it seems that he was injected with Succinylcholine, or SUX it's a neuromuscular paralytic drug. The toxicology reports confirm it.

SUX paralyzes all the muscles of the body, including those used for breathing, so he would have been wide awake while this happened and unable to do anything. He then slowly died of asphyxia.

You got a real sicko on your hands, Walsh."

"You got any good news, Doc?"

"Well, you can't buy this stuff over the counter at Walgreens. So, you're looking for someone who has access to these sorts of drugs, like hospitals, doctor's offices, medical supply companies, and someone would have to have some sort of medical background or training."

"Have we identified him?" Walsh asked.

"He's John Alexander, a petty criminal who worked at Coney Island Hospital as a janitor. Had his prints on file. It's all in the folder."

"Thanks, Doc," Walsh said, taking the file folder.

Walsh turned to Roscoe, "Roscoe?"

"Well, if it were my case, I'd start looking at any doctor's offices and medical facilities around the Boardwalk. Also, check any known accomplices and acquaintances of Mr. Alexander.

Let me know if you need any help. Oh, you might grab Officer Harris to help with the leg work. I gotta go and see my pair of baby killers."

"Thanks, Roscoe, I'll keep you posted."

Walsh headed back to his office to start the tedious job of slogging through paperwork and background checks, Alexander's known accomplices, past arrest records, and his autopsy report.

He had the unpleasant task of informing John's parents of their son's death. Mr. and Mrs. Alexander live in Long Beach, California, and plan on coming to New York to claim their son's body. Walsh agreed to meet with them at the morgue after they had identified their son.

Walsh found seven medical offices, two pharmaceutical companies, and Coney Island Hospital near the Boardwalk. This wasn't going to be an overnight arrest. It looked to be several months of investigative legwork, endless hours of following up with leads, countless dead ends, and weeks of interviews, all in an effort to separate the truth from the half-truths, the facts from fiction.

He brought in Officer Ron Harris to help him make a list of possible people to see. They started by going to John Alexander's apartment on 608 Brighton Beach Avenue, above Rosenbaum's Gourmet Deli.

The studio apartment looked more like a crash pad than a place where one lived. A thin mattress lay in the corner with only a rumpled top sheet; next to it was an ashtray full of Camel cigarette butts, a half-full bottle of Jack Daniels, and a stack of gay porno magazines.

There is a pile of dirty dishes covered with roaches and mouse droppings in the kitchen area and nothing in the cabinets. In the refrigerator, two rotting carrots, a half carton of sour milk, and an unopened can of Mountain Dew. There weren't any photographs, letters, or correspondence of any kind.

After finding nothing of value at the apartment, they called the boys from CSI to dust for prints, then headed over to see the head of personnel at Coney Island Hospital, Mr. Nussbaum. Walsh would interview Nussbaum, while Harris would talk to the head of hospital security.

"Mr. Nussbaum, thank you for taking the time to meet with me," Walsh said.

"Detective Walsh, how may I help you?"

"Mr. Nussbaum, I'm investigating the homicide of a young man who worked here as a janitor, John Alexander. He was murdered of a drug that isn't common knowledge to the average layman, and we believe that it had to be administered by someone with a medical background."

"Oh my, I hope you do not think anyone associated with our hospital would be involved in such a thing?"

"No, of course not. I'm wondering if there might be anyone who was released recently that may have exhibited improper or unlawful behavior. Anyone who might have access or knowledge of the drug Succinylcholine or SUX?"

"No, no one comes to mind at the moment. But, if you give me a day or two, I'll go through my files and see if there is anyone that I feel might be a possibility."

"I would appreciate it. Also, if you could send me a copy of John Alexander's file as well."

"I certainly will, Detective. Would tomorrow be all right?"

"That would be fine; thank you for your time, Mr. Nussbaum."

Walsh met Officer Harris at the squad car parked out front of the hospital. Walsh asked, "Any luck?"

"Maybe, the head of security said there was one guy who was a real punk. A guy named David Evans. Apparently, he worked as an orderly in the Anesthesiology Department and was let go because some drugs came up missing. They couldn't prove he took them, but they had enough other complaints against the guy to cut him loose."

"That's interesting; old Nussbaum told me nobody came to mind when I asked him if anyone was let go because of improper or unlawful behavior. I wonder what that's all about?"

"Aw, you know hospitals are always paranoid and overprotective, so afraid of getting bad publicity."

"Yeah, maybe. But he better come up with the name David Evans, or he and I are going to have a come to Jesus meeting."

"By the way, I got the name of the head doc of Anesthesiology: Doctor Steven Mulholland. The security guy says old Doctor Steve is a bit of a wild man."

"How so?"

"He's a real ladies' man, and the Doc likes to party hardy. Aside from that. He is supposed to be "The Guy" when it comes to anesthesiology."

"Maybe I should go talk to him."

"Not today; on Wednesdays', he's sailing off Long Island Sound on his Pearson Vanguard yacht."

"Well, excuse me, matey. Okay, let's see if we can track down this David Evans."

"Aye, aye, captain."

Vincente Hernández sat in his cell at Rikers Island, New York's most famous jail, while cursing at the correction officers for the lousy food.

Hernández was referring to his dinner, which consisted of 5 oz. Turkey soy casserole, dinner roll, 1 cup mashed potatoes,1/2 cup of fresh fruit, 1 cup glazed carrots, and one brownie served to him in his cell on a plastic tray.

"Hey, pig, this shit isn't fit for human consumption!" Vincente snapped at the guard.

"Well, then it's perfect for you 'cause you ain't no human, you fucking baby killer!" The guard snarled back.

From down the cell block, a voice shouted out, "You're a dead man, Hernández! You fucking baby killer."

Suddenly, there came a chorus of other inmates chanting, taunting, and threatening his life.

Two days later, on the day of his arraignment, Vincente Hernández was found in his cell, beaten, burned, and stabbed to death. On his chest was carved the words asesino de babés (baby killer).

Vincente's wife and now widow, Maria Hernández, was sentenced to fifteen years in Albion Correctional Facility in upstate New York, where she met the love of her life, a muscular Latino woman named Isabella. Like many other women, Maria adopted the attitude, 'Gay for the Stay' for comfort and a relationship.

Walsh and Harris returned to the Precinct to find that Roscoe had taped a note on Walsh's black Olivetti typewriter, 'Got info on D.E.'

They walked down the hall to Roscoe's office, where they found him reading a copy of Mad Magazine.

"Really, Mad Magazine?" Walsh asked.

"Keeps your mind limber," Roscoe replied without looking up.

"You said you had some information on our David Evans?"

"I heard from a reliable source that your Mr. Evans is currently working at the Coney Island Cyclone as a roustabout. After the word got out about his misbehavior at the hospital, nobody in the medical field would touch him, and this was the only job he could get."

"How'd you hear about him?"

"I have my sources."

"Your source wouldn't happen to work at Nathan's Famous, would he?"

"I'm sorry, but that's a confidential source; besides, I told you that eating at Nathan's was a good thing."

Walsh stood staring at a grown man, a Detective Sergeant in the New York City Police Department, reading a Mad Magazine.

Roscoe peered over the periodical and said, "There's a good satire on Bonney and Clyde in here called Balmy and Clod. Want to read it when I'm done?"

"Mmm, tempting, but I'm reading a great book called, Chariots of the Gods? By Erich Von Daniken."

"B o r i n g."

"No, it's an international bestseller."

"It sounds like an international snooze fest."

"Goodbye, Roscoe. Come on, Harris, let's go ride the Cyclone."

The Coney Island Cyclone is a wooden roller coaster built in 1927. It has a total length of 2,640 feet, a maximum height of an eight-story building, and an initial first drop of 58.1 degrees. It's the world's third steepest wooden roller coaster, reaching speeds over 60 miles per hour, and riders sustain G-forces of 3.75.

The popularity of Coney Island and the Cyclone declined due to increased crime, insufficient parking, and poor weather. During the day, the area was reasonably safe, but at night the area around Steeplechase Park had been taken over by gangs, druggies, and hookers.

Walsh had Harris change into his civilian clothes so as not to scare off their suspect. Word of a Police Officer in the area quickly spreads, and the low lives disappear faster than roaches in a kitchen when the lights come on.

It was a little after two in the afternoon, and a small crowd was waiting to ride the wooden monster. From a distance, you could hear the clickety-clack of the roller coaster cars and the people screaming as they were being whipped around on what looked to be death on wheels.

They bought their ticket at the little ticket shack and went to stand in line. As Roscoe and Walsh waited, they spotted their suspect, David Evans, who was one of two ride operators helping people get in and out of the cars. Walsh and Harris decided to question Evans after they rode the Cyclone since, after all, they did buy a ticket to ride.

Walsh and Harris happened to get the coveted first car seats, to the dismay of their fellow riders. As the coaster left the platform, they double-checked to see if the seat restraint was properly secured.

The car started slowly curving to the right, past the next batch of waiting riders waving and cheering them on. They went by several signs posted, telling passengers of their last warning to remain seated and hold on to the hand bars at all times; this means DO NOT PUT HANDS UP and do not rest head on lap bar.

They were rewarded after the slow, angled sixteen-second climb to the apex of the Cyclone before the 85-foot drop by passing under two American flags and a final reminder to remain seated. Then, it was a sheer drop, leaving both Walsh and Harris' stomachs somewhere above. Then came a body-wrenching grind down into the bottom of their seats before rushing up and whipping around a hard left curve, then down and up and up and down, left then right, over and over again. The total time for the ride was two minutes and thirty seconds, but to the two Detectives, it seemed longer.

Once the ride was over, they exited the car and approached Evans. Walsh flashed his badge and said, "David Evan, I'm Detective Walsh. I need to speak to you."

"Hey, man, can't this wait? I'm almost done with my shift."

"I'm afraid not. Is there somewhere where we can talk privately?"

"No, man, not around here."

"Okay, then let's go to the station. Harris, go square it with the manager."

While Harris went to talk to the manager, Walsh escorted Evans to the squad car.

"Hey, what's this all about? I didn't do nothing."

"We'll talk down at the station."

"Am I under arrest?"

"No, we just need to talk to you about something."

"Well, whatever it is, I didn't do it."

All the way to the station house, Evans kept saying, "I didn't do anything." And Walsh kept repeating, "Look, we aren't accusing you of anything, so just relax."

"Okay, but I didn't do anything."

Walsh looked at Harris, who was driving, and said, "I guess I'll just have to kill him if he doesn't shut up."

Harris smiled and said, "I know a good place to dump the body."

Evans straightened up in the backseat and didn't say another word.

Detective Walsh brought David Evans into interrogation room two; Officer Harris waited outside.

"David, would you care for something to drink?" Walsh asked politely."

"Mountain Dew."

"All right, sit tight, and I'll be right back," Walsh said as he left the room, locking the door behind him. He walked down the hall to the soda machine, dropped ten cents into the slot, pushed the Mountain Dew button, and blonk, a bottle shot out at the bottom. Walsh took the bottle and snapped the bottle cap off with the built-in bottle opener on the vending machine.

"Here ya go," Walsh said as he placed the green bottle with a cartoon of a hillbilly shooting at another hillbilly, running towards an outhouse printed on the glass.

Evans picked up the bottle and drank the entire contents in one long drink. He slammed the empty bottle onto the table, smiled, and let loose a thunderous burp.

Walsh stared at him for a minute without saying anything, just in case Evans felt the urge to belch again.

"Okay. Let's start with your full name."

"David Waldo Evans."

"How old are you, David?"

"Twenty-six."

"How long have you worked at the Coney Island Hospital?"

"Almost two years."

"And what did you do there?"

"I was an orderly."

"What department did you work in?"

"The Anesthesiology Department."

"What sort of things did you do as an orderly?"

"Oh, assisting patients, moving them from one place to another, helping them get in and out of bed, eat meals, clean up, you know, general stuff."

Walsh wrote notes of everything Evans said; he opened a file, placed a photograph of John Alexander in front of his suspect, and asked, "David, do you know this man?"

"No, man, I ain't never seen that guy."

"He worked at Coney Island Hospital the same time you did."

"So, there's like a million people working there. I don't know them all, man."

"He was a janitor assigned to the Anesthesiology Department. Are you sure you never saw him? Because we have several people who say that they saw you two hanging out."

Evans picked up the photograph and looked at it, "I might have seen him once or twice, I don't remember."

"Now, David, I'm not accusing you of anything. I'm just trying to find out what happened to him. Do you know if he was friends with anyone in the Anesthesiology Department?"

"I don't know."

"Well, do you know if there was anyone who didn't like him, who might have had an argument with him?"

"Not that I know of."

"Well, I think the Anesthesiology Department is a tight-knit community, and somebody will know something. I wanted to talk to you first, to hear what you had to say before I talk to everyone else."

The suspect sat looking at the photograph without speaking for a couple of minutes.

"David, why were you let go from the Hospital?"

"Aw, the head nurse didn't like me; she said I was stealing drugs, but I didn't."

"Why would she say that you stole drugs?"

"I don't know; she never liked me; Mrs. Marini is a real bitch. She didn't like it that I was friends with Doctor Mulholland."

"You and Doctor Mulholland are friends?"

"Yeah, so?"

"Oh, nothing. Are you still friends?"

"Yeah, he's a good guy."

"Couldn't he have saved your job at the hospital since you're such good friends?"

"He tried, but that bitch had it in for me. She had a couple of the other nurses say that they saw me in the room where the drugs are kept."

"Did they?"

"Did they what?"

"Did they see you in the room where the drugs are kept?"

"No! I was framed. They needed to blame someone when the drug count came up short. So, they blamed me."

"Okay, David, I want to thank you for talking to me. I'm going to have Officer Harris take you home."

"Don't bother."

"By the way, what is your current address, David?"

"891 Avenue Z."

"Oh, I know that area; it's right down the street from the Avenue Z Jewish Center. You live there alone?"

"Naw, I live in my folk's basement. I have my own pad down there and my own entrance and everything. I come and go as I please."

"How adult."

David Evans walked out of interrogation room two, out of the Police Station, and proceeded to walk the 1.5 miles to his parent's basement bunker.

Once Evans left, Walsh took his handkerchief from his coat pocket, carefully picked up the glass Mountain Dew bottle, and walked it downstairs to the CSI lab to be tested for fingerprints.

"Detective Walsh."

"Hello, Detective Walsh; this is Mr. Nussbaum from Coney Island Hospital."

"Ah yes, Mr. Nussbaum."

"Detective, I wanted to get back to you with the names of those recently let go due to improper behavior."

"Okay."

"Well, it seems that there are only three people that we had to terminate. Shall I give you their names?"

"That would be helpful."

"Yes, sorry. The first one is Mary Jacobs, a nurse. She was removed from her position for getting into an altercation with a patient. That was ten weeks ago.

Next is Jeffery Sotomayor, a security guard terminated six weeks ago for stealing hospital property. The hospital pressed charges; I believe he is still incarcerated.

Finally, there is David Evans, an orderly who was released for suspicion of stealing drugs. That was three weeks ago."

"On the David Evans case, was there proof that he actually did steal drugs?"

"No, like I said, he was suspected, but the department he was assigned to has some very serious drugs, so we erred on the side of caution."

"Do you know if there were ever any reports of the drug Succinylcholine that had gone missing?"

"Could you hold on while I check?"

"Sure."

Walsh could hear the sound of papers rustling through the phone; moments later, Nussbaum was back on the phone.

"Yes, Detective, there was a report of a vial of Succinylcholine that couldn't be accounted for."

"Was this around the time of David Evans' dismissal?"

"Err, yes, it was."

"Mr. Nussbaum, why didn't you have this information yesterday when I asked about people being let go?"

"Detective, the hospital was to be so very careful these days. I do apologize, but I felt it was my duty to first check with our attorneys. I wasn't trying to hide anything; I hope you understand."

"Mr. Nussbaum, if you would be so kind as to send me a complete copy of David Evans' employment folder, as soon as possible."

"You will have it this afternoon. Is there anything else?"

"Yes, was there an investigation into David Evans' thief charges?"

"Yes, of course. Several nurses said that they saw him go into the room where the drugs are stored, and afterward, they discovered drugs missing."

"Did anyone vouch for Mr. Evans?"

"Why yes, Doctor Mulholland, head of the Anesthesiology Department."

"And the nurses carried more weight than the head of the Anesthesiology Department?"

"Doctor Mulholland was speaking to Mr. Evans' character, not to the charges. In fact, it was Doctor Mulholland's testimony for us not calling the Police."

"Thank you, Mr. Nussbaum, you've been most helpful."

"Doctor Mulholland, my name is Detective Walsh, and this is Officer Harris; we'd like a few minutes to speak with you."

"About?"

"We're investigating the murder of one of the hospital's employees, John Alexander."

"I'm sorry, but I don't know a John Alexander."

"He worked in the janitorial department in the Anesthesiology Department."

"I'm sorry, but I don't know anyone in the janitorial service."

"Well, how about an orderly named David Evans?"

"Yes, I knew David; he no longer works here."

"Yes, we know, we talked to Mr. Nussbaum. He informed us that Mr. Evans was terminated for allegedly stealing drugs."

"Yes, I know, but as I said in my deposition, I never saw him steal any drugs. I testified that I found him a hard, diligent worker."

"Were you and Mr. Evans friends?"

"Friends? No, I wouldn't say that. We were friendly, but I like to think I'm friendly to all the hospital staff."

"So, you never socialized with him after work hours?"

"Well, Mr. Evans said that he thought you two were friends."

"Like I said, I was friendly to him here at the hospital, but we weren't friend, friends. You know what I mean? I never socialized with him outside of work."

"Do you know if he would have had access to the drug Succinylcholine?"

"Not officially."

"Were you aware that a bottle of Succinylcholine went missing around the time of David Evans' termination?"

'I do believe that I had heard something about it, yes."

"And yet you gave Mr. Evans a positive character review."

"Well, nobody actually saw him take it."

"Succinylcholine is a dangerous drug, is it not?"

"It can be if not used administrated by a trained professional."

"John Alexander was recently killed with an overdose of Succinylcholine, Doctor."

Silence.

"Thank you for your time, Doctor; if we have any more questions, we'll be sure to contact you."

Roscoe stuck his head into Walsh's office, "How's it going?"

"I have a suspect but nothing concrete to tie him to the murder. He was an orderly who was fired from the hospital for suspicion of stealing drugs, and a vial of the drug that killed our victim went missing around the same time he was let go. The victim also worked in the same general area as my suspect."

"It's not concrete, but there's a ton of circumstantial evidence going on. I bet good old Judge Travis Beesey would grant you a warrant to search the guy's residence."

"Judge Beesey?"

"Yeah, he's every Policeman's friend. I've seen him grant a warrant just because he didn't like the suspect's name. They call him old Easy Beesey."

On the way over to Judge Beesey's chambers, Walsh filled Roscoe in on all the goings-on: Alexander, Nussbaum, Doctor Mulholland. They went over the original notes from the interview with Evans.

"Have they gotten any matches with the prints from the soda bottle?" Roscoe asked.

"Nothing yet, but it's only been a day."

"Well, I'm sure something will pop up; this Evans guy sounds dirty."

Walsh only got halfway thru the circumstantial evidence he had when the Judge held up his hand and said, "Say no more, Detective, this scum shouldn't be allowed to walk our streets. Here's your warrant."

"Thank you, your honor," Walsh said, taking the warrant as he and Roscoe left the Judge's chambers.

"What did I tell you, Easy Beesey," Roscoe said.

"Amazing."

"You want I should go with you to serve the warrant?"

"You working on anything?" Walsh asked.

"Nothing that can't wait."

"Cool. Let's rock and roll."

"Groovy."

"Groovy? Roscoe, you're so hip."

"You just gotta stay up with the times."

"And the fedora?"

"Hey, now don't be disrespecting my chapeau, Walsh! That's my trademark, like the Bat Masterson's derby, Sherlock Holmes's Deerstalker, or Bogart's fedora in the Maltese Falcon."

"I get it, but you have to admit you're one of the last of a dying breed."

"You know, maybe you should try wearing a hat. It'll give you a certain je ne sais quoi."

"What? You don't like this suit?"

"No, I didn't say that; it's very nice, but…"

"But what?"

"Well, you look like all the other detectives; you need a trademark to set you apart from everyone else. If someone wants to let someone know who I am. They say, "Oh, he's the detective with the hat and mustache."

See, I mean, you need a colophon, a brand, a signet. You need something that sets you apart so you don't blend in with everyone else."

"I got just the thing," Walsh said as he pulled out a pair of Ray-Ban sunglasses, black frames, and dark green lenses.

"Whadda, you think?" He said as he put them on proudly.

"I like it. You know if you go down this road, you'll have to wear them all the time, day and night."

"No problem."

"Okay, 'Shades,' let's rock and roll."

891 Avenue Z was a two-story brick home with a one-car garage. Over the garage was a covered patio with planters overflowing with daffodils all the way around the patio. There were two staircases, one leading up to the main

entrance of the house and one leading down to the basement entrance where David Evans lived.

Walsh and Roscoe started downstairs at David Evans' residence. They knocked on the door and rang the doorbell. No answer.

They went upstairs and knocked on the door. A middle-aged woman wearing a simple house coat answered the door.

"Yes? May I help you?"

Walsh held out his ID and badge, "Ma'am, I'm Detective Walsh, and this is my partner, Detective Sergeant Brown, with the New York City Police. Would you know if your son David is at home?"

"No, he's at work. I'm his mother, Ruth. David works over on the Boardwalk at the Cyclone Rollercoaster. I'm afraid he won't be home until eleven this evening. Is there something I can do?"

"We have a search warrant to search David's residence. Would you happen to have a key to his door? Otherwise, we'd have to break in, and we don't want to do any undue damage to your property."

"What has David done now?" She said she was resigned to the fact that her son was in some kind of hot water.

"I'm sorry, Ma'am, but we can't discuss that as it's an ongoing investigation," Walsh explained.

She went and got the key and handed it to Walsh.

"Please be careful. I have some of my mother's belongings down there that are very precious to me."

"We'll be mindful of your belongings, Ma'am," Roscoe said reassuringly.

The apartment was dark; all the blinds were closed, and the curtains were drawn shut. Roscoe left the front door open so Walsh could find a light switch. They could barely see even with the entrance light on; it wasn't until they drew open the curtains and opened the blinds.

The place was a dump with a sink full of dirty dishes, empty pizza boxes all over the kitchen and living room, newspapers stacked up almost to the ceiling. There weren't any sheets on the bed, and clothes were strewn throughout the house. The place looked like it hadn't been cleaned in months, if ever.

They began to search for anything they felt might incriminate Mr. Evans, although they didn't find any drugs, illegal or OTC, and no vials of Succinylcholine. They did find several unused hyperemic needles and miscellaneous medical paraphilia that looked like they might have come from the hospital.

Overall, no concrete evidence was found to tie David Evans to John Alexander's murder, but Roscoe suggested that Walsh bring in David Bowles and the boys from CSI to give it the once-over.

"Good idea. I'll give Bowles a call." Walsh said.

"How about you hold the fort, and I'll head back to the station and have Bowles, and his lab rats come out asap?"

"Sounds like a plan."

David Evans was on his way home to have his mother fix him lunch when he observed two men standing on the porch talking to her, then going downstairs and entering his apartment. He recognized one of the men as Detective Walsh, who had interviewed him the day before.

He sat on a swing set in the P.S. 209 Margaret Mead Elementary School playground, which was catty-corner to his house. He watched a Police CSI van arrive and a team of people wearing white jumpsuits carrying small suitcases storm inside.

Evans watched and waited for over an hour before heading back to his job at the Cyclone. As he walked back to the Boardwalk, he tapped his back pocket, making sure that his "kit" was still there.

Roscoe was sitting in his office going over his trial notes for a murder case involving an 18-year-old twin brother and sister who killed their parents with a shotgun while they slept. They said their parents wouldn't allow them to have sex with each other. Detective Louis Hernández knocked on Roscoe's door and said, "Hey, Roscoe, there's a Doctor Mulholland here looking for Walsh. You want to see him?"

"Yeah, where is he downstairs?"

"The Sergeant's desk."

"Thanks, Hernández."

Roscoe went down to the lobby, and he saw a well-dressed distinguished-looking man standing in amongst a sea of hookers, petty criminals, and low-lives.

Roscoe called out to him, "Hey, Doc. over here."

Doctor Mulholland made his way over to where Roscoe was standing on the staircase.

"Doctor Mulholland, I'm Detective Sergeant Brown. Detective Walsh is out. I was hoping that I might be able to help. Let's get out of this madness; follow me."

Roscoe led the good doctor up the stairs to the Detective's squad room and into his office.

"Please, have a seat."

"Do you work with Detective Walsh?"

"Yes, I'm his partner."

"So, you are aware of his investigation of David Evans."

"Yes, I am."

"Well, after Detective Walsh visited with me, I received a call from David. He sounded irate and threatening towards Detective Walsh and me. It sounded to me like he was tormented and felt persecuted. I fear he might try and do something reckless or even dangerous."

"This is quite a change from the recommendation you gave him a couple of months ago."

"Sometimes, when things are going well, a person with a mental illness will show no signs of their neurosis until some major event occurs, then the neurosis will come to the surface and manifest itself into either a bipolar disorder or possibly schizophrenia. I've already alerted hospital security to be on the lookout for David."

"Sounds almost like Doctor Jekyll and Mr. Hyde."

"That's a very accurate description. I just wanted to warn Detective Walsh and you to be careful when dealing with David. I think he's dangerous to himself and others, especially if he feels cornered."

As Roscoe showed Doctor Mulholland out, the doctor handed Roscoe a small package.

"Good luck, Detective."

"Thanks, Doc."

Roscoe stopped by the Sergeant's desk in the lobby and left a written message with Sergeant Morricone, who was the officer on duty, to give to Detective Walsh as soon as he came in.

Walsh had received a call from David Bowles with CSI that they had found several fingerprints belonging to John Alexander in David Evans's apartment.

Walsh contacted the District Attorney's office to have them issue a warrant for his arrest for the murder of John Alexander. Once he picked up the warrant, he called Officer Harris to meet him at the station. He wanted Harris to back him up when he went up against Evans.

Harris got Walsh's call as he was booking one Tommy P. Shrump, a local scuzzball who he arrested for beating up and extorting gays. Shrump would be waiting outside the public men's room on the Boardwalk, and if someone approached him, he would lead them to a secluded place and then threaten them, "Either you pay through the nose or bleed through it."

Unfortunately for Shrump, he threatened a New York City undercover Policeman, who just happened also to be gay. Shrump grabbed his would-be victim by the lapels, shoved him against the alley wall, and produced a switchblade knife. The undercover officer brought his assailant to his knees with a swift knee to the groin and a crushing right hook to Shrump's temple, causing him to land face-first onto the wooden Boardwalk, resulting in a broken nose. On this day, it was Shrump who was the one who bled through the nose after accosting Officer Harris.

As Walsh pulled up to the precinct, he noticed Harris walking out of the station, so he decided not to park and go inside. He gave a quick car honk to get Harris' attention; Harris spotted Walsh's 1968 light brown Mercury Comet.

"Hey, Harris, ready to take a wide ride on the Cyclone?"

"It's do it!"

After ten o'clock, the Boardwalk's action slowed down, especially on a Wednesday night. They spotted their suspect as they approached the rollercoaster entrance; Evans and two other workers were assisting riders on and off the coasters. As they reached the line queued up for the next group of riders, Evans noticed Walsh and Harris; he quickly said something to one of his coworkers and left through an employee's only exit.

Walsh and Harris flashed their badges to the workers and began the chase. They saw Evans head towards some company trailers in the back of the property parked close by an exit to the Boardwalk. The lighting was harsh, with deep, dark black shadows contrasted by bright white light; it was difficult for the eyes to adjust to.

Walsh stopped Harris and whispered, "Let's split up. You go right, and I'll go to the left. Remember, he's dangerous."

"Right."

Harris edged his way right, walking between two parked 18-wheeler Mack Truck semi cabs with trailers loaded with machine parts. He was concentrating on searching the space under the truck trailers, thinking that Evans would be hiding where there would be little or no light. He was wrong.

Evans stood where the truck cab and the trailer were attached, holding an eighteen-inch S-wrench. It was too late when Harris sensed the suspect's presence. White light pain, stars, and blackness engulfed Officer Harris.

Walsh was unaware of Harris' condition and continued his search when he spotted Evans running towards the Boardwalk exit. He pulled his revolver and shouted, "Police! Freeze, or I'll shoot!"

Evans stopped and slowly turned around.

"Drop the wrench and put your hands up!" Walsh said as he cautiously approached.

Evans did as he was told, dropping the S-wrench and raising his hands.

Walsh reached behind his back to get his handcuffs, but they weren't there; they must have fallen out during the chase.

"Damn! Harris, I'm over here by the exit."

Evan's smiled, "I'm afraid your partner is outta commission, Detective."

"Where is he?"

"Over there somewhere, want me to show you?"

"Turn around slowly with your back to me. You try anything, and I'll blow your brains out, you dig?"

Evans said nothing; he did as he was told, slowly turning his back to Walsh. Walsh grabbed Evans by the back of his shirt collar and pressed the barrel of his gun into Evan's back.

"Move slowly!" He commanded.

Evans led Walsh into the area where Harris was lying. Once they were in the deep, dark black shadows, Evans made his move. He spun around, grabbed Walsh, and pushed him up against the side of one of the tractor-trailers so hard that he knocked the wind out of the Detective, forcing him down on the ground on top of the unconscious Harris.

The next thing Walsh remembered was a sharp, painful pin prick into the back of his neck, then being rolled over onto his back so he was facing the black of the sky.

"Detective Walsh, that pain you felt in your neck was an injection of Succinylcholine. You're going to die a slow, painful, agonizing death while I just stand here and watch you die." Evans said, leaning over smiling.

Walsh was beginning to have difficulty breathing, and his vision was becoming blurred. He tried to relax and not panic. Walsh fixed his gaze on Evans' smirk as all-round him, sounds became enhanced, colors seemed brighter, more vibrant, and things started to move in slow-motion. He steadied himself for death.

Suddenly, there was a flash of light, a thunderous boom. David Evan's left shoulder exploded, soaking Walsh with a shower of blood. His assassin fell out of sight; then, a familiar face appeared. The figure was wearing a fedora. Was it really Roscoe, or was he hallucinating? There was a sensation of another pinprick in his right arm. As he closed his eyes, he felt someone slapping his face. The more Walsh wanted to go to sleep, the more someone kept slapping his face and pinching his cheek. Slowly, the fog that surrounded him began to lift.

"Walsh, stay with me, don't go to sleep. Come on, open your eyes." Roscoe said as he slapped his friend's face.

"Come on, open your eyes." *Slap!*

Walsh made a slight moaning sound.

"Come on, Walsh, stay with me!" *Slap!*

Walsh opened his eyes, blinked a couple of times, and finally muttered, "Roscoe, if you slap me one more time, I'm gonna kick your ass."

Eight weeks after the attempted murder of Detective James Walsh and Officer Ron Harris, both James Walsh and David Evans were released from the hospital. Detective Walsh from Coney Island Hospital and David Evans from Rikers Island Infirmary. Evans was brought back to the 60th Precinct for questioning.

Detective Sergeant Roscoe Brown and Detective James Walsh were sitting across from Evans and his public defender.

Evans sat smugly in his chair, looking at Walsh smiling.

"It's so nice to see you again, Detective Walsh. How are you feeling these days?"

Walsh was prepared not to show any weakness or animosity but to be flat-out professional and show no emotion.

"I'm doing well, and how are you? How's the shoulder?"

Evans seemed disappointed he hadn't gotten a rise out of the Detective.

"Oh, I'm just peachy; how's the other pig? Did I at least kill him?" Evans asked.

"Thank you for asking; Officer Harris is recovering nicely. I'll be sure to tell him that you asked about him." Walsh said.

"Now that the pleasantries are out of the way, I'd like to get down to business, David. Would you be so kind as to tell me why you killed John Alexander?" Roscoe inquired.

The public defender quickly interjected, "I object. David, you do not have to answer any of these questions."

"No, man, I want to. I want the whole world to know who the Cyclone Psycho is. I just love the name that the Post gave me; it's so damn cool. Don't you think it's cool, Detective Walsh?"

"Yes, I do. I think they captured the true essence of David Evans."

"Thank you, Detective Walsh; coming from you, that means a lot."

He gave his attorney a short disapproving glance, then looked at Roscoe and said, "So, Detective Sergeant Brown, you wanted to know why I killed John. It was because he wanted to have sex with me."

"He thought you were homosexual?"

"I don't know. We were hanging out at the Cyclone one night after my shift. We were back by where you shot me. I chose to go that way because it was the quickest way to the Boardwalk, but he must have thought I wanted to have sex with him."

"What happened to cause you to kill him?"

"He starts coming on to me, you know, wanting to kiss me. I said I'm not into that. I said I like girls. Next thing I know, he's down on his knees, giving me a blow job. Afterward, he wants us to go back to his place. I said no fucking way, I ain't no homo."

"So, you killed him?"

"No, it was after that. He flips out and starts threatening to go around, telling everyone that I'm a faggot. I tried to calm him down, but he was freaking out. He gets mad and tells me to go fuck myself; that's when I decide to kill him.

I originally stole the Succinylcholine to party with, but he was going all ape shit on me. I tell him I'll party with him if we both try this stuff; I tell him it'll get us high.

So I inject him first and pretend to inject myself. He takes off his clothes and lies down. I get him hard, and then I see he's starting to become immobile; that's when I take my pocketknife and cut his dick off, roll him over, and shove it up his ass. That'll teach him telling me to go fuck myself."

"Then what did you do?"

"I waited until the place closed up and the area was deserted, then I dragged his sorry ass across the Boardwalk and down to the beach; the tide was coming in, so I left him at the water's edge. I figured the tide would carry him out, and maybe some sharks would eat him. Then I went home."

"No regrets?"

"Sure, I regret that he wasn't eaten by no sharks, and I got caught."

"I meant, do you have any regrets about killing John?"

"Hell no! I'm the Cyclone Psycho."

"They're going to love you in prison."

"I ain't scared; nobody better fuck with the Cyclone Psycho."

Roscoe turned to Walsh and asked, "Is there anything you'd like to ask, Detective Walsh?"

"Yeah. David, you're twenty-six years old, and chances are you are going to spend the rest of your life in prison; doesn't that frighten you at all?" Walsh asked.

"Look, out on the streets, I'm a nobody, a loser, but in prison, I'm a somebody, I'm the Cyclone Psycho. Besides, it's better to reign in Hell than serve in Heaven."

"Well, Mr. Evans, you got your wish; you'll spend the rest of this life in Hell. Come on, Detective, I think we're done here." Roscoe said to his partner as he stood up to leave the interrogation room.

The trial turned into a media circus. Not only did it make the national news, but it was also covered worldwide. David Evans finally got his wish; he finally was a somebody.

The trial lasted three weeks, and in the end, he was found guilty of one count of first-degree murder, two counts of attempted murder, two counts of aggravated assault, two counts of assaulting a Police Officer, and one count of possession of a dangerous drug.

The Judge passed down a sentence of 215 years, with the possibility of parole after 99 years served. The year would be 2067, and David Evans would be the ripe old age of 125 years old.

Roscoe, Walsh, and Harris were sitting on a bench in the Coney Island Boardwalk Garden facing out towards the ocean after an official awards ceremony honoring the bravery and valor of one Roscoe Brown, James Walsh, and Ron Harris.

Roscoe Brown received the Medal of Valor, and James Walsh and Ron Harris received the Police Combat Cross and the Purple Shield.

Roscoe's wife, Betty, was in attendance along with Walsh's girlfriend, Veronica Lennox, and Officer Harris' mother. There were speeches from Captain Sean O'Rourke, Police Commissioner Raymond Kelly, and even Mayor Richard F. Wagner Jr. The local press and TV stations covered the event. Of course, there were the obligatory photo ops with all the higher-ups.

After all the hoopla was over, the three of them left and went for a walk along the Boardwalk decked out in their dress blue uniforms. They ended up sitting on a bench looking out towards the ocean, silently reflecting on the course of past events.

"Roscoe, I meant to ask you how did you know that we were going to be at the Cyclone?" Walsh asked.

"I didn't; I was working on preparing my notes for the Farkas brother and sister murder trial when Doctor Mulholland stopped by looking for you.

We spoke at length about Evans and, in particular, the extreme danger the drug Succinylcholine was. Before leaving, he gave me a syringe and vial of Pyridostigmine, Succinylcholine's reversal agent.

I left a note at the Sergeant's desk with instructions for you not to approach Evans without a large backup team. However, I couldn't take a chance that you might not get it, so I decided to go out and try to intercept you and Harris, but I was too late." Roscoe explained.

"Well, maybe late, but definitely not too late, partner," Walsh said.

"Yeah, thanks, Sarge." Harris coyly said.

"Hey, that's what partners do." Roscoe proudly said.

Roscoe heard a small commotion to his right. Vinnie, the counterman from Nathan's Famous, and three other

Nathan's workers were heading their way, waving and carrying several bags of food.

"Yo! Roscoe, the gang at Nathan's wants to provide yous guys with lunch, courtesy of Nathan's Famous. This is in recognition and gratitude for all that you and these other brave men in blue do by risking their lives in the line of duty." Vinnie distributed the bags of hot dogs, fries, and drinks.

"Hey, Vinnie, tell everyone that this means a lot to me, Detective Walsh, and Officer Harris."

"Will do. Bon Appétit."

The three of them ate in silence, enjoying their free chilidogs, fries, and sodas. They drew a lot of stares from passersby, and after they finished, they started casually strolling back to the station.

Roscoe asked, "Walsh, do you know why love is like a roller coaster?"

Walsh shook his head in feigned disgust, "No, Roscoe, why is love like a roller coaster?"

"Because first, you rise, then fall, you rise again and then fall….then you puke."

Harris let out a belly laugh.

Walsh quickly admonished him, "Harris, for God's sake, don't encourage him!"

THE END

The Case of the God Squad

Two fresh-faced young men with buzz cuts were wearing white short-sleeved shirts with name tags attached to their shirt pockets, dark ties, and black chinos. They carried backpacks and carrying copies of the "Watchtower." They smiled at everyone they passed on Neptune Avenue as they began their morning mission calls.

They turn off Neptune Avenue, heading south on Brighton 1st Street, past several semi-attached homes until they enter the block's center, where the houses stand alone. They start with the first house on the left side of the street.

"Hello, ma'am, we're missionaries from the Church of Jesus Christ of Latter-Day Saints, and we'd like to…"

SLAM.

The next house.

"We're encouraging folks to read their Bible. The answers that it gives to important questions often surprise people. For example…."

SLAM.

The next house.

"Hi, my name is Elder Barton, and this is my companion, Elder Ward. We'd like to share a message with you about…"

SLAM.

The next house.

"Good morning, do you believe in Jesus Christ as the Son of God…"

SLAM.

The next house.

"Good morning. Have you ever asked yourself, where did I come from…"

SLAM.

The next house.

"Hello. We're just making a brief call to share an important message with you. Please note what it says here in the Bible. What do you think about that?"

SLAM.

The next house.

"Good morning, we're Jehovah's Witnesses, and we'd like to…"

SLAM.

They decided to try the houses on the right side of the street.

The first house on the right was a two-story, white aluminum-sided with brick trim, a faded red awning covering the entire first-floor porch that stretched the whole width of the house.

The two men scanned the neighborhood and found no one out on the street as they opened the chain-linked fence gate and made their way to the front door.

Ding Dong

Elisa May Griffin, a recent widow in her late sixties, answered the door. Elisa had been going through her late husband's clothes, deciding what to donate and what to throw away when the doorbell rang.

"Hello?" She said as she stood in the doorway wearing her flowered housecoat and slippers with her hair in curlers.

"Hello, ma'am. My name is Elder Barton, and this is my companion, Elder Ward. We're missionaries from the Church of Jesus Christ of Latter-Day Saints, and we'd like to share a message with you about God's plan. Could I offer you a copy of the Watchtower?" The man calling himself Elder Barton said, smiling.

"Oh, would you boys like to come in?"

"Why, thank you, ma'am, that's very kind of you," Barton said as he led his partner into Mrs. Griffin's house.

Mrs. Griffin offered them to sit on the sofa as she sat opposite them on an overstuffed chair.

"Tell me, boys, I'm a bit confused. The Church of Jesus Christ of Latter-Day Saints are Mormons, and aren't the folks who distribute the Watchtower members of the Jehovah's Witnesses?"

It was only after her next-door neighbor, Jack Wilson, noticed an overpowering stench coming from Mr. Griffin's house that Police were summoned.

Mrs. Elisa May Griffin was found bound and gagged, lying on her stomach with a dry cleaner's plastic bag tied over her head. She died of asphyxiation. According to Doctor Olsen, the ME, she had been severely beaten, tortured, and mutilated before having the plastic bag placed over her head.

Mrs. Griffin had been dead and lying on the kitchen floor for over two weeks. The neighbors all said that it wasn't uncommon not to see her for weeks at a time; ever since her husband died, she had become a recluse.

By the time Roscoe and Detective Walsh arrived, Doctor Olsen had finished his preliminary findings and was having the body taken down to the morgue for a complete autopsy.

"Hey Roscoe, Walsh, this one's is particularly heinous; they beat and tortured her before suffocating her."

"Sexual assault?" Walsh asked.

"None that I can tell, but I'll know more this afternoon."

"Thanks, Doc. We'll talk later." Roscoe said.

The two detectives went over to talk to the first responding officers on the scene, Officers Beechwood and Klinner, both men seasoned veterans.

"Hi, fellas," Roscoe said.

"Hey, Roscoe. Man, this one was brutal. We arrived around 10 am and found the neighbor, Mr. Jack Wilson, standing in the driveway with a handkerchief over his mouth. Once we got out of the car, we knew why. The stench knocked us on our asses."

"Any sign of forced entry?" Walsh asked.

"None that we could see. CSI is going over the house now."

"How'd you get in?"

"The neighbor Wilson had a key."

"Tell me what you saw," Roscoe said.

Honestly, at first, it was hard to see anything; our eyes were watering so badly. The first thing we did was open some windows; then, we spotted the victim lying on the kitchen floor. We searched the rest of the house, and then we called it in."

"Talk to any of the neighbors?"

"Not yet; I wanted to make sure we talked to you first."

"Okay, thanks. See what you can find out from the neighbors. We'll touch base with you later."

Roscoe and Walsh entered the house; even after two hours with all the windows open, the lingering smell of decomposing flesh hung heavy in the air. It was truly repulsive, and the hordes of aerial and terrestrial insects crawling and flying all around were a considerable and constant nuisance.

All the CSI folk, including David Bowles, wore hazmat suits, gloves, booties, and face masks. Roscoe and Walsh stood just inside the front door holding handkerchiefs over their noses and breathing through their mouths, which didn't help all that much.

Bowles walked over to them, reached into his hazmat pocket, and pulled out a small jar of Vicks VapoRub. He held it out for them to take a dab and stuff a little in each nostril to help kill the stench.

"Here, you go."

"Thanks, Bowles," Roscoe said.

"Got anything yet?" Walsh asked.

"I think we may have found some things, hairs, fibers, fingerprints. I don't think these guys were pros, but it will be an all-day project."

"Guys? Why guys and not one guy?" Roscoe queried.

"Look over here on the coffee table, three cups of tea, too many cookies on the plate for just two, and look at the cushions on the sofa. Doesn't it look like two people had sat there, with that chair moved close to the sofa as if three people had gathered?"

"Bowles, you should have been a detective."

"Not my style, Roscoe. Me, I like to observe the scene, gather evidence, theorize the crime, and then move on to the next one. I get bored spending days, weeks, or even months snooping around thru garbage cans and having to interact with murderers and such scum. Then, having to tell a mother that someone just gutted, garroted, or greased their baby. No, thank you."

"I know what's the matter with you, Bowles; you're just a compassionate guy." Roscoe teased.

"Hey, Roscoe, I've got your compassion right here!" Bowles said, grabbing his crotch.

Roscoe and Walsh slipped on a pair of booties over their street shoes so as not to contaminate the scene, then took a walk through the house.

All the rooms in the house, even the bathrooms, had been ransacked. Anything that had any value had been stolen, nothing big like the TV or stereo, only small items, jewelry, cash, anything made of silver or gold, and a couple of pieces of artwork had been taken off the walls. The paintings had been ripped from the frames lying on the floor, then either folded or rolled up for easy carrying.

Bowles approached them with a piece of paper in an evidence plastic bag and handed it to Roscoe.

"What's this?"

"Read it; it's a handwritten note of what looks like an obscure Bible verse. It was found under the body." Bowles said.

Roscoe read it out loud so Walsh could hear, *"See, the day of the Lord is coming—a cruel day, with wrath and fierce anger. . . . I will put an end to the arrogance of the haughty. . . . Their infants will be dashed to pieces before their eyes; their houses will be looted, and their wives violated. Isaiah 13:9–16."*

"What is that mean?" Walsh asked.

"Beats the Hell out of me," Roscoe said.

Officers Beechwood and Klinner stood outside the front door waiting for Roscoe and Walsh.

Beechwood stuck his head in when he saw Roscoe and shouted, "Hey, Sarge, when you get a minute."

"Be right out," Roscoe replied.

The two detectives tossed their shoe coverings into a collection bin on the porch.

"How about we talk over by the garage? I'm getting a little nauseous from the stench of death." Roscoe suggested.

The four of them walked over to the one-car garage where Mrs. Griffin's white 1962 Ford Fairlane 500 was parked. The car looked to be right off the showroom floor. CSI officers were going through it, and the contents of the garage, which was so spotless it looked like you could have eaten off the floor.

"Whadda got?" Walsh asked.

"Well, as usual, no one remembers seeing or hearing anything, but some of them remember a pair of Jehovah's Witnesses knocking on their door that day," Klinner said.

"They described them as two Caucasians, short hair, clean cut wearing the standard uniform, white shirt, tie, black pants with backpacks." Beechwood recounted.

"Sounds like Mormons. Do they think they might recognize them if they saw them again?" Roscoe asked.

Klinner glanced over to Beechwood, "No, although there was one woman, Mrs. Joan Newton, who was the only one who gave a detailed description of the two. I think that if we could get her with our sketch artist, we'd have a good chance of getting something solid to go on."

"Do we know if Mrs. Griffin has any next of kin?"

"The neighbor Jack Wilson says she has a daughter living in Los Angeles," Klinner replied.

"Okay, thanks, guys. Jimmy, would you call Veronica and see if the two of you can meet with Mrs. Newton?"

"Sure thing, Roscoe."

Veronica Lennox, the 60th Precinct's Police sketch artist, is Detective James Walsh's girlfriend. She looks more like a model than a hardened Police artist. She's five foot eleven, one hundred and ten pounds, and has long blonde hair, silky smooth skin, and baby blue eyes. She has aspirations of becoming a legitimate fine artist, but in the meantime, she works as a Police sketch artist while she takes classes at New York's School of Visual Arts.

"Hey, Ronnie, it's Jimmy."

"Hey, babe."

"Listen, we need you to do a couple of sketches of two suspects. Think you might have some time today for me to come by and pick you up?"

"I have a life drawing class at four today. Could we do it around one this afternoon?"

"No problem; how about I pick you up at noon?"

"Sounds perfect; where does she live?"

"She's at 2940 Brighton 1st Street. Her name is Joan Newton. They tell me she is a single mother of three boys, so I think you'll definitely have your work cut out for you."

"Three boys, you owe me big time, Walsh."

When they arrived, all three boys, ages 2, 4, and 6, were out playing in the fenced-in front yard. The mother was sitting on the front porch, keeping a motherly eye on the mayhem, chaos, and pandemonium going on in front of her eyes and drinking a Schmidt's Beer.

The front yard looked like a tiny war zone. The three pint-size commandos were wreaking havoc in a small plastic sandbox filled with a variety of toy soldiers, army trucks, and decimated cabins made from Lincoln Logs.

"Mrs. Newton, I'm Detective Walsh, and this is Ms. Lennox, the Police sketch artist. May we come in?" Walsh said, holding up his badge and ID.

Mrs. Newton waved them in, "Sure, come on in. Please ensure you lock the gate behind you; Bobby, the oldest, likes to wander, given a chance."

Walsh opened the front gate and allowed Veronica to enter. He followed her in, turning and locking the gate and checking it twice.

"Would you all like a beer?" She asked.

"No, thank you, not while I'm working," Veronica said.

"Not allowed while on duty," Walsh added.

"Well, come on in the house. I think I'll have another," Mrs. Newton said.

The house was clean but unkempt; toys and kids' clothes were strewn everywhere. Over a modest fireplace, there was a photograph of a man in an Army Ranger uniform on the mantle.

Mrs. Newton came back into the living room from the kitchen, "Please, have a seat. I'm sorry the house is such a mess, but with my three little pigs, I can never seem to get ahead of the game."

Veronica smiled and said, "No need to apologize; boys can be an overpowering force. I have three older brothers who were terrors."

"Are you married, Ms. Lennox?"

"Ronnie, please, and no, not yet?"

"Detective?"

"No, ma'am."

"That's my husband, Doug." She said, pointing to the photo on the mantle.

"He was killed in action April last year in Vietnam in Operation Rolling Thunder, with 52,000 casualties and 21,000 dead in an unmitigated failure."

"We're so sorry, Mrs. Newton," Walsh said.

"Eight years as an army wife, and all I have is a small pension, a handful of medals, and a flag to show for it." She said as she started to tear up.

Veronica went and sat down next to her on the couch and put her arm around her shoulder.

"Do you have any family nearby?" Veronica asked.

"Doug's mother lives in New Jersey, and my folks live upstate, near Buffalo. Doug's life insurance paid for the house, thank God. But, for now, it's just the boys and me.

Listen to me blabbering on; you didn't come here to hear me go on about my troubles. I only hope I can be some help for poor old Mrs. Griffin."

"Mrs. Newton, you say you got a good look at the two men who came to your door?"

"That's right, and please call me Joan. They said they were Jehovah's Witnesses, but their introduction sounded more like they were Mormons."

"Please describe them to me the best that you remember," Veronica said as she held her sketch pad and pencil at the ready.

"The one who called himself Elder Barton had olive skin, a squarish shaped head, short dark hair, brown eyes set kind of close together, full lips with a small scar over his left eye. He was about five foot seven, stocky built, and had a flower tattoo on his upper right forearm."

As she spoke, Veronica feverously sketched and occasionally used an eraser to make minor changes and alterations. Once done, she turned the sketch pad around to show Joan what she had sketched for her opinion.

"What do you think?" Veronica asked.

"Oh my God, that's him."

"Great, now describe the other man," Veronica said as she handed the finished sketch to Walsh with a hint of professional pride.

"The other one, who was called Elder Ward, had a round face, no, an oval face, short hair but long enough to have a part on his left side. He had bushy eyebrows, green eyes, thin lips, fair skin, and was about five-eleven. I didn't see any tattoos or scars on him."

As Veronica continued to sketch, Walsh asked, "Joan, may I ask, why didn't you let them into your home?"

"There was something about them that seemed not quite right; it was just a feeling. As they were speaking to me, they seemed to be looking past me as if they were casing the place to see if I had anything of value. Although, with three screaming kids, I don't get too many visitors, if you know what I mean."

Veronica finished up the second drawing and showed it to Mrs. Newton.

"Wow, Ronnie, you are good. Did you ever consider being an artist? Not that doing what you do isn't art."

"It's okay, Joan, I know what you mean, and yes, that's what my aim is. I'd like to give up the glamourous life of a Police sketch artist and become a real-life starving artist one day." She said jokingly.

From outside, where the kids were playing, came a thunderous crash, then silence.

"Bobby, what happened!" Joan yelled out to the kids.

"Nothing."

While Walsh and Veronica were interviewing Mrs. Newton, Roscoe finally tracked down Mrs. Griffin's daughter, Carol Hughes, in Los Angeles.

"Hello?"

"Hello, this is Detective Sergeant Brown of the New York City Police. May I speak with Carol Hughes, please?"

"Speaking."

"Mrs. Hughes, I have some bad news: your mother has passed away."

"Heart attack?"

"I'm afraid she has been murdered."

"Oh my God! Nooooooo!"

Roger Anderson slammed the door on two door-to-door holy rollers who'd come knocking on his door wanting to sell him their weird, phony religion.

"Roger, who was that?" Sally, his wife, asked.

"Ah, just a couple of them Jeehoobie Witnesses. I told them to buzz off."

Sally went to the front picture window and saw two neatly dressed men invited into Mrs. Walters, her neighbor's house.

"Roger, Anne just invited those two Jehovah's Witnesses into her house."

"Well, it will serve them right. She'll bore the Hell out of them. I bet they'll come running out of there in less than ten minutes."

"Roger, be nice."

"Why don't you nice boys come in." Mrs. Walters said as she opened the front door.

"Why, thank you, ma'am." Elder Barton said.

"Can I get you something to drink, some iced tea, or maybe a nice cold Coca-Cola?"

"A Coca-Cola would be wonderful. Is there anybody else in the house, ma'am?" The man said as he followed her into the kitchen.

"No, my husband is at work, and my two girls are in school; it's just me."

The man who called himself Elder Barton stood at the kitchen counter while Mrs. Walters gathered the glasses and ice. She never saw him remove the butcher's knife from the rack. The last thing she remembered seeing before she died was the flash from the morning sun glinting off the polished steel of the butcher's knife's blade as Barton started stabbing her in the neck.

Sally Anderson had been dusting in the living room as an excuse to keep an eye on Anne Walters. She had a bad feeling; they had never had Jehovah's Witnesses in the neighborhood before. It just seemed odd.

It wasn't the ten minutes that Roger had predicted that the two men would come running out of the house; it was more like thirty. But run out; they did, and one of them had what looked to be blood on his otherwise clean white shirt.

They bolted out of the house and ran right down towards Neptune Ave, where, as Sally later would describe to the Police, some sort of hippie van picked them up and drove away.

"Roger!" Sally shouted.

"Yeah, what is it? What are you yelling for?"

"I just saw two men run out of Anne's house, and one of them had blood on him."

"Aw, you're nuts."

"Roger, you got to go over there and see if Anne's alright!"

"Okay, okay, just let me go get my Louisville Slugger. Call Terry from next door and have him meet me over there."

Roger Anderson, a retired New York City sanitation worker, and his next-door neighbor Terry Bowman, an ex-long haul truck driver, were what most New Yorkers would call a couple of blue-collar toughs. Roger from Hunts Point and Terry from Navy Hill grew up in some of New York's roughest neighborhoods. They had both served and fought in the Korean War and had seen some pretty horrific things, but nothing prepared them for what they saw in Anne Walter's kitchen that day.

Roger threw his breakfast up all over his shoes, and Terry fainted, falling backward, cracking the back of his head open, requiring eleven stitches when he hit the corner of the coffee table.

Officer Andy Devine, a twenty-year veteran of the force, stood outside the house waiting for Roscoe and Walsh. An ambulance was parked on the street, and the two paramedics were treating Mr. Bowman's head wound.

Doctor Olsen and his medical examiner's crew arrived at the same time as the CSI boys.

"What do we have, Andy?"

"It's a freaking butcher shop in there. I've never seen such a bloodbath in my twenty years on the force."

Doctor Olsen, Bowles from CSI, and the two detectives walked into the house together. Just like Mrs. Griffin's house, every room had been ransacked. Furniture was overturned, drawers opened or emptied on the floor, and clothes were strewn everywhere.

In the kitchen, Mrs. Walters's body lay in a sea of blood. She was lying on her back, with multiple stab wounds on her neck and throat, cut from ear to ear. Her left eye was lying on the floor next to her; she had her dress ripped open, her stomach had been sliced open, and her intestines were pulled out and placed on her chest.

On the wall was the bloody butcher's knife stuck in the wall opposite the refrigerator with another handwritten note with a Bible verse scribbled on a piece of paper.

"Ye shall utterly destroy all the places, wherein the nations which ye shall possess served their gods, upon the high mountains, and upon the hills, and under every green tree: and ye shall overthrow their altars, and break their pillars, and burn their groves with fire; and ye shall hew down the graven images of their gods and destroy the names of them out of that place. Deuteronomy 12:2-3"

From outside the house, Officer Devine shouted, "Hey, Roscoe, need you out here as soon as you can."

"What's up?" Roscoe asked.

"We have a neighbor lady who thinks she saw the perpetrators."

Devine led Roscoe over the street to the Anderson's house. Roger and Sally were standing in their front yard watching all the goings-on. Roscoe walked over to where the couple stood, showed them his ID and badge, introduced himself, took out Veronica's sketch of the two suspects, and showed it to the Andersons.

"That's them; those are the two Jeehoobies that came to our door," Roger said.

Mrs. Anderson quickly corrected her husband's smart-ass remark, "Jehovah's, they're called Jehovah's Witnesses, Roger!"

"Yeah, whatever. Those are the two guys, Detective."

"Did they offer you any type of magazine?"

"Yeah, it had like a castle on the cover."

"Could it have been something like this?" Roscoe asked as he produced a copy of the Watchtower from his leather portfolio.

"Yeah, that's it."

Roscoe asked, "Mrs. Anderson, are these the two men you saw going into Mrs. Walters's home?"

"Yes, sir." She answered.

"Thank you both for your help. By the way, Mr. Anderson, how's your friend doing?"

"Oh, he'll be alright, but he's going to have a gargantuan headache for a couple of days. I tell you, Detective Brown, he and I saw some pretty heavy combat in Korea, you know, hand to hand, but we never saw anything like that. Man, I don't know how you get used to it?"

"You don't."

Roscoe and Walsh met with Andrew Danby, the Coordinator of the Body of Elders, at the Coney Island Kingdom Hall of Jehovah's Witnesses on 16th Street.

The Hall was a modest structure, one story, white stone, waist-high black wrought iron fence with two well-manicured trees on the sidewalk, very tasteful. The only signage was lettering on the upper right front of the building, KINGDOM HALL of JEHOVAH'S WITNESSES.

When they arrived at the Hall, a well-dressed man was sitting on one of the wooden benches under the canopy reading 'The New World Translation of the Holy Scriptures.'

He rose as the two Detectives entered the grounds, "May I be of some help?" He asked.

Roscoe showed his badge and ID and said, "Good day, I'm Detective Sergeant Brown, and this is my partner, Detective Walsh. We're here to see Mr. Danby."

The man held out his hand and said, "I'm Elder Danby; what can I do for you?"

"Elder Danby, there are two young men going around Coney Island killing and robbing people, who we believe are posing as Jehovah's Witnesses."

"Oh, dear. I can assure you, Detective, that we are a peace-loving religion."

"Elder Danby, do you recognize these two men?" Roscoe said as he showed Danby the Police sketch.

"No, sir, I can assure you they do not belong to our congregation."

"Would it alright if I left this sketch with you to see if any other congregations might know them? They might be a couple of men who became disgruntled with the Church or just a couple of punks going around pretending to be who we believe are posing as Jehovah's Witnesses."

"Detective. I will make copies of these men and send them to all the Kingdom Halls in the tri-state area. You shall hear from me sometime tomorrow."

"Thank you, Elder Danby; I look forward to hearing from you tomorrow."

"Would you gentlemen care to come into the Hall for some fellowship and prayers?"

"Sorry, Elder Danby, but we're kinda busy."

"Too busy to pray?"

"I know; how about you pray while we go and try and catch these killers," Roscoe suggested.

"You'll be in all our prayers, Detectives."

"Thank you. I don't know about Detective Walsh, but I sure as Hell know I could use some. Thanks again, Elder Danby." Roscoe said as he and Walsh were halfway out the gate.

Walsh and Roscoe's next stop was to the Church of Jesus Christ of Latter-Day Saints on 86th Street to meet with Bishop Patrick Ahern.

To Roscoe, the Church looked pretty much like every other Christian Church: red brick, white trim with a large white steeple on the roof.

They went in and were greeted by Mr. Ahern's secretary, Mrs. Montgomery, an attractive middle-aged woman with long red hair, green eyes, and black cat eyeglasses with rhinestones. She wore a dark grey pencil skirt suit with a matching jacket and white scoop neck top.

"Hello, may I help you, gentlemen?"

"Good day, I'm Detective Sergeant Brown, and this is my partner Detective Walsh. We're here to see Bishop Ahern."

"Oh yes, Bishop Ahern is expecting you if you'd follow me, please."

She led them to the Church offices, where over twenty people were doing clerical work, assembling programs, and meeting in conference rooms. Classes were being held, and sitting alone in a small office was an elderly man with more gray hair on his face than on his head, reading the Book of Mormon.

"Bishop Ahern, this is Detectives Brown and Walsh."

"Gentlemen, please come in and sit down."

"Thank you, Bishop, for taking the time to meet with us," Roscoe said.

"What is it that I can do for you?"

"Well, sir, I don't know if you are aware, but there are a couple of men going around posing as members of the Church of Jesus Christ of Latter-Day Saints. They have been dressing like Mormon missionaries and gaining access into people's homes, then robbing and murdering them."

"Dear Lord."

"We have a composite drawing of the men I'd like to show you to see if you might know them or maybe have seen them hanging around the Church."

Roscoe handed a copy of the drawing to Bishop Ahern, and he studied it carefully for several minutes and shook his head.

"I'm sorry, I don't recognize them. May I keep this to show others? Maybe someone here might recognize them?"

"Please, keep it; show it around to see if anybody recognizes them. If they do, please contact me at this number." Roscoe said as he handed the Bishop his business.

"I will get this around today."

"It's urgent that we stop these guys, as people are dying," Roscoe said.

"We send our thoughts and prayers to the victims, Detective."

"Thoughts and prayer are nice, Bishop, but what we need are solid leads."

Elder Barton and Elder Ward are, in actuality, Lance Barton and Eddie Ward, two recent parolees from Attica. Both had been serving time for armed robbery, assault with a deadly weapon, and manslaughter. They had served twelve years of a twenty-year stretch, coming out of prison harder than they went in. While in Attica, they met Billy Ray Sullivan, a Mormon who tried to better himself by preaching the word of God to the inmates after getting arrested for bank fraud.

After listening to Billy Ray a couple of times, Lance and Eddie hatched what they called the God Squad dodge. They began asking Billy Ray a ton of questions about the whole missionary racket.

"So, Billy Ray, you mean to say that just by hyping the Bible, people actually let you into their houses?" Eddie asked.

"Groovy, baby." Lance smiled.

As they were working out the details for their new scam, a member of Jehovah's Witnesses would come to preach at Attica. Lance and Eddi always sat in the front row center, taking notes. They benefited by gaining more material for their con game and getting brownie points as a couple of do-gooders in prison, which helped them get an early release.

When Lance Barton and Eddie Ward walked out the gate at Attica, they each had a Bible, a Book of Mormon, half a dozen copies of the Watchtower, a Greyhound Bus ticket to Rochester, New York, and thirty-seven dollars and forty-two cents' cash.

The first thing they did when they got to Rochester was to walk the mile trek to the Goodwill Thrift Store to buy themselves each a white shirtsleeve shirt, a pair of black pants, a pair of black street shoes, and a backpack.

It only took them two hours before someone let them into their home. Mr. and Mrs. Scanlon were both in their late seventies the day they let Barton and Ward into their home.

The Scanlon's were busy packing for their dream vacation down in Miami Beach the next day and attending the opening of spring training. What occurred that day was not a dream but a nightmare. Police found the elderly couple hog-tied on the kitchen floor with both their heads bashed in with Mr. Scanlon's most prized mementos, a baseball bat that Yankee legend Mickey Mantle had personally signed.

By the time the Rochester Police discovered the Scanlon's, Barton and Ward were halfway to New York City on a Greyhound bus with over eight hundred dollars in cash and all of the old biddy's jewelry that Lance figured they could pawn for at least three hundred.

"Pretty nice haul," Eddie whispered to Lance.

"Yeah, who knew that being in the God business would be so lucrative."

"It's like the good book, sez, Lance. God moves in mysterious ways," Eddie said, laughing.

"Amen, brother. Amen."

When Lance and Eddie arrived at the Port Authority a quarter after eleven in the evening, Lance called his hippie sister, Rachel, who legally changed her name to Sunbeam. Sunbeam lived in Coney Island, in a crash pad above a dog grooming salon slash bagel shop with another hippie, Suzie. She referred to herself as Suzie Cream-Cheese.

"Hey, sis, can you come pick Eddie and me up? We're in the Port Authority."

"Oh, wow, Lance. What are you doing here? I thought you were still in the joint."

"We got paroled. Come pick us up."

"Oh, okay, I'll be there as soon as I can. It might be a while. I'm kinda tripping at the moment."

"You mean you're tripping on acid?"

"Yeah, but it's cool; so far, it's been a real mellow trip, man."

"Are you sure you're okay to drive?"

"Oh yeah, Lance, I'll be there soon."

As he hung up the receiver, he heard her say, "As soon as I find my hands." *CLICK.*

The Port Authority Bus Terminal and immediate surrounding area is New York City's capital for whores, pimps, smut, porn, sleaze, scum, junkies, dealers, con men, hustlers, crooks, thieves, evangelists, missionaries, holy joes, ministers, and pulpit warriors.

Walking down 42nd Street, you'd encounter them all within two blocks. Lance and Eddie decided to kill some time at the Booby Hatch until Sunbeam arrived. It was an all-nude strip joint across from the bus terminal on 8th Avenue.

Lance saw that next door to the strip club was the Pawn Pirate pawn shop.

"Hey, Eddie, let's go get some cash. Come on, let's go hock some of the loot."

When they walked into the pawnshop, it was so brightly lit that Eddie put on a pair of his victim's Ray-Ban sunglasses. The place was better fortified than Fort Knox, with thick bulletproof glass, gun ports from all sides, dozens of internal cameras, and a self-locking door that one had to be buzzed in and out. There were several signs posted around the shop, "Please remove ski mask before entering." and "Shoplifters will be beaten to death and or shot!"

A gruff voice bellowed from behind the protective glass, and then a glass-distorted face emerged, "What can I do yous for?"

"Like to see about pawning some stuff," Lance said.

"We don't buy stuff." The old geezer said sarcastically.

"Well, do you buy Rolex watches?" Lance said as he took a man and a woman's Rolex Oyster Date Precision Hand Winding Watch.

"Let me see 'em." The fossil-faced old man said excitedly.

Lance dropped them into the pass-thru, and the old man snatched them up, dropped his eye loop over his coke bottle glasses to examine them scrupulously.

"Hmmm, are these yours?"

"No, they were our parents. They passed away last week."

"Sure, sure, another heartbreaking story from two loving sons, am I right?"

"That's right, old man," Eddie said.

"I'll give you five hundred for the pair."

"Five hundred, are you out of your fucking mind!" Lance shouted.

"I'll tell you what, you tell me the names on the back of the watches, and I'll double it. But. I'm betting these watches are hot, so tell me, what's the names?"

"Ah, just gimme the five hundred, you old fucker."

As the broker started to pass five one-hundred-dollar bills through the small opening, Lance asked, "How much for the .38 Smith & Wesson?"

"Three hundred."

"Gimme the two hundred bucks and the gun."

"You got ID?"

"No."

"Well then, it's four hundred for the gun and a hundred for the watches."

"You really are an asshole, aren't you?"

"Hey, you want the gun or not?"

Lance was pissed off, but he knew that the old geezer had him by the short hairs.

"Bullets?" Lance asked.

"I don't sell them; that would just be asking for trouble, now wouldn't it?"

The old man was right, and Lance knew it; if he could get his hands on bullets, he'd try and kill the old coot.

"Okay, gimme the gun and the hundred," Lance said, frustrated.

The old mossback dropped the pistol and two fifty-dollar bills into the pass-thru tray. Lance took the revolver, examined it carefully, lifted his jacket, and put it in his waistband. He picked up the two fifties and handed Eddie one of the bills.

They made their way to the locked door and waited to be buzzed out, but nothing happened. Eddie turned around and yelled, "Hey, grandpa, let us out!"

Buzzzzzzzz. Buzzzzzzzz.

Lance opened the door and held it open; he turned to the face behind the glass and asked, "Hey, man, what were the names on the watches?"

The distorted face smiled and answered, "There weren't any. Ha. See ya boys; ya'll come back now, ya hear. Ha."

After dropping twenty bucks in the strip joint and didn't even get their bells rung, Lance and Eddie returned to the Port Authority to wait for his sister Sunbeam.

They didn't wait long when Lance spotted the 1966 Volkswagen Micro, all painted with peace signs, painted flowers, and images of Mr. Natural cruising up 8th Avenue.

Lance stepped out into the street, waving at her. He was lucky she didn't run him over, as she was still high as a kite. She slammed on the brakes, just missing them. Eddie and Lance jumped into the van. Lance hopped in the front passenger seat, and Eddie crawled in the back. There wasn't a seat in the back; she had taken them out and put in a mattress, and love beads hung over the rear and side windows.

"Hey, sis, how're you doing?"

"Wow, I'm really stoked that you're here. You really are here, right? I'm not just tripping."

"No, I'm really here. Do you remember my friend Eddie?"

"Oh, sure, Eddie. Didn't I give you a hummer last time I saw you?"

"No. It wasn't me."

"Well, I'll give you one if you remind me later."

"Uh, okay?" Eddie said, looking at Lance, whose expression was that he couldn't care less.

"Listen, sis, Eddie and me need you to help us out by driving us around. Is that okay with you?"

"Hey, that's far out, man. Is it like, for your job?"

"Yeah, for our job, we're, ah, Tupperware salesmen."

"Far out."

The next day, Sunbeam dropped Eddie and Lance on Neptune Avenue on the corner of Brighton 1st Street. She then parked at the end of the block at the corner of Brighton 1st Street and Ocean View Avenue and waited.

She watched her brother and Eddie walk up and down the block, going to people's houses, getting one door after another slammed in their faces until someone let them into their home.

While she waited, she smoked a joint and listened to the Grateful Dead on her eight-track tape player. She eventually fell asleep and was only awoken when Lance and Eddie opened the van door, shouting for her to get going.

"Hey, Lance, lighten up, man. You're harshing my mellow, man!" She snarled.

"Sorry, sis. You know how it is, the first day on the job and everything." Lance said as he gave Eddie a devilish smile.

"Just what is your job, Lance?"

"Huh, Eddie and I are door-to-door salesmen. I told you last night when you picked us up, remember?"

"Yeah, I remember. So, what do you sell?'

"Tupperware." Eddie blurted.

"Tupperware?" Sunbeam asked.

"Yeah, we took a sales course in Attica," Lance said.

"In Tupperware?"

"Yeah, in Tupperware. So, we're cool?" Lance asked.

"Yeah, we're cool. So, you guys working tomorrow selling Tupperware?"

"If it's cool with you?"

"Absafuckinglutley. I love Tupperware. I use it to keep my stash in."

Roscoe called a meeting of all the detectives in the Six 0, "Listen up, we have got a couple of actual psychopaths running around in our precinct, posing as Mormons and Jehovah's Witnesses robbing and killing folks.

I want these sketches sent to every Police department in the tri-state area. I'm also sending them to all the networks and newspapers; somebody has got to know these mutts.

We've put out an APB about an hour ago for these two, and we believe that they have an accomplice who's driving them around in what has been described as a "hippie" van.

Now, these punks are believed to be armed and extremely dangerous. So, approach with caution. They've killed three people that we know of so far, so be careful."

"Detective Sergeant Brown, sixtieth precinct."

"Detective Brown, this is Warden Jason Miller, Attica Prison."

"Yes, sir, warden, how can I help you?"

"I think it's I that can help you. I saw your composite sketch, and it appears the men you're looking for are two convicts who were paroled last week from Attica. Lance Barton and Edward Ward, who had been serving time for armed robbery, assault with a deadly weapon, and manslaughter. They had served twelve years of a twenty-year stretch and were cut loose over my objections last Tuesday.

We believe that they brutally murdered an elderly couple in Rochester the day they were released. We believe they made their way down to Manhattan, and it sounds like they're now operating in your area."

"Thank you, Warden, for the heads up. At least now we know who we're dealing with. I'll touch base with Rochester PD right after I hang up with you."

Detective Walsh walked into Roscoe's office just as he finished his call with Warden Miller. Roscoe filled his partner in on his conversation with the warden.

"Jimmy, I can understand those two goons coming down to Manhattan to try and get lost in the city, but why Coney Island? Unless they have some sort of connection here."

"I'll go and check the files on Lance Barton and Eddie Ward, see if either of them have known associates or maybe family here."

"Great, now, I have to go down and speak with the press. Hopefully, somebody has seen these thugs."

"Good luck."

"Yeah, keep a good thought."

Sunbeam ran into the living room where her brother and Eddie were sleeping, all excited.

"Lance, Lance, wake up! Your picture is on the TV. wake up!"

Lance and Eddie bolted up and jumped off the sofa bed; they stood there in their prison-issued boxer shorts, looking dazed and confused, trying to shake the cobwebs out of their heads and orient themselves in the room, looking for the TV that was sitting right in front of them.

"Where!" Lance shouted.

"Right here!" Standing next to the portable Philco black and white TV perched on three stacked concrete cinder blocks, Sunbeam said.

"Good morning, New York; we have breaking news. The New York City Police are asking you to help to see if you can help them apprehend these two men, Lance Barton and Edward Ward. They are wanted in connection with the robbery and murder of Mrs. Griffin and Mrs. Walters, both residents of Coney Island.

If you have any information or know these two men, do not approach them, as they are considered armed and dangerous.

If you see these men, do not approach them; you are instructed to contact the NYPD immediately. There is a ten thousand dollar reward to anyone who gives information that leads to the arrest and conviction of these two men. You can call any precinct or the NYPD T.I.P.S. Hotline.

And now a check of this morning's weather..."

"Fuck me," Lance uttered to himself.

"Lance, we got to get the fuck out of here, man! It won't be long before somebody recognizes us and turns us in." Eddie roared.

"Don't you guys sell Tupperware?" Sunbeam quizzically asked.

"Rachel, your head is full of mush, honey. Too many acid trips. Now, sis, you stay put, don't leave this apartment, and don't be driving that hippie van anywhere; they'll probably be looking for that, too."

"Lance, we got to leave right now!" Eddie implored.

"Okay, get dressed, let's go."

They put on jackets over their white shirts, ball caps, and sunglasses, hoping to help disguise themselves. They put their loot into their backpacks and headed down the street to hail a cab.

Lance's idea was to take a cab to the Greyhound Station in downtown Brooklyn and catch the first bus to anywhere out of New York state. They walked over to the main drag, Coney Island Avenue, and caught a Checker Yellow Cab.

"Where to?" The cabbie asked as he dropped the flag on the meter.

"The Greyhound Station, 206 Livingston Street," Lance replied.

"Any particular way you want to go?"

"No, you know best."

"Right."

To Lance, the cabbie keeps looking at them suspiciously in the rearview mirror. He wished that he had taken the time to buy some ammo for his .38 revolver, but he and Eddie were too busy killing and robbing old ladies.

Paranoia sets in quickly when you are running for your life. Lance's paranoia peaked right around the time the cab was paralleling the Green-Wood Cemetery on McDonald Avenue. It was then that he thought for sure that the driver had identified them. That's when he pulled his pistol out and told the cabbie to pull into the cemetery.

Pedro Martinez had been a cabbie in New York for over eight years. He had been robbed six times before and was fed up with these punks taking his hard-earned money; enough is enough.

He had fled Cuba and moved his family to New York right after Castro seized power in 1959. His daughter became a cardiologist at Lenox Hill Hospital, and his son had just started at Annapolis. Pedro once foiled a jewelry robbery in progress that he saw while parked at a red light on 47th Street in the Diamond District.

A man with a gun was holding up a Hasidic Jew diamond merchant when Pedro came up from behind holding a tire iron and pressed the iron into the robber's back, telling him he had a gun. He held the man there until the Police came and arrested the would-be thief.

The diamonds were worth over a quarter of a million dollars. His picture was in all the local press, and he refused a reward from the owner, saying that's what any good citizen would do.

Now, these two hoods trying to get an easy score from him was too much. He thought this aggression will not stand. Acting on sheer instinct and adrenaline, Pedro made a hard left turn off the street, crashing over the curb and sidewalk onto the lawn of the cemetery, bouncing the cab up into the air, forcing Lance and Eddie up off the bench seat, making them hit their heads on the roof. As the cab landed, Pedro continued making the taxi steer left, throwing Lance and Eddie deep into the right corner of the backseat, one on top of the other.

Pedro noticed a large mound of freshly dug dirt off to his left; nobody was nearby, so he aimed the taxi at the embankment.

CRASH.

The sixty-three-year-old Cuban cabbie rolled out of the taxi, landing on the dune of soil; he was unhurt. He got to his feet and drew the .38 Police special that Mayor John Lindsay had awarded him as a thank you from the city for his selfless act of bravery.

As Lance and Eddie fell out of the cab disorientated, Pedro, pointing his gun at Lance, who was still holding his unloaded pistol, yelled, "Drop the gun!"

Lance's first reaction was to use his weapon; as he raised his hand, he realized the gun was empty. Unfortunately for Lance, Pedro's revolver wasn't.

The New York City cabbie fired four times, all hitting Lance in the chest and stomach, none proving fatal. As Lance was getting his ass blown off, Eddie grabbed his and Lance's backpacks and ran into the wooded cemetery.

Eddie began to walk slowly to avoid drawing attention to him; he walked clear through the graveyard's opposite side to 5th Avenue, where he headed north towards the bus terminal.

As he was walking, he saw and heard what seemed to be dozens of Police cars going to where his partner was shot. It took Eddie over an hour to make his way to the Greyhound station. He cautiously walked by the depot several times to see if he could spot a Police trap, but nothing. He waited across the street in a greasy spoon, eating a burger and fries, looking out the window. Nobody that came in or out looked like a cop. There was a middle-aged couple that looked to be waiting for a bus, sitting in the lobby close to the ticket counter. The woman wore a shabby coat and a cheap-looking faded floral dress, and her companion wore a tattered cardigan sweater, baggy chinos, and an old beat-up fedora. They each carried a small, worn-out suitcase.

On the other side of the lobby was a young pregnant Hispanic woman with three screaming brats running around the lobby, and outside stood three sailors in uniform with duffel bags having a smoke.

Eddie felt he couldn't afford to hang out in the diner much longer without raising suspicion, so he decided to chance it. He walked out of the restaurant and walked away from the bus station. He walked entirely around the block to see if he could spot anything hinky, nothing.

He finally committed. As he walked in, nobody seemed to pay any attention to him; no one even looked up. The three sailors didn't move, and the mother of the year with the screaming kids was so overwhelmed that she probably didn't even know what day it was.

"Can I help you?" The ticket counterman asked.

"I'd like a one-way ticket to Dallas," Eddie said.

"Yes, sir, that will be twenty-two dollars."

As he reached for his wallet, a voice behind him said, "Don't you mean a one-way ticket to Sing-Sing, Eddie?"

Eddie casually turned around to see the old man with the fedora holding a Police badge and pointing a gun at him, as well as his female companion. The three sailors and even the young haggard mother were aiming a gun at him.

After capturing the three suspects, the New York press had a field day. The best headline came from the New York Daily Herald when they dubbed them the "God Squad."

The entire city was united in their hatred for these heartless hooligans, and it took seven weeks to find any semblance of a quote, unquote fair jury.

Poor Eddie Ward stood trial first as Lance Barton recovered from his gunshot wounds. His trial lasted four weeks, resulting in a guilty verdict for three counts of robbery, assault, and four counts of murder for the deaths of Elisa May Griffin, Anne Walters, Deborah, and Neil Scanlon. He was sentenced to death in the electric chair.

Lance Barton's trial lasted three weeks. He was also found guilty of the same offenses as his partner in crime, and he too was sentenced to die in "Old Sparky," Sing-Sing's electric chair.

Rachel Barton, aka Sunbeam, was arrested and charged with aiding and abetting in the murders of Elisa May Griffin and Anne Walters. However, the court found after a thorough psychiatric evaluation that due to her extensive use of LSD and other hallucinogenic drugs, she was too unstable mentally to stand trial. Sunbeam was sent to a mental institution until such time as she would be capable of standing trial.

It took ten years of appeals and requests for stays, but their day of reckoning finally came in the winter of 1976. Lance Barton was the first to be led to meet his maker. He was defiant till the end, refusing the counsel of the clergy. His last words before they dropped the switch was, "I'll see you all in Hell!"

Eddie Ward was contrite, begging for forgiveness and repentance. He got so weak-kneed that three guards had to drag him into the death room and strap him into the chair while he wept and sobbed. The Priest mumbled some prayers over him and gave the sign of the cross. Eddie's last words were a cry for his mother, who had refused to come and visit him.

Pedro Martinez received New York City's Citizens Heroism Award from a grateful Mayor Lindsay, who, when presenting the award, whispered, "Pedro, we got to stop meeting like this."

Roscoe and Walsh each received a commendation from Vincent Broderick, Police Commissioner, co-signed by Mayor Lindsay.

Sitting in Roscoe's office after the presentation ceremony, He and Walsh were having a couple of beers when Captain O'Rourke stopped by.

"Just want to say good job, well done," O'Rourke said.

"Thanks, Captain," Walsh said.

"Say, Captain, care for a cold one?" Roscoe asked, holding up a bottle of Rheingold.

"Well, maybe just a couple."

Roscoe handed the Captain, who sat across from Roscoe in a chair next to Walsh, a beer.

Walsh took a drink and said solemnly, "How cruel to use God as a way to kill and rob those poor people."

"Jimmy, people have been using God to kill others through millennia, the Crusades, the Spanish Inquisition, and, of course, Hitler, just to name a few. That's why I'm an Agnostic." Roscoe proclaimed.

"You don't believe in God?" Walsh asked.

"Oh, I believe in a God. I just don't believe in organized religion."

"Most religions believe that their God is the true God and therefore other people's Gods aren't worthy, or they're not equal, so they must die. Christian versus Jews, Jews versus Muslims, Shiites versus Sunnis, and everyone versus Atheists." Captain O'Rourke said as he finished his second beer.

They sat there for several minutes, silent, thinking, and contemplating when Roscoe smiled and said, "I think I just figured out the differences between religions."

"Oh, really. Do tell." Walsh asked.

"Well, a Catholic believes that shit happens because they're bad.

A Jew thinks, why does shit always happen to us.

A Protestant believes that shit happens because you don't work hard enough.

A Hindu believes that shit happened before.

A Muslim believes if shit happens, it's the will of Allah.

A Buddhist believes if shit happens, it's not really shit.

And an Atheist believes no shit."

"What about the Agnostic?" Walsh asked.

Roscoe thought for a second and replied, "An Agnostic believes maybe shit happens, and maybe it doesn't."

Captain O'Rourke smiled, raised his beer, saluted Roscoe, and said, "Right on."

THE END

The Case of the Mamba Murder

Jesse Jenkins kissed his wife, Cindy, goodbye as he headed off to work. It was a day like any other workday. At 7:30 am sharp, Jesse was on the way out the door, grabbing his briefcase and car keys, going out the front door to his parked brand new 1967 Chevy red Monte Carlo, his pride and joy. He got inside.

Usually, Jesse would give a quick honk on the horn just to let Cindy know he was leaving.

But on this day, there was no honk. Cindy was in the back of the house doing laundry, so she figured she didn't hear the beep with the washer and dryer noise going simultaneously.

It wasn't until ten o'clock that she noticed the Monte Carlo was still in the driveway. She opened the front door and ran out to discover Jesse slumped over the steering wheel. Cindy banged on the car window, screaming. She tried the door, but it was locked. Her next-door neighbor, Mr. Hoffman, a retired Fuller Brush man, came out to see what all the commotion was about. He peered into the passenger window.

"My God, a giant rattlesnake is lying on the passenger seat! Go call the Police." Hoffman screamed.

Officer Ron Harris was the first on the scene, and he immediately called Roscoe, Doctor Olsen, the Chief Medical Officer, David Bowles, and his CSI team. He also called for someone from animal control.

Roscoe and Detective Walsh arrived first.

"Whadda we got?" Roscoe asked.

"Mr. Jesse Jenkins, apparently a victim of a fatal snake bite by that monster coiled next to him. His wife is inside. She claims that he left the house at 7:30 to go to work, and approximately two and a half hours later, she discovered the car was still in the driveway.

She came out to investigate, and that's when she saw her husband sitting in the car. She tried to open the door, but it was locked. Her next-door neighbor, Mr. Hoffman, heard her screaming and asked if he could help. He's the one who saw the snake on the passenger seat.

I arrived at 10:22 and proceeded to call you, the ME, and the CSI. I also called animal control. I told them it was urgent, and they said someone should be here within an hour."

"Good work, Harris. Jimmy, get a hold of animal control, and if you have to kick some ass, you tell them they better have someone here in ten minutes, or their ass is grass.

I'm going in to speak to the wife."

Mrs. Jenkins was sitting at the kitchen table, being consoled by Mrs. Hoffman from next door.

"Mrs. Jenkins, I'm so sorry for your loss. I'm Detective Sergeant Brown; if you don't mind, I'd like to ask you a few questions."

She nodded.

"I understand that your husband left for work at 7:30 this morning. Is that right?"

"Yes, he was very punctual, 7:30 every morning on the nose."

"Did he seem like anything was on his mind? Did he seem worried or nervous?"

"No, he was in a good mood; he kissed me goodbye like he did every morning."

"Where does your husband work?"

"He's the store manager at Waldbaum's."

"The big supermarket in Brighton Beach?"

"That's right."

"How long has he worked there?"

"Seven years."

"Do you know if he has had any problems with anyone at the store?"

"Not that I know of."

"There's no one that you can think of that would want to hurt your husband?"

"No, no one."

"Is there someone you'd like me to contact that could come and stay with you?"

"I've called my mother; she's on her way over now."

"Well, when she arrives, we'll bring her right in. Now, if you would please, stay inside until we're through. And again, I'm so sorry."

When Roscoe got outside, the snake had been extricated from the car. Doctor Olsen was examining the body; the Police photographer was shooting every conceivable angle; Bowles and his CSI lab rats were fingerprinting every square inch of the car, porch, and outside door and roaming looking for any shoe prints and tire tracks.

Several uniforms went door to door, asking the neighbors if they had seen anyone or anything suspicious. Walsh was talking to the neighbor, Mr. Hoffman, when Roscoe approached.

"Mr. Hoffman, this is Detective Sergeant Brown. Roscoe, this is Adam Hoffman. He was the neighbor who came to Mrs. Jenkins's aid.

Mr. Hoffman, did you happen to see or hear anyone around your neighbor's car last night or this morning?" Walsh asked.

"I'm afraid not, Detective. Since I've retired, my wife and I tend to go to bed rather early these days."

"I'll leave you in the capable hands of Detective Walsh," Roscoe said as he walked over to see what the ME had found.

"Hey, Roscoe, this is a new one, even for me. Death by Mamba."

"No other trauma?"

"Nope, it appears that he was bitten several times in the face, then he went into a state of shock and died a rather painful and excruciating death."

"That's scary."

"Although Black Mambas are fast and nervous, unlike most adult snakes, they usually only strike once, but Mambas will strike repeatedly."

Bowles was standing close by, listening.

Roscoe asked, "Any idea how the snake could have gotten into the car?"

"Yeah, it appears that the passenger side rear window had been tampered with."

"So, it's murder."

"Well, for one thing, Black Mambas aren't indigenous to this area of the country, and second, there is no way that a snake tampered with this window and crawled into the car unless by some divine intervention," Bowles stated.

"Where is the snake now?" Roscoe asked.

"Animal control has taken it. My guys are going to do some tests on it to see if, in fact, it has been doped up." Bowles said.

"Okay, I'll leave you two to do your thing. I'm off to Waldbaums."

"Off to do a little shopping, Roscoe?" The Doctor asked sarcastically.

"No, smartass, that's where the victim worked. I'm going to go see just how cutthroat the world of bodegas, delicatessens, and supermarkets can be."

Roscoe saw Walsh still talking to the neighbor Hoffman, "Yo, Jimmy, gotta roll, let Harris finish up." Roscoe said with a wave of the arm.

Walsh handed off the interview with Hoffman to Officer Harris, then joined Roscoe in the green and black Chevy Biscayne Police car.

"Where are we going?" Walsh inquired.

"Waldbaums, and no, we're not going shopping."

"Hey, I didn't say anything?" Walsh said with a smirk.

The Waldbaums' parking lot was full when they arrived a quarter after twelve. Roscoe parked by a fire hydrant in front of the store in the only spot available.

A teenage bagboy was passed by, pushing a food cart full of groceries for an attractive woman shopper. He stopped as Roscoe and Walsh were getting out of the car and said, "Hey, man, you can't park there. You're going to get a ticket."

"Kid, you see this is a New York City Police Car, right?" Roscoe said.

"It ain't fair, man."

"Yeah, well, there's a lot that ain't fair, kid. It's called life."

As they walked away, they heard the kid mutter under his breath, "Fucking pigs."

"Well, Roscoe, I think you handled that rather well." Walsh quipped.

"Yeah, I think that kid has gained a newfound respect for the Police."

They entered the store and asked the first checkout cashier where to find the assistant manager. She pointed to the office area on the opposite side of the store.

"That would be Mr. Martini. You can't miss him; he's short, balding, and wears black round glasses."

"Thank you, Miss," Roscoe said.

They spotted the assistant manager standing and talking to a butcher. Martini was holding a pencil and clipboard, the butcher a cleaver. As they got closer, Martini spotted them and dismissed the butcher, then turned his attention to Roscoe and Walsh.

"Yes, may I be of some assistance?"

Roscoe took out his ID and badge and said, "I'm Detective Sergeant Brown, and this is Detective Walsh. Is there somewhere where we can talk privately?"

"Yes, of course, right this way," Martini said as he led them into the office.

Inside, there were a couple of women who appeared to be account types.

"It might be better if we could speak alone," Roscoe suggested.

"Ladies, could you give me a few minutes?"

After the women left, Roscoe said, "I'm afraid I have some rather bad news; Mr. Jenkins was found dead this morning."

"Oh my God!"

"How well did you know, Mr. Jenkins?"

"We've worked together at the store for about six years."

"Was he well liked?"

"Oh my God, yes, Everyone here at the store loved him. Can I ask how did he die? He was so young."

"We believe that he was murdered."

"Murder! I can't believe it. Did somebody try to steal his car? He loved that car. He had a special parking spot in the back of the parking lot."

"No, at the moment, we don't believe it had anything to do with his car."

Walsh asked, "And you can't think of anyone here at the store who might have a grudge or problem with him?"

"No. No one at the store. Like I said, everyone here really liked Jesse and got along with him."

"Is there someone who was recently fired that might have been disgruntled?"

"What about any customers?" Roscoe inquired.

"No, I can't think of anyone."

'And you say you got along with him okay?" Roscoe asked.

"Yes, in fact, he and Cindy and I and my wife have had each other over for dinners, and we have gone to the movies together. I would say that we were very close."

"Okay, Mr. Martini, we appreciate your help. We will need a list of all your employees, present and past, as soon as possible." Roscoe requested.

"I'll have them ready for you this afternoon, Detective."

"Mr. Martini, here's my card; please feel free to call me at any time if you remember anything, anything at all," Roscoe said.

As Martini walked them out of the office, Roscoe stopped and casually asked, "By the way, Mr. Martini, do you own any snakes?"

"Snakes? No! I abhor them; they give me the creeps. Why do you ask?"

"Just curious."

Out on the street, the bagboy whom they met going in looked at the Police car and saw that Roscoe, indeed, had received a ticket. The boy laughed and said, "See, I told you."

Roscoe took the ticket off the windshield, ripped it up, and said, "See, kid. I told you, life ain't fair."

Dennis McDonald from Animal Control called and left a message for Roscoe to call back when he got into the office. Roscoe had Walsh come and sit in for the call.

"Hello, may I speak with Dennis McDonald? Detective Brown is returning his call."

"Ah, Detective, thanks for getting back to me. Well, the snake is a fourteen-four Black Mamba. They are considered one of the most, if not the deadliest, snakes in the world."

"Where would one get such a snake?" Roscoe asked.

"Mmmm, it's illegal to own or keep such an animal unless you are a zoo or have a special government permit to keep them. But just like anything, if you want something bad enough and are willing to pay, there's a black market for venomous snakes."

"Any idea how we could trace to see if someone recently purchased a Black Mamba?"

"Not offhand but let me nose around and put the word out."

"Yeah, I'm not out to bust the seller. I want the buyer."

"I'll see what I can do."

"Thanks, man. I appreciate your help."

David Bowles from CSI gave a quick knock, came into the office, and handed Roscoe his preliminary report.

"Whadda find?"

"Well, we found a partial palm print and an index print on the car, but there are no matches so far. We also found a single footprint, which looks to be a man, size 10. The sole has a distinctive waffle pattern. I'm having the team work on a search. We should have something later today. I'll keep you posted."

"What about the snake?"

"Nothing, we didn't find it to be drugged; it's just one mean mother of a snake."

"Well, I asked McDonald over at animal control to snoop around to see what he could uncover about the black market snake trade."

"I'll see if any of my guys can come up with something, too."

"Thanks, Dave."

They sat in silence until Walsh blurred out, "Hey, let's go to the Bronx Zoo and talk to their snake guy."

"Now that, my friend, is an outstanding idea."

"Doctor Michaels is our lead Herpetologist; he should be in the World of Reptiles, checking on Suzy." Doctor Roger Aberdeen, the Zoo's manager, said.

"Who's Suzy?" Walsh asked.

"She's our thirty-foot anaconda Suzy is expecting any day now."

"Do you know who the father is? Just kidding." Roscoe quipped.

Aberdeen was not amused, simply saying, "Yes, how droll. Like I said, Doctor Michaels should be in the World of Reptiles."

"Thank you, Doctor," Roscoe said as he grabbed a map of the zoo on the way out the door to the park.

They passed Tiger Mountain, Northern Ponds, and Grizzly Corner over the bridge to the World of Reptiles.

It was cool, dark, and humid inside the World of Reptiles. Mostly, young boys were staring at sleeping or just plain disinterested snakes, frogs, and alligators. Doctor Michaels wasn't in the public area, so they went around to the back of the reptile house. A young woman wearing a khaki shirt and shorts was standing by the entrance to the exhibit.

"Excuse me, but you're not allowed back here; this is for zoo personnel only." She said sternly.

Roscoe took out his ID and badge and said, "I'm Detective Sergeant Brown, and this is Detective Walsh. We're looking for Doctor Michaels; we were told we might find him here."

"Yes, he's busy at the moment."

"Oh, is he with Suzy?" Roscoe asked.

The young lady, whose name badge said that her name was Sharon, looked surprised.

"Why, yes, he is. He should be out in a couple of minutes."

"Do you work with Doctor Michaels?"

"Yes, I'm Sharon Hughes. I'm a student at Fordham. I'm studying biomedical science, and I work here part-time."

"That's great. Do you like working with snakes?"

"Yeah, they're fascinating creatures, although I do have a soft spot for the primates."

"And what about Doctor Michaels?"

"I have to say, the man really knows his stuff; he's amazing."

"That's terrific; say, would it be okay if we waited here?"

"Sure, I guess so."

It wasn't but a couple of minutes before a tall man, looking to be in his mid-forties, with long blonde hair and a short-cropped beard, wearing an identical khaki outfit to Sharon, came out the exhibit door. He was surprised that two men \in suits were waiting for him in a restricted area, and he shot his assistant a disapproving look.

"Now, Doctor Michael, don't go giving this young lady any grief. I'm Detective Sergeant Brown, and this is Detective Walsh. We need to talk to you for a few minutes. We're investigating a homicide that happened this morning involving a Black Mamba."

"A Black Mamba?"

"Is there somewhere that we can talk, Doctor?"

"Sure. Sharon, why don't you go ahead and feed Cookie."

"Cookie?" Walsh asked.

"The Emerald Tree Boa," Sharon answered.

The Doctor led the way back to the administration building to his small office decorated with all things reptile.

"Make yourselves comfortable, gentlemen," Michaels said as he sat at his desk. Roscoe and Walsh did as they were told. The room was so small their knees touched the front of Doctor Michaels's desk.

"Now, then, Detectives, how may I be of service?"

"Well, like I said, a man was murdered this morning by a Black Mamba that was placed inside the victim's car. It appears that the snake stuck the man several times in the face, resulting in the man's death." Roscoe explained.

"I'm surprised the man wasn't able to get out of the car and call for help. The Mamba's bite doesn't kill instantaneously."

"The medical examiner thinks that the victim went into shock and was unable to open the car door."

"I see. Well, what can I do for you?"

"Since no one at the ME's office and our folks in the CSI lab aren't experts on snakes and, in particular, the Black Mamba, we'd like to go and get as much information that we can."

"Just to be clear, although I am a Herpetologist, I'm not an expert in Black Mambas. But I'll try and tell you what I do know.

The Black Mamba's scientific name is Dendroaspis polylepis; they're carnivores. On average, they live wild and can live eleven years or more. They can grow to 14 feet and weigh up to three and a half pounds. They live in the savannas of southern and eastern Africa. They're quick little devils, slithering at speeds up to 12 miles an hour. They are known to strike repeatedly when attacking, injecting large amounts of potent neuro and cardiotoxins with each strike.

I understand the bite gives a tingling sensation at the site of the bite. It may be the only initial sign of envenomation. Other neurological symptoms include miosis, ptosis, blurred vision, bulbar symptoms, paresthesia, fasciculations, ataxia, and loss of consciousness. Death can occur as quick as 30 minutes or up to 3 hours."

"How easy is it for a private collector to obtain one?" Roscoe asked.

"A Black Mamba? It's nearly impossible; I only know of zoos and some research labs that have any."

"What about illegally?"

"You mean black market?"

"Yeah."

"I honestly wouldn't know."

"Never heard anything about the black market, even in college?"

"Not personally, but there was a classmate of mine who got into some trouble for purchasing some endangered species. Nothing deadly, mind you.

His name was Erik Howard. He was a year behind me in vet school, so I don't know whatever happened to him or where he's at currently."

"Erik Howard. Great, thank you, Doctor, for all your help. Here's my card in case something might occur to you later." Roscoe said as he handed Michaels his card.

Back at the old six 0, Roscoe and Walsh received the list of names and addresses of all the Waldbaum employees for the past five years.

"How about you take everyone working at Waldbaum's, and I try to find this Erik Howard?" Roscoe said.

"How about *you* take everyone working at Waldbaum's, and I try to find this Erik Howard?" Walsh countered, slightly perturbed.

"Well, let's see, if my memory serves me correctly, you hold the rank of Detective, and I, on the other hand, have the rank of Detective Sergeant, which means that I outrank you. And as the saying goes, rank has its privileges.

But, being that I am a thoughtful, kind, and benevolent person, I've arranged for Officer Ron Harris to assist you on this difficult and arduous task; fair?"

"Fairish," Walsh said begrudgingly.

"I've arranged for Harris to meet you here in the morning. Okay?"

"Sure."

"Seriously, you okay?"

"Just remember what Ralph Kramden said to his neighbor Ed Norton, "Be nice to the people you meet on the way up because you'll meet them on the way down," Walsh said, grinning on his way out of Roscoe's office.

"Hey, don't forget, we got a date to go bowling with the girls tonight!" Roscoe yelled after Walsh, who just raised his hand in acknowledgment.

Minutes later, Roscoe received a call from the coroner's office.

"Hello, Roscoe, this is Doctor Olsen. I have the lab results for Mr. Jenkins. As we expected, he died as a result of multiple snake bites. There was no other trauma; his tox screen was clean. Poor guy, he should have lived to be well into his 90s."

"Okay, Thanks, Doc."

At Surf Avenue and 32nd Street, where the Surf Theater once stood, was now the Surf Lanes Bowling.

Bookended on either side was Al and Dave's Candy Store on the corner, and at the other end was Frances Dress Shop.

Even on a weeknight, Surf Lanes was jumping. Roscoe and Betty arrived a little before six, picked out a lane, got their shoes on, and practiced a couple of frames. Walsh and his girl Veronica got there closer to six-thirty; since neither of them owned their shoes or ball, they had to go through the ritual of renting shoes and choosing a ball from the dozen racks of orphaned bowling balls, with all sizes, weights, and colors.

After bowling a couple of frames, Roscoe suggested that he and Walsh get their pizza order in and get some Rheingold's for the group.

Veronica works as the precinct's sketch artist while attending the School of Visual Arts in Manhattan at night. She had heard about the snake murder that morning and asked Betty if Roscoe had mentioned it to her.

"No, Roscoe doesn't usually share his work with me. He knows how it upsets me to see all the cruelty and evil in the world right on our doorstep. I don't know how people can be so cruel, callous, and heartless as to be able to hurt and even kill another." Betty said.

"I'm sorry if I upset you." Veronica apologized.

"Oh, it's all right, dear. I know I can't and shouldn't be shielded from such things, but sometimes, the sheer magnitude of evil distresses me. And unfortunately, it's not getting any better; if anything, it's getting worse."

Veronica spied the boys coming with the pizza and beers.

"Looks like the cavalry has arrived, and just in time, too. I'm starved." Veronica said.

"Who's hungry? We decided on getting the large." Walsh proclaimed.

"Wise choice," Betty said, winking at Roscoe.

"Better not have any anchovies on that puppy!" Veronica announced.

"No, just Italian sausage, pepperoni, onion, spinach, mushrooms, and extra cheese." Walsh declared.

Roscoe grabbed his ball after gobbling down a slice and acknowledged it was his turn. He stood motionless, eyeing his shot, then took two small shuffle steps while bringing the ball back and gaining momentum before launching his ball just as his left toe reached, but it didn't go over the foul line. The red, white, and blue swirl ball barreled its way down the lane, crashing mightily into the 1 and 3 pins, mowing all but the eight-pin standing, wobbling until it too fell.

It was decided early on that these would only be games for fun, so there would be no pressure, no competition, and no ridiculing of others. The two ladies dictated these rules and were strictly enforced.

By ten o'clock, the score was pretty lopsided, as Walsh and Veronica were more interested in each other than bowling.

"Ah, I remember when we were more interested in fooling around than concentrating on the game," Betty whispered.

"Hey, speak for yourself," Roscoe said as he nibbled the back of her neck.

She giggled, "Stop it. Save it for later."

Roscoe peeked over at Walsh and Ronnie, sitting on the bench kissing and chortling like a couple of teenagers.

"Well, why don't we call it a night. Whadda say, Walsh?" Roscoe said.

"Huh? Oh, okay, are you sure? We could go more time." Walsh feigned interest.

"No, it's getting late, and tomorrow we got to snag that snake charmer."

"Whatever you say, Ssssarge," Walsh said, throwing a verbal jab at Roscoe for pulling rank on him.

"Sssssmart ass."

Crazy and Cold Blooded was an exotic pets and oddities store on Stillwell Avenue just south of the Stillwell Avenue Bridge. It was right in the heart of Coney Island's auto collision and body shop capital; there were over fourteen individual and separate auto body repair shops along a two-block stretch of Stedwell Avenue.

The C&CB pet store was sandwiched between Big Lou's Repair & Body Shop and Vinnie's Wicked Wrench Body Shop, whose slogan was "We cheat the other guy and pass the savings on to you."

The one thing that Roscoe found to stand out more than the exotic creatures in Crazy and Cold-Blooded pet store, were the customers. Dozens of people were standing around chatting to one another while lizards, snakes, frogs, iguanas, scorpions, tarantulas, and assorted other hexapod invertebrates crawled and or slithered all over the bodies.

Sitting behind the sales counter was an ill-dressed, chubby, balding, middle-aged man reading the Daily News with a hedgehog resting on his shoulder. He didn't look up from the article that he was reading about the British Secretary of War having to resign amid a sex scandal. "Can I help you, mate?" The man said with a British accent."

"I'm looking for Erik Howard. I understand he works here."

"And who might you be?" He asked, still not looking up from his paper.

"I might be the King of England, but let's say, for now, I'm Detective Sergeant Brown, NYPD," Roscoe said, flashing the badge and ID under the guy's nose.

"Now, where is Erik Howard, mate?"

"He's in the back; want I should get him?"

"If it wouldn't be too much trouble."

The man and his hedgehog walked over to the office door, stuck his head in and shouted, "Oye, Erik; there's a copper here, sez he wants to have a talk with you!"

As Roscoe was patiently waiting for Erik to appear, a young woman wearing a six-foot Burmese python around her shoulders told the Limey at the register that she needed two mice for Snowflake, her snake.

The Brit called back towards the back of the store to a young man who was feeding a glass tank full of mice. "Yo, Tommy, bring me up two mickeys for the bird."

Roscoe watched as the boy reached into the tank and fished out two brown mice and carried them up to the counter by their tails, dropped the pair of *Mus musculus* into a clear plastic container, and asked, "Eat in or take out?"

"To go, please." The woman said.

It was about that time that a scruffy dressed man, unshaven, long unkempt hair wearing reader glasses, stepped out from the office.

"Erick Howard?" Roscoe asked as he showed his ID and badge.

"I'm Detective Sergeant Brown. May I have a word, sir?"

"Look, if this is about my ex-wife bitching about my late alimony payments…"

"No, Mr. Howard, I'm not interested in your domestic affairs. I'm from homicide."

"Homicide? Hey, I didn't kill anyone."

"Relax, I didn't say you've done anything wrong. I'm just here to ask you a couple of questions. Okay?"

"Okay."

"Now, the person who was killed was killed by being a bite from a Black Mamba."

"Jesus!"

"We believe that someone purchased the snake on the black market, and I was hoping that you might be able to help me."

"Oh, so you heard about that. That was a long time ago, I've been clean ever since. That stupid act ruined my life, I got kicked out of vet school, my wife divorced me, and now here I am working in a freaking animal house."

"Mr. Howard, I'm not accusing you of any wrongdoing. I was just hoping that you might be able to give me a name, that's all, to help me catch the person responsible for this tragedy."

"I don't know if the man I dealt with is still doing business."

"Well, there's only one way to find out."

Howard stood there thinking, staring out into space, lost somewhere in the recesses of his mind.

"Erik?" Roscoe said, snapping him back into the moment.

"Ah, David Smokoska."

"Smokoska?"

"Yeah, David Smokoska."

"David Smokoska, okay. Thank you, Mr. Howard. I appreciate your help."

As Roscoe walked past the Brit at the counter, he snipped, "So long, copper."

"So long, wanker." Roscoe said as he doffed his hat.

Roscoe made his way back to the station house via a quick stop by Nathan's Famous on the Boardwalk to pick up his customary mid-day regalement of two chili-cheese dogs, crinkle-cut French fries, and recently, he's started drinking a large Coca-Cola.

Detective Walsh and Officer Harris were back from interviewing the employees at Waldbaums when Roscoe walked into the squad room. Harris and Walsh were in his office, Walsh had his back to the door, but as soon as Roscoe walked past to get to his office, Walsh knew by the fragrantly spurious aroma of Nathan's chili-cheese that Roscoe was in the building.

"Roscoe, have any luck?" Walsh shouted.

Roscoe did an abrupt U-turn back towards Walsh's office.

"As a matter of fact, I did. How was your day?"

"Well, ours was quite illuminating, if you must know."

"Really? Do tell."

"So, it seems that our Mr. Jenkins was having a romantic interlude with the head cashier, Mrs. JoAnn Tanenbaum."

"Jenkins was shtupping the head cashier?"

"That's right, and from all account, the hubby was none too pleased when he found out."

"Have you spoken to Mrs. Tanenbaum?"

"Not yet, but she's agreed to come down to the station for an interview this afternoon."

"Do we know what the husband does for a living? Anything to do with snakes?"

"No, David Tanenbaum works for Pan Am."

"At Kennedy?

"Yeah."

"Well, we'll need to speak to him after we talk to Mrs. Tanenbaum. What time is she coming in?"

"She said after her shift at Walbaums at four o'clock, so sometime before five."

"Great, good work."

"So, what did Erik Howard have to say?"

"He gave me the name of his contact, a fella by the name of David Smokoska."

"Smokoska?"

"Yeah, that's what I said. Hey, Harris, could you run this guy Smokoska thru the system to see if he pops up? If he's been smuggling exotic creatures into the country there's a good chance that we may have snagged him at least once."

"Sure thing, Sarge," Harris said as he went downstairs to run this Smokoska character through the National Crime Information Center (NCIC) database.

"Oh, and while you're at it, see if there's anything on this Tanenbaum character."

"You got it, Sarge."

"Meanwhile, my chilidogs are getting cold."

"More like fermenting." Walsh jabbed.

"Real funny, Walsh, you're a real laugh riot."

"We want to thank you for coming in to speak with us, Mrs. Tanenbaum. I'm Detective Walsh, and this is my partner Detective Sergeant Brown."

JoAnn Tanenbaum was an attractive woman, thirty-six years old, short black hair, bright blue eyes, with an infectious smile. Both Walsh and Roscoe could see that she had applied extra makeup to cover a black eye and that she was obviously nervous about being there.

"Now, Mrs. Tanenbaum, let me say right off that you are in no way under any suspicion. As you have undoubtedly heard, Mr. Jenkins, the store manager, has been killed.

So, we're speaking to everyone at the store; it's just standard routine procedure. Now, how well did you know Mr. Jenkins?"

"Ever since I started working there, four years ago."

"Okay, but just telling us how long you've known him, I'm asking you how well did you know him?"

"I don't understand?"

"Mrs. Tanenbaum, were you having an affair with Jesse Jenkins?" Roscoe asked.

She sat quietly sobbing, looking down at her hands clenched in her lap.

"Yes." She uttered.

"And how long had the affair been going on?" Roscoe inquired.

"About six months."

"When did your husband find out?"

"Two weeks ago."

"And is that when he gave you that black eye?"

"Yes."

"Did you report him to the Police?"

"No. David just went crazy when he found out. He's never hit me before, and I ended the affair once David found out. I haven't been with Jesse since."

"Mrs. Tanenbaum, what does your husband do?"

"He's a Station Supervisor with Pan Am."

"Do you know what that entails, being a Station Supervisor?"

"He's responsible for overseeing all the loading and unloading of all international cargo and making sure that everything is either picked up or delivered. It's a big job." She said proudly.

"I bet it is," Walsh said.

"Mrs. Tanenbaum, when David found out about you and Mr. Jenkins, how did he react aside from striking out at you? Did he threaten Jesse?" Roscoe asked.

"No, David isn't a violent ma…" She cut herself off, bringing a hand up to her eye.

"Where was your husband two nights ago from the hours of midnight to say 6 am?"

"He was at home with me?"

"Is there any possibility that he could have left the house that night without your knowledge?"

"No."

"Are you a light sleeper, Mrs. Tanenbaum?"

"Well, no. But I'm sure David was with me all night."

"Really, would you swear on the Bible that he never left the house that night?"

She sat in silence, deep in thought.

"Does the name David Smokoska mean anything to you?"

"Smokoska?"

"It's interesting; everyone has the same response," Roscoe noted.

"No, I've never heard that name before."

"Do you have any pets, Mrs. Tanenbaum?"

"We have two cats. Why?"

"No, reason, just curious. Thank you for coming in, Mrs. Tanenbaum; one of my officers will take you home."

"David Smokoska has a Police record for violating the Lacey Act." Officer Harris announced.

"The Lacey Act?" Walsh asked.

"It has to do with illegally importing or exporting animals." Harris divulged.

"Very good, Harris. The Lacey Act prohibits the trade in wildlife, fish, and plants that have been illegally taken, possessed, transported, or sold, and that includes snakes." Roscoe stated matter of factly.

"He served one year at Danbury and was fined eighty grand," Harris said.

"Eighty grand? Harris, did he pay it?" Walsh asked.

"In cash!"

"We need to talk to Mr. Smokoska. And the sooner, the better!" Declared Roscoe.

"I have his last known address; it's an apartment at 3 Shore Parkway."

"I know where that is. It's right across from the Coney Island Creek. Let's go." Roscoe said.

Harris brought the squad car around and drove over to 3 Shore Parkway. Parked in the driveway of number three was a silver 1965 Mercedes-Benz 220SE.

The complex was a series of three-story attached brick house-looking structures. The bottom apartment was next to the one-car garage; two separate apartment entrances were located on the second-floor landing. One led upstairs to an apartment on the third floor, and the other was for the second-floor apartment. The third-floor apartment was the jewel of the complex, with two large windows on either side of French doors that led out to a sizable balcony; Smokoska lived on the top floor.

Roscoe sent Harris around to the back of the complex in case Smokoska made a run for it.

Roscoe and Walsh climbed the fifteen stairs leading up to the second-floor landing and rang the doorbell.

An elderly woman dressed in a gray maid's outfit answered the door.

"Yes, may I help you?"

"Good afternoon, I'm Detective Sergeant Brown, and this is Detective Walsh; we're here to see Mr. Smokoska."

"Do you have an appointment?"

"Lady, I'm the Police. I don't need an appointment. Excuse me." Roscoe said as he and Walsh made their way past her and went up the stairs to the third floor, followed closely by the maid.

The maid skirted around the two Detectives when they reached the top landing, explaining to her employer that their presence wasn't her fault.

"They pushed right past me, Mr. Smokoska. I couldn't stop them."

David Smokoska sat on a large brown leather sofa, wearing a red silk smoking jacket with a paisley ascot, drinking tea, and reading the Wall Street Journal.

Smokoska, sixty-two years old, and the spitting image of David Niven: thin, well-coiffed hair, bright blue eyes, and a pencil mustache.

"That's quite alright, Margret. Gentlemen. Please have a seat. Can I offer either of you a cup of tea?"

"Mr. Smokoska, I'm Detective Sergeant Brown, and this is my partner, Detective Walsh, and this isn't a social call."

"Well, that doesn't mean we can't be civilized, so please have a seat. Margret, tea for our guests. Now, what can I do for you, gentlemen?"

"Mr. Smokoska, we're investigating a murder. A man was killed recently. He was a victim of snakebite, a bite from an African Black Mamba."

"Oh my, those can be extremely dangerous."

"Yeah. You were found guilty of the Lacey Act two years ago and served time in federal prison."

"And don't forget the fine, eighty thousand dollars."

"Yes, and I heard you paid the fine in cash."

"Well, I do hate bothering with financial institutions. I prefer cash, don't you?"

"We know that you still engage in importing and exporting exotic animals, am I right?"

"Yes, Detective Brown, but as they say, I paid my debt to society and have learned my lesson. So, I now only trade in legal wildlife."

The conversation was interrupted by Margret bringing in tea and cookies. "Ah, Margret, thank you dear. Oh, and I see you brought in some cookies as well. Detectives, you're in for a treat. Margret makes the best chocolate chip cookies. I kid you not. Thank you, Margret, you may go.”

“Yes, Mr. Smokoska.” She said as she finished serving the tea and cookies and left the room.

“Mr. Smokoska, I really don’t give a damn about your business practices, except I have a man who was killed by a Black Mamba. Now, we both know you can’t go into a pet store and buy one off the shelf. So, either you give me the name of the man who you sold it to, or I promise you I will make your life a living Hell. I’ll get a warrant and turn this place, your Mercedes, and your life upside down and inside out.”

“No repercussions?”

“Did you know the man wanted the snake to commit a murder?”

“Certainly not.”

“The name.”

“No investigations?”

“No.”

“No charges?”

“The name is Mr. Smokoska. Who was it?”

“Knudsen, Alfred Knudsen.”

“Knudsen? Who the fuck is Knudsen?

“He’s the gentleman who purchased the Black Mamba.”

“Where can I find this Knudsen fella?”

“No idea; we always met somewhere neutral.”

“You have a phone number for this guy?”

“I do.”

“Has he ever ordered anything else from you?”

“As a matter of fact, he has an order coming in tonight: a dozen Brazilian Wandering Spiders. They are considered the most venomous spiders on Earth.”

“Is this Knudsen a regular customer of yours?”

“No, this is only his second order. I did it as a favor. He was referred by one of my long-time customers, a zookeeper who is strictly legit. Honest, Detective, I've gone straight. This was a one-off."

"We need to talk to this Knudsen. Where is the drop-off?"

"The Aquarium parking lot, tonight at eleven."

"Okay, all of this better be on the up and up. Don't bother looking for us. We'll be watching you. Just go about your business as usual, understand? Here's my card, call me if anything changes, got it."

"Got it. Don't forget; we have a deal!"

"Deal. Right."

"How'd it go?" Harris asked as Walsh and Roscoe got into the squad car.

"It just gets curiouser and curiouser," Roscoe said.

"Alice and Wonderland." Walsh proudly stated.

"Very good, Walsh."

"Gee, Roscoe, I didn't know it had been written back when you were a kid."

"Yeah, my mother used to read it to me by the light of our cave fire as we were roasting the stegosaurus my father killed."

Harris started laughing, "Ha, that's a good one, Sarge. Stegosaurus."

"I'm glad you liked it. Now, Harris, I want you to find out what we have on Alfred Knudsen and his connection to Jesse Jenkins or David Tanenbaum. While Tweedledee and I go have another chat with Mrs. Jenkins."

When they got to the station, Harris jumped out to run a check on Knudsen, while Roscoe and Walsh drove over to the Jenkins place to talk to Jesse's widow, Cindy Jenkins.

"Mrs. Jenkins, we're sorry to bother you, but we'd like to ask you a couple of questions if that's alright with you?" Roscoe asked.

"Of course, please come in."

She led the two Detectives into her living room, where an older woman was seated on the sofa.

"Detectives, this is my mother." Mrs. Jenkins said as she sat down next to her.

"How are you doing, Mrs. Jenkins?"

"I keep expecting to wake up and find this has all been a bad dream. Won't you have a seat?"

"No, thank you. We just have a couple of questions. Do you know or have you ever heard of Alfred Knudsen?"

"No, is he the man who killed Jesse?"

"How about David Tanenbaum?"

"No, although I've met a Mrs. Tanenbaum. She's a cashier at my husband's store. Who are these people? Is one of them responsible for my husband's death?"

"At this point, they're just people of interest."

"Is there anything that you can tell us? Is there any progress, Detective?" The mother asked.

"All I can say is that we're following a couple of leads, and I promise I will let you know as soon as we know anything definite."

"Thank you, Detectives."

"So, Harris, whadda find out?" Roscoe asked.

"Well, Sarge, I couldn't find anything linking Tanenbaum to Smokoska, but that guy Knudsen looks like he's an enforcer for Seamus Riley."

"Mad Dog Riley, the loan shark?" Walsh asked.

"The one and only," Harris replied.

"This Knudsen must have a rap sheet as long as your arm if he's one of Riley's men."

"You got that right, Sarge. Here, take a look at this." Harris said as he dropped a stack of Police records over an inch thick on Roscoe's desk.

"Well, well, well. Our Mr. Knudsen has been a busy and naughty boy—assault, battery, rape, domestic abuse, harassment, vandalism, and attempted manslaughter.

So, I'm guessing Mr. Jenkins somehow got tangled up with Riley, got in way over his head, and paid the ultimate price." Roscoe said.

"You want to have us bring him in?" Walsh asked.

"No, let's wait until after we pick up Knudsen tonight. We'll see what he has to say about this."

Roscoe's phone rang, "Detective Sergeant Brown. Oh, hey, Corrigan. Really! Tell him to stay put. We'll be right down."

He hung up the receiver, stood up, and said, "Tanenbaum's downstairs. Let's go see what he has to say."

Roscoe picked him out of the crowd straight off: short, stocky, black wavy hair, clean-shaven, dark-skinned, and Eastern European looking.

"Mr. Tanenbaum, I'm Detective Sergeant Brown, and this is Detective Walsh. Let's go somewhere where we can talk." Roscoe said as they walked down the hall to a small conference room.

"Now, Mr. Tanenbaum, what can we do for you?"

"I wanted to come in to tell you that I had nothing to do with Jesse Jenkins's death. I'll take a lie detector test or anything else, but I didn't kill anyone."

"We know."

"You do?"

"Yes, we know. But we also know that if you ever lay a hand on your wife again, I'll see that you get thrown into Rikers Island so fast your head will spin.

Do you have any idea what the cons in Riker would do to a shmendrik like you?"

Tanenbaum's eyes grew wide with fear. "Yes, sir, I promise it will never happen again." He blurted out.

"Okay, now get out of here," Roscoe ordered.

Tanenbaum bolted out of the room and the station at supersonic speed.

Roscoe looked at Walsh, smiled, and said, "Ready to go catch the spider man?"

"Yeah, let's gather the posse."

"Let's be sure to get that guy McDonald from animal control. Because I sure as Hell don't want to handle the deadliest spider in the world myself."

"Scared?"

"Fucking A."

The sky was pitch black, there wasn't even a sliver of the moon over the Aquarium, and most of the parking lot lights were out. There were two parked cleaning vans near the Aquarium buildings. One would assume they were the cleaning crew's vehicles, but they would be wrong.

In one of the vans sat Officer Harris and Detectives Walsh and Brown; in the second van were two uniformed officers and Dennis McDonald from animal control. Parked outside the entrance of the parking lot were three unmarked Police cars randomly parked, with two plainclothes officers sitting in each.

At 10:45 pm, David Smokoska's black Lincoln Continental drove into the parking lot and parked three-quarters of the way in, positioning itself facing the exit.

At 11:00, a green Ford Fairlane slowly drove into the parking lot; the vehicle drove completely around the entire circumference of the lot for several minutes, stopping where the vans were parked; feeling safe, he drove and stopped next to the Lincoln.

Smokoska got out of his car, went to the trunk, and waited. The driver of the Ford did not get out right away; when he did, he carried a small canvas gym bag to the back of Smokoska's Continental.

They shook hands; Smokoska lifted the trunk hood and removed what looked to be a black hatbox. There was some discussion going back and forth. Finally, the driver of the Fairlane traded Smokoska the gym bag for the hatbox.

As soon the Ford driver got back into his car, Roscoe yelled into the Police radio, "Now! Go! Go! Go!"

The three unmarked cars quickly parked behind one another, blocking off the parking lot exit while the two cleaning vans sped towards the Fairlane to box him in with lights flashing and sirens blaring.

At one point, a dozen Police officers were aiming their guns at the Ford driver. Roscoe took a bullhorn from the van and announced, "This is the Police; come out of the car with your hands raised above your head."

The driver sat in the Ford, not moving for several minutes, forcing Roscoe to repeat his order, "Come out of the car now with your hands raised above your head. I'm not going to tell you again."

Finally, the car door opened. As the man was wearing all black, it was difficult for Roscoe and the other officers to see that he was holding the black box with the lid off. Once out of the car, he flung the spiders out of the box toward Roscoe, Walsh, and Officer Harris.

Having made an aggressive gesture towards the Police officers, one of the plainclothes officers fired two shots at the suspect, wounding him in the right shoulder and forcing him down on the ground on top of all of the venomous spiders.

Brazilian Wandering Spiders are well known for being aggressive under normal circumstances, but they become highly combative when they sense that they are attacked; Mr. Knudsen sustained over fourteen bites. If it hadn't been for the forethought of Dennis McDonald from animal control bringing several vials of antivenom, Knudsen would have died within thirty minutes.

Roscoe and the other officers were able to kill 11 of the 12 Brazilian Wandering Spiders, leaving one unaccounted for. They franticly searched the parking lot, the Ford, and each other, and then Walsh happened to shine his flashlight on Roscoe.

"Roscoe! Don't move. The spiders on your hat. McDonald, come quick and bring some serum!"

Harris snuck up from behind, grabbed Roscoe's fedora, threw it on the ground, and started jumping and stomping the hat for a good five minutes. There were at least four flashlights focused on the crushed fedora while Roscoe carefully examined the flattened millinery. When he turned the hat over, there was the squished arachnid on the front brim.

"Oh, hey, I'm really sorry about your hat, Sarge," Harris said apologetically.

"You killed my fucking hat."

"Sorry, Sarge. I panicked; I didn't mean to ruin your hat."

"It used to be a hat; now it's a Frisbee," Roscoe said, holding his prized chapeau. Hey, it's okay, Harris." Roscoe said, patting the officer's shoulder.

"Roscoe, come on, they're taking Knudsen to Coney Island Hospital," Walsh said.

"I'm following you."

Harris asked, "Hey, Sarge, what about Smokoska?"

"Arrest him."

"Hey, Brown, you said we had a deal; you'd let me walk if I cooperated!" Smokoska yelled.

"I lied."

Knudsen lay in intensive care for over a week, and doctors weren't sure if he'd pull through. With the combination of spider bites and gunshot wounds, it could have gone either way.

After twelve days in Coney Island Hospital, he finally was stable enough to be transferred to the prison hospital ward at Rikers Island.

"Mr. Knudsen, I'm Detective Sergeant Brown, and this is Detective Walsh. We'd like to ask you a few questions."

"Fuck off, pig!"

"Boy, Knudsen, that's gratitude for you. We could have just let you spaz out in the Aquarium parking lot, but no, we saved your ass, and this is the thanks we get. And on top of that, I got my favorite hat stomped on."

"Too bad your head wasn't in it at the time."

"Hey, Walsh, not only is this guy a murderer, he's a comedian, too. They're going to love him on Death Row in Sing-Sing."

"You got nothing, pig."

"No? See this." Roscoe said as he held up a small notebook.

"We found this in your apartment. You're not very smart to leave this out so us pigs can find it, are you, Al? This here notebook has the names, addresses, and the amount each owes on their loans to Mad Dog Riley.

See right here, its name and address of Jesse Jenkins, the man you murdered with a Black Mamba."

"You're crazy. I have never seen that notebook in my life. You pigs must have planted that in my desk."

"I didn't say where we found it."

"Ah, go fuck off."

"So, this is where it gets interesting; see here in the back of the book; you wrote yourself a reminder, Tuesday. Smokoska – Mamba.

Now, Al, that was just plain stupid for such a trained professional as yourself. And on top of that, throwing those deadly spiders at Police officers, that's attempted murder. I'm afraid even if you don't get the death penalty, Al, one way or the other, you're going to die in prison."

"I want a deal."

"Deal? What do you have that we'd even consider talking deal?"

"Mad Dog Riley."

"You got nothing. No, it would just be your word against his."

"I got proof."

"Listen, dirtbag, you better not be yanking my chain and making me look bad in front of the DA. I'm already considering stomping on your head for ruining my hat."

"I'm not jerking you around. I really have proof. But. I want a deal."

"Walsh, go give DA Gladwell a call."

The murder trials of Seamus "Mad Dog" Riley, Alfred Knudsen, and David Smokoska went big on the national news. The New York City tabloids had a field day with cheesy headlines like The Snake Pit Trials, Den of Vipers, The Serpent King, The Basilisk Brothers, and The Mamba Murders.

All three defendants were convicted, "Mad Dog" Riley was found guilty of murder, and Alfred Knudsen was found guilty of murder, attempted murder, and violating the Lacy Act. Both were sentenced to life in prison without the possibility of parole. Seamus Riley was sent to Attica to serve his sentence, while Knudsen went to Sing-Sing to separate him from Riley since he testified against his former boss.

Two months into his life sentence, the guards found Alfred Knudsen stabbed to death with a dead rat stuffed in his mouth.

David Smokoska was convicted of violating the Lacey Act, was sent back to Danbury Prison, this time for five years, and fined half a million dollars.

Roscoe walked into the detective's squad room the morning after the trials, sporting a brand-new gray fedora. As he made his way to his office amongst the cat-calls, jeers, whistles, and hoopla, he was greeted by Walsh and Officer Harris waiting for him in his office.

Before he hung up his new fedora on his hat rack, Roscoe turned to the squad room and announced, "Anyone who touches my hat, whether on or off my head, will be shot!"

"Nice hat," Walsh said.

"Yeah, but I miss the old one. It fits me perfectly."

"Say, Sarge, I'm really sorry for crushing your hat, but I want to give you something to make amends."

"Aw, you don't have to. I know you only did it out of the goodness of your heart, Harris."

"I know, but here," Harris said as he handed Roscoe a wrapped package shaped like a painting.

"What the Hell is this?"

"Go ahead and open it, Sarge. I hope you like it."

Roscoe unwrapped the package to find his old, crushed fedora framed under glass, with the squashed Brazilian Wandering Spider front and center.

"Oh, hey, that's fantastic. Thank you, Harris."

"Well, Sarge, I can't take all the credit. Detective Walsh helped, too."

"Hey, thanks, Jimmy. You guys…"

"Where are you going to hang it, Sarge?"

"Right across from me on that wall so that I can keep my eye on that damn spider. I don't trust that it's dead. See, I think he's looking at me right now."

"Glad you like it."

"Come on. I'm going to take you fellas out for lunch."

"Wait. Don't tell me, Nathan's Famous." Walsh said.

"Nothing but the best for my guys." Roscoe grabbed his new hat and put it on with a slight tilt.

"That's a new look for you, Roscoe," Walsh commented.

"As old blue eyes, Frank Sinatra always says, "Cock your hat – angles are attitudes.""

Sitting on a bench facing the ocean on the Coney Island Boardwalk, eating chilidogs and fries, Roscoe smiles and asks, "Hey, Jimmy, What do you get if you cross a snake with a hotdog?"

"I give up, Roscoe; what do you get if you cross a snake with a hotdog?"

"A fangfurther."

"Damn it, where is a Brazilian Wandering Spider when you need it." Walsh lamented.

THE END

M. Ward Leon – the Author

M. Ward Leon is a former advertising creative director who started his career at Doyle Dane Bernbach, New York, during the Madmen era. While at DDB, his writing on the Volkswagen Rabbit campaign won him inclusion in the Smithsonian Institution Advertising Archives. His writing recently earned him two Emmy Awards for Public Service advertising.

He is a California State University Los Angeles graduate and an Art Center College of Design alumnus.

Other books by M. Ward Leon: *Blood of the Beast* • *Revenge of the Beast* • *Wounding of the Beast* • *The Strange and Curious Cases of Roscoe Brown, Detective NYPD* • *Ambush at Fig Tree Gulch* • *City of Angeles Trilogy* • *Ishmael. My Life After Moby Dick* •